TALE OF TWO BROTHERS

BY

DANIEL FERNÁNDEZ MASÍS

Tale of Two Brothers
By Daniel Fernández Masís

Editing by The Pro Book Editor
Interior design by IAPS.rocks
Cover design by Daniel Gómez

ISBN: 978-1499289169

Main category—Fiction
Other category—Thriller

First Edition

DEDICATION

Life is all about those who surround you, who make you want to improve yourself as a human being and persevere at it. Not an easy task by any means. So, this book is dedicated to those who have become such an immeasurable guiding force to my life.

My mother, father, and brother, who have always walked with me, held me tight to keep me from trailing off my path, and ensured I never lost sight of who I am and where I come from. No words can convey my gratitude.

My beautiful girlfriend, who has become a paramount motivation to do what I want to do and always feel supported, encouraged, accompanied, and loved. Additionally, her constant desire to steal a sneak peek at my book and urging to hurry up and finish pushed me on until it became a complete book. I love you.

My friends and family who have somehow, even unknowingly, supported me in this process. Their lives, their comments, their personalities, and their coexistence with me were a never-ending source of inspiration and motivation. Thank you.

Last, to my reader, whoever you may be. Your decision to spend time reading my work is an honor I don't take lightly. Thank you for being you, for loving to read, and for sharing this experience with me. Because of you, this exists.

Hope to see you soon,
Daniel Fernández Masís

PROLOGUE
FIRE

A GROUP OF ROAMERS CAME DANGEROUSLY close to our home yesterday while walking straight toward an old lady with a small child. We could not tell them to run, and they had not seen or heard the threat yet. The lady stumbled with every step, dehydrated almost to death. The child was small and frail, probably born after The Day and too young to realize in what type of world he lived. Their steps echoed on the cream-colored walls of the houses around them, their shadows dancing on the broken street. Vines slowed the lady's steps by tangling her bare feet, while the child played at stepping on dandelions. They were completely defenseless, and their luck had run out.

Oh, God, the roamers were merciless. They saw the lady and child and started running and shouting at them. The poor lady had a small supermarket cart with hardly any supplies; they were probably dead way before the roamers spotted her. What they did to her, I don't want to remember, ever. It was a bloodbath; it was...

I can't.

My brother was beside me, staring at the horrible scene. Before, during, and after the killing, he did not move. He just stared at the group of roamers with hatred in his eyes and his fists clenched at his sides. Maybe he wanted to save the old lady and the kid but suffered in silence because he couldn't. His eyes did show suffering, but no words came from his mouth. My shocked mind must have been playing tricks on me as I even saw smoke coming out of his clenched fists and his eyes turned slightly yellow.

Without a word, my brother stood up, opened the hatch on our roof, and left me alone. The wind was rustling the leaves, giving me goose bumps. I heard him grab his equipment and leave our house. I knew he was going to kill them; he would not risk having those men so close to us. "A timebomb best exploded before its time is up," he'd said before when bad people got too close. I understand why he does it, and I hate that he must be the bad guy.

The roamers left the bodies in the middle of the street as if disposable. Those devils did not deserve to live. Even though my brother is not entitled to take someone's life, I know God will forgive him. In this world, someone must do justice by making the toughest decisions. Otherwise, we are all doomed to the most brutal death and the world will be for those unworthy of its beauty.

The devils started setting up a camp about a kilometer away from our house. They lifted a camping tent in a heartbeat, with a green camouflaged exterior on top of black metal bases surrounded by a playground. How sick to use such a joyful place, a child's haven. Two more built a fire using what seemed to be clothes they had stolen from their victims. I despised them. They seemed to be having the time of their lives, working together, joking, throwing water at each other, fake fighting and trying to burn each other with small, burning twigs. How could God allow them to enjoy life instants after they had taken away two innocent souls? Their laughs, even if inaudible from our rooftop, were darts to my heart.

I watched my brother walk toward their camp, silent and quick. One second, he was in my view; the next, he'd disappeared. He can blend with his surroundings and is the fastest, stealthiest runner I have ever seen. You will never hear or see him coming unless he wants you to. Trust me, I have received thousands of blows to my head for not being able to foresee him. Surprise attacks are inevitable when you live with an untrained fifteen-year-old scarecrow as a sidekick.

Ten minutes later, I saw one of their scouts thirty meters from the last place I'd seen my brother. I started panicking, my heart racing. Where could he be? Did he see the scout? Was he heard? My God, what would I do if he's caught? The scout was armed and staring straight at my brother's last location. The scout was standing still, trying hard to see through the night shadows. Moving side to side, confused, believing he'd heard something. His stance was rigid. He was afraid.

The scout turned around suddenly, then fell to his knees with an arrow straight through his throat. A quick shadow ran over him, taking the arrow too as he vanished into the night.

That was way too close. The scout must have heard or seen him. What if he'd alerted the others? What if my brother was defeated? It felt like being seat-belted into a car being pushed toward an abyss, and unable to do a thing about it. That is how I feel every night he goes out.

Fifty meters away from the dead man, I saw my brother again, creeping up to a tent. Close to the tent, he started to back away.

Where was he going? Why back away? Were there too many? Surprise attacks are invaluable. I wished I could hear what he heard to at least have an idea of what he was facing.

He stood completely still about ten meters away from the tent. He bowed his head for about twenty seconds. Why would he do that? Was he praying for the souls of the victims he was about to take? I really didn't think so as I have never heard him pray before. He should have attacked them before they saw him or come home if he was having doubts!

Abruptly, the tent burst into fire. A giant fireball consumed the tent, roaring toward the sky above, illuminating the playground where they had set up camp. We've suffered thirteen days of rain; how could a tent catch fire? I guessed they had a gas leak and my brother was lucky. Maybe he backed away after hearing the gas leak and lit it up. Thank God for fire. It was burning fiercely as if fire could hate and shout in anger. The whole night sky was illuminated with the light coming from the torched-up tent.

Those men and their suffering were hard to take. But, at the same time, they were evil. They would have done to us what they did to that old lady and the child, massacred us without a doubt. How can something so important for survival be so deadly? Fire is amazing. Staring at the giant flames roaring from the tent, I'd felt in peace until the screams from the tent's occupants brought me back to reality. My brother, where was he! Was he caught in the fire? Did he get burnt? Did he die?

I looked around the flaming tent, down the road, to the houses nearby, straight to the surrounding trees. He was nowhere to be seen. He'd simply vanished again. Uncontrollable anxiety filled my body and mind. I felt my skin get cold, and my teeth started chattering. Trembles ran across my body, real fear of losing him, physical fear. Fuck me, where was my brother?

As swiftly as the fire had started, it turned into a tornado and collapsed in on itself. No more fire, no more screams, only silence. The only proof of it were the ashes where the tent used to stand. What happened? That was extremely weird, though the gas could have run out. What if he was caught up in the fire? He would be careful not to go close to it. I hoped he was coming back home.

Five meters to the right of the ashes stood my brother, holding his sword and staring into the night. He was waiting for something. Why didn't he run back home? Somehow, he knew the battle was not over. I needed him back. Standing there was way too dangerous. He was completely exposed, and at night especially, death lurks around every corner.

Then, out of the woods came four roamers running straight toward the tent. One was an almost two-meter-tall man, bearded, with an army shirt and destroyed cargo pants. He held a seventy-centimeter-long knife that shone with the moon's reflection on its blade. It sent a chill down my spine to see that blade heading toward my brother. And the man made my brother look small by comparison. On either side of him, two hooded figures held wooden sticks with nails sticking out of their tips. They were about the same size as my brother, and they were laughing at him. Their awful laugh echoed all the way to my rooftop, seeming to come straight from hell and filled with hate. The fourth was a small man holding a bow and arrow at the ready as he struggled to keep up with his cohorts. A single arrow he had. One miss and he'd be dead. But one hit, and he'd be...

What if they managed to defeat him? I struggled with whether to stay there or leave and try to save my brother.

He hadn't moved. He wasn't showing any reaction to these new foes. They stopped their run six meters away from my brother. Why was he so calm? All of them had a death grin on their faces. Predators staring at prey. How could one man stand a chance against four seasoned, armed men? He did not back off as they walked closer and closer, each step seeming to duplicate my heartbeat. Four meters away and they started circling around my brother, all flanks menaced.

They stopped three meters away, and the tall man approached him with his knife stuck out in front of him. My brother held his ground and stared right into the man's eyes. The man grabbed him by his forearm and started shouting at him, then held his knife right at my brother's throat and tried to grab his quiver. He stared at the man as if he were not there threatening him. It was weird how peaceful he looked, and this did nothing to calm my nerves.

Suddenly, the tall man screamed in agony, staring at the hand he'd just used to grab my brother. In the blink of an eye, the small bowman fell to the ground with an arrow splitting his forehead, and the tall man grabbed his throat, trying to stop a rush of blood from flowing out of a deep gash. The large blade fell to the playground's floor. No more reflection came from it as its previous owner died on top of it, protecting it from the bright moon.

My brother still stood as if nothing had happened. I had not seen him move, yet he'd defeated two adult men in the blink of an eye. How? He does not have an ally, at least none I know of. He wouldn't trust anyone to help him. If he was alone, what had happened was impossible.

The twins started to circle him, talking to each other and yelling at my brother. Men always try to hide their fear behind useless threats and screams. They moved quicker and quicker circling him, trying to find a weak spot to attack. They were still two guys with weapons, but I felt they had no chance. Maybe my brother's peacefulness was a sign of what was about to happen. He is never thoughtless, so I knew he was measuring the perfect moment to end those men's lives. They did not stand a chance.

He turned his head and stared straight at me. Did he know I was watching?

1
THE ELDER
THE BEGINNING

MAY OUR JOURNEY START AND *end the same way...together.*

It's been said that our world is beyond saving, but I believe this saying was conceived by a narrow mind. Our world was beautiful—mesmerizing views of waterfalls, forests, lakes, abiotic and biotic components of nature blended with cosmopolitan, man-made structures. That has been destroyed, but another type of beauty survives. After all, beauty is subjective. It is a state of mind bound to be distorted and changed by human experience. Some might argue that humanity destroyed the world, so this might be a recovery. I see beauty in this world, the beauty of surviving surrounded by the most adverse conditions imaginable. Beauty in perseverance.

Yes, our world, our lifestyle, our history was shaken by a force so devastating that no human can understand it, at least by what I have learned from the people I've met without killing them where they stood. Don't get me wrong—I am not a murderer, not by choice. Few people have opted for a greeting rather than the more common shot or arrow at my head. I have no choice but to protect what I value most. Those who greet instead of killing, scarce and uncommon, have traveled long distances, met terrible foes who enslave others and massacre entire villages for pillaging, though none have brought any explanation as to what happened to our world. These visitors keep my faith in humanity alive, barely. Several years have gone by since the last time I spoke to a traveler.

Seven years ago, we lived inside houses with high-speed internet and drove internal combustion vehicles over potholed asphalt streets. Now, every centimeter of the planet has been invaded by the only other force known to be as powerful as the one that shook humanity back to its roots—nature. As soon as the world collapsed, nature stepped forward to reclaim it.

The shift was devastating. I still remember watching houses crumble, people running in fear, children searching for their families in the rubble, scavengers pillaging and even killing people who desperately sought to run away from the destruction. It truly saddens me to remember the early days of this new era.

That this world destroyed human decency and morals was bound to happen because of scarce resources. People started to feel the need to overpower others in order to survive at all costs. As soon as a stomach growled, or a throat withered, we fell back to our baser animal instincts and became either predator or prey. Nothing separates us from the animal kingdom.

My house is two stories high with a brick façade and a clay tile roof, so it is safe to assume my parents were—or are? —old school. A three-and-a-half-meter concrete wall separates our front yard from the sidewalk and the outside world. Back in the day, we used to feel safe inside our house. Nowadays, there is no safe place, no haven, no second of peace and tranquility. Security means living by defeating mentally, physically, and psychologically any foe. However, you never really feel safe. At night, sleep is no longer fulfilling, and you are always slightly fatigued. Alertness is key.

In the front yard, a U-shaped brick driveway leads to a mahogany front door with one of those huge bronze decorative doorknockers no one ever used. How could someone use a doorknocker on a door behind steel fences and electric wiring?

A bench still sits beside the front door; no clue why it is there, though. Now it works as a watch station to our frontline defenses, so I cannot complain about it being there. In the middle of the U-shaped driveway stands a concrete fountain with three cylindrical basins at different levels, creating small waterfalls. I remember how peaceful it felt to stare at it while dusk crept down on the horizon. Mom used to go wild if moss grew it. Now the fountain is a moss sculpture; she would be so pissed. Water has not flowed from those basins in seven years. It is an ironic masterpiece to our naivete.

That sculpture reminds me every day of the reason why I must fight and never surrender. Underneath, away from plain view, rests a garden fountain. I am sure my family can be reunited. The fountain and sculpture are whole, so all we need to do is work for it, remove the moss, clean up, and persevere. My family was torn apart by forces beyond my comprehension, beyond my power, but not beyond my saving.

Once you enter the front door, you are met by a wonderful autumn painting by my grandmother. It captivates my attention with its uniqueness. Constantly I find myself staring at it silently, as if waiting for it to come to life. She was an amazing woman who taught me key lessons to confront this world's challenges. "Live life to the fullest, as you may not win at it, but you have to make it worth living," she used to say, and now I understand what she meant.

There is no other thing in that painting besides trees and dust. You could say it is a live representation of our current lifestyle. There is no civilization, only woods, only wind, only leaves blowing without direction. We are just like leaves at the end of the day; forces larger than us sway us toward destinations we don't know of. That feeling of being impotent is upsetting.

Underneath the painting, we used to have a wooden table with two orchids and a bowl filled with candy. Butterscotch candy...damn, I really miss candy. I should try to cook some candy, though it will probably be uneatable. The table is still there, but now serving as the first storage point for defensive supplies. Any day, enemies could outrun us and overpower our defenses. During our retreat or last stand, those supplies could be crucial to survival.

Besides candy, I miss friends and that unnerving sensation you get when you know a girl likes you and you must make a move before it is too late. How many survived? Where are you now, my old friends? Will we ever see each other again? No clue, and trust me, no hint about it being possible. Hundreds migrated to "safe places" sold to us by liars when all this started. In seven years, I have never heard about a successful safe place. I miss the peacefulness felt at the beach. I miss the freedom felt while driving. I miss waking to the sweet scent of coffee being brewed. I miss the marvelous sound of laughter. But above all, I miss my parents.

How improbable that seven years ago, the day of... *The Day*, they were away from home. We haven't seen them since.

My name's Nathan, and I am not alone. "We" includes my younger brother James. Well, I call him Jay because James is excessively serious for him. I am a strong-willed young adult battered by adversity into a survivor. At least that should be the intro to a movie trailer based on my life. I think I would go watch it too. My life's all about wreaking havoc and adventures, so it would probably be a great action flick. Well, truthfully, my life is about suffering and survival. It is about fighting every single day with every bit of strength my body can muster to ensure one more minute for my brother. I would not have been able to survive this far if I had not felt the urge to ensure his safety. His life, not my own, is my most precious asset.

I cannot accept that Jay's youth is this torment. When I was fifteen, just as he is now, my biggest concern was how to speak to the girl I liked at school, closely followed by how to reach the next level in the latest survival horror game. We used to play about surviving and being the tough guy fighting against the infected. Trust me, it is not like the games we played. It is hell. Something that is reflected properly on those videogames is humanity and how it crumbles so quickly to nothing but survival of the fittest.

Jay's biggest concern is fucking survival. I have vowed to myself that he will survive and get the life he deserves, even if I must give my own in return. There is absolutely no possibility of failure in my mind when it comes to his safety. My strength grows every second, though I am not capable of controlling it thoroughly. Nonetheless, when needed, I do not fail and will not fail.

Right next to the beautiful painting is a long hallway leading to the kitchen and dining room. We have a cream-colored ceramic floor that is a pain in the ass to keep clean, especially because Jay seems to have butter for hands. Besides his constant spilling, dust and moss are a nightmare. It is not a matter of aesthetics, but of safety. If an enemy ever manages to go through our perimeter defenses and get into the house, moss and dust make you slip and leave footprints behind, risking exposure. Might as well lie down and wait for death. No, I will not risk it.

The kitchen is full of wooden compartments topped with a marble surface. How could it be possible that seven years ago every single compartment was full of food? I would simply head down to the first floor, open any drawer, and get a bite to eat. Now, we pile up all our food to have a mental picture of our inventory when I leave to find more. We are running so low on supplies, probably the lowest we have ever been, but not the lowest we will be. As time goes on after The Day, fewer and fewer neighboring houses have useful supplies. Venturing farther might be suicidal, but it is necessary.

I usually tell Jay I will eat after he does and work on house repairs or weapon repairs or something to keep my mind off the hunger. The truth is I cannot remember the last time I had three meals in one day. My dad is an agronomist, and a damn good one. Our backyard is one big vegetable garden with big, red, firm tomatoes; huge, leafy lettuces; small, orange carrots; rosemary bushes; basil leaves; and potatoes.

I finally understand how hard it was for my father. Every single larva, fly, wasp, disease, moss, and vine on the face of the Earth tries to attack our crops. There is never enough water, as we have none to spare. Jay works hard on our vegetable garden; he looks funny as hell wearing Mom's gardening hat, but skin cancer will not fuck all the work I've done to make him survive this far. Though the sun seems colder and duller since The Day.

Next to the kitchen, we have a round table working as a dining room. It is not so much a room, as a big space next to the kitchen. Here I sit, sharpening a couple of shivs and arrows and trying to find peace within before venturing to the outside world tonight. Jay calls it an adventure, but I call it a necessity. Going outside is a rush from the moment you step a foot outside our front wall. Imagine guerrilla warfare in the sense that every house, window, corner, stranded car, overgrown bush, cracked structure, nook, and cranny is a suitable hiding place for anyone waiting to kill me, to kill us.

However, we are running low on supplies, and I will not tolerate another grumble from Jay's stomach. That sound crushes me. So tonight, the steps ahead of me are beyond our home and into the wilderness. Jay knows he will not come, not today, not ever. Roamers, slavers, wild animals, venomous spores, and macabre assassins are out there just waiting to capture, torture, and kill with no warning, no mercy, and no second chance. I don't need a second chance. I will have no mercy, and I do not forgive. This world has made me ruthless; I cannot remember the last smile not caused by my brother.

Every day goes along similarly. We wake up at sunbreak and make an inventory of supplies, inspect and repair the scarce weapons we have, review our defenses, and then I get up on the roof and inspect everything around us with my mom's old birdwatching binoculars. If something has changed, even the slightest thing like a roof tile on any house, we strengthen our defenses.

The large wall around the house could be scaled, but we have a clever ploy. The east corner crumbled because of the intense tremors unleashed during The Day. I managed to create a large pile of rocks, construction rods, and soil blocking that breach. From the outside, it seems as if the wall collapsed and access is blocked. Contradictory to the past, an incomplete wall is safer now, so adversaries assume the house must have been looted long ago. On top of the wall and the pile of rubbish, and invisible from the outside, we have barbed wire, sharpened construction rods with snake and frog venom, and small bubbles filled up with acid waiting for anyone stupid enough to try to enter.

Under the rubble, there is a metal security blind I stole years ago from a store left behind by its owners. I moved the remains of our fallen front wall to open a path where I managed to place the blind within the rubble and cement rocks to its front face. This way, if you stand outside of our house you see a pile of rocks and fallen debris, and no one will be able to spot that under the rocks there is a metal blind.

This blind can be opened from the inside easily, since I worked on a small pulley system that we pull using a large chain. At first it was almost impossible to pull since the rocks weighed it down, but the pulleys have made it easy enough to pull. From the outside, we can open the blind by pulling a thin metallic wire attached to the same pulley system. However, this is far more difficult since a wire is much smaller than the chain we use inside the house, and this demands much more strength.

This system has saved us more than once. Enemies have come close to our house and discarded it as they assume a house without a front wall must have been scavenged long ago. Additionally, this way, the front garage doors are never opened. Both are cemented to the ground and our long dead cars are pushed against them, holding them closed. All this scheme may seem exaggerated or overly cautious to anyone who does not live in this world. Trust me, it is far more than necessary.

Through the years, I have set up numerous wire-activated bear trap lookalikes, venom-soaked barbed wire, unstable rocks, sound alerts, and slippery surfaces around the property's perimeter. All of them are worsened by the small lookout I built on the highest point of our roof, which gives me and my arrows a 360-degree view from within. There is a way to leave our house through its west border, the one opposite the front yard, but only we know the intricate sequence of steps and trap deactivations.

Unfortunately, all of this is a consequence of what I have seen and lived. Our world is not what it once was. One of the most valuable assets nowadays is guns. It feels miserable to live in a world where knowledge, art, music, friendship, cooperation has stepped down, and survival and murder are the new normal.

Guns are very scarce nowadays since some people understood their value and took them by force right after The Day. Bullets and gunpowder are even harder to find because people used them in excess during the horrifying first days of this mess. People traveled ridiculous distances away from their homes, looking for armories. The first murders from humans falling to their baser animal instincts happened right outside of gun shops. When the world's end was still being discussed by some, others foresaw it was our reality for the long run and followed that path of no return, the path of killing.

My first decision when all hell broke loose was to work hard on our defenses, to keep people from entering our house. Cementing our gates closed and pushing our cars toward them to ensure they could not be opened. Even being only nineteen years old back then, something told me to tend to our defenses immediately. Human selfishness was soon to subdue those naive enough to think cooperation could last. Now I congratulate my past self, because the first month was all about human cooperation and support, and rare attacks and homicides.

The second month after The Day showed our true species' face. No more help from one another, no more friendly greetings and sharing supplies. Everyone soon understood no government, no police, no army was going to be able to revert the situation. Massive protests turned into massive massacres. People who dared exit their houses were soon shot to death. Those gunshots caused the current bullet shortage and defined the ambiance of our lifestyle. Outside is danger; each step away from the confines of your shelter is a step closer to death.

Once the bullets ran out, guns started to wither owing to misuse and lack of maintenance. That is why nowadays you barely see someone holding a functioning and loaded gun. On the other hand, that makes them drastically important as an advantage at the battlefield. Range, precision, and instant kills are the perks of being one of the lucky bastards holding a gun.

***

My brother is already asleep after having a great deer stew for dinner. Nothing pleases me more than knowing he is safe and well fed, sleeping in a world of dreams a thousand times better than the one we live in. I like to come to our rooftop at night and check our surroundings accompanied by the stars and moonlight. Here I am, sitting with outstretched legs, my left arm extended behind to hold me up and my right arm holding our binoculars to my face.

To my right, the north neighboring houses and the road's dead end are unchanged. Behind me, the wind rustles through the unconstructed lot. The pine tree sings the night away, and I imagine its smell as if it could reach me. A long time ago I enjoyed that same tree's shade accompanied by... No need to reminisce in pain. To my left and front, more than one hundred houses stand, all uninhabited, as I know because I have inspected them innumerable times. All of them are battered by nature, time, and humanity's collapse. Countless people have died on these streets since The Day; it's a real ghost town without ghosts.

I remember the chaos, the confrontations between old friends, the first murders over supplies, the harrowing screams and cries expanding across our city. Now, only desolation and memories are left. Small details remind me of the horror we endured. Mr.

Jefferson's old 1982 Mercedes is turned over about three hundred meters from our house. He was one of the last to have gasoline, and our neighbors did not allow him to leave, fearing that car was their only way out toward an imaginary haven in another city. In the end, they fucked up the car, and all had to leave on foot, probably to their deaths.

Before my thoughts wandered farther away, I continue inspecting our neighborhood. At a house maybe five hundred meters away, something atop a table on a garden terrace catches my attention. I cannot believe my eyes, so I clean the binocular lenses and look again. I'll be fucked...a rifle! We've survived the last seven years without a gun powdered weapon. Each enemy I've faced who had a weapon has been heart-stoppingly close to killing me. It's been a few years since I've seen a working gun.

Back in the day, diamonds, gold, and fashion were expensive. We paid so much money for useless shit. The funniest stupidity was money. We thought a piece of paper had value and power enough to make us happier, better, safer. Nowadays, value is whatever will give you a fighting chance against adversity. Value is measured by the seconds it will add to your painstaking life.

A rifle must be one of the most valuable material assets to have nowadays, no matter if it has no bullets. If it works, it gives you range of attack, bargaining power, and the possibility of surprising enemies. On the other hand, if it does not work, you at least get an intimidating weapon that might prevent a fight.

I must get it. My heart rushes, making me ponder between running now without a plan or waiting for tomorrow. The risk is extreme, as I have no idea how many enemies are surrounding it, if it is the only one they have, if it even works. Nonetheless, the opportunity outweighs the risk, and I have made my decision. Tomorrow I will retrieve that rifle. I cannot allow someone so close to our house with such a disruptive power. I will not tell my brother; he does not need to know.

May my senses be advertent, and my aim be unerring... I will write again if I come back.

2
THE YOUTH
MY BROTHER

NATHAN FORCES ME TO DO stupid stuff every single day. He makes me stand on one leg for a long time. He makes me stand on my tiptoes and walk like a ballerina. We play this game where I must put my hands palms down on top of his palms up, then he hits my head hard if I fail to protect myself in time. He makes me stand on the patio and throws stuff at me that I must try to dodge while grabbing a ball he hid somewhere. We play hide and seek, and he shouts at me when I miss some clue he left for me. He forces me to wrestle with him even though I will never be able to defeat him. He jumps out of nowhere and starts hitting me, leaves wires tightened around corners to trip me, wakes me in the middle of the night and forces me to run around the house avoiding a ton of obstacles he has set up. I really don't get why he does it. I hate it, but I won't say a thing. The world is bad enough as it is; I don't get why he must make it hard for me inside our house too. Our parents would scold him for being so mean.

Despite that, I really hate when he leaves. I know how dangerous it is, why he does not allow me to go with him. Panic always fills me up the moment he steps outside and won't leave until he returns. Our supplies are very low and even our weapons are running scarce. They don't last very long as much as we must use them. The reason why I put up with all he does is because he is a real hero and has suffered much to ensure my safety. Maybe what I resent is feeling useless here, all day playing stupid games and never helping.

I wish I could go with Nathan, fight with him, but he won't allow me. He says he needs to focus on the battlefield, and I will only distract him. I believe him, having seen him fight. He doesn't know, but during his hunts, I get up on the roof and watch him. Lying on my belly, on the cold roof tiles, I use our binoculars to follow him. At least if he is in my line of sight, I can be sure he is okay. I panic when I can't see him.

Our home is on a hilltop with a view of our entire neighborhood. To the north, seven houses separate us from a dead end where tall grass has covered the steps heading down to the Inter-American Highway. To the east, across the street, a vast unconstructed lot is an inner-city jungle now. Moss, grass, dandelions, and fallen leaves blend as a green ocean. At the center of the lot, a pine tree stands tall and strong with its trunk half covered by the creeping vines. To the south, the hilltop descends gradually and leads toward dozens of diverse houses long uninhabited. Last, to the west, our neighborhood's downtown seems an urban maze. Some old businesses mixed with houses, rusty playgrounds, electric poles, unoccupied lots, our church, and the dried-up riverway.

All clearly visible from our rooftop, from my spy spot, and all so different from the way I remember it when our parents were here. The streets are destroyed by overgrown tree roots, covered with trash and unkempt grass. Most houses have broken windows, destroyed fences, and shattered walls. Blood stains from the early days taint walls, useless cars are parked all over, and not a single man or woman lives here anymore. We are completely alone.

Nathan says when the world collapsed, so did humanity. People will kill before even questioning you. He says life expectancy is now determined by how quick you pull the trigger, if you even have a gun. We don't have a gun, or much else to help us survive, which is why I'm amazed by Nathan's skills and how long he's kept us alive.

I was not able to see him hunt today, since he forced me to work on all the supplies he retrieved yesterday from the roamers. He managed to retrieve one metallic arrow from the dead bowman that I had to sharpen, two bars of soap I had to clean thoroughly, the long, shiny knife whose grip needed to be slimmer for my brother's grasp, and a book. He loves reading and forces me to read every single night. Anything with words is valuable to him. I even believe he reads the ingredients on food cans, just for the fun of it as the interior is long expired.

I walk toward our front door and open it as I can hear him coming through our secret entrance under the rubble. He slowly pulls the metal blind down to enclose our home and starts walking toward me. He is pulling a small white-tailed deer, visibly exhausted from the hunt, and carrying his bow around his waist. The deer's legs leave two straight lines on our garden's grass, annoying me as I oversee landscaping here.

He gives me a knowing look that said he was aware I was not able to watch him hunt, unable to be on the roof because of my chores. He never talks about his adventures, and this was not an exception. Nathan comes inside our house and walks across our inner hallway, past our dining room to his left and our laundry room to his right. He sets the deer on our kitchen table for me to prepare as supper and goes across our glass doors onto the backyard terrace.

Upon his return he just sits on our terrace in silence, staring in silence at our backyard, at the small palm tree in the middle, at our vegetable orchard to the right and the back wall separating us from neighboring houses. Only wind accompanies him while he rests his chin on his fist, and his eyes dance around. I think he worries I'll think of him as a murderer if he shares more about what he does, but I know he became what he became to avoid having me suffer, even if he had to be destroyed in the process. He is a good guy in a bad guy suit.

I work hard skinning the deer at the kitchen, removing his soft fur and sticky hide. By now I am accustomed to this bloody process. Carving the delicious meat, applying the few condiments we have left, and trying to store the pieces as hermetically as possible to avoid rot. As I start washing the blood off my arms, setting two perfectly cut pieces of meat for Nathan to cook, he finishes his silence and walks back toward me. He grabs the meat and heads back out to the terrace, where our rusty grill is waiting for his culinary skills. His mouth is lopsided after those silent meditations as usual, grieving.

I follow him and sit down on our terrace chairs and see how he cuts the meat into small pieces. Using some carbon and one of our last thirteen matches, he fires the grill, and sets a small cauldron with water on it. While the water boils, he inspects some vegetables I had prepped from our garden. Slowly, he starts adding the ingredients to the hot water and the sweet scent of hot food fills our house. He serves me a deep bowl, and I see joy in his eyes, not because he killed enemies, but because we will live another day.

He raises his bowl and says, "To the lady and the child. May they rest in peace, fortunate to have been spared this world's atrocities." His face darkens slightly with sadness at the memory of what happened to them, and probably about being unable to save them.

"Thanks to you, they shall rest in the peace of God, having been avenged," I say proudly so Nate knows I have no remorse about what he did, and he has my complete support.

A frown wrinkles his forehead and his mouth tenses into a slight line like he is angered. "Jay, vengeance is never an answer to our problems. Whatever I did, and whatever I will have to do, is done to ensure our safety, but it is not justified by any means. Death is not something that should be decided by men for other men. You believe in God, so you must understand that life is the most important thing we all have."

He continues in a deep, gravely tone of voice he uses only when scolding me or teaching me a hard lesson. "Those men used their lives to do despicable things that I will never forget, and truth be told, it fueled the anger I used to defeat them. Nonetheless, it was their choice and destiny, or God's, or whatever really is beyond life, if there even is something past our death. I only hope something will put them up for trial and punishment. Do you understand? Never encourage or use vengeance, little brother, or it will consume you, taking you down a road from which no one can return safely."

My hot head makes me blurt out, "But they deserved to be burnt up, they deserved to be killed, they deserved to be dealt what you did. God would not and will not forgive them for their actions. They did things to the lady and child that no human being should have to endure, so what you did is only fair. What if you are the means God uses to do his justice?" My arm hair is rising from fear of having contradicted my brother with something I am slowly reconsidering before he answers back. *What a stupid comment.*

"I agree their crimes should be punished, but it was not my place to do what I did, not even in this world. You don't understand because you have never faced a dying man, when all his courage, hatred, and evil fades away as he begs to live. It is truly heartbreaking to be the one causing their death, even if they deserve to die for the horrors they have forced upon others. Please, James, understand this world has collapsed, civilization has collapsed, but humanity must be saved within those who can still be honest, respectable, benevolent, and altruistic. I cannot be that type of man and survive, so I decided to do what was needed for us. But you don't have to, so do not follow me down this road. That is why I won't allow you to join me, I'd rather die in battle alone than expose you to that feeling where someone's life is ended by your hands." He looks half angry and half miserable as he speaks, trying to convince me with all his will.

Maybe he is right. He is not evil...he is not the bad guy, at least from my point of view. Yet it seems as if he sees himself as the bad guy sometimes. I know God will forgive him since his intentions have always been for good, for the defenseless, for the betterment of our disintegrating world.

"I understand." While nodding in approval, I stand up to clear the dishes and wash them with as little water as I can because they are the only ones we have.

Nathan stands up, walks over and hugs me, and says, "Good night, little brother." His warm embrace makes me feel protected, sure about a tomorrow.

"Good night, BB," I answer.

As I drift off to sleep that night, I can't help but wonder how he became such a fantastically skilled hunter? How is he able to face death with a smile and defeat it every single day he goes outside? How am I worthy of his protection? How in God's name did yesterday's fire start in the roamer's tent?

3
THE ELDER
THE HUNT

I LIED TO HIM. I TOLD him I am going out to hunt for food tonight. He does not need to know I am going out on such a dangerous mission. That beauty still lies unattended at the backyard table where I saw it, and it will be ours. My heart has not slowed down since last night, and I barely slept at all. The few moments when exhaustion overcame my excitement, I dreamed about the rifle. I could see myself running toward that backyard, crawling inside the house, retrieving a working rifle, and coming back home victorious.

You see, I had to face that group of roamers with my bare hands, a few arrows, and a rusty "sword," as my brother calls it. It is not so much of a sword as it is a club. Its sharp edges are curved now and frail. At least one of my enemies had given me an upgraded sword. I know my way around enemies, even when outnumbered, but hell, I can't risk confronting a group with guns without having my own firearm. That night was a blend of luck, power, and experience that won't last forever, and each time I risk my life, I risk my brother's as well. Unacceptable.

Our inventory holds three revolver rounds, which are useless without a revolver. Even if I get the rifle, they will still be worthless, but I'd rather have them taking up space on our shelves than in an enemy's satchel. The same applies to the rifle—maybe it has no rounds, maybe it is not working properly, but it's best hidden behind our walls than being held by our foes.

To be honest, I'm never scared for my safety, not as you would imagine. Tonight, I am uneasy because if I die, my brother is not ready to survive on his own. If a rifle was so carelessly placed, it means it is not the only asset its owner has, making the risk worth taking. All my tribulations could be lessened by this rifle, and Jay's security vastly enhanced.

***

The rifle is still waiting for me on the same spot, as if expecting me. I leave our house around midnight, in a hurry. I am deadlier when accompanied by shadows. Turning right as soon as I leave our house, I descend the hill running as close as possible to our neighboring house's outer walls. At the corner, I stop and peek around to check my surroundings. The usual silence hints me to proceed, the only sound being my heart pounding at my ribcage. Another one-hundred-and-fifty-meter sprint brings me even closer to my destination. Around three blocks away from the house where the rifle waits for my embrace, I start searching for tracks, any hint or trace of another human being…the most dangerous game, as Richard Connell's book says.

A small lump of grass peeking out of a crack on the sidewalk has been stepped on. According to the direction of the slanted grass, they were, or he or she was, going north. So, I go north, straight to the house where my prize is carelessly set in plain sight. *How naive and imprudent in this survival-ruled world.*

My first step presses the same lump of grass, slanting it farther. I am way too excited, which is not ideal when lurking. Stealth must be executed with a steady heart and intricate attention to details…but it is a fucking rifle. What if someone else spotted it and is dashing toward it at this moment? What if I'm second to it and lose my chance to build up our defensive and offensive capabilities? What if I get there and am killed with that same rifle just by being a second too late?

No way. Breath in. Breath out. Feeling my heartbeat slow down and my awareness go up. Now's the time to go on.

I dash toward the house containing my prize. It is funny to imagine Mr.…and Mrs.… Damn it, I can't recall their names. This will not be the first time I've entered their house since The Day, though the bastards never invited me in when they lived. A real shame, because their daughter was a ten out of ten. Trust me, a real smoking bombshell, about my age, with ruby cheeks, wide lips, green eyes, long brown hair, and an attitude as if she could cherish you and destroy you simultaneously. She is probably long gone as well.

I stop about twenty meters away. Crouching, I focus on any noise, smelling any smell, and seeing any abnormal movement. That's one of the perks of living in the apocalypse, everything is usually steady, unchanging. Change means an opportunity or a threat, both of which need to be assessed with caution.

Nothing, no noise, no smell, no movement. Still, I feel uneasy. Ten minutes pass by, the longest minutes. Standing, frozen, the only sound is my heart's pace and the whistle of wind charging through nature. Beautiful, unnerving, dangerous. There is no greater fear than uncertainty. Now it makes sense—uncertainty means a false step could trigger a series of unfortunate events.

Time to get that rifle. I sprint to the metal fence, place my foot on a ledge, and vault over. Almost flawless, but one of those damn spikes scraped my shirt and torso. A drop of blood falls, tainting the concrete driveway. The owners would kill me, or at least try to. I allow myself a silent laugh, then continue my run toward the front door. The uncomfortable burn of a new cut brushing against clothing tries to distract me but fails.

Now, not so much of a run as a silent crouch. All windows and doors are closed and locked. I don't have to check to know. That's how most homes were back then, and so still are now. However, enough heat and a measured amount of pressure will make any lock fail, doors open, windows crack. Besides, a wide-open door calls for attention from the inside and the outside. The best way to enter a house nowadays is by avoiding main entrances. That way you only deal with enemies who are already inside before having to deal with the ones lurking outside.

I enter the house through a small window into a bathroom. Beautiful bathroom, but it smells like shit. Well, not shit, because no one has used it for that in a long time, but like putrid moss and dead leaves. Right outside its door, there's a beautiful living room that welcomes me with a large ear-to-ear smile. Two big leather armchairs face a huge smart TV, which is now an ultra-expensive mirror. A Persian rug made of red and golden threads covers the center of the room. It depicts Alexander the Great's war against the Persians around 330 BC. How amazing would it be if in a couple of centuries, people spoke about Nathan the Great, Nathan the Literate Warrior, Nathan the Destroyer, Nathan the Infinite Fire, Nathan the...

Unfocused idiot. The rifle. Go for the rifle and leave as quick as lightning.

Weird, the carpet is fully stretched, no sign of folding caused by footsteps or someone tripping over it. The rest of the house is filled with toppled furniture, broken pictures and knickknacks, and large plants that long ago exceeded their pots' capacity. Paint is peeling off the walls. A roof fan hangs desperately by its electrical wires. I can see to my right, through an open door, how the kitchen drawers and refrigerator door are wide open and empty. The back door is broken, yet the carpet is perfectly in place.

Something is not right.

Time to move and move fast before someone arrives. I exit the bathroom and run straight across the living room. The TV mirror to my left shows my reflection jumping over all obstacles on the floor, avoiding broken glass and roots and splintered wooden floor tiles. I hasten through one of the broken door panels and arrive on a small terrace in the backyard. There it is!

Right where I saw it sitting on a small outdoor table. My heart is pumping. My forehead is sweating. My hands are shaking.

I dash the few meters to the table and grab the rifle, thinking about how much it will improve my brother's safety.

Idiot.

A bell attached to the rifle tingles my safety away. Apparently, that's how death chimes, unforgiving, melodic, and continuous.

No one in this world would leave such a prize just sitting on a terrace table. Seven years of this shit teaches us to be extremely cautious. Apparently "us" does not include me, a fucked-up idiot. Of course, someone stretched the carpet to feel normal, to see and feel normality in between the severity and dangers of daily survival in this world. This house is being set up by somebody as a shelter, but it is a long way from being finished.

I feel the cold metal of an extremely sharp knife pressed against my neck, my right knee receives a violent blow, and I fall to the ground. My new sword is snatched away, and someone lands a kick straight to my forehead. A ringing noise fills the inside of my head as warm blood gushes out of my neck. I cannot focus, rendered useless, unprotected, no power.

Focus, Nathan. Try to survive.

My power struggles against this confusion and pain but doesn't manage even a heat spurt. My hand feels the heat rising inside, but my thoughts are scattered and incapable of focusing. *Please, don't fail me now,* I think, trying to clear my distraught mind. But with thousands of ideas, feelings, and nerves shooting signals of agony from all around my body, fire is not coming.

I try to turn my head to identify my assailant.

An elbow is thrust to my back and I am "helped" to stand. A right hook to my left jaw, an uppercut to my nose, a knee to my groin, a jab to my liver...

Hello, Ali, I think, then laugh at my own idiocy. I am getting the beating of a lifetime and yet I am laughing, probably at my death. Blood is still running from my neck and my swelling cheekbones are reducing my vision. Just like boxers fighting by instinct, my right fist flies straight into the night searching for some jaw-like destination. My heart wants to feel flesh being crushed by my knuckles, but only air is hurt by my desperate attempt. My left hook follows closely behind and manages to collide against a human torso.

The dark figure jumps back at the unexpected blow, but just for the blink of an eye.

As I am in no shape to fight back, my foe steps forward and punches me in the face. Wish I had faced this enemy without being surprised so the fight could have been fair, intriguing, matched, and probably to the death.

As I am trying to stay upright, I see a lightning quick stride come toward me. Maybe if my sight was not so blurred, I could dodge some of these attacks. Completely overpowered by this surprise attack, I know deep down death is looming. My heart breaks at the thought of Jay being left all alone…no parents, no Nathan, no nothing. Blazing wrath gets me back on my feet and just as I'm ready to attack with all I have left, a definitive round kick to my jaw impedes any possible comeback.

Light fades and obscurity sneaks upon me. I am losing consciousness, nonetheless I feel at peace. Peace of death, is it? No, peace because I know I'll survive. Somehow, something tells me this is not my time to depart, this is not my destiny, and my life is not fulfilled yet.

I smile.

"Love your smile, dead man," says a lovely female voice like the sweet caress of a morning mist being felt while drinking a freshly brewed cup of coffee.

From darkness, her face emerges. She is a dashing beauty, a redhead just like autumn, white skin just like snow, and a wide red mouth not needing a damn bit of lipstick. Death is my dream woman, at least I know angels exist.

No words come out of me. *Yes, Nathan the Deadman is my name.* I fall unconscious.

4
THE YOUTH
UNCERTAIN

I WAKE UP TO A TYPICAL hazy, gloomy day and sit on my bed as I usually do for my five-minute routine of staring at the wall before getting on my feet. Nathan hates it. He gets up at the break of dawn with no hesitation, no fighting the need to stay between the bedsheets. No way will I be doing that anytime soon. The world is cold and dark now, making it very tempting to just lie in bed and hide. There is nothing out there exciting enough to get up for.

The metal door Nathan built to keep people from reaching our rooms if they come from the main stairs is wide open, the lock and chains on the ground. Weird. Nathan usually uses our secondary exit. To open it, you must slide the second wooden panel that covers our bedroom window, from left to right. Its hinge aligns with a small channel in the lower panel, allowing it to open from the inside. That's cunning work done by Nathan. I would never be able to build something like that.

Now, I stare at my shadow's silhouette, confused. Why would Nathan use the main exit and leave it open? Well, I must go and find out, so I exit through the main metal door and close it behind me. Walking slowly through the hallway, I turn right toward our wooden main stairs. Thirteen steps in a U shape covered with obstacles and booby traps to decelerate an enemy's approach. At the second-to-last step, a small, almost invisible wire is fixed to a generator. The slightest contact and you will fall in pain, immobilized, so I avoid it carefully.

Right at the bottom of the steps, to the left, our grandma's autumn painting hangs on the wall. Nathan stares at it for long periods of time, speechless. I have never asked why, but I guess he just likes the painting. I would never dare touch it; it has something special to him. Maybe he misses our grandma, or he likes autumn, or something like that. By no means would I get into that sort of trouble. I know when not to annoy him.

To the right, our house's main mahogany door is closed, so nothing else is weird so far. Even our defense kit is sitting on the table under grandma's painting. I turn left and walk toward our kitchen. Of course, I don't call out for Nathan because he always told me never to shout for help as it is "the same as asking politely to be killed." Sometimes I believe he is just exaggerating with comments like that. How could the world be in such a state? Do people really kill each other without even trying to see beforehand if they are enemies? I know the men and women Nathan has faced have attacked him, but maybe that is not how everyone is now.

Then it hits me—this is a test! Nathan is playing with me, and I have been very careless so far. I throw myself to the ground and roll inside the kitchen. Bellow the sink we have a small dagger, a couple of bottles of water, and a box with medical supplies consisting of two Band-Aids, two acetaminophens, and about a quarter-liter of alcohol—not the drinking type but the one you use for wounds. My brother explained expired medicine just has a less potent effect, so it still important to have these days. A headache could mess up your focus and lead you into a trap.

I tie the box and two bottles of water to my waist using a small rope hanging beside the sink. I grab the dagger just the way Nathan taught me, blade away and down, pointing out the bottom of my hand. This way my wrist will not budge if I must use the knife against a solid target. I hold it tightly, careful of its razor sharp blade thanks to my brother's constant maintenance of our supplies and weapons. My worried eyes reflect off its blade.

The TV hanging by the table works like a mirror to check out my surroundings. Nothing abnormal to be seen. Instead of going out of the kitchen through its main entrance, I hop on the counter and go out the inner window leading into the living room. Even if the TV showed me no hint of trouble, heading straight out is risky because I'd be left with too many directions from which I could be seen and attacked.

However, this is not the best place to be when hunted either, as it has three main entrances. One doorway to the table, one hallway leads to the dining room, and a glass door behind me leads to our terrace. Too much exposure. Oh, and it can be seen from the TV room on the second floor since its wall is only a meter tall to improve lighting between the two floors. I hold in a small laugh at thinking just like Mom.

If I remained, I could imagine getting scolded by Nathan, so I crouch and crawl to the terrace to get a 360-degree view from there. No disturbance, no movement, no clue on or around the house. I go around our small palm tree and move silently to the external hallway that connects the backyard with the garages at the front. It is a long hallway, about ten meters long, which gives me only one escape route if confronted. I start to move silently but quickly to avoid this risk.

I mistakenly step on our orchard's soil. I can't leave footmarks behind, so I kneel and gently rub my hand over it to make it seem as if I am going the other way. As I walk to the garage, I feel my heartbeat start to race. Is it really a test? Where is Nathan? I have never been able to avoid being caught for so long, which is either amazing or worrying.

Checking around corners, crouching, creating wrong clues about my direction, searching for signs of Nathan's location inside the house, and retracing my steps is worthless. He is not in the house. He has never left without telling me or at least without being obvious for me to know he was leaving. Uneasiness starts to get ahold of me—something is wrong. What should I do now?

I open our front door and run to the roof, jumping the steps two by two, carefully leaping over the electrified wire. Sliding a chair underneath the wooden panel, I move it to enter our room. A second before stepping into our room, I push the chair away with my foot, just like Nathan taught me, and close the wooden panel. I know for a fact no one is inside our room unless Nathan's hiding spot was always here, and I just fell into his trap.

The roof's entrance is located inside our walk-in closet, which has another door hard to open. First, I go around the door, to its right, where a large iron rod must be pushed into the wall, just the right amount to shove a rotary axle that blocks the closet's door from the inside. Success! The axle clicks, signaling I pushed the rod perfectly. The metallic scrape causes me to feel a flash of pride. No time to see if it is a test. I am genuinely worried for him.

Then I get in front of the door and look for a small thread that hangs from the top frame, almost unnoticeable. By pulling on it, a small pulley inside the closet tugs on the bolt to open it. Done! The door's hinges open and the door creaks to let me in. I toss one of my shoes inside to lure any threat out of it or at least cause a reaction to be seen, but nothing happens. Once again, my fear of Nathan not being home takes control. Without thinking, I run toward the roof in desperation.

Jumping on a small wardrobe, I push a gypsum panel that covers the final entrance to our roof. It has been a long run, having to overcome all of Nathan's obstacles. All of these are meant to stop our enemies from finding us if we are invaded. As you see, no one would be able to get here without knowing all the secrets to our entrances. And from the roof, we can access the east exit of our house, through our neighbor's roof. Our final escape if needed.

I find Nathan's binoculars and a small piece of paper with

notes and drawings. It reads: "500 m to target. 20 m pause. Dash over fence, force window. Grab prize. Escape route A via garden wall to adjacent park. Escape route B..." But no Nathan to be seen.

That hollow feeling of uncertainty upsets my stomach. This seems very strange to me. Nathan did not even plan a second escape route. Either his mission is extremely easy, it is a clue for me, or he left in a rush. He never thinks something is extremely easy and this does not feel like a test for me. He must have seen a prize so valuable that he had to hurry for it before someone else got it. A nervous tremble shoots across my body. He left without thoroughly planning a way out. How long ago did he leave?

Escape route A meant he went somewhere with a garden right next to a park. I scan our surroundings with his binoculars and find three houses with gardens separated by walls to a park. Now what matters is the distance to those houses, as Nathan's target is five hundred meters away from this spot. Out of the three houses, only one is about five hundred meters away from our home in a straight line. It is that weird white house owned by Mr. and Ms. Van de Kruit.

The house's driveway is covered with moss, rubble, and debris. Then I notice one of the windows up front is open. This is a typical Nathan move, since he always says, "Don't create signals that will attract attention, but don't force normality on anything as nothing is normal anymore." Again, that hollowness at my stomach strengthens at the thought of losing him. I don't have his genius and skill, and if he is not coming back, I am doomed.

I continue inspecting the house until I see the garden next to the park. There is a table with a cloth on it or a towel. That does not make any sense as wind and rain and sunshine would have already messed it up unless someone put it there recently. Nonetheless, we don't have any neighbors, at least that we know of. Our neighborhood has long been deserted and only visited by roamers.

Wait a second... My mouth flies open, astonished. A cold chill runs through me, giving me goose bumps as my brain registered horror. There is a stain on the ground. Fresh blood pooling at the house where my brother is supposed to be. A thousand thoughts run disorganized through my mind, suggesting plans beyond my skillset. Nathan could be injured, captured, or even…dead.

Tears flow uncontrollably down my face and my mind screams, *Oh God, oh God! What should I do?*

5

THE ELDER

DEATH

I WAKE UP SLOWLY, FEELING AT arm's length from my memory and wanting to fade slowly back into obscurity. I experienced that awkward feeling where you are coming back from the realm of dreams, slightly confused, slightly tired, and with a sense of remembering the forgotten. The void in my head starts to clear up, and a wonderful dream comes to mind.

I got the shit kicked out of me.

This dream feels excruciatingly real. Every centimeter of my body is silently moaning in pain. My neck must have a cut, and something warm and terrible is dripping from it. Blindfolded and muted by a cloth tightly strapped around my jaw and head, I stand defenseless. Lying on a furry surface, face down, and unable to move, I realize all of this is real. The soft caress of the carpet against my forehead and cheeks soothes me enough that I don't panic.

Well, I lie defenseless. My hands are tied behind my back with what feels like socks tied together. It must be a well-tied knot because I can't budge my hands. My legs are separated and pinned down, so I can't stand up. You never know how cumbersome it is to be held down until you are in this position. My muscles tense and my teeth grit as I try to move and fail. Nothing seems to work.

Someone knew what he or she was doing because I am truly detained, contained, and even somewhat afraid. Someone and no one; no one and someone.

This is infuriating and uncomfortable. And the dusty carpet is triggering my allergies. Sneezing all over the place might attract more enemies. I start to feel an uncomfortable itch inside my nose.

As quickly as the first blow began the beating of a lifetime, I remember what happened. I had been sucker punched and attacked from behind when I idiotically took the rifle without noticing the small warning bell attached to it. How careless I had been, a shameful defeat. The soft carpet brushing against my cheek is a reminder of all the mistakes I have committed. Of course, someone had straightened it; otherwise, it would have been a mess like the rest of the house.

Fuck.

This means I must still be at the same house, close to home and alive. This headache is making it hard for me to remember what happened exactly. Jay must be back home worried sick about me, even on the verge of doing something erratically stupid by now.

An image instantly comes to mind. A sweet caramel voice heard before I lost consciousness. I had been attacked by a woman. Well, more than attacked—destroyed. This gal has amazing agility and stealth skills. I was barely able to see her silhouette during the entire episode. Since the moment I had forced the window, entered, scouted the room, and exited toward the backyard, I had not seen or heard any sign of her presence. My training had never failed me before. The rifle had clearly made me reckless and now has gotten me into a terrible mess.

My stupid male emotions remind me of her beauty, making my mind wander through a scenario where we're flirting and talking. How unpredictable our thoughts... How senseless a man throbbing for a woman's touch?

Now is no time to imagine improbable scenarios. It is time

to get myself free, find Jay, and ensure he is safe and sound, then decide whether to find her and settle our score. I really miss a woman's touch, a woman's smell, a woman's smile, a woman's laugh, a woman's body tucked up under my arm while I stroke her silky hair. The Day took more than my family away—it took her away, my girlfriend, the woman of my dreams. Chrissy.

About a month and a half into this mess of a world, I had gone to her house, naively unaware just how much the world had changed. I had prepped our defenses, but still had some faith in our leaders finding a solution. A simple visit to my girlfriend's house, I'd thought, with flowers in one hand and my heart in the other, but her front door had been in pieces, apparently shattered by an axe, judging by the splinters and wood shards all over the front porch. The living room had been turned upside down, with cushions on the floor, furniture broken and slashed, and dirt from the plant vases all over. The farther I'd gone inside, the more destruction I'd found, making me fear the worst. I can still feel the worry and anxiety of that day when I think about it.

I had run up the staircase through what those fuckers left behind. Clothes, drawers, lamps, bedsheets, and pillowcases littered the stairs and floors in a makeshift pathway, having fallen from their filthy thieving hands while they'd escaped. My heart had been racing and my hands trembling. Turning right at the end of the stairs, I'd rushed to her white door painted with green and pink flowers in her childhood, finding it wide open with the knob broken as if someone had forced entry. Her body had been lying on her bed, her right arm hanging from the edge. A bronze candlestick on the floor below her hand had blood on it. She had fought valiantly against whomever attacked her. She had been just lying there, undressed, filled with peace as if she were just taking a quick nap before coming back to me. But she never came back to me. That image has haunted me for seven years. The notion of not being able to save her crushes me.

How hurtful it is to believe you could have done something to save a loved one but failed? There's a gnawing sensation on your heart that never actually leaves. Wild thoughts of what I could have done to save her had stirred up a whirlwind of emotions: anger, vengeance, love, pain, suffering, loss, denial, all at the same time.

That day I had sat beside her and prayed for one last time, with tears running down my face and my entire body shaking, my heart shattered. She'd been a woman of dreams, of hope, of faith, and of love. Yet evil had taken her away from me, away from this world, which desperately needs her and her benevolence. She had taught me so much in her life, and in her passing, taught me more—she'd taught me not to ever give up. She had fought till her last breath, protecting her life and her family, and I will always love her for that.

I don't believe God would have allowed such cruelty to happen. He must have left this world before The Day, left us to ourselves, alone and unprotected. And if He exists and allowed it, He is not a God I'll worship. The pain inside me is excruciating every time I picture her, her laugh, her stare, her grin, her soft hands caressing my face, her positivity, her beauty, her spirit. Part of me went into the grave I painfully dug that day, and the flowers I'd intended to give her rested on her deathbed.

Three tears roll down my cheeks to the carpet. An uncomfortable ache spreads through my chest at the memory of never being able to avenge her. The sting of my mistakes. *Use it, Nathan. Use this pain to get yourself back to Jay. Use it to ensure Chrissy's passing away was not in vain.*

Now's the time to get myself out of this mess and go save my brother as I should have saved her. I have no idea how long I was out, and he must be scared, desperate, or even reckless. Did he leave the house to find me?

Somehow the first enemy that manages to defeat me is not a killer, Irish luck for me. The pain starts to turn into anger. My stupidity riles me up, the beating enrages me, and the memory of never having avenged my girlfriend infuriates me.

My eyes close to focusing, I still need to feel it within me to work. I need to get control of my mind and block all the thoughts rushing through my head like a high-speed highway through the desert. Breathe in, hold it, breathe out. Get my mind to a clean slate, nothingness. This is the only way to get it right, to get control over it and avoid chaos.

My heart starts pumping faster and louder, my back and wrists tighten up, my teeth grit, my eyes are amber now; I know even though I cannot see them because the rug starts to smell burnt. Almost ready to get out of here. The owner of that beautiful harmonic voice better be far, far away. She should run, for I am focused now.

The sweet scent of fumes intensifies and lingers around me. Heat waves shoot up and down my body. This usually doesn't take this long, but I am hurt. Defeat is hard to overcome, and pain is hard to contain. Temperature rises constantly, and my arms are about to blast into flames.

Almost ready, Nate. Chrissy, thank you for being my guardian angel.

I pull my arms away from each other and toss away the burnt-up ropes. The rug is burning, flames dancing around me as I am their owner, their leader, their master. Fire listens to my orders and is constantly waiting inside me to be commanded.

I remove the blindfold and stare at my reflection on the TV. The fire shoots upward and starts smoking the ceiling. My body is larger than normal, tensed up, my eyes shining brightly across the room with an incandescent glow evocative of the fury inside me. And my cheekbones are puffed up from crying at my girlfriend's memory and the beating of a lifetime. She is part of the fuel that intensifies my inner fire.

A fiery column shoots from my right hand, directly to the TV, knocking it to the ground as it bursts into flames. My inner heat is rising steadily to levels I have never felt before. The flames around me scorch the ceiling as my footprints leave burn marks on the wooden floor. Striding heavily out of the living room, to the terrace where the rifle had been, I see she has left no tracks. What a mistake to leave me alive.

Walking back inside, I cross the living room and walk toward the front door. All the pain and rage are still building. I stand in a lunge-type stance, point my right hand toward the door, and whisper "Go." A massive fire-whip sends the door flying twenty meters outward to the fence. The walls ripple with flickering yellow and red waves.

My right arm shivers the way people react when inadvertently surprised by cold. The shivers worsen, and my surrounding flames start to diminish. I feel exhausted suddenly. Gasping for air, feeling my strength falter, I fall to one knee. Fire extinguishes from my finger tips and leaves me burnt out.

Turning around, I see the chaos I caused inside this house. The rug and TV are still burning, the ceiling is gone, and the door is nowhere to be seen. Smoke and fire quickly consume the house as it bursts into flames. My powers are beyond my comprehension and control. With the remaining strength in my body, I manage to stand and wobble down the front yard toward the exit.

Time to go home. Time to find Jay.

6
THE YOUTH
NEXT STEP

THE SMALL PATCH OF BLOOD on the terrace's floor has stopped moving. It must have dried up in the three hours I have been stalking the house. These have been the worst hours of my life, since I have no clue as to what to do next. I need Nathan to tell me what to do, but at the same time, he is probably the one who needs me to make up my mind. Alone and afraid, too scared to move, and too worried to stay.

My head is spinning and hurting from all the crying. My arms are having weird contractions, maybe because of the tension I feel crawling over my body. I must do something, but my body will not move as I want it to. Let me think the way Nathan does. Vomit seems to be on the verge of gushing out of my throat.

My first option is to get back to our backyard warehouse and prepare a scouting kit with weapons and provisions to search for Nathan. This would be smart if he needs my help. Maybe I could somehow save him from whatever has managed to stall him for this long. My last seven years have trained me for this moment; he has trained me for this moment. The sole idea sends harsh trembles up my arms.

Am I ready?

I would have to scout for clues starting right outside our house. The only clue I could find within was the piece of paper.

Based on the clues I manage to gain the moment I leave, I would crawl close to the ground for two purposes: (1) to avoid being spotted by enemies and (2) to search for any hint about Nathan's direction and whereabouts. Yes, that is what he would do.

An issue would be if I head out and Nathan returns home before I find him. This would send me down Death Road since he would undertake a swift search for me, which wouldn't last long. I am sure I would leave numerous bread crumbs inadvertently guiding him toward me, and he would be extremely pissed off at my recklessness. Maybe I should not leave; maybe I am just being the panicky kid I've always been.

My second option is waiting here, using the binoculars to search for him until I manage to see him and calm down the mild heart attack I'm having. The problem with this is that I have no idea as to how much time is enough to wait before changing back to my first option. Seconds seem like hours; every sound makes my heart skip a beat, and several times I've seen things that are not there.

Besides, what if Nathan is hurt or caught right now? Every second wasted is an advantage for his foes. He could be enslaved, or worse… I cannot say it. On the other hand, my skinny, weak body and the scarce weapons we have are no match for any of the foes I have seen Nathan defeat. If someone or a group of people or strange beings managed to overcome him, I have no chance to save him. I mean, if a car outruns a Ferrari, a simple VW Beetle like me won't do any good as a replacement in a quarter-mile race…

I am biting my nails again.

Suddenly I remember the last thing Mom told me: "You take care of your brother during our trip. He looks after you, but someone has to be there for him if all else fails." My fists clench and I grit my teeth, feeling my muscles burn with anger. It is time to move, to go find my brother. My mother entrusted me. She would want me to move, to be a grown-up and do what is needed. She wouldn't want me to be a coward.

While standing up, my mind is trying to mess up this courage burst, but I will not allow it. Nathan needs me, and my mother trusts me to be there when all else fails. First option it is! Several flashes of Nathan hitting me when I was failing to be stealthier come to mind. I must get my A-game ready if this is to work for both of us. Making this into a bigger problem is not an option.

At our backyard warehouse, I grab three shivs and a sweater, the couple of bottles of water, and the box with medical supplies I collected from beneath the kitchen sink. Now I am ready to go and find Nathan and get one of the worst scolds of my life for leaving our house by myself. I must go straight to him and set him free or get him back in the game with the weapons I carry.

I leave through our hidden exit. It is one of those old metal security blinds used on stores, cleverly hidden behind what seems to be a collapsed wall blocking the way. When you manage to open it, you create a small sixty-by-forty-centimeter window amongst the rubble.

The cleverness goes beyond the apparent. Nathan managed to make them resist rust and stickiness from the humidity, so the blind opens clean as a whistle. No sound can be heard, and no movement can be seen from the outside. I open the blind all the way up and attach the rope to a concealed hook to avoid being crushed. This way the pulley system holds the blinds while I crawl out. I hope it doesn't close on me and leave me trapped.

Wriggling my body, I manage to get out. Well, truth be told, I don't have to wriggle that much since my scrawny body more than fits. Once outside, detaching a thin metal wire from a metal climbing hook releases the metal blind and hides our entrance. Once again it slides fluidly without a sound and our house is sealed.

If I manag—*when* I manage to find Nathan, he will be able to open it from outside using that wire and his strength. One more reason why finding him is key to my survival. There is no way for me to open it from the outside, as the thin wire requires way more strength than the inner rope and pulley system. This was the only way to disguise the opening mechanism from any enemy who managed to get close to our house. During these seven years, few enemies have reached one hundred meters from our front door before being misled by Nathan's ruses, and the few who have managed to get closer have been deceived by the crumbled wall.

Suddenly, my body freezes and cold, steady drops of sweat slide down my cheeks. First time outside our house since The Day. I used to skateboard down the sidewalk and played soccer with my neighbors, who must all be dead by now. The sweat drops turn into tears, icy and steady as well but no longer caused by panic. Life, human life is over. I will die soon. Mom, Dad, friends all gone, and now maybe even Nate gone. This is my reality, and for too long I have lived in a bubble.

This silence is unnerving. Only the wind whistles through the trees, moss and dead leaves crashing onto walls and deserted streets. The moon is full, so lighting is not an issue for my search. How strange that this scenery, so passive and silent, is so deadly. Where I could see peacefulness, I now see invisible danger. Where I heard nothingness, I now hear silent peril. Desperation gets ahold of my mind, since I am living in a world with no turning back. This is our normal now, and seven years have done nothing to make us more used to it.

My mom's words sound strong again inside me, getting my head back in it. I may die soon, but at least it will be because of my brother beating me for leaving our house to save him when he was totally okay. I have seen him defeat packs of roamers without a scratch; of course, he is fine without my help. This makes me laugh silently at my foolishness, at the idea of his being in trouble right now. But the creeping doubts remind me of the possibility of losing him.

Fuck.

Remembering the roamer group gives me a second of peace. I don't know how many succumbed inside the burnt-up tent. The tall man and the archer were destroyed in seconds, and the twins shared one last thing in their lives, the way they'd left them. An entire army would be needed to overpower Nathan, but it wouldn't be able to outsmart him. He would foresee them and avoid them. He was built to survive in this world; somehow or something early on had made him resilient and fierce. I never understood why he changed so quickly. Probably Chrissy leaving the country with her family made him colder.

Maybe he is running late because he found something so valuable, he just could not leave it behind, and he is waiting for a group of enemies to spread out or leave. Stealth is not like the videogames where you succeed by moving slowly. "Sometimes stealth requires patience beyond time, patience to be able to hold your breath, your position, and your eagerness to dash into danger and be exposed to a threat you ignore," as Nathan says. I can recite it, but evidently not put it into practice.

Unfortunately, Stupid Jay has acted impulsively and got himself locked out. I grab the wire and pull as hard as I can, just to burn both of my palms. To avoid screaming in pain, I snort loudly. Then I grab it again but cover my hands with my shirt. A trickle of blood drips down the wire. Damnit, my right palm is cut.

As hard as I pull, the blinds barely move. Maybe two centimeters from the ground before falling back in place. Nathan wouldn't design an entrance easily accessed by anyone who spotted it. Staying here is suicide. Total exposure beneath this glowing moonlight, no shelter close by, backed up against a wall, and no knowledge of where I should run if I were chased. Besides, if anyone sees me, I would guide them straight to our safety, into our house.

I have no choice but to go on. My next step must be in Nathan's direction or I am as good as dead. Time to find him and have him save me as usual.

7
THE ELDER
FIRST THINGS FIRST

When my inner fire burns at its fiercest and my amber eyes intensify my sight, I lose control. Anger is what drives my focus and guides my flames, not calmness or control or clarity of mind. I don't allow myself to use my power because giving free rein to the full extent of my anger could send me down a path from which I will not be able to return. Hatred and darkness.

My brother could be in danger right at this moment.

My eyes turn back to their customary hazel and my inner fire starts to feel like ashes. Before hunting that bitch, I need to ensure my brother did not get out of our house in a desperate attempt to find me. I know my mom must have told him something regarding my safety. I have overheard him when he has imaginary conversations with her. It saddens me how lonely he feels and how much he misses them. By protecting and training him, I have left him alone in this world. I'm not a brother, but a drill sergeant.

The front door is gone because of my outburst and the front gate is open, the only clue Ms. Fuckyou left for me. I will need to return here when I start hunting her, and something must point me in the right direction. The difference is that this time, she will not outthink me. She will end up charbroiled for her insolence.

Wait. Do not become the evil you have long fought against.

A long sprint takes me back to our house, to our safety and peace. Except this time, something feels awry the moment I approach. My eyes inspect our front wall, the reinforced gates, the barbed wire on top of them, the clever rubble to lead our foes' suspicions astray. Uneasiness grabs hold of me, the notion of Jay leaving our house into this world of aggression and unpredictability fuels my worst fears.

The secondary entry with the metal blinds is closed as it should be, each stone and crumble seem to be in place, but the wire…the wire is loose. As the wire sways with the wind, so does my hope for Jay to be safely home. The dancing shadow of the wire mocks me. He must have left in search of me, terrified to leave safety behind, not thinking straight. How frail is the human mind in front of adversity, of fear? It corrupts into doubtfulness, clouding sound judgement, leading my brother to escape.

My heartbeat accelerates. Where should I go now? Where would he go in search of me? If he was caught by someone, how could I know? Left, or right? To our neighborhood's center or the suburbs? To the north or the south or the east or the west? What if he stumbles into Ms. Fuckyou?

Come on, Nathan, get your mind under control. A train of thought without control will turn into a train wreck and death for both of us. My eyes widen as thoughts start organizing themselves like building a Lego structure, each piece adjusting perfectly to the one underneath. Of course, Jay left to find me, but first he must have thought I was playing a game on him, a test. He has improved considerably on those tests.

When I left to retrieve the rifle, I did not plan as usual. The urge to get it overcame my training, and I was reckless. What did I do, exactly, that Jay might have found as a hint? A small piece of paper jumps to mind abruptly. Planning was interrupted, but not entirely ignored. The piece of paper included the distance to the house where I got my ass handed back to me. If it did not blow away from the roof, Jay must have found it and used it as an indication to my whereabouts.

"500 m to target. 20 m pause. Dash over fence, force window. Grab prize. Escape route A via garden wall to adjacent park. Escape route B..." Even the binoculars were there, and he knows how to triangulate distances. His route was not uncertain or idiotic; he must have walked toward me but didn't get there, as we would have met.

Damn it, what happened to him?

Taking a knee, I inspect the sidewalk and start crawling downhill from our house. He is not stupid and must have hidden his tracks to the best of his knowledge. After a hundred meters of crawling without any hint, I turn right and advance two hundred more meters without any clue left behind by Jay. I'm proud of his advances; maybe he is ready to get out and accompany me in my adventures, our adventures. One more reason to find him.

One hundred more meters in the direction of the house, almost scratching my abdomen on the sidewalk to avoid missing any trace of Jay. I can even see the house from here. I see the windowsill I detached to get in. He must have reached the house. I cannot think of any risk that could have detained him from this successful trip. By identifying the windowsill, he must have been sure I was in there.

A cold quiver starts at my toes, runs up my thighs and torso, through my back, and tenses my neck and jaw. My fingers start to tremble, and no fire is left within me as I see a blotch of blood on the sidewalk beside me. It was not there when I started my rifle mission. It is right by the stumped grass that had alerted me of my foe's direction when searching for the rifle. I know this sidewalk in detail and blood was not a part of it.

I fall to my knees and curse the loudest my voice ranges. He must have been so close to me, almost reaching the place where I was strapped to the floor, unconscious. My fault. My naivete with the rifle, being careless about my surroundings, not being cautious about my enemies, had me caught for hours. Jay must have been miserable and scared enough to search for me. Mom, Dad, Chrissy, and now Jay, all gone without my being able to do shit about it. A turmoil of sorrow and ire blends into disbelief within me.

While my tears continue falling like an endless stream of water down a rock wall, something catches my eye. Two small shivs of my own creation are stuffed under the garage door beside the blood splotch. Large drops of salty tears drop to the patch of grass and blend with the drops of blood.

Jay is gone. Someone has him.

All my strength, all my courage, all my knowledge and experience, all that makes me survive runs away from me and escapes into darkness. The hollowness left behind is worse than death. Failure haunts my thoughts, tears strike the floor as I am completely still on my knees. No mom, no dad, no girlfriend, no brother, no reason to live.

A memory comes to my mind clear as a motion picture. My parents waving as Jay and I boarded the school bus. Before even sitting down, my cell phone vibrated and, strangely, a message from my mom popped up. It read, "You know him better than anyone, so take care of him." My answer, concise as usual, was, "Always." What would she think of me today?

Wait! Those shivs should not be under that garage door. As quick as the memory faded in, it fades away. They have been clearly forced underneath. Someone assaulted my brother, probably he spat those blood drops onto the sidewalk as he fell. Cleverly, while lying immobile, he must have stashed them forcibly as a message to me. Jay is not dead; he is waiting for me to rescue him.

This is not the work of the bitch who sucker punched me. She works cleaner than this. The culprit or culprits don't mind leaving signs of their brutality behind. Hitting a defenseless fifteen-year-old like that and taking him away must be the work of enslavers. My brother won't suffer slavery, not while I live and breathe. Now is the time for me to find him, to send those responsible into oblivion.

My inner fire has never felt this way before. I feel heat waves through all my limbs. My chest is pumping visibly at the rhythm of my exalted lungs. Fire creeps up my wrists, covering my forearms and circling around them like a tornado. My breathing accelerates, and I don't feel my energy draining as it should. An image of my brother with grief on his face, pleading for me to rescue him, enrages me.

The windows in front of me show my new form. Luminescent red eyes are staring directly at my reflection glowing with fire surrounding my curled-up arms. I curl my back and charge up all the intensity building up inside of me. My mind is blank as if waiting for something to happen, just like a horse with all its power waiting for the doors to open in a hippodrome.

As I shoot my arms upward, fire bursts from and surrounds me while I shout at the top of my lungs, "Fiery death is coming."

8
THE YOUTH
SCREWED UP

BARELY TWENTY-FIVE METERS AWAY FROM the house with the hanging windowsill, so close and still so extremely far. Excitement can be such an idiotic thing to feel in this world. Running directly to the house was stupid, yet I did it. My footsteps sounding like a drumroll on the sidewalk alerted him. Suddenly, a blow to my chin knocks me to the ground. So damn close to Nathan.

He hits me the hardest I have ever been hit. I spit blood on the sidewalk from my cut lip. Almost flat on the ground, with my attacker beside me, I know I must do something quick. Escape is not an option—he is stronger, faster, and better equipped than me. My heart races and panic fights with my need to do something smart. What would Nathan do? I must stop trembling and do something. What should I do?

Got it!

Moaning, I reach slowly inside my jean pocket. The two small shivs feel cold at my fingertips. Using them to attack this monster would be a big mistake. I am not Nathan, not at all. I groan and roll away, so I can try to stuff the shivs under the garage door beside me. Dizzy, I fumble, and my hands won't do exactly what I want them to do.

A cold voice says, "Get up, or I'll get you up piece by piece."

A split second before I feel his strong arm grab me by my armpit and hurl me upward, I slide both shivs right under the garage door. My blood is splattered all over, and the shivs are way more than Nathan will need to know something's off and start the hunt to rescue me.

A heavy hand on my aching shoulder forces me to walk northward, away from the house with the hanging windowsill. So close, yet so far.

***

My capture was seven days ago. My brother must be pissed at me and worried to death. That day, after I managed to get up, stumbling as I walked, my captor tied my hands up and strapped me to a chain. We walked north for about two hours, leaving my home town for the first time in seven years, until we arrived at a small camp where other people were chained as well. All the way he slapped my head, spat on me, punched me, and pulled the chain until I fell, but not a single word came from his mouth. He is not alone.

To this day I have counted seven more men who follow his instructions. All of them have a large scar on their right forearm that resembles the way you draw a gust of wind, with curvy lines toward their biceps. They call him Cold, and I could swear they are all afraid of him. Their attitude toward him is of obedience and subjugation, a type of willing slavery. They walk behind him, and never in front of him. To address him they are the live representation of a scolded kid asking for permission; head down, back hunched up, wide open eyes and hands to their sides. How come all these evil men are fearful?

Today is the seventh day we walk. No one can speak, or they are hit until they fall unconscious. I really have no idea where we are going or what they will do to us, to me. My mind reels in horror every single day at the possibility that they are cannibals. I have read about that—it is when people eat each other. A chicken wing would have more meat than my body, yet they would still kill me for the pleasure of it.

Children, mothers, fathers, adults, families are all the same to them. We are strapped to chains and walked like dogs, or more like pigs to the slaughterhouse. If you could smell fear, this group of people would stink. Everyone cries silently. I cry silently with them as we walk into exhaustion and beyond. The world is destroyed, houses are crumbling, vines and moss cover everything, and only the wind travels the roads with us. Humanity is gone.

Every day we stop, and some of the bad guys go out. Each one in a different direction. Usually, at least one of them brings another victim to camp. All beat up, bloody, scared, chained, with puke, shit, and piss on their clothes. Everyone has a desperate frown, no one believes we are living to tell this story. I don't believe we are going to survive. Nathan would, but not me.

Everyone caught goes through the same ritual I had to suffer. They tie us to a chair, naked. Then a rope is tied to the chair's legs, stretched, and soaked with gasoline. You can smell the gasoline as they pour it on your legs, on your body, on the chair's wooden surfaces, and on dry leaves they scatter around you. The end of the rope is lit up. You see the flames coming slowly toward you, gasoline burning, knowing it's impossible to move, to run, or to stop it. They all laugh and throw stuff at you while you try futilely to escape the approaching flames. You feel your legs heat up and then terrible streaks of pain shoot through them. All those small hairs on your legs light up, and it starts to smell like roast meat. Tears start to dry up as the fire rises around you.

In the end, when your legs are almost blackened, they pull you out of the fire and throw dirt on you as if they are doing you a favor. You are left alone, unable to move, in agony and silence on the ground. The ache of burnt skin is unexplainable, constant, and worsens with time. Even the slightest mist causes agony so unbearable that you fall unconscious. The human body is unable to withstand such an extreme level of pain. It shuts down. Every part of your body coils and screams, but fear of being killed makes you mute.

And all the other slaves must watch silently. The only one I've seen try to stop this ritual was set on fire and used as a wooden log for the ritual he desperately tried to halt. He was trying to save his wife, who was killed after seeing him burn to death. Some people have died during this ritual, and they just finish burning the corpse. Then they tie clothes from the body to our chain, to remind us we could be next. These demons have no place in hell, they are just too evil. I am dead.

The day after your ritual, they make you walk with the others, in a straight line, no matter how burnt up your legs are. If you fall, Cold brands you with a "-1" on your forehead. I don't know what it means, but I have it on me. I really tried not to fall, to continue walking even if my legs were burnt almost to the knees. But three hours in, I stumbled on a root and was not able to stand. How depressing to be this feeble. Before standing up, the iron rod burned deep into my forehead. The smell and sound of my sizzling skin still haunts my nightmares.

Cold is an enormous bald man with a black beard that has white patches. He has a "+10" branded into his forehead and several tattoos on his arms and neck. I have never seen him wear a shirt, and he exercises constantly. His khaki pants are cut off below his knees. A massive sword with blue engraved lines on the blade is always strapped to his back. He has thick eyebrows; a slim, long nose; and two piercing blue eyes, cold as ice. You never want him to stare at you, because you know you are as good as dead. Cold is the leader of this pack of cannibals, or whatever they are.

I see a large metal fence with wooden walls behind it pop over the horizon, beyond the trees we are walking through. As we get closer, I can see barbed wire and guards standing on top of a scaffold above the fence line, overseeing the forty meters of bare land separating them from the forest. Their bodies are covered waist-down by a wooden wall attached to the fence, probably for cover or protection. All of them carry a bow around their torso and arrows in a quiver. It seems to be a huge stronghold; the end of the wall disappears off to the left and right. Marching straight at it, Cold has perked up as if he owns this place. He always walks as if he owns the world, and his followers fear him. He will kill anyone, friend or foe, without a second thought; he seems to feed his fucking ego with suffering.

We stop thirty meters from the fence. Cold walks ahead and speaks to the guards. They see him and take a knee, bowing to him. As soon as they open the gates, Cold stares back at us, indicating we must start walking. I can't stop thinking this looks just like those concentration camps in the history books Nathan made me read. A line of skinny slaves forced into a fenced-up place, led by an evil man, with no indication as to what is going on. Our silent group marches inside the walled stronghold, toward a thousand different sounds.

I stare behind to see the forest that leads back home, as the gate is closed. I am trapped. Every single soldier bows to Cold as he leads us across an open area, but it doesn't seem to be out of respect. Some of the younger soldiers shake as he goes by, even though he doesn't acknowledge their existence. All of them have the same scar on their right forearm, it must be a brand of allegiance or something like that. They're bowing out of fear.

The smell is the worst I have ever smelled. Shit, sweat, rust, mud, smoke, all blended into one nauseating fragrance. We walk through a large hall of rusty metal walls without a roof. It's cold and every breeze makes the metal pieces scrape each other. Sounds horrible. Every time it happens my hands tense up. I hate that sound, metal over metal. Feels like the walls are closing in on us.

The zinc walls end, and we turn to the right. We start going up wooden stairs that are all broken and rotten. They creak under our feet.

Cold takes us out on a stage facing a riled-up crowd, shouting and cursing and drinking and dancing. These people are dirty, with hideous teeth and a blend between armor and rags for clothes. I see people kissing and having sex, fighting, and bartering, and the noise is unbearable. This looks like a zoo filled with the worst type of animals. They are not human beings.

Suddenly everyone is silent. Cold walks to the center of the stage, points to his forehead where he has his brand, and everyone does the same while kneeling toward him. He just lowers his arm, stares to the crowd, and shouts with his horrible, terrifying voice, "Begin."

All hell breaks loose again. A kid beside me is taken by force, two soldiers carrying him as he kicks trying to release from their hold. He fights uselessly, until he is thrown like a rag on Cold's feet. The wood sounds hollow as his body bounces and leaves him breathless. I want to do something but feel impotent.

His mother shouts and cries and hits the soldiers trying to control her, but she is fighting a lost battle. One of Cold's men knocks her out with a vicious hit to the back of her head.

I feel terrible, knowing what it feels like to have your family torn apart forever. I shall never see Nathan again or get to know if my parents survived. Tears fall down my cheeks, but I won't allow my face to show grief. I know better than to show weakness right now. Soon my time will come to be auctioned to one of these bastards.

Cold grabs the boy's arm and raises him like a fish in a trophy photo, showing him to the audience. He stares at the crowd while the kid cries and pisses himself, then smirks at the boy.

Cold looks back at the crowd and reads, "Negative one."

Now it smells like piss and blood, and I am about to puke.

A woman with a large body steps forward, pregnant and wearing armor, which seems weird. A skinny man, bald and frail with a short beard, steps forward. He is wearing one of those bags carpenters used to hold their tools in, bulging with what I can't tell, and has a long whip in his right hand. A young man, maybe Nathan's age, steps up. He is the only one I have seen in this world with impeccable running shoes. He is wearing armor as well, but it looks different, lighter and like it was made specifically for his body. He is holding a helmet in his right hand that looks like a war helmet with a small visor and horns toward its back like the Dodge symbol on my dad's car. Last, a woman in a filthy dress steps forward. She has blond hair almost down to her waist, a beautiful face, green-bluish eyes, and large red lips surrounding blackened teeth.

The blond woman raises her hand, and none of the others move.

Cold knocks the kid unconscious and passes him off to the nearest soldier to be delivered to the blond woman. The woman points the soldiers to a rusty old wheelbarrow next to the stage. One of the woman's henchmen rolls the wheelbarrow and the kid through the crowd and disappears into a shed at the back. The creaking of the wheelbarrow fighting to roll across the mud as the poor kid is being taken away like construction materials, dispensable, an expendable resource, is heartbreaking.

The same happens with the other child, but this time his parents know better than to fight back. Cold reads, "Negative one." The same blond woman raises her hand. The boy is hit unconscious and taken to her. This kid has convulsions after Cold hits him, and his parents can only cry and hold each other in desperation.

I don't know that I ever stopped crying but am crying harder than ever now and trying not to vomit. This is the end of the world, hell on earth. How can these people live like this, enjoying so much pain? All those bastards just stare at Cold as if he is a king, a god even, while breaking families apart.

The mother of the first child is dragged upstage still unconscious. Cold reads, "Plus one." She is picked by the fat woman. The father of the second child is taken by the skinny bald guy, while his wife is taken by the fat woman.

The adult man branded with a "-2" is taken to center stage. Cold reads his score and stares at the four devils. All of them have a satanic grin. None of them raise their hand. He had earned two negative marks by falling once and fainting from exhaustion once during our trip.

Cold smiles and looks up at the sky, whispering, "So weak, not worthy of life."

Cold looks back down at the frail man, and in the blink of an eye, breaks his neck and kicks his body off the stage. Something inside me explodes, and I run toward Cold, tackling him. He barely moves, only hitting me with a backhand to my cheek. While I am down, he hits me twice on my forehead and kicks my torso so hard I vomit. I will not faint this time. I would rather die than suffer this humiliation. No Nathan, no Mom, no Dad. I don't give a fuck if I live one more day.

Cold picks me up and shouts at one of his soldiers to bring the burning rod. I kick him and bite his hand as hard as I can to free myself. A small punch lands on his ribs but gets no reaction. As a guard runs toward me, Cold releases me, and I dash toward the guard, making him trip. Kneeling on him, I land punches desperately, with all my strength. The crowd is mute, and no one is moving.

A couple of guards run toward me, but Cold shouts, "Leave him!"

The guard finally raises up, pushing me down, and hits me in the back of my head. Then he kicks me across the stage. Approaching, he kneels on me, but as he gets ready to start beating the crap out of my head, a sword bursts out of his neck. A river of blood falls on my face, even inside my mouth. It is acid and sticky, and I start regurgitating.

"Weak," Cold says in his unnerving voice from behind the dead soldier.

Cold drags the dead body to the edge of the stage and slings him toward the crowd. The body lands right on top of the frail old man, knocking him flat. They laugh hideously even though the guard was one of their own. Cold drags me to center stage, pulling me up to my feet. With one look, he makes it clear that I messed up.

At least I will go down fighting. Not worth it to live like this.

I face the audience, eying the four bastards picking people like cattle, and tense my teeth. Today I die, but I did not die in vain. Nathan would be proud, and I hope he kills all of them. He will. I know he hasn't lost hope and is trailing our steps with vengeance in his heart. It is a shame I will not be alive to see it happen.

I close my eyes and wait to be beheaded, but instead feel fire on my forehead as Cold presses the iron rod on it. I scream in agony but won't move. I will not give him the pleasure. He isn't smiling, but I see joy in his deep blue eyes as he brands me again. He must have changed my score to ensure no one picks me, to kill me, to break my neck and kick my dead body off stage like that poor old man.

Bye, Mom. Bye, Dad. Bye, Nate.

He finishes his job, and that smell of burnt flesh fills my nose again. About to be killed and disposed of, I think maybe this is better than surviving long enough to see what those four bastards do to you. After being set on fire, branded, beaten and terrorized and humiliated every minute of the day, only to be auctioned off like cattle, I don't want to live long enough to see what else these people are capable of.

I stare directly into Cold's eyes, unafraid.

Cold turns to the crowd and shouts, "Plus three!"

The young man with the ram-looking helmet raises his hand. I am his first and only pick.

9
THE ELDER
HOPE FALTERS

I HAVE BEEN TRACING JAY'S STEPS for several days now, and my hope is faltering. Whoever caught him was experienced and left almost no signs of movement behind even though he or she would have had to cover up at least two pairs of footsteps as they went. At least my brother was ingenious enough to leave a clue behind.

Right after finding the shivs and then calming down, I went back to our house. I have never run so fast as I did that day. I pulled as hard as I could on the string attached to the secret entrance to our house, dashed inside, and kicked our front door open. In the kitchen, I noticed Jay took some supplies with him. Smart move. He was going to save me, or at least try to. My body was still smoking from using my power, so every one of my steps left a black imprint on the floor. There was no time to worry about leaving a trail. Every second counted, and I needed every hint I could find about what Jay took with him, to know what clues to look for during my hunt.

Other than figuring out what items he'd taken from the kitchen and warehouse, the first floor gave me absolutely no indication about Jay's intentions, so I went upstairs, avoiding the traps.

Our room's metal door was closed from the inside, just as I

taught him. Maybe he is ready to overcome what is happening to him right now. Maybe by overprotecting him, I didn't realize he's not a child anymore. Nonetheless, my responsibility is to amend my errors and retrieve Jay safely while eradicating from this world whoever caused him pain.

The wooden panel aligned properly, allowing me entrance to our room. My large backpack was hanging from a hook nailed to the wall. I grabbed a jacket, gloves, socks, a pair of thermal pants, and my black sunglasses and headed out to the roof. There I saw my handwriting on that damned piece of paper. 500 m to target. 20 m pause. Dash over fence, force window. Grab prize. Escape route A via garden wall to adjacent park. Escape route B… My binoculars were beside it, so I took them and placed them in my backpack. Jay must have been there not long before me, deliberating whether to risk a rescue mission. He made the wrong, but valiant, choice. At that moment, I promised myself I would make it up to him. I had and still have no idea when or if I will return home…we will return.

I dropped to my knees, inconsolable, frantic thoughts clouding my judgement. What if I had not left that note? Maybe he wouldn't have risked leaving without an idea of where to find me. Maybe if I had taken him with me in past ventures, he would have been ready to avoid being caught. What if? Those scenarios angered me and spooked me at the same time.

Chrissy came to my mind. "Live in the present, learn from the past, and prepare for the future, as it is the place of dreams." My lovely lady was right as usual, even stealing a smile from me when I was at my darkest. There was no gain from dwelling on the past, and a whole lot to gain by going on and saving Jay.

I sprinted downstairs with my backpack to fill it up with supplies: food, water bottles, my medic-kit, shivs, wire, matches, our only lighter, armor, the remains of our camping tent, and a small notepad and a pencil. Finally, I strapped my bow and quiver with thirteen arrows to my back. Fueled by Chrissy's memory and Jay's need for rescue, a renewed vigor raged inside me.

Before leaving, I said those words that haven't yet failed me. "May my senses be advertent, and my aim be unerring." Once again, I feel heartbreak. It truly feels painful inside your chest to consider the possibility of losing everything you have left. First my parents, then Chrissy, and now Jay. If this is to be true, I am lost and alone, without a reason to fight on.

Leaving our house that day, through the rubble, I stopped to hide the string used to open the secondary door. No one shall invade our home, as we will be back...together. Securing our home was calming. Made me really believe I could save him, and I still believe. All else may be beyond my grasp, but hope is within me.

When I arrived back where he was caught, I made a long, detailed search of the place. My wrath constantly tried to divert my judgement, but my heart fought bravely to maintain concentration. No detail could be missed, as seconds counted when hunting. Yes, this was and is still a hunt to the death.

North. Fourteen steps away, Jay had painted the smallest "N" on the wall with his blood. I couldn't risk going too far north based on Jay's clue, since he wouldn't have known their destination. Therefore, I covered a five-kilometer radius over the next twenty hours to ensure nothing would lead me anywhere but north. North was the way back to him.

My body shrieked for sleep that night, but fire erupted uncontrollably from my fingertips, and my jaw was numb from clenching my teeth. A two-hour nap was all I managed before continuing my pursuit. A half-hour run northward took me to the edge of the five-kilometer radius's border I had inspected the day before. Every step beyond that point would lead me into territory I had not explored yet. The landscape was no different from our house's landscape: moss, vines, mud, broken walls, blood splotches, garbage, fallen signs, trees, and wildlife. However, similar is not the same.

I did not stop for a second at that uncertainty. The only one who should live in fear was and is the motherfucker who took what I value most. As time goes by, my need for revenge feeds my rage. At times I find myself only thinking about his death, about the moment when I see whoever took Jay and send him to hell.

Today, the third day after his kidnapping, I am walking northward, stopping at nothing that does not remotely relate to Jay or his captor. Forty meters in front of me, I spot a campsite of some sort. A small opening in the woods reveals the remains of a fire. Dashing toward it, taking long strides on the tough soil, I touch the ashes. Cold. At least a day has gone by since there'd been a fire.

The camp has two fire pits. This first one is set up for cooking. I inspect the second one, thinking it is different, the ashes are not surrounded by stones and are spread out with a burnt-up chair on top of them. About eight pairs of footsteps seem to have danced around it, and some places smell like alcohol and gasoline. A ritual must have been executed, but no blood was spilt. What went on here?

I inspect the fire remains closely, my torso scraping the ground and ash blackening my shirt as I search for any indication as to what happened. Under the ashes, I find what's left of an Under Armour CrossFit tennis shoe, black with blue lightning bolts. Jay's favorite shoes. He cleans them every single day and cares for them as if they are alive. I am considerably behind but in the right direction. But instead of swelling with hope, the burnt pieces of his shoe unleash the hatred coiled inside of me. All sorts of images cloud my mind and my inner fire loses control. Did they burn Jay? Did they kill him? Heat bursts all over my body and into my mind. The temperature rises all around me, the soil underneath me starts to smoke, and my back tenses like rock. I have never felt so enraged, so powerful, so unconquerable.

Fire lashes extend from my fingertips for meters and dance

around me like a fire tornado. Quicker and quicker it accelerates around me, burning everything in its way. Higher and higher this fire tower ascends without control, my ultimate power. Hatred feeds the fire, and it is beautiful and fearful and uncontrollable.

***

This time I lost consciousness. My power exceeded my body's capacity and knocked me out. I guess fire lives within me but not for me, I can control it but not master it yet. My mouth is dry, and my eyes have lost all moisture, making it hard to speak or blink. My muscles feel drained, even bruised. My arms and legs are spread wide as I lie on the soil, facing upward, with the worst hangover. A clear sky peeks through a burn hole partway up through the forest canopy. My fire had soared upward at least five meters high and four meters wide before I collapsed. Now, I am swallowing hard and agonizing as tears sear down my cheeks. Probably the only water left inside of me turned into tears.

What have I done? Anger and vengeance made me lose time, lose my senses, even risk saving Jay. How long have I been out?

Standing up, I feel hollow and fear of being once and for all alone in this unforgiving world sweeps over me. Pain starts to turn into anger again.

Do not give in, Nathan. Don't lose control again. "Fire, obey my command!" My voice breaks the silence through the forest, dominating the slight whisper of wind through the bushes.

Long fire lashes whip from my hands and start dancing around me. Energy starts to drain from my body again. I feel dizzy and numb, but at my command, the fire falters and fades. My power is not limitless—it needs my anger and concentration—but my body is not yet ready to provide enough energy for it. From now on, daily practices are going to be needed to learn how to control my inner phoenix. I'm going to obliterate anyone who has Jay.

Using the energy left inside of me, I stand up feebly, unstable. Walking around the camp is starting to be frustrating as no footsteps can be seen. Where did they head after camping here? It seems as if wind covered their path, but no regular wind is strong enough to disappear all traces on this unforgiving rough terrain. Rain could disappear them, but we've had a month-long drought.

Just as my hope is starting to falter, I see a small shiv, clearly of my own creation and taken by Jay, pushed into the ground, pointing north once again.

Fire is closing in, and forgiveness is not an option.

10
THE YOUTH
HUMANITY NO MORE

A MONTH HAS GONE SINCE THE day I was handpicked by the young man with the ram helmet. If Nathan's training was hard back then, this asshole's training is unforgiving. He allows me to sleep for two hours a day at most, then training ten hours a day, being brainwashed for eight hours, and serving my "masters" for the remaining four hours has been my life.

There is no way to know how many they are. Cold is their leader, everyone bows down to him as he walks by and few manage to look into his eyes when spoken to. During this month, he has killed twelve members of his clan, or family, or I don't know what they are, and at least forty slaves. You cannot fail in any way or it is your head. This angers and frightens me. I have not been able to sleep soundly so far, not under this kind of stress and feeling constantly at the edge of death.

He just slaughtered a friend of mine, Mr. Ridley. He was old and weak; I mean, it was not his fault at all. He slipped while carrying a basket with bread loaves. The floor was all slippery with moss and humidity, and they had broken his walking cane, so he was barely able to move by himself. As soon as those loaves touched the floor, he was a dead man.

I ran as quickly as I could to help him pick them up and

clean them, but Cold saw it happen. While on my knees helping, I could sense his deadly stare. Without turning around, I knew he was coming by his rattling armor that always sends goose bumps up my neck. Mr. Ridley stared up at me in peace, knowing it was his time. His brown eyes and wrinkled smile projected serenity, even though I felt deeply shattered at the sight.

With no notice, Cold's heavy sword fell onto Mr. Ridley's head. I feel drained of my strength and my faith.

I have always believed in God, but today He has left us. Hollowness is all that's left within me; no more friends, no more family, not even the slightest hope to survive this. No more God and no more humanity. May you rest in peace, my friend. He did not deserve this. No one does.

I move quickly to resume sharpening our arrows' points, my mind wandering. The sound of the rock scraping the metal does not stop me from hearing the old man's body being dragged away. This happens almost every day. A despicable act, a murder, and we must go on living in this nightmare. Tomorrow, my body could be dragged while others are forced to turn the other cheek and continue doing their chores. My life has ended.

Cold's actions are despicable, but he is not the source of all evil here. The four people from the auction are Cold's henchmen, the leaders of his four main branches. He is personally in charge of the army and of managing this hell. The large pregnant woman oversees reproduction; her name is Lizbeth the Bringer. She chooses adult women who are healthy and then forces them to accompany Cold's soldiers, to live with them, to even have their children. Every single one of them cries every single night. It breaks your heart to hear to grieving women sobbing desperately as they are forced to do horrible things against their will. I feel empty and impotent.

The skinny bald guy runs forced labor; he is Pete the Perpetual, as he needs no sleep. He chooses adults, mainly male, who are in shape. Not because they can handle more work or be better at it, he chooses the strong ones because they may be able to survive his workload. I get two hours a day of sleep and feel burnout constantly, my mind running as thoughtlessly as a dancer without music most of the time. They maybe get two hours a week at most. They carry large food bags to storage rooms, enormous metal scrap parts to the foundry, mine coal and other minerals, log in the surrounding forests to keep the furnaces going and build every single structure in Cold's realm. The forced labor men don't cry at night; they just stare straight ahead with eyes so dark, so lost, and so hopeless. If God exists, their souls must have left to heaven way before their deaths will release them—those men are no longer alive inside.

The young blond woman is the leader of servitude, and her name is Miley the Enabler. She chooses those who are not fit enough for forced labor or old enough to have children. They must be available 24/7 for the masters, and I have seen no boundaries to their responsibilities. They cook, wash, entertain, and babysit while being whipped, slapped, and constantly humiliated. Since I got here, I have not seen one of them look up from the floor. Trying to get their spirits up is useless. No talk of escaping gets even the slightest hint of a reaction from them—my words crash against their hollow minds, nothing left but pain and surrender. Even their hunched over backs seem to be carrying the burden of their existence, of their humiliation. Only Mr. Ridley held on to his true self, and he is no longer with us.

And last, the young man with a helmet shaped like a ram is Ex the Relentless. He leads those who are strong, young, and feisty. Ex's goal is to turn us into their followers, to be shaped into fearless slaves willing to take on the hardest missions. Sadly, they eventually succeed. I have witnessed unspeakable actions done by people who were caught like me and turned into loyal servants. Time breaks us.

That is why we train so long every day on upper body and lower body strength, camouflage, survival, problem-solving, suicide. We are meant to commit suicide if caught or cornered to avoid ratting out our base camp's location and numbers.

Brainwashing is a term used to cover up torture. I have been almost drowned, lit on fire, stoned, whipped, slapped, hit unconscious, and I have not shed a tear. My agony is held back like a dam holds a river, by my anger. Not because of what they do to me, but because of what I have witnessed.

Nathan taught me to endure, to go past the point where your mind and body want to break down and give up. I don't know if he is alive or not. Maybe he was killed inside that house; there is no way to know what happened to him. A long month makes me wonder if he is dead, but at the same time, something inside will not let me accept that. Heat is within me, just the way you feel when reaching out to a fire at a night camp, but inside of me.

My tears tend to dry up before leaving my eyes because of this immense heat inside me. Some days it feels stronger, and some days it feels weaker. Some days it turns into grief, which doesn't feel like mine. Some days it transforms into hope and excitement, the way you feel when you find something you've long been searching for. These emotions are foreign to me, yet inside of me. It feels just like a déjà vu, something real and unreal at the same time, familiar but unfamiliar.

I walk with all the sharpened arrows to the armory, that gloomy, wooden warehouse built beside the filthy sheds where we are forced to sleep. The soldier in charge of inventory receives my day's work and inspects it with disdain. You will never be thanked, as you will always be an outsider, a slave.

The heavy rain of the past days has messed up the dust pathways, so my bare feet slip and slide on the mud leading to my shed. I've never gone to the end of the sleeping quarters, but I know there are more than fifty rotten, flaking buildings. As I walk up the three steps to my shed, one breaks, and the splinters scrape my ankle. Blood spurts, but I feel no pain; we have been trained with constant agony.

The shed has almost nine square meters of space and is inhabited by at least ten slaves. Sometimes more, and sometimes less, since death has become a common part of our life. Mr. Ridley was not the first to die here, and he will certainly not be the last. The innumerable water drops leaking through the roof wet the rags on top of which I sleep. No point in trying to dry them.

While lying on my pile of rags, one of those foreign emotions takes hold of me. The fear of being caught makes my heart race, and I can feel how a violent gust of wind pushes on my body. My hands clench as if I must hold on to something to avoid falling, but it is all in my imagination. Suddenly, someone drags me out of my covers and tosses me to the ground. Between the paralyzing fear and sudden attack, I'm frozen, unable to react. Ex comes right at me, his metal pointed boot striking me in the stomach and leaving me breathless. Gasping for air is pointless. He picks me up once more and lands a punch to my jaw. My knees turn to jelly and dizziness threatens to fade into blackness. Blood fills my mouth, the repulsive taste making me gag.

He tosses me down the sheds' steps, and I roll on the sticky mud. Before I faint, I see his kick coming at my head and I roll to the right. He misses. Adrenaline has woken me up and spitting out the blood in my mouth relieves me. All my remaining strength goes into standing up and ducking under another angry right hook. Lunging toward his knees, I manage to knock him down. Then I land a one-two jab combo to his face, causing a trickle of blood from his lip. His eyes flare up with hatred and a slight hint of fear.

A kick to my right knee wakes me up from the illusion of hope that I might be able to defeat him and sends me back to the ground. Before I manage to stand up, he tackles me and lands at least three punches to my head. He keeps punching, hitting my jaw, cheeks, forehead, ears, head, and neck.

He gets off me and forces me to sit upright and pushed against a wall, to hold myself up. My head is ringing and aching, bleeding from several cuts, and my eyes are swelling closed. I feel myself nodding off, my remaining strength drained from my body, leaving me helpless against this monster. His blurry silhouette is the only thing I can see; everything else is dark. Mr.

Ridley's peaceful smile comes to mind and soothes me—maybe he was right to smile at death.

"You motherfucking, thieving cunt! Cold says this will be the last time he tolerates your disrespect. Once more and you will be fed to the hounds, alive!" Ex's voice breaks my inner harmony, just the way an unexpected thunder causes panic in fearful dogs. His voice is cruel and menacing, yet has a hint of fear, even of doubt. Before I put my finger on it, he marches angrily away.

As my head swims, fighting the blackness threatening to consume me, another silhouette comes at me. *Not another beating, please. I should pass out once and for all.* But this is not a male silhouette trying to bash my head in.

I say, "Hello, Silver. Mind telling me a story to help me go to sleep?"

She says, "What the hell happened, Jay?"

Of course, she doesn't know, or maybe she does and wants to hear it from me. No sense in arguing with her. Besides, I may fall unconscious anytime now. Her pissed-off attitude amuses me, and a short, painful laugh escapes.

She stares at me with pain in her eyes.

"I stole a small loaf of bread a couple of hours ago for Ms. Barnaby. You know she will die of famine soon unless we do something, Silver."

Her disapproving look gives her away: she's afraid of losing me too. She has lost all her loved ones. Her two younger sisters were caught in a crossfire when all this hell started. They were playing out on the street, no idea of the danger. Silver feels responsible for their deaths, though she won't say it.

Silver is twenty-one, a redhead with green eyes and pale skin with tiny freckles around her nose. She has the kind of smile that brightens up your day, but she can break you with a simple glare. Maybe at first sight she looks frail, but trust me, she is the strongest person I have ever met, the slightest, the quickest, the smartest, and the most vicious. Well, maybe only second to Nathan. She has been an amazing companion within these walls, in this unforgiving semi-life we are forced to live. No one deserves to have wandered in this world alone for such a long time, unable to relate to others because of the intrinsic violence that shapes humanity nowadays. However, she has survived all this time by herself.

Since the first day Ex picked me, we bonded. She was caught the same day I was, and she has a "+5" branded on her forehead. No idea how she managed such a high score. Maybe she killed several of her attackers before they could enslave her. I've seen her dominate as many as five trained men during our practices. She moves like a ballerina, swiftly, fluidly, but each strike has the brute force of a hammer. Her moves are elegant but potent, like a dancing cobra. Timing is her best trait, measuring her opponent for the exact moment to strike for the kill. She knows her limitations but is proud of them as they are part of her humanity. Hope for humanity rests on people like her, who will fight until their last breath to live on within the people she helps, like me.

She has my back, and I have her back. For every time I have been whipped, she has been whipped twice for protecting me, lying for me, or taking the blame. She tends to my injuries, making me feel back at home, before The Day was our worst nightmare, when my mom picked me up and my dad covered my scraped knees with Band-Aids. Their memory inspires a mix of hope for days like those and sorrow at the idea of never seeing them again.

I have told her about my parents and how we have no clue if they survived. She says there is no reason why we should be certain they died. I am fully aware of how far they were, and why they have never managed to come back, if alive. I feel hopeful for my parents, and at the same time, afraid for what humanity might have done to them.

Silver helps me up and takes me stumbling to the small basin outside the shared bathroom. My arm is around her shoulder, and I am limping slowly. The bathroom is a filthy hole behind plywood walls, with no roof, which is used by all forty or more slave sheds. She grabs a brownish towel that dangles on top of the bathroom's wall, humid from the rain, and cleans the wounds Ex inflicted upon me. It burns as she scrapes the dirt off—a necessary pain I am well-acquainted with by now.

She mutters angrily, "Go to your shed. I'll try to find something to tend to your messed-up face." Every step sends a stinging to my head, a terrible ache. I feel how at least a rib must be broken and my right knee is busted. The three steps to my shed are excruciatingly painful to go up. Before entering, I spit some blood outside, as if the inside were any cleaner and I should not spit. How funny the way old habits do not die?

She comes back to my shed as soon as I manage to lie on my rags. She covers my wounds skillfully with a cloth to ward off infection and helps me lie back in bed. We have less than two hours before it's time to get up again. A smile forces its way through my tears.

"Silver, how were you trapped? I cannot imagine your being trapped."

"Okay, Jay, I will tell you to shut you up and keep you awake. Those blows to your head might have caused a concussion, so I need you to stay up. All right?"

"Yes, my red captain."

She glares at me.

"I will let it pass since you are definitely stupefied by that beating. Well, I was caught close to where you were caught. Running away from an encounter. I was careless. Ran straight into Cold's motherfucking camp. To this day it angers me, the thought of how easy it would have been to not be caught. It feels as if I grabbed the fucking hook, placed it inside my mouth, and helped them reel me in.

"I ran from that encounter not because I lost—trust me, I won that fistfight. A tough guy, though. No one had ever managed to counter me after a surprise attack. A fury of blows, and yet he managed to strike me with a helluva right hook. In the end, my surprise attack had been enough to stun him, and

I finished it. My carelessness was the fact that I had mistakenly gotten too comfortable and ran into this enemy right inside the house I had chosen to fortify as my safe house. In my experience, you must defeat your foes and leave quickly, no turning back and no traces left behind, because enemies will come searching for revenge. You know, I have never killed an enemy.

"This time I was surprised because this enemy managed to get into my safehouse without forcing entry. No sound, no hint, no nothing, Jay. A complete ghost, silent as the night. At times I think about that night and how lucky I was to be the one who surprised my foe, and not the other way around. That man could have killed me. Fortunately, I was upstairs prepping my bedroom's defenses when I heard it."

Her eyes narrow down exactly the way they must have done at that moment.

The enemy must have made a noise. What a hapless foe to run into her surprise attack. She'd have run straight at them, punching and kicking again and again until they collapsed unconscious. *What an unfortunate foe to find Silver, but no jewelry,* I think with a chuckle.

A sly smile appears on Silver's face. "A small bell I had attached to a rifle sitting on a table right outside, in the backyard's terrace. That's what alerted me, Jay. Truth be told, that rifle didn't even work. I used it to scare enemies, and it was as dangerous as any club. And it worked great for making sure any potential threats gave themselves away."

All the warmth inside my body leaves in a rush, and I'm frozen. My eyes widen and, trembling from head to toe, I stare blankly at Silver and blurt out, "No! Nathan!"

11
THE ELDER
PERSEVERANCE

A MONTH AND A HALF HAVE gone by, and yet I feel as if everything stopped around me. Time moves, but everything else is the same. My patience is failing. I feel void, nonexistent, hopeless. Then I feel enraged and heated up from the inside out, and then pleasure in the relief of blasting fire all round me as my inner strength fights against my seeming surrender.

Jay must be alive; he must be.

No fucking signs point to him being dead—no mounds of dirt and no unburied bodies left behind. Not even those devils can disappear a body.

For every step I've taken north from that camp, I went two steps back in fear of missing any of Jay's clues. Hunting a ghost who leaves no footprints and barely finding any signs of camps, it's impossible to know if you're going in the right direction. The only thing left behind are those strange ash patterns and burnt up chairs. Those fires are surrounded by absolutely no footprints, so I cannot know if all were made by the same group or which campfire burned first to point me toward a marching direction. Desperate, just like Alice going down the rabbit hole. No sense of direction, of time, of the end of it all. And I worry that my excessive meticulousness is allowing them to vanish for good. This doubt clouds my judgement and sends me in spirals of confusion.

Today I decided to go against my fear of missing a clue. It is time to march due north without hesitation. Too long has gone by and my training has failed me. Time to risk it. Right now, there is no greater loss to me than time. Wandering around, searching for the invisible has proven to be the worst loss of all.

I walk north through a dense forest where almost no light touches the ground. There's almost no wind and only the faint crunching sound of dry leaves as I walk. As the day ages, the humidity rises, making my skin sticky. I have plenty of water, so exhaustion or dehydration will not be a problem. Today is a day where I've got an edge if some foe crosses my path. Rested, hydrated, covered by moving shadows from the canopy, and fire raging explosively within.

Suddenly I hear a deep voice, commanding and filled with pride, straight ahead. Crawling through the dense forest slowly, I sneak my way through the bushes and manage to see the voice's owner.

A tall, bald man with a black beard is standing twenty meters in front of me, staring into the forest away from me. The trees' shades dance on his wide back. He is strongly built and has a meter-long, shiny metal knife strapped to his back and a large shield in his left hand. Wearing armor around his torso, thighs, and shins, but no helmet, he stares at the forest before him as if waiting for something. His arms and neck are tattooed all over, but they don't look like they're made exclusively with ink. They look cut into his skin before being painted over. Death depictions framed with dates and numbers.

I'm staring at a murderer, an evil creature no longer human. I feel disgusted.

In a one-on-one confrontation, I might be overpowered by him. He is clearly well-trained, his stance seeming to be naturally ready for assault even while he must believe he's not in danger.

The notion that he might be Jay's abductor surges within me, heat shooting all over my body. My face tenses as I fight against the urge to explode, to release all the power I possess and kill this man. Maybe he is not Jay's captor, so he should not be murdered. Or maybe he is, so I must wait patiently for him to guide me to Jay for his rescue. So evident and logical, yet the urge to torch him is fighting for control.

Don't, Nathan! You have failed to contain fire once and days were lost. The raging anger that consumed me last time heats my body, but I contain myself to stop this anger from possessing me. I am not sure yet if he is alone or not. Better to follow him slowly and silently before making a rash move. This is the first seemingly good lead since finding Jay's shoe. Time to become invisible.

He walks away toward the trees in front of him and away from me. As I move a step forward, I notice he is not leaving any footprints behind him. I turn around and see the trail of my footsteps on the dry ground. Confusion grabs hold of my thoughts for a second. He must be the one I am hunting; this asshole has something to do with Jay's disappearance.

Deadly fire whips emerge from my hands, ready to char him into a pile of ash. My eyes feel like they are flaming red, but my training is proving effective. Fire slows down, flickers, and then vanishes.

Out of the woods in front of the bearded man come four more men. I lie down on my stomach and watch them through the tall grass, just as a predator on prey. They bow down to the man, then he growls something, and they stand up. One of them says something and gets knocked out with a powerful yet quick blow. This bald man is a force to be reckoned with. The soldier falls heavily to the ground, his neck snapped. That man does not give a damn about what just happened; he walks away without even checking whether the man survived.

A nervous twitch in my neck alerts me to fear, fear that I must overcome if I am to face him.

The other three men pick the body up and walk behind the bearded man, northeast from my position. He pauses, turns, and casually says something with a cold smile and penetrating gaze. The men drop the body and leave it behind without turning back.

What the hell was that all about? No time to wonder. Crawling behind them, I see how again no footprints are left behind, even now that they are four heavy men. No clue as to why that happens.

As I reach the body, I inspect for vital signs. His head is turned almost to his back. He was a heavily built man, with a small arched nose, several scars across his face, and brown eyes. His armor is rugged, handmade, heavy, and not built to his size. His long bow was taken by those who used to be his companions, and no sign of his allegiance is left behind, no mark as to who they are. A dead end once more. While taking a knee, my senses alert me to no danger close by, so I dash in the direction the men and their terrible leader went.

Right ahead, they march, formed up in case they are attacked. They walk silently northward, not even stopping to grab pitanga fruits. Those are great sweet and sour fruits shaped like a pumpkin but the size of a small strawberry, filled with nutrients and carbohydrates, making them well worth the picking.

Why are they ignoring such a rich food?

When I reach those trees, I do take some fruits. Biting one, I relish its red juice and bittersweet flavor. This sugar injection boosts me up and strengthens me. It reminds me of a childhood memory when Jay and I ate them while throwing some at each other. As they'd struck our clothes, we pretended the red stains were gunshot wounds. Sadness once more takes ahold of me. Please, Jay, be safe, be ready to escape back home with me.

Are these men leading me to Jay? My heart and mind seem to agree for the first time in a long time that this is leading me in the right direction. I'm harnessing all my power, building it up to maximum levels; soon all of them will perish while I rescue my brother. My sadness turns into hope, my downcast eyes into red luminescent fierce eyes, and my doleful expression turns into an angered grin.

Foolishly, I step on a dry branch, all covered with moss and dead leaves. Before even discovering whether my foes heard, I climb up the nearest tree using my bow as a harness. Up and up and up until the canopy covers me. Silence is now my enemy as it hides their advances. A hollow feeling in my stomach, a tense back, and a racing heartbeat rule over me, as my eyes shoot in all directions trying to see anything that might endanger me.

Suddenly, a hurricane-like wind makes me struggle to keep hold of the tree's branches. The dense leaves keep me covered, but the skinny bushes on the ground are destroyed, and my mind is simply unable to understand what just happened.

Snapping out of my surprise, I watch through the leaves as the bald leader and his soldiers scout around, searching for the cause of the creaking sound. They circle around, even under the tree I am hiding in.

The bald man stops underneath. He stares upward, right at my position, as if he knows I am here. Tense seconds go by, as I wait to be spotted and forced to fight. One of his soldiers tells him something while pointing southward. He lowers his gaze and follows his subordinate. That man just saved me, and based on what I have seen, killed himself by guiding this bald savage into an erroneous direction. My breathing starts to slow down to a normal tempo.

Minutes go by and they seem to give up, maybe thinking it was just a squirrel. They continue walking, not even worried the sound could have been the comrade they left for dead. No respect for human life whatsoever, as if he were completely disposable like a Kleenex after a sneeze.

When they've gone thirty meters away from my hiding place, I slide down and continue following, this time fully aware of my surroundings. That wind was not natural; something devious is happening here.

Thirty minutes after the unexpected hurricane almost blew my cover, fear is trying to convince me I am following a dead end, maybe my dead end if I'm spotted. Nonetheless, fear is a mere water drop trying to extinguish the forest fire flaming inside of me. The fact that they leave no footprints has me convinced of their connection with Jay vanishing.

I halt my pursuit. By focusing on them and my thoughts, I almost walked out of the forest covering and into what seems to be their camp. A large metal fence with wood walls behind it stretches off to the left and right without an end in sight. On top of it, barbed wire seems to be the first line of defense. The second line consists of three guards holding crossbows, standing atop a ledge and staring straight at the forest without flinching. They take a knee and bow quickly toward the bearded man before resuming their positions.

The gate opens slowly yet smoothly, uncommon as rust has done its work for the past seven years on gates and fences. Those must be new; they must have a foundry. Counting the three surviving men, the leader, and the bowmen, there are seven enemies, three bows, a large sword, and the knives held by the three soldiers. Yet the size of this camp makes evident they are just a small pack out of the entire force.

Briefly, through the open gate, I see a large hall lined up at each side with rusty metal walls. Those are not new, but they do the job of concealing what is beyond them. How can I get inside to recon if Jay is in there without being spotted? While I'm observing, the wind brings a revolting scent. Metal and sweat and dried-up blood and human feces and smoke are all blended into a nauseating mix. Within those walls, unspeakable things must occur, and I must stop it. Chrissy would insist on my doing something, especially if my brother is being held. No matter how many enemies stand in my way, all will fall into an abyss of eternal fire.

Dusk is already darkening the skies. Nightfall will come soon, and that is when I shall venture inside. Until then, I will scout around to find a weak point, a possible entrance, a solitary guard exposed to a predator like me. That is the best and only way. No way will I expose my cover without being sure Jay is in there. My carelessness during this mission could quickly lead to a war against an army of trained and well-equipped savages.

Someone moves up to the guards on the scaffold. He is a couple of years older than me and walks like he owns the place. A wooden wall attached to the fence covers him waist-down, so I am only sure he is wearing armor to cover his torso. He puts a helmet on this head. It looks like a horned bull or a ram. My bow and arrow are pointed straight at him. I could pierce his neck and watch his blood paint the floor beneath him, but not yet.

The guards nod slowly without staring at him directly. He points at something to the north, inside the camp and out of my view. He then points outside of the camp and makes a slow gesture, moving his thumb across his throat, threating someone about escaping. Helmet guy moves out of sight for a couple of seconds, descending behind the wall. The archers don't move or speak, clearly afraid of this man. Seconds feel like minutes as I feel this has something to do with Jay, sensing my footsteps have guided me in the right direction.

Again, he emerges on top of the fence. This time he is holding someone by the arm, but his body hides this doomed soul completely. He throws the man to the floor and kicks him, then picks him up, punches him in the liver. As the man falls to the floor again, helmet guy spits on him.

The skinny little man trembles, then stands up slowly with his head bowed, avoiding eye contact with helmet man. His body is skinny but not entirely unmuscular, just the way someone looks when they start exercising before completing puberty. His back is toward me, arched down from the blow. Shirtless, I notice how his back is bloody from whiplashes. The tortured man manages to stand up straight and turns around to stare at the guards while the helmet guy leaves.

I squint hard, trying to focus. His profile is familiar to me…

Fire bursts out of me, brightening the night sky, and a fierce shout filled with death and vengeance emerges from my lungs, piercing the silence of night.

I have found you, little brother.

12
THE YOUTH
HOPE RESTORED

SILVER WAS THE ONE WHO had attacked my brother. She only left him for dead, and I am not angry at her. She did what she had to when faced with someone unknown to her. Destiny played with us, but it did not manage to break what we have built. Despite blurting out his name, I managed to cover up my mistake. I made it seem as if I fell asleep during her story and spoke out from a nightmare.

Nathan was still inside the house when Cold knocked me out that day. Silver had just run out and was foolishly trapped. At least I am certain now that Nathan was not dead when I last left our house; he was unconscious but alive. That could mean he was never found and killed by Cold and his men. My hope is restored at the faint possibility of his being alive and well and in search of me.

I know my brother as well as I know myself. He must have woken up and followed our tracks, found my shivs planted under the garage door, the small "N" I painted, the shoe I buried in the ashes of our first night camp. But why has he been unable to find us? Unfortunately, I could not leave any more hints as Cold started being suspicious and his men followed my every move. Probably as we got closer to this hellhole, they grew warier.

One night while acting asleep, I started to scrape a rock with a stolen metal spoon. Slowly, to avoid any noise my captors might hear. That night I had heard them talk about a large town, and it was the best hint so far that I could leave behind for Nate. I was terrified of getting caught but had to try.

The possibility of leaving the clue was shattered. One of Cold's soldiers saw me moving slightly under my covers and picked me up violently.

"Masturbating, sick punk?" He yelled, tossing me to the ground.

A kick to my head was the last I remembered. The next day, they kicked one of my legs almost until broken and then forced me to hobble on one leg all day. The searing pain taught me I would never be able to leave more clues behind. Now, I regret it. Nathan lost the trail.

Now, since the moment Silver accidentally told me about her encounter with my brother, this feeling inside of me has strengthened. Fire seems to burn inside of me stronger and stronger every day. Sometimes it feels wobbly like a candle hit by wind, fighting against being put out, but then it comes back twice as strong. Nathan's on my mind day and night. He will save me—save us, Silver and me. I am sure of it.

Two days ago, Silver was summoned by Ex into a courtyard. A small child of maybe seven years old was on her knees, with legs holding her down, clinging to a horrendous doll in her trembling hands and weeping hysterically. Her eyes met Silver's, pleading for help.

Ex whispered into Silver's ear and then stared back at the child. That filthy stare meant death. He had asked Silver to kill the child right in the middle of the courtyard while the innocent soul stared up at her. I was frozen by this scene, feeling empty inside at the depths of cruelty someone could force upon others. All around me people froze, unable to do anything to save her. We knew better. One wrong move and you are dead, and the child suffers twice. We had seen it before.

My emotions changed from sadness into anger and then fear and back to despair, a rollercoaster I'd grown used to. Something stung in the back of my mind. A deep struggle took hold of my thoughts, as if I had to make the hardest decision of my life. Yet it did not feel like my own struggle, but rather belonging to someone or something else.

Silver raised her bow and arrow slowly toward the child. Ex was screaming and laughing at the small child, who was unable to run away. For every centimeter Silver's bow raised, the deep struggle inside of me worsened.

Kill quickly and painlessly or let Ex do unspeakable things to an innocent soul. Kill Ex.

No! That would only make it worse for all.

Me? How can I kill Ex?

While I swam in all those emotions, some my own and some apparently Silver's, I closed my eyes. Without opening them, I felt it the moment the child moved on to a better life, straight to heaven. All those feelings and thoughts broke like a glass falling to the ground, as if my heart had been ripped out of my chest. I cried in silence, suffering twice with my pain and Silver's.

Somehow Silver's emotions bonded with my own and took control. This bond is beyond friendship and empathy; it is mental, natural, psychic. The deep scars in her are now fused with my own. Silver did it to save the child from further pain, but it shattered her heart. She had never killed anyone before, had survived without the need for it, until today when everything changed. What she had avoided for so long, withstanding impossible trials and still not taking a life, rips at her. Her soul shattered, her eyes dulled, her entire body shakes as she sobs. The innocent child's passing reminds her of the horrible moments when she lost her sisters. Her pain is beyond my comprehension even as her memories flash in front my eyes. I feel as if I made that terrible choice and shot the arrow. Tears roll down my cheeks uncontrollably.

Silver is changed. As days and nights pass us by, she becomes rebellious, suffering twice as much punishment as before. Her resilience doubles as her desire to cause change in this world triples. She speaks day in and day out about doing something, finding a way to survive, escape, and change the world. She becomes more cynical, ready to kill enemies who cause suffering to innocent people. A constant hatred taints her soul, reminding her about the consequences of her past naivete. Even though escaping is impossible, even if we are always moments away from dying in this camp, her desires evolve from survival to a broader sense of the greater good.

I know all of this since from that day on, our emotions are connected. Her ideas, plans, thoughts, feelings, and deep desires are visible to me, tangible. Since that day, I know what Silver feels. Concentrating allows me to sense her thoughts and feelings even though she is far away. She doesn't know, or at least hasn't said anything to me about it, and I'm not able to do it every try or hold it for more than a couple of seconds. Only on that horrible godforsaken day had it lasted very long, maybe because those feelings were extremely powerful and painful.

I've felt like fire has been spiking inside of me every day for more than a month. And I sense that someone feels my fire, someone filled with wrath and vengeance and repentance. Someone else is connected to me and is searching for hope. Those are not Silver's feelings, so I believe strongly that Nathan is coming.

Why fire? I don't know.

***

Today I am having my first test. These assholes think two months here have broken me. My beliefs stand as firmly as ever, and Silver has been key to this. We talk every time we can about what happens, what we see, what we feel, what we want to do, and what the future holds in store for us. She has prepared me to do the bare minimum at these tests to avoid torture, but at the same time, escape from doing evil.

They are going to send me out on a mission or place me at a lookout or some task that could put me in a position where I would have to prove my allegiance to them. I know I must do it, just the way Silver did back then with that poor child. Sometimes offering death to people who cross Cold's path is the best choice. I don't know if I will be able to do it. My mind feels shackled and empty and rattled. I know it makes no sense, but that is exactly what happens…senselessness.

Today I feel completely distracted by the strongest sense of fire within, seemingly being stoked from something or someone close by. It feels enraged, strengthened, and powerful beyond my comprehension. I feel cautiously hopeful, just like a chess player thinking twice before making a checkmate move.

Ex is coming toward me, holding his ram helmet at his side. He is fully armored and has a slight grin on his stupid face. He grabs my arm and pulls me up to follow him. My hatred boils inside, contained. My arm burns with pain in his brutal grip, but I will not give him the satisfaction of seeing my pain.

We are walking toward the main gate. Cold went on a mission about a week ago, so Ex has been in charge. Since he returned today, Ex returned to his regular duties. Something terrible is going to happen to me today, I know it. This bastard has something against me, a personal vendetta. Insecure idiot.

He releases my arm and orders me to wait before going up to the scaffold to give orders to the guards. He must be going to tell them to kill me if I do not follow their orders. As he is climbing up on the lookout's ledge, someone's thoughts take ahold of my mind. Who is it? Silver is not here, and they are wondering about Ex. Who is he? Why is he giving orders to the guards? Is he wearing armor on all his body? Is his helmet a ram? Confusion clouds my thoughts. I know the answer to all these questions, and yet I feel real doubt. This connection feels as strong as the one I share with Silver, as clear and as present as ever.

Running over my thoughts about what Ex has in store for me, ideas about how to get into the stronghold and outthink the archers distract me again. All this is extremely baffling, so much so that I am not even listening to what Ex is telling me, shouting at me. He climbs down and shouts harder at me. Focus is lost on me. Why am I thinking about where he went, even though he is in front of me?

He grabs my arm again as he pulls me up the stairs to the ledge. Thrown to the floor in front of the bowmen, my knees scrape on the wood floor. A surprise kick to my side breaks my connection to the strange feelings. Pain shoots up and down my torso. Ex picks me up and lands a punch to my liver, doubling me over. About to puke, my knees bleeding, a nasty spit lands on my face.

This anger is my own. All the pain escapes in a hurry as anger takes control of me, desperate to kill Ex, to grab one of those arrows and end his life, and mine with it. Not today, especially with Nathan coming to find me soon. Silver, Nathan, and I will make a deadly team, capable of fleeing this hell and killing any of Cold's men who dare to face us.

Fighting against all the soreness in my body, I manage to stand up straight, once again not giving him the satisfaction. As I turn to be told my instructions for this disgraceful test, confusion and curiosity swiftly turn into an uncontrollable wrath inside of me, but it is not my wrath. I know whose it is. It feels so familiar to me, so close to me, and so unforgivingly powerful.

As an unprecedented force fills every single part of my body with intense, uncontrollable heat, a tower of fire explodes right at the forest line fifty meters away from the fence. Once more a familiar, external thought takes control of my mind, this time filled with hope and vengeance. Clear as an uncloudy night sky, his thoughts say, *"I have found you, little brother."*

13
THE ELDER
SKY-HIGH FIRE

THE SECOND I IDENTIFY MY brother, all plans, all meticulous searches for a safe entrance, and all possibilities of a stealthy approach burn to the ground like the forest around me. I can sense the fire column raging, fueled with the anger and fear that has possessed me for too long. The heated air blurs the view in front of me, as the guards and the asshole hurting my brother duck behind the wall. Two months of searching and worrying and fearing for him and suddenly he is found. Today is no day for cautiousness—today is a day for revenge.

The horned-helmet guy grabs Jay and tosses him over his shoulder, then runs beyond my view, enraging me further. The bowmen are dazzled as they watch fumes and fire reaching up toward the dawn sky. I walk slowly, taking each step full of certainty that everyone will pay for all they have done.

I emerge from the burning forest with my glaring red eyes centered on the guards who are coming back to their senses, identifying me as an enemy. They decide incorrectly to attack, but too late. As soon as they maneuver to take a shot, I discharge a tornado of fire at them. They are not even suffering, just gone. There is no need to tire myself by running, so I take every step at a casual pace. I turn around and see how beneath every footstep a burnt mark is left behind. Vengeance is fueling me, and it feels everlasting.

Control it, Nathan. Don't pass out.

I hold both hands out, cupping them together to create a small sphere of disordered flames. I can feel my power accumulating gradually until it screams to be let loose. I spread my legs in a wide stance and push hard in the direction of the main gate. A wall of fire rushes forward, sending the gate flying inward and bursting the entire zinc hall into a runway of fire, a true red-carpet event.

Continuing my walk surrounded by intermittent fumes and smolder and fire, I grab my bow and an arrow. The burning wall around me is illuminated against the dusky sky, and I can hear screaming enemies running toward me. My strength is somewhat drained, and my mission has barely begun, so I must ration it. Now is time to hide again, to run away from the flames and continue my search. I command whips of fire to emerge once again from my right hand and blow one of the zinc panels out of place. My body comes back to normal, no more fire emanating from it.

I cross the recently opened pass slowly, watching my surroundings carefully as I enter unknown territory. Two dozen scarecrow-like figures are spaced out in what must be a sort of training ground. The ragged figures are full of holes, and some even have knives thrust into them.

Twenty meters to my left, parallel to the burning wall behind me, a guard is staring confounded at the flaming wall. I get into a crawl and walk slowly toward him. The slight sound from my footsteps is undiscernible from the creaking noises from the fire. He dies silently without even noticing me. To be cautious, I pick his armor and cover myself up. At least it will buy me some seconds if I run into more enemies. Fortunately, he used a black cap that covers my face.

Dozens of enemies with bows and arrows and knives and clubs are coming in my direction from the north, aroused by the brutal attack that just shattered their frontline defenses. Another group of men run toward the flames with water buckets to extinguish the flames destroying their main entrance.

To avoid suspicion, I grab a bucket of water and run with them, throwing gulps of water at my sons and daughters. All these men running to extinguish what could be fed up again whenever I want makes me smile beneath my face mask. The helmet guy is nowhere to be seen, so after throwing my seventh bucket at the flames, I vanish behind a small warehouse to continue my pursuit.

Inside the building, I see a stage overlooking an area large enough for a massive crowd, probably used for executions and slavery auctions. True malevolence happens within these walls, and the thought of saving more people crosses my mind. While running, I extend my arm back and shoot a small fire river at the stage. It creaks wildly as its support beams shatter and break. The sound of destruction pleases my rage.

About a hundred meters in front of me, I discern forty plus silhouettes running in my direction. Quickly, before being spotted, I enter a small cabin at my right to let them pass, the dancing smoke covering my path. Faces not yet blackened by smoke, these heavily armored men must be new to the party. Surprised by how many of these assholes there are, fear threatens to weaken me but is immediately sent to oblivion by my need to save Jay. No way in hell I can handle such a force by myself, but I won't have to.

This cabin smells like moss and grease. It is made of wood, wood darkened from rot. It has pots, pans, cups, bowls, glasses, forks, and knives enough to feed more than half a hundred. These disgraceful sons of bitches probably keep them for themselves and make their slaves use their hands, if they are even fed. Two months, James has endured this—two months taken away from him, two months of suffering as something less than human.

I'll kill as many as I can to ensure no one else goes through this.

Through a door at my left, I enter a small hallway connecting the cabin to a large container modified into a kitchen. Three men are standing three meters ahead, facing away from me, with blades strapped to their waists, clearly more than cooks. They stare through a small window in front of them, arguing about what could be happening. As soon as the forces outside run out of view through the window, the man closest to me swallows one of my arrows and, before his blood touches the ground, the other two men are each served.

Looking out the small window on the far wall, I see the bald man with the black beard stomping calmly toward the stage. Bolting down to avoid being found, I convince myself he is the leader of this clan. No one else would dare walk so casually toward the flaming disaster. I retrieve my arrows and push the three dead men against the door to make it difficult for anyone to enter. I leave through a hatch where these men served the others. These many men led by such a savage is beyond my prowess. It's time to run. Go, go, go.

I run away from the burning wall and the kitchen, feeling the damp soil under my heavy steps. The moon has started to rise as nightfall creeps closer. A two-hundred-meter sprint running parallel to the stronghold's outside wall two meters to my right gets my heartbeat running. To my left, buildings like the kitchen are laid out in a disorganized way, with a road leading toward the front wall that is burning down still. Somehow, I know Jay is within the neighborhood, I can hear his voice inside of me. He is desperately wishing for me to find him; he knows I am close!

What looks to be somewhat of a neighborhood rises fifty meters in front of me. These buildings were built after the apocalypse, with battered-down wooden, zinc, and adobe walls. They are seemly inhabited, probably used as sheds for the slaves being held in this stronghold. Each step closer shows me how crude this reality is. A light wind brings a putrid smell toward me, of feces and rot. The houses are unevenly distributed around a central path. As soon as I reach the path, I halt my run and lower my body to inspect the first house to my right.

Two undernourished men, a woman, and a couple of children

fearfully sneak a peek from the windows, doors, and small slots between the wall panels of this first house. These slaves have been tortured into ghouls who can barely stand by themselves. My heart breaks at the horrifying sight, but I cannot stop to save them, not before saving my brother.

I walk toward them and ask them for help. "Have you seen a boy called James? Fourteen years old, skinny, and caught not that long ago?" But no one answers me, staring lifelessly at me. They are unsure if they can speak to me without getting in serious trouble. The woman even trembles in fear at the sight of me. The moment I turn around to go on in my search, one of the children says softly, "You are Nathan?"

My body feels aroused and goose bumps crawl over my arms. Without thinking, I hug this guiding angel in the form of a small, skeletal child. "Where is my brother James? Help me, little friend, please." She weakly raises her arm toward the central path in front of me, deeper into the neighborhood. "Ex took him down there." Tears run down uncontrollably from my eyes as hope returns. The woman blurts out, "About ten houses down the road. He must have taken him to his shed. You will see it to your left. Now, go! Leave us or they'll kill us." Her comment brings back the urgency to my mind.

Running down the main street of this godforsaken neighborhood, doubts of Jay's status start fighting my fortitude... Jay must be in one of the three sheds to my left, but which? The door to the first shed, the one closest to me, opens. I can see four dirty faces peek from the door. These people know something has occurred as they slowly, fearfully stand inside their sheds staring at me. The sight of me causes an almost palpable fear in their eyes. Before a word escapes my mouth, I feel a shooting pain sear my leg.

An arrow pierces my right thigh, shooting pain through my body. My sprint ends as I fall to the ground, screaming in agony. Based on its direction, someone to my right, down the neighborhood's central path, shot at me. As I slowly raise my sight, I distinguish the helmet with the horns in front of the third shed, about ten meters away from me. The man who has my brother.

He is walking toward me and pulling his string backward with another arrow. The pain is blocking my focus, so only small flames are dancing from my fingertips. A second before he manages to shoot me dead, a small figure surges from the shed to his right and tackles him to the ground. The helmet guy easily discards the attacker with a kick and jumps to his feet.

The kid stands up to face him, giving me time to break the arrow and pull the head out of my leg. As I recover from the fresh jolts of pain, I watch helmet guy get a knife out of his holster and run toward my hero. His first slice misses when the kid gracefully dodges. The second slice misses by millimeters as the kid jumps and rolls to the right. A third attack cuts the kid's torso deeply, racking him with pain.

He will kill him if I don't do something.

The kid backs away and into the breaking moonlight. Now I know who my mystery savior is, but this will be the last time you will have to save me, Jay. The entirety of my power surges back from the tips of my toes and up my limbs, while my eyes turn devilishly glowing red. Just like water escaping a dam, my fire rages to its maximum. My body swells from the pure strength building within me, and fire swirls around my forearms.

The helmet guy turns toward me at the sudden brightness and before a terrified shriek escapes his throat, a stream of revolving fire blasts him into oblivion. The shed behind him burns wildly, its windows breaking, and the wood creaking with flames reaching the night sky. This man will never spread evil again. The pain my brother has suffered is finally avenged.

Jay stands up and turns around at me, his face betraying shock and fear at my transformation and, to him, my newfound abilities. His eyes are wide open, and he stands motionless staring at me. I understand his fear and confusion, but it is time to escape before more enemies come our way.

Walking feebly toward him, my usual self slowly crawling back into existence and my alter ego hiding once more to patiently wait until needed again, I say, "Hello, little brother. Time to go home."

"Maybe God does exist," Jay replies, then grabs my arm to help me walk and leads me farther into the neighborhood.

At what appears to be the sleeping quarters next to his, he leans me against a wall and goes inside quickly searching for something. He comes back out exasperated, and calls out toward the next shed "Silver?" I can see him worried, running down the path searching for this Silver thing. Out of the corner of my eye, I see someone running toward us from the sheds on the other side of the central path. I roll painfully to avoid being attacked and turn around toward the foe. On the other side of the three-meter path, I see her, the redhead magnificence. My body tenses at the infuriating sight. She works for *them*.

My fire power is sluggishly extinguishing as I have overused it today, but some of it can still be mustered. She turns to stare at me, surprised as I point at her and say, "Love your voice, dead beauty." My grin is accompanied by fire revolving around my hands, building up for a final strike. A fraction of a second before shooting my remaining power at the sweet sight of revenge, Jay steps in front of her, arms wide open, stunning me.

"Get away from her, Jay! She is the reason for our being here." He angers me further and more power fuels me.

"No, brother, don't do it!"

How foolish of him to trust her. "I am your brother, Jay!" Anger and anxiety reach high levels once more as I struggle to contain it, to avoid hurting Jay, who's in my way.

"Please, Nathan, I owe my life to her!"

"Jay, you are wasting time! Get the fuck away from that bitch!"

A knife flies past Jay, barely missing them both as it zings past his ear. My anger is diverted to the direction of the attack. A woman covered in armor composes her stance back after missing to attack again. Before foolishly attacking my brother again, she falls to her knees with a small knife in her forehead. The redhead is in a fighting stance, having just saved Jay. Surprisingly, she is not one of them. Time to go now, the time to settle my score with the redhead postponed.

"Let's go! Both of you!" I redirect the remaining fire power burning within me to my leg to avoid feeling the pain from the arrow.

We run toward the wall perimeter beyond the slave neighborhood. The entire force of this clan's footsteps resounds behind us, sprinting in our direction. They must have extinguished the fire on their front wall, and my attack on Ex alerted them of further danger in their slave quarters. My leg aches terribly and our run is slower than their fearful stride. They are catching up to us.

We have maybe sixty meters of a head start, and the wall is growing closer and closer. Forty meters to go. My heart is pounding, half from exhaustion and half with adrenaline. My fire is fighting the pain in my leg, so I can run again, the wound bleeding badly, leaving a red-stained trail behind me. We must get out somehow, but I am running out of strength to blast the wall.

"Jay, I may not be able to open an exit!" My voice sounds as weak as my body.

Time is running out as my power falls rapidly to its minimum. My eyes are heavy, my limbs are numb, and my legs are running more by inertia than by my own doing.

The girl dashes ahead and opens a small door at the wall by cutting the pulley system holding it closed. She turns around with desperate eyes, yelling at us to run faster. My brother is staying behind to aid me in my painful run. We race through one at a time, then I turn and stop, allowing them to go ahead.

"Nathan, what are you doing? Please, come with us! Please!"

I barely hear Jay's desperate voice behind me as I kneel, feeling the humid soil underneath. I concentrate, letting all the sounds around me fade away. No more enemies running toward me, no more Jay screaming wildly… calmness to get ahold of my inner fire one last time for tonight. Even if I die, they will survive. I whip flames toward the hole in the wall, and it bursts into flames. A waterfall of fire illuminates the night, cutting off our pursuers.

Even as relief fills my thoughts, the fire drains from me, and I collapse. *They will survive, and my mission is done.*

Bye, bye, little brother.

14
THE YOUTH *TRIO*

"NATHAN, WHAT ARE YOU DOING? Please, come with us! Please!" A panicked scream escapes from me as Nathan stops and faces our pursuers.

The army is almost to the hole in the wall.

Before I take a first step toward him, he steps forward, opens his stance, and shoots both arms forward. An ocean wave of fire stems from his palms, advancing menacingly against our pursuers. The flames ignite the wall all over, closing their path just as Moses closed the sea on the Egyptian army. Nathan's tense body shakes, trying to hold the fierce attack. Through the creaking flames I can see the enemy army stopping their run and staring fearfully at the impenetrable barrier.

It ends as quickly as it started.

Nathan falls to the ground unconscious. Silver and I run to him but can't wake him, so we each grab one of his arms, fling it over our shoulders, and continue our escape. His body is burning up and hurts my skin. *What if he is dead?*

Silver shouts, "Jay, get ahold of yourself. Without you focused we are as good as dead!"

We run and jump over branches and leaves almost blindly with so little moonlight making it through the forest canopy.

Somehow the fire is still raging though Nathan is knocked out. Then I notice his fists are clenched tightly, and he is whispering under his breath. Thousands of images cloud my mind, distracting me from the heat assaulting my neck and shoulder—Nathan transformed, engulfed by fire; his violence; his power; and all the destruction he managed to cause.

The flames' sound is growing faint in the distance as we are running away as fast as we can. As soon as we are unable to hear the menacing screams of our enemies, we stop to catch our breath.

"What are we going to do, Silver?" Through my heavy breathing, my words try and fail to hide my fear. My heart racing, I listen for any enemy who managed to follow us.

"Cold will avenge this, no doubt, Jay. We must go far away, someplace safe and hidden." She seems to be uneasy but in control, the only way I have ever seen her under distress.

She is right—we must decide quickly where to go and go straight there. Those men are not going to be able to leave the way we left, so going all the way to the front entrance and around to our location gives us a good thirty-minute head start, plus they'll have to fan out and search for clues to know which way to go.

"What about our house?" Homesickness aside, we could stay hidden there for a long time. Maybe long enough for Cold's men to believe we escaped forever. It is far away from here and well protected, but the thought of having to outrun them for such a long time through the wilderness, carrying Nathan, is terrifying.

"I don't know, Jay. Cold caught you close to your house. Maybe he'll tie the loose ends and look for us there."

Right. She's right.

Silver stares at the ground, thinking.

"It is the best choice we have, Silver, even though it is risky. Nathan must rest, and we must tend to his wound. According to what he has told me, Cold is not the only worry we have out in the open like this. At least back home, he'd be the only thing to watch out for," I say.

"You are right. It still feels wrong, but let's go!" She picks up Nathan's arm once more, throws it over her shoulder, and starts treading to her right. It is time to start going around Cold's stronghold and heading south toward home.

I catch up and grab his other arm, settling into a steady pace with her. His body is getting cooler every minute, back to normal human temperature. The fire holding back our enemies must be slowly turning into embers.

God, if you do exist, please accompany us in this journey.

***

We have walked for eight days with almost no rest, carrying Nathan. As we stumble through the camp where my legs were burnt when I was first taken, my mind shifts to anything else but my pain and exhaustion.

How could those men follow Cold without question? Never will I comprehend such evil. Nathan controls fire somehow. Why won't he wake up? How long has he had this power? Is he the same Nathan I got separated from two months ago?...

We should get back home today without a doubt. My legs are starting to fail even as my mind is struggling valiantly to keep going ahead. Silver is panting, and I am close to fainting. I wish to get home and rest for days. We should only be about three hours away now. Such an image grants me one last breath of strength.

How nice to have a decent meal from our orchard and sleep on our soft, comfy beds once more. Our home is the best place in this world to be, safe, warm, well supplied or at least supplied, and familiar. It is all that is left of my family, and that makes it invaluable. We don't usually talk about Mom and Dad, but the truth is that I miss them and pray every day for their safety to God or whomever listens.

We exit the forest, leaving its last trees behind and entering our neighborhood. The houses are covered in moss, with broken windows, left uninhabited long ago. The street in front of us is cracked as roots have grown large and strong under it. The sun is glaring at us, showing how no one is in our way toward our house.

Now, after witnessing first-hand what the world has become, I pray for my parents' safety or at least a painless end to their suffering. Maybe dying was better than living at a fortress like the one Nathan rescued me from.

Don't think like that, Jay. We must fight on, and someday reunite.

My mind still struggles to understand Nathan's power. Fire bursts out of him as if it was always inside, and he can make it reach toward the sky and direct it in any direction he wants. Ex was completely consumed by a beam of Nathan's fire. Even though I was standing maybe two meters away from him, it did not hurt me at all. It felt like sitting in front of a campfire, away from danger but warmed. How does he control it to that degree of precision? When did this happen? Is he really in control when transformed? I pray I haven't lost him to something incomprehensible.

He has always been able to light fires, even when the logs seemed to be dripping wet, and now I know his secret. He can summon fire whenever he wants, but apparently, he is not powerful enough to maintain it forever. He can't make fire when all the energy he has left is the bare minimum he needs to live. Could it kill him? Is he ever going to wake up? His breathing is slow but constant, and his body temperature has been normal for a long time. He has even taken some sips of water, instinctively.

I have tried to forget it, but I cannot let go of the image of my brother in flames, shooting flames to destroy. He looked terrifying while attacking Ex. His back and arms and legs grew maybe twice his normal size, and he looked slightly bent forward. Fire danced around his arms in a spiral just before shooting out and vanishing Ex. Even if I did not manage to see what was left of him, it was a brutal way to kill him. So much vengeance and hatred in my brother must not be healthy.

The worst of all were his eyes. Glowing red eyes pierced the night. They were filled with anger and loathing. What frightens me is if Nathan is not capable of controlling this. That power seems to be under his control when awake, but what if he did not faint and it overcame him?

Where did his power come from? Has he always had it or was it developed? Is he the only human being with powers? This brings a memory flashing back to me. Just like a raindrop hitting your face on a sunny day, surprising, even scaring you momentarily before you notice what just hit you. What I felt during my enslavement, the fire inside of me that felt external and not my own must have been Nathan's. My theory must be correct. Is my power being able to feel other people's emotions? That seems awfully lame and useless. My head droops at the thought of not having a power as incredible as Nathan's.

Silver interrupts my wandering thoughts. "This is where you were captured, Jay."

I look up, seeing that we are forty meters away from the house where Silver and Nathan had their unfortunate encounter. Her worried eyes look straight at me, clearly sensing something is wrong. She knows me too well and can tell I am afraid and confused and disappointed all at the same time.

We lay my brother gently against the garage door where I left a shiv months ago to point my brother in the right direction to rescue me. I can see the Van de Kruit house, the one where Nathan and Silver had their encounter, three blocks down to my left. Silver tells me, "I will go to that white house. Maybe no one has taken the weapons I had stashed before being captured by Cold's men."

She runs as quickly as her tired legs allow. I can see her skillfully jumping over the front wall and through the front entrance that lost its door. Nathan is breathing unevenly at my side; I sit down beside him and notice how his face has returned to its usual coloring. His legs are extended, and his arms hang heavily at his sides. Five minutes go by until Silver exits the house carrying a bow around her torso, a quiver with some arrows, and Nathan's sword.

"Thankfully no one stole my stuff. I left it hidden before leaving your brother unconscious in case I managed to return after losing your brother's trail." Her eyes glow slightly, excited about our improved offensive capability. She has a reddened face from the effort, and I have never felt as exhausted in my life.

One last break, before finally reaching our house safely, against the odds. She sits beside me and my brother. "Jay, your brother's power is marvelous, but honestly, it feels dangerous. When I surprise attacked him, he must not have been able to use it yet. But what if he had been able to? Do you think he is able to control it, or is it beyond his control?" She is visibly uncomfortable and trying to hide her fear from me, almost successfully.

"I have no idea. I never saw him do anything like that before. He never let me go with him to scavenge, though I always wondered how he was able to protect and provide for us like he did, without ever getting hurt. And when attacking Ex, he precisely avoided hurting me, even though I was way too close." We had been walking in silence but thinking the exact same thing. Is Nathan more powerful than fire, or is fire more powerful than him?

"Let's keep going, Silver. This place is not safe, and my house is not much farther away." Nathan is breathing normally now, and it finally looks as if he is just sleeping rather than fighting for his life. At home I will be able to tend to him properly. The injury from Ex's arrow is as clean as we could keep it but needs proper cleaning to keep it from getting infected. Silver has tended to it every single day, and I am thankful for it.

Silver grabs Nathan from his right armpit and pulls him to his feet. I grab his left arm, and start walking once again to our right. After two blocks of carrying my brother, we turn left at a crossroad. Suddenly, we are surprised by a dozen of Cold's men standing next to the playground diagonal to our house, all armored up and holding crossbows. I freeze in place. There is no way we are going to be able to outrun them while carrying Nathan, and Silver and I are not capable of defeating them head-on. A screeching shout breaks my panic.

"Jay, get the fuck out of here!" Silver is moving, taking Nathan with her.

They are starting to run toward us. My body reacts instinctively as I dash off the street to the edge of an overgrown lot. I can see our house behind them, extremely close and now impossibly far. Silver is crouching behind a messed-up car in the middle of the road with Nathan's body laid down behind her. She has her bow ready and is waiting for them to come in range. They are shouting insults and their heavy footsteps on the asphalt sound like a stampede we cannot outrun.

I get my bow ready and take a stance. Using the skills those assholes taught me will be ironic. Their crossbows have a better range than our bows, so arrows are falling around us, hitting the car with metallic sounds. Each clang makes me tense up even more. I feel surrounded, sure I'll be dead soon.

Silver's eyes are focused on them. I feel her inner struggle, wanting to kill them but wishing there was another solution. She remembers the child she had to kill and both of her sisters, and her heart aches with wishing death never had to be an answer. The images flashing through my mind are interrupted by the arrows swooshing around her, the heavy steps of our enemies, the sound of a light wind through the bushes to our left. She is desperately trying to avoid the inevitable—becoming something she despises. This world constantly forces us to do what we would have never wanted to do.

She strings the arrow with trembling hands, her mind still in debate. She looks at me with pleading eyes.

I nod at her. "We must do this, Sil, even if we don't want to. My brother, you and me, have a long road ahead of us. We must do this if we'll ever be able to change the world later."

She smiles slightly even though her eyes don't play along. Her first arrow flies upward, arcs, and then dives straight into an enemy's head. He drops to the ground. Tears fall down her cheeks as she prepares for the next.

Poor Silver and damn this world!

Eleven to go now. Their armor plates clanging as they run toward us has a different metallic sound than the arrows hitting the car, but just as scary.

My first arrow flies over the car and straight at our enemies, but this time they are more careful and zigzag as soon as they see me release the string. It hits the road and breaks in two, just like my hope. I fucked up. The men are now forty meters away.

"Suck it up! We have no choice! Shoot! Shoot, damn it!" Silver screams at me, not in panic but in need. She needs my support, or our trio is going to be history.

As I try to get the bow ready once more, the arrow slips from my hands to the ground. My hands are trembling with fright, making it impossible to pick up the arrow. *Fuck, fuck, fuck. My time has come. I am so sorry, Nathan, for failing you. I am so sorry, Silver.*

She stares at me with a gaze I have never seen from her beautiful green eyes...defeat and resignation. A smile starts to take control of her as she rapid fires a second, a third, a fourth, a fifth, a sixth, yet six more foes are only twenty meters away and readying their knifes.

As I kneel beside Silver, I whisper, "I'm sorry."

She clenches her jaw and stands up, willing to take them on in a straight melee combat. She refuses to die without a fight. Her stance is noble, just like a warrior from old stories about to face death without flinching.

Her courage makes me stand and copy her. We will die together, but these men will not take our lives easily. Silver is holding her knife and I, Nathan's sword, which she stole from him in their meet-up. Standing in our fight poses, ready to face them, ready to be killed, a rash of scalding wind brushes past my body from behind. We stumble forward at the sheer strength of it.

Out of my peripheral view, Nathan emerges in his transformed self. He turns to Silver and me and calmly says in a deep voice I have never heard from him, "My turn." He is on his feet and already lunging forward. Both his arms are engulfed with fire, and he's circling his hands around one another, harnessing his strength, getting ready to attack.

I lose sight of the remaining men as a wall of flames shoots from my brother's hands. As the fire wall reaches its prey, I can see all of them burst into flames and become nothing more than ashes. Such an amazing power, but terrifying in its ability to take all their lives in the blink of an eye.

Nathan is standing in that same pose, heavily breathing as his shirt inflates with each breath. He is staring downward, visibly in pain. Tears fall from my brother's eyes, and he drops to his knees, seeming defeated. He is painfully accepting what he has become to save me, to save us.

15
THE ELDER
A NEW DIRECTION

WE HAVE ARRIVED SAFELY BACK home, at least for the time being. Those men who attacked us are ashes now, cleaned away by the wind as if they never existed. My tears were the sum of all the pain I have caused my fellow man. This world is nefarious, and starting to rub off on me. At least those tears remind me I am still human, and my relentlessness to save my brother at all costs has not turned me into a senseless killer.

Did I really have to murder all the men and women who have opposed me since The Day? Have I not had different choices? The more I think about it, the more convinced I am that they did not give me a choice. And this time especially. All of them were running at us, shouting, and prepping their weapons to kill me and my brother. No dialogue or negotiation would have stopped them. Fighting against a stormy wind by blowing air out of your mouth is useless.

I still feel empty inside, and thoughts of what happened, what I have caused, keep flashing across my mind, tormenting me. I create a flame on my hand and stare as I command it to dance there silently. It reminds me of all those who have been irreversibly consumed by my power. I stare up at the night sky, listening to the silence that reminds me in the end nothing will prevail. We will all be silent eventually, and many have been sent into it by my hand. This is not the way we are meant to live and to relate as human beings, but what else can I do?

"Nathan, you have been terribly quiet for a long time. Are you okay, big brother?"

His worry-filled voice breaks my train of thought. He is the reason I am and will always be who I am. He is the reason why all those decisions make sense. What I have become is a result of need, not of choice. I extinguish the flame on my hand and turn toward him. He is sitting a couple of meters to my right on a black plastic chair in our backyard, playing with a baseball, and the girl is standing in front of me on the lawn, illuminated by the gloomy moonlight.

"Sorry, Jay. You know me and how I get carried away by my thoughts." I look from Jay to her and back. Now, both are staring at me with what looks like a mix of curiosity and fear. "I guess you two want to know about my powers?" I can't help but grin.

Both nod, looking like a pair of raccoons staring dubiously at some fruit handed to them by a human, ready to take it and run before it is too late. They are sincerely afraid behind their nods, and rightly so. I would be scared too. The uncertainty about the extent of my powers and my ability to control them still frightens me.

"Well, as you have seen, I am capable of creating and manipulating fire. I can summon it whenever I want, if I can focus. That is why you are not a pile of cinders. What is your name again?"

"Silver," she answers while taking a seat to my left.

Jay slides his chair closer to me, interested in my explanation.

"The issue is that it consumes my vital energy, just like exercising but to an extreme. If I let loose of all my power, I fear I might succumb to it and die of exhaustion. Nonetheless, this time it merited pushing myself to the limit to save you, Jay. Well, to save both of you, even though I did not agree at first."

Silver chuckles and gives Jay a side nod, making fun of me.

"Where did you get this power from?" Jay asks, a question I knew was coming sooner or later.

"All I know is that it came to me after The Day. As time passed after the destruction of everything we knew, maybe to ensure our safety, my body started changing. Every time I was angered by some peril threatening us, I felt a heatwave surge within me. Then it evolved into a fierce temperature increase, my body growing slightly, strengthening my muscles and raising my endurance. Its effects on my body have increased each time I've had to use it."

Their wide eyes and half-open mouths hint they are still confused. Silver crosses her arms, the way people do when uncomfortable, and Jay is moving anxiously on his chair.

"The first time my powers hinted at their existence was when this world took Chrissy away from me. People, alleged human beings, entered her house, killed her and her family, and scavenged everything they could. The pain this caused fueled my inner fire with a desire to avenge her. That day, my heart was torn away as I kneeled in front of her body, touching her lovely face with those big, brown eyes, and something changed within me. I remember feeling fire—not heat but fire—burning my insides without hurting me. If only I'd been there to stop those people. The notion of being too late getting to her still consumes me."

Jay's eyes get watery and Silver's face contorts with empathetic sadness at my tale.

"Then, as I carried her body downstairs, the pain soothed my powers away. At least for the time being—I think my body was just not able to process the immensurable agony and the raging, fiery hatred simultaneously. With each thrust I made with the shovel to dig her grave, a piece of my heart, of my goodness, of my hope for humankind was shattered. That hollowness must have been filled up with fire, with revenge and loathing."

Jay's dumbfounded stare reminds me that I had never shared Chrissy's story with him. "I am sorry I never told you about Chrissy, Jay. I wanted to protect you from the cruel reality we live in. Now, you have lived such a reality and seen first-hand how humanity has collapsed."

He stands up and hugs me, incapable of expressing what he feels beyond the brotherly grasp. I pat his back, squeezing him close, until he goes to sit back down and continue listening. It feels like our bond has grown tenfold stronger. He is the reason I decided to use Chrissy's memory for good instead of surrendering to the challenge of survival.

"After tending to Chrissy's burial, I sat on the white garden bench she had built and painted for her father. I stared at the burial mound for hours, as agony took hold of myself. My train of thought was running wild. Small fire sparks started to burst from my hands while I cried uncontrollably. This was the first time I created fire."

Both are staring intently and are motionless as the minutes of the night fly by.

"On the following days, as grief continued, and heat waves ran inside my body, I understood whatever was happening inside me was bound to my emotions. Only extremely powerful feelings sparked them, so I started working on my concentration and self-control. I could not allow you to see me, Jay.

"To do so, I went to her house almost every day to pay my respects and allow myself to feel the extent of my pain. Each time fire emanated from my fingertips I tried to extinguish it with my mind. Failure was constant for weeks, even if the heavy rains of May fell on me, fire continued on my hands every time I sat to stare at my girlfriend's final resting place."

Silver stares away from me, slightly turning her head while she removes tears from her cheeks with the back of her right hand.

"I prohibited myself to think about Chrissy while you were around, Jay. I could not risk showing you my powers, as you were only a child who would not understand the full extent of their implications. Eventually, four or five months after struggling, I succeeded at deciding when small flames ignited on my fingertips and palms even while grieving at Chrissy's memory. Long hours went into being able to control this power, and at the time I thought the only cause was pain."

They nod simultaneously with relief.

"After that, you and I struggled to adapt to this world. We learned to live by ourselves and figured out how to survive. That occupied my mind away from my powers. I continued training, but the evolution was slow. My capacity felt stagnant at creating small flames at my will. Nothing managed to enrage me sufficiently to expose them fiercely until about three years ago. When we saw those men rape and kill that poor young woman from our rooftop, I lost complete control. Her futile struggle, their violence and complete disrespect of her life was unbearable. The notion of them being the ones who did that same despicable thing to Chrissy angered me to my limits. The feelings I had managed to successfully confine inside of me for such a long time were released to their full extent.

"You remember, Jay, how I ordered you to shut yourself in our room until I returned, right? Well, that night as I stalked toward those bastards, the same heat as the night when I had to dig my girlfriend's grave came back to me. Fire emerged from my forearms, swirling around them. Rage consumed me completely as they had completely disrespected and taken another human being's life. When they dared to challenge me, fire waves and bolts shot from my fingertips and into their bodies. All my anger and vengeance. They burst into flames. Surprised by this new-found power, I lost focus, and the fire died out in the blink of an eye. However, that short moment was enough to end their lives. In a split second, fear took ahold of me—fear of myself and of what happened. So, I understand—*truly* understand—what both of you are feeling right now."

They look at each other, speaking without words. They feel comforted by my sincerity. The moon behind them is low as the end of the night creeps closer.

"Honestly, I panicked at the sight, at the fierceness with which revenge had led my emotions and actions. Those men had absolutely no chance against me and no warning that it was best to back off. I don't regret that night, though. To this day, their actions are unforgivable to me, the same as my actions are unforgivable to others.

"What I have been meditating about tonight is whether this power has killed my humanity and transformed me into someone or some*thing* else. I believe you, Jay, are the reason why I can still control it. You give me a reason to live, someone to fight for. Without this motivation, I might succumb to the temptation of overusing my power. Without you, it could take control of me, and the path I would end up taking might not be the one I would like to follow."

Both are staring quietly at me, a hint of fear in their eyes and a river of thoughts clearly dominating their minds. To break the tension, I command a couple of tiny fire twines to reach Silver's red hair and burn it at its tip. She breaks out of her silent spell, jumps to her feet, and starts patting hurriedly at her hair as Jay and I share a laugh for the first time in a long time.

"You stupid idiot!" She kicks the ground and tosses dirt in my face.

The three of us laugh it off, and it feels simply right. The void inside me seems less empty and allows me to enjoy that beautiful feeling you get when surrounded by the people you value, where you truly smile inside and feel as if nothing wrong will ever change this happiness. An old forgotten feeling is resurging when needed most.

"You are just annoyed by the fact that I am more powerful than you. Little wimpy Charmander!" Silver says mockingly while sitting back down Indian-style on the chair, frowning as if angry.

"You truly are a worthy opponent, just like a grain of sand standing courageously in front of the sea. But not even a million of you built like a sand castle could stop a sneeze from me," I reply, still smiling.

She answers my taunt by getting up on her feet and assuming her fighting stance. Just like a boxer, she moves right to left, dancing elegantly as she punches at the air, inviting me to spar with her.

I stand and get into my fighting stance, stretching my right arm with my palm upward and challenging her by closing my hand defiantly a couple of times. The moment she steps forward, I curl myself up in surrender. "I'm sorry, Silver. You are truly stronger, braver, quicker, and much more beautiful than me."

She squints suspiciously at my reluctance to face her.

I command a wall of fire to emerge between us, and I stare straight at her eyes. "Make your move."

She falls to the ground, toppling the chair, and starts laughing with that gorgeous laugh she has. "You cheating dirtbag," she says between laughs while drying tears from her eyes.

Jay is laughing too, and it's so heartwarming to hear his sweet, innocent laughter again.

"I learned from the best, the only one who has managed to outmaneuver me."

Acknowledging her prowess feels right. Helping her up from the ground, I stare into her deep green eyes and we share a quick smile. "Thank you for guiding my brother. Thank you for saving what means most to me. Thank you for being a part of us, Silver." My heart goes out to her, as I owe her all my gratitude for what she has done to save Jay long enough for me to come back to him.

She nods graciously before grabbing Jay's head in a death choke and telling him, "You, I can definitely still beat you."

Jay smiles his approval, or perhaps relief at my acceptance of Silver.

And all of this feels right. Finally, a home once again filled with laughter and plenty of reasons to live, even to die for.

***

How amazing it is to wake up in your own bed, to have a sound sleep all night long knowing you are protected. For the first time in a long time, I feel really rested and back to my normal self. Jay is still sleeping next to me, drooling a bit. Cautiously, moving to get out of bed without waking him up, I look around our room. Silver is nowhere to be seen, riling me up with doubt about her intentions. This world makes you exceedingly cautious.

I run down the stairs, avoiding the traps, and rush into our kitchen, almost crashing head on with Silver.

"Good morning!" she says, startled. "Well, you explain the noise I was about to investigate." She steps back to the camping stove beside the kitchen sink and pours the food mixture she'd been stirring into a cast iron pan. "I'm sorry if I woke you. I just wanted to make breakfast as a thank you to both of you for welcoming me."

I step over to the table and look in the pan. She is cooking what seems to be an omelet with some of our orchard's vegetables and eggs that I have no idea where she got.

"No worries, Silver. Just my training leading the orchestra. Look, I wanted to talk with you alone."

She looks at me and nods before saying, "Do you resent me for attacking you?"

I gasp containing my laugh and smile at her widely, trying to see if she is mocking me or asking honestly. I believe she is serious, so I say, "I understand this world, Silver. You either attack or die, as simple as that. You were inside your personal stronghold and I was a menace, either a thief, an assassin, a scavenger, who gives a fuck. You did what you had to do, and I would have done the same to you had you entered this house." Silver stares at me, listening intently.

She moves the contents of the pan with a spoon while saying, "I am glad James has you. He has grown and learned how to face this world to an extent, but he is still in need of guidance. You know the world as I do, and it is the best protection he can have." I nod in agreement; I feel close to her and at the same time wary.

I shift nervously from one foot to the other, look her in the eyes, and say, "I have never trusted anyone but my brother. You are the first person we have ever allowed into our house since

The Day. You have proven loyal to my brother, risking your life time and time again for his wellbeing, taking charge when I was unable to. For that, I swear on my life I will protect the three of us. You are a blessing to us both, and I am deeply grateful for your decision to come with us. Please, stay with us for as long as you want. Speaking for both of us, we want you to stay forever. Your friendship, your charisma, your sense of humor is appreciated. Your abilities and your resilience are a necessity. Please."

She smiles. "I will stay with you knuckleheads. I almost killed you, and Jay has become quite a loose cannon. You do need me."

We laugh at her remark, sharing a tender hug. Her breath warms my neck as her body nestles between my arms, against my chest. A much-needed moment of human connection for both of us. She looks up at me with that lovely smile and her piercing green eyes, sending guilty feelings running through me. We separate abruptly, like two teenagers ashamed of showing their true selves to one another.

"Thank you, Sil," I say, while starting to inventory the food stocks sitting on the table two meters to my right. *Where did she get all this?*

Silver returns to the camping stove and fidgets a cooking knife around in the pan's ingredients. "Before Jay comes down in his zombie morning mode, I wanted to comment on something you said last night. This world truly has forced us to do unspeakable things. Things we never would have done before, and I am proud of you for fighting so long without becoming like…*them*. Men and women who no longer value human life, who enjoy killing and hurting others. Even children…"

She stares off at nothing out the window to her left for a moment, then continues, "Same as you did, I lost a loved one to this world's violence. It taught me to be unforgiving, cynical, deadly. I have done harm to others. But there is a difference between defending yourself from certain death and being able to attack, kill, control, hurt just because you can. If you care about your humanity, you don't have to worry about losing it."

"What happened to you, Silver?" I ask hesitantly, waiting for her reaction to understand if I am intruding on her personal life. She strengthens her grasp on the frying pan, uncomfortable with what I ask and fighting against her feelings. A couple of seconds go by, and I see pain in her eyes that redden as she is deciding whether to share all the memories flashing through her mind.

"My sisters. Ellie was four years younger than me and Louise was six years younger. I am twenty-one now, so back then I was forced to take care of them by myself even though I was fourteen. They were babies and I fucking failed. My parents were killed as soon as this hell started, trying to protect our supplies against half a dozen men who ravaged our home. I was unable to see what happened, as my mother hid us in our basement's closet. I remember hearing my parents screaming wildly, fighting for all our lives and failing until their screams were muted forever. Their murderers stomped on the floors above us, stealing what they could and breaking everything else." Her voice crackles with the agony she feels, and her eyes blink quickly, failing to contain her tears.

"We stayed hidden for hours, maybe a complete day, since we were shocked at the incomprehensible attack. As the hours went by, staring at my sisters silently sobbing, hugging me, I understood I was to protect them from evil, danger, and people in general." I grab Silver's hand and walk her to the kitchen table, helping her to sit at the chair closest to the kitchen. I nod slowly for her to continue, while I continue preparing breakfast as she proceeds with her tale.

"I decided to leave, contrary to what you decided for Jay. We could not stay where our parents were killed. Ellie and Louise never completely understood what happened to our family or to our world, and that was my fault. I concealed my pain, crying long hours after they fell asleep, to protect them from the cruel reality. We walked for a couple of months, mostly at night to avoid being kidnapped, and sleeping under bridges, amongst overgrown bushes, inside abandoned cars." Her sight wanders as she turns to stare through the door to our yard, remembering her tribulations.

"We finally found a place to live. A beautiful abandoned house with a tall wall surrounding its lot, a large staircase leading to an amazing wooden wall. My sisters celebrated all night long as they were finally princesses with a castle. They never knew how difficult it was for me to set up precautions to avoid outsiders from entering such a huge mansion. We were able to live some beautiful months in that house; it was home." Silver stares back at me and her face disfigures with red eyes, tears rushing down her rosy cheeks, her lips cracked and her nose runny. I can feel my tears bundling in my eyes, ready to accompany her while clumsily cutting our breakfast's ingredients through a blurry sight.

"One day they were playing on the street outside our house. I was so naive to allow them to go out. I was supposed to be careful, to protect them, to be smart. I could see them through a window encased by a wooden frame, standing in the living room while cleaning our house. They were so happy at that moment, laughing, running, getting sunbathed while enjoying life." I place the frying pan in the sink and walk toward Silver to console her with a hug. She holds her hand up, telling me to wait, while she cleans her tears away to continue the story.

"A crossfire ended their lives. Two groups of people shooting at each other to steal each other's supplies, ignoring any possible danger they caused to other human beings. By the time I managed to open the front door, run down the long, front staircase, dash the thirty meters of the front driveway, and exit through the concealed entrance between the front ferns, they had passed away." Silver sobs uncontrollably at the memory she does not share. She must have had to carry their small bodies back inside to bury them, fighting alone against that hope you always have when a loved one dies. The hope of it all being a nightmare, unreal and temporary.

"After losing them, I left that house forever. I could not bear living there with all the memories those months gave us.

Since then I have survived by myself, moving constantly to avoid being trailed, and avoiding contact with human beings as best as I could. I have encountered enemies and tried to help those in need when of utmost necessity, but within me I feel void and desire solitude. I fear death and desire it at the same time. If I could be certain death will take me to see them again, I would kill myself in an instant." She clenches her jaw as anger takes control of her. She must blame herself for her sisters' passing and all the pain she has had to endure.

"Now, in retrospect, I know the mistakes I have made. I swore to myself I would never harm anyone who was not directly involved with my sisters' deaths, but the world is a funny place, where what you plan never happens. Even if I had never killed before being enslaved at Cold's camp, I know people have died because of my actions. I have stolen their supplies, I have misled them outside of their homes to scavenge, and I have denied them my help. Ironically, by deciding not to murder, I have caused deaths." Silver stands up and starts walking out the door to her right, away from me.

My eyes start watering as I reply, "It hurts deep inside to think I have turned into a monster. What I saw at Cold's camp has riled me up, and I want to change this world. I want to live for some bigger purpose. I shouldn't have such power and not use it for good. But I'm terrified that road leads me to becoming something I don't want to become." Silver halts and turns around at my unexpected comment.

Silver looks at me and says, "If no one does anything, what will Jay's future look like?" She walks toward me and grabs the frying pan from my hand.

I step closer and kiss her cheek for sharing and listening to what troubles me. Then I go about checking the traps on the exterior doors while thinking about her words. If I do not use my powers for good, then I am only postponing our deaths by hiding while others suffer outside our home. However, going out could risk everything I have worked so hard for during this last seven years. Jay's life, his survival, would be in peril as soon as we step outside. He would never allow me to leave him behind.

Besides, something has changed now. We are not only two anymore. Silver is experienced, she has endured harsh personal trials and survived. She is mature, wise, smart, skillful, and extremely pretty. *Idiot. Do not lose sight of what is important, Nathan.*

If we work together, the three of us could slowly start freeing people from Cold's unforgiving tyranny. What if that is our destiny, the reason why we are here, and the reason why I have my powers?

All these thoughts won't allow me to concentrate on my chores, so I decide to go back inside and continue speaking to Silver. Together we must find a path toward something. There is nothing as futile as living without a goal, without motivation to transcend.

Returning to the kitchen, I hear that Jay is already up, walking on our second floor. Our talk will have to be postponed, so I say with a smile, "How can I help with breakfast? And where did you get all the eggs?!"

The kitchen smells amazing. The sweet scent of spinach being fried in a hint of olive oil with tomatoes and onions and scrambled eggs is making my stomach grumble. She is a great addition to the team, really makes it feel like home once more.

Wait a second. A long-forgotten scent fills my nose and causes me to nearly drool. *Coffee!* "Sil. How?" I blabber, pointing at the steaming coffeepot I finally see sitting just behind the camping stove.

She smiles. "I managed to steal these half-pound cans of grounded coffee from those fuckers a day before you torched the whole camp."

We share a laugh at her ingeniousness as she pours me a cup. The sweet scent perfumes my spirit as I raise the cup to take a sip.

Clumsy footsteps announce Jay just before he stumbles half asleep into the kitchen. "What is that beautiful smell? I guess it is not you, Nathan." He is rubbing his eyelids and looking for the source of the drool-causing smell as he comes to stand by me.

We lean against the kitchen cabinet, staring at Silver cooking, just the way we did back when our family was whole, and Mom cooked for us.

"The cabinet won't fall over if you aren't leaning there, and the table won't set itself, if you two want to be useful," Silver says with a glare over her shoulder.

Jay and I look at each other, then jump to getting the table set for three. As quickly as I realize how comfortable it all feels, my instincts have me questioning if comfortable is a good thing anymore. I say to no one in particular, "This is perfect, but perfect may not be the best way to survive. Should we stay, or should we head southward in search of a new place to settle?"

Silver nods as if she had been wondering the same thing. Jay looks surprised but doesn't say a word.

Silver says, "Jay had a very valid point when he told me about this place, Nathan. Here, our only true worry is Cold, since he might guess our whereabouts. If we leave, we risk being exposed to the numerous threats hiding around every corner that we both know exist out there." The three of us carry our plates to the table as we prepare to have a delightful breakfast and a serious talk. I sit at the table's head with our yard straight upfront, Jay sits down to my right with a curved back over his plate, and Silver crosses her right leg while setting her plate and coffee down.

I answer her, "That is true, and even though the three of us make a great team, we are not ready to face even just the different threats I have dealt with or avoided in the past. Not even with my powers, and your experience, Silver." I am reluctant to go out, we are not ready, but I am also reluctant to stay since our enemies were so close to home. The first bite fills my mouth with long-forgotten tastes, and my stomach grumbles with the memories.

Once more, she defends my brother by assuring me, "Jay has new abilities that still must be polished. However, he is not the child who left this house months ago. He has been trained in melee combat, archery, stealth, offensive and defensive strategies, and endurance. You must test him and see. I do not know if it is best to stay or leave; nevertheless, we should not decide it because we mistrust Jay's skills." Jay nods, approving Silver's comments, unable to speak because he was gulping a large amount of coffee.

"Do not do that, Jay, it is disrespectful." He half smiles as I scold him, and stares at me sadly. He must feel I do not trust him and his newly acquired skills, but it is beyond wariness. *What if I fail and he is kidnapped again or killed because of me? I would never forgive myself.*

Jay speaks out for the first time, "Please, brother. I would love to stay here, and we are now three capable soldiers defending our home. Why should we risk all of this? Are we not having the best time we have had for a long, long time?" Jay comments naively, thinking a great breakfast foreshadows easy times.

Within the numerous thoughts rushing through my mind, two seem to become stronger. *Is it fair to have powers and not use them for others? Why am I set on deciding between staying or leaving, instead of deciding whether to help others or not?*

I lean on both elbows, while moving my breakfast on its plate with my fork. Against my better judgement, I ask about the brands they have on their foreheads. I need to understand our enemy better and the reason for those brands could give us an insight to his working, so I say, "I am sorry for asking this, but I have noticed how each of you have a brand on your forehead. I did not want to ask as I believe neither of you wants to remember what happened, but I need to know." They stare at each other with disappointment as though they wish those brands to fade away.

Silver answers my question, while Jay chews on his breakfast listening intently, "When you are caught by Cold you go through many trials and tortures. Based on how you endure their evil tests, they will brand you with a red-hot iron rod, searing your skin. My "+5" and Jay's "+3" are high grades on their disgusting scale, and that is why we were trained as soldiers. Other people with lower grades will suffer another type of enslavement, and some are even killed if their brand is too low." She sets her fork and knife on the table, disgusted at the memories coming back.

She adds, "It is the most pain I have ever felt and based on this mark you are assigned to different tasks during your enslavement." She caresses her forehead with her index and middle finger while remembering the moment when she suffered such agony. Jay stares at his plate, unable to comment about it.

After listening to her harsh story about their branding, fighting back the hatred I feel against Cold's ruthlessness, I say, "Tell me more about this Cold and the enslavement camp. I need to get a better picture of their numbers, tendencies, strategies to understand how risky it is to stay put, whether we'd be exposing ourselves to their armies marching into our neighborhood, sacking every house in search of us." We are almost done with our breakfast. Silver and I are sipping coffee with empty plates in front of us, while Jay is still eating slowly as usual with half a cup of coffee left.

Jay says loudly to grab my attention, making me turn to him surprised, "Cold has four captains under his leadership. Lizbeth the Bringer oversees reproduction. She owns women who can carry children and forces them to act as wives for his soldiers. They suffer so much, Nathan. They are truly hopeless." Jay's voice waivers, but he continues. "Then there is Pete the Perpetual, since he is a work machine. He leads forced labor and makes men, women, and children work into their graves. I have seen people die right in front of him, in the middle of his giving out orders, and he seems not to notice them. Just continues ordering the others around and punishes anyone who even looks at the corpse. He leaves them there until they rot. He is evil, completely evil." His eyes fill with tears. I turn toward Silver, who nods, approving the veracity of Jay's comments.

Silver stands up and walks around me to stand between Jay and me. She places a comforting right hand on his left shoulder, getting a funny look from Jay.

He swipes tears from his cheeks and goes on. "Third is Miley the Enabler. She supervises servitude. Cold's men treat them as garbage, humiliating them by spitting, shouting, forcing them to do embarrassing tasks, and even sexually assaulting them. Not one of them raises their head while walking, as if the ground gives them comfort." His skinny jaw clinches as his pain and sadness is joined by anger. Silver notices I am uncomfortable, as I need to hear this story but cannot endure my brother suffering. She grabs my right hand with her left and squeezes to support me.

"Finally, Ex the Relentless. Well, you got rid of that bastard, but Cold must have already appointed someone else. His task was to brainwash us into compliant soldiers. This was done by beating us constantly and forcing us to do unspeakable things to innocent men, women, and children. Silver and I have experienced hell under his reign. Please...please don't make me tell you more." Jay starts crying inconsolably.

I can't even imagine what my little brother endured. His tears bring back my inner demon, but this time controlled. How I wish I could finish what I started and eradicate that plague from the face of the earth. All those people, innocent at heart, found guilty by Cold's satanic judgement. He has no right to do what he does, and the time for him to pay for all his sins will come.

Silver steps back as I grip his shoulder, pulling him to look up at me. "I'm sorry, Jay. I should have trained you for the possibility of dealing with things I foolishly thought I could always protect you from. I am sorry you had to face them unprepared."

My denial of Jay's need to be prepared for the world made him powerless when caught by Cold. That is a mistake I will never make again. From now on we are equals, not protector and protégée, but a team of brothers. I stand up to carry the empty coffee cups to the kitchen.

"That is not the only camp." Silver breaks the moment while grabbing the empty plates from the table and carrying them to the kitchen sink where I stand.

Awestruck by that comment, I turn to see Jay sitting back at the table and notice he is surprised as well. He says, "What do you mean, Silver?"

She elaborates, "Since The Day, as you call it, I have traveled all around in search of safety. At first it was to take care of my sisters, but they passed away." Her voice stumbles but gets back to its normal authority in a heartbeat. "After losing them, I understood that safety is just an illusion in this world, something temporary, if existent at all. We lived in the United States back then, when countries existed. Maybe three months on foot away from here or more. Since snow can be such a challenge, I decided to march south toward a tropical climate. I'd rather have sunshine and rain than snow and cold. Besides, our parents had passed away soon after The Day, so nothing tied us to our birthplace. It had been just the three of us for months. And for them, I decided never to kill a soul, to protect their minds. Now I understand that sometimes this world will put us into a position where killing evil is the only way to have a future." Before going on, she sets the plate in the kitchen sink and goes back to the kitchen table, sitting down again.

She continues, "Along my journey, I stopped every now and then and hunkered down for a while, always advancing southward. I have crossed rivers and mountains and forests, walking along the Atlantic Ocean if I did not encounter people, potential enemies. When I saw someone along the coastline, I would walk deep into the forest, avoiding cities, and walking south until the threat vanished. The beautiful sights were the most painful, since I had no one to share them with." Silver smiles sadly, remembering how much she misses her sisters. I rinse the plates and cups while listening her story.

She adds, "After almost five years I reached what used to be this country and have lived in it for about two years now. I knew about Cold's camp, but not exactly what they did inside or who was in charge. People around here are constantly and brutally attacked, menaced, enslaved, and forced to pay tributes. Most of the victims who survived that I managed to talk with, remembered the soldiers had a curvy scar on their right forearm and were led by a brute of a man with devilish light blue eyes." Before she goes on, I invite them with my hand to go to the living room to continue her story. Both get up, Silver pushing her seat under the table, while Jay leaves his chair misplaced. I push it under the table as usual before heading behind them to the living room.

I think about what early travelers told us about an evil man ending humanity. Cold has been destroying lives for too long. I hate him to death.

Silver sits on our long velvet sofa, on the farthest wall from the living room's entrance. I walk toward her and sit beside her, with my legs on top of the couch. Jay sits on the floor, on top of our red, hairy carpet, staring up at us. Silver looks straight at me and continues, "Every single time I spotted one of those armored men, I hid and covered my tracks meticulously. The first time I saw them was two or three days after I left the coast behind. I decided to venture farther inland to avoid the wide-open coast. Dozens of Cold's men were attacking a small village hidden within the woods, burning down both trees and huts, while killing everyone. I hid silently and motionless, staring depressed at the sight, feeling completely impotent." She stares past me and into the backyard, losing herself in her memories.

Her gaze sets back on Jay, and she goes on saying, "I have seen Cold's reach within your country, wreaking havoc in almost every place I have visited. As soon as I settled, believing I was safe, I would see a group of Cold's men marching close to my safehouse or attacking a nearby village or kidnapping anyone I knew lived close to me. Cold's MO is simple; he enslaves small groups of people who seem to be fit for service, kills and pillages small villages that barely subsist, and demands tributes in the form of food, water, or materials from larger towns that can supply him with constant resources." Jay stands up and tries to squeeze uncomfortably between Silver and me. I push him off and point him to the rocking chair beside me, at my left.

Silver continues, coming closer to her conclusion, "When I said Cold has more camps, I specifically was referring to the largest one I ever encountered. About two months north of the place Jay and I were held stands the tallest wall I have ever seen. It is made of white adobe heavily guarded night and day. Some of the armored men I had avoided headed there, taking dozens of people. That must be the capital of Cold's empire or maybe Cold's superior's kingdom. The closest I managed to get was about half a kilometer away, so I could only see the wall. The few men and women I ever managed to talk with wouldn't speak of that camp. The mere thought of it made them shiver and babble warnings to avoid it at all costs. The camp where you and I were caught, Jay, is just a small experimental site built around mining and the foundry."

A loud noise breaks my concentration and I turn to find Jay has fallen from the rocking chair and is convulsing, his head banging on the floor. His entire body is jerking right out of his chair. Panicked, I send the chair flying with a violent push to make room. Foamy saliva is overflowing from his mouth, and his eyes are jumping left and right quickly. I guide his body to the floor and cushion his head with my hands. My heart is racing, and I tremble, helpless to stop this.

Silver kneels beside me and softly lays a hand on Jay's shoulder.

This cannot be the way he dies. What the hell is happening? "Come on, Jay. What is happening? Please, brother, don't do this to us. Don't leave us!" I shout, terrified at the sight of him appearing to worsen by the second.

Then in the blink of an eye, it stops. He lays still, with his eyes closed and his body relaxed. He opens his eyes slowly, blinking with pain. His face wrinkles, and he swallows hard, like waking up from a terrible hangover and trying to remember a dream that will never come back. Slowly he sits upright with our help and looks at Silver and then at me. His complexion changes suddenly from confusion and discomfort into surprise and excitement. His mouth opens, and his eyes shoot wide open as he stands up with my aid.

"Nathan, Silver, I know where Mom is," he blurts out with great excitement.

16

THE YOUTH

EMPATHIC CONNECTION

"Nathan, Silver, I know where Mom is." I truly know where she is, no doubt about it.

However, Nathan and Silver are still half panicked about my blackout and now bewildered at the words I just muttered. How am I going to explain it and be convincing?

"Jay, what the hell just happened?" Nathan says in a loud, angry voice, still kneeling beside me on the carpet. He is so worried. "You just convulsed all over the place, came back seemingly lost for a second, and now you know where Mom is? Speak, now!" His voice is still shaking.

At my left, also kneeling, Silver is watching me with her arm on Nathan's shoulder, trying to calm him. "Go on, Jay. Tell us what happened."

Neither of them will understand how I know where she is, but I simply do.

I try to explain, "When you were telling that story of the huge camp you believe to be the capital of their clan or group, images came to me. You know, you just get mental pictures from your own imagination. Nate must have imagined it differently than I did."

So far, their nods hint that I'm making sense. I sit up, and they stand up and take a step back to give me more room. My hands feel the carpet, soothing me while I'm trying to think how to explain this.

Maybe they will understand if I describe everything I saw, "But, as you continued with your description of the wall from the outside, something changed in my mind. I found and felt myself walking toward that wall, my hands shackled to a chain being led by a group of armored men. But they weren't my hands; they were feminine hands. Long, bony fingers with just a couple of wrinkles and a skin whiter than mine. And those hands felt known to me. Slowly, the wall came closer, getting larger and taller, an enormous obstacle to anyone trying to get in. It smells even worse than Cold's camp, and the sound the gates make when opened goes for miles. Metallic creaks and chimes make your skin get goose bumps. I felt the goose bumps, I smelled the infestation within those walls. Death, shit, and tears."

Nathan starts pacing around the living room in front of me, exhaling heavily while pulling his hair backward anxiously. Silver sits down at the tan couch to my right. I stay still to avoid triggering my brother's anger by standing up.

Before he speaks, I continue, "Then my memories flashed forward in a rush and a blur. That moment when entering the wall must have been a long time ago. The next image felt more real, more current, as if happening right now. At that moment, Sil, I was no longer listening to you. It had nothing to do with whatever you were telling us. I was just gone into memories or visions from where you were talking about. The same hands, yet far weaker and feebler than those I saw while entering…White Tower! Yes, that is what they call it. That is the name of the walled city. Those hands are skeletal now from working in the mining camps, waist deep in mud. Imagine a first-person view, just as if looking through the eyes of someone else, but it felt real."

Nathan blurts something I can't quite understand. Before he repeats it, Silver stands up and quickly reaches him, whispering something I cannot hear. He stares at her for a couple of seconds before nodding. She grabs his hand and leads him to the couch again. Both sit and look at me intently, as Nathan signals me to go on with his index finger.

"It was raining hard, loud, and it was almost impossible to move in the mud. People's bodies were in front of her, lying in a horrible pile, a nightmarish sight. I could feel the desperation and hopelessness within her, her exhaustion. Then a terrible pain shot from her back and into me through the memory. A kick below her neck and a gruesome voice ordering her to work harder and wipe that sad-looking expression from her face. With the remaining strength in her body, she got back up, and started picking rocks faster. The voice was Pete The Perpetual's."

Nathan's eyes turn to amber, and I can see how smoke emanates from his shoulders. He stands up quickly to avoid burning Silver and clenches his fists in front of me, giving me his back, grunting and tensing his entire body. Silver stares at him surprised, silently. He is struggling to contain his powers. The news of our mother suffering is crushing him, but he fights courageously. I stand up in a rush and grab his right hand from behind. My grasp breaks his concentration as he turns his head slowly without turning his body and smiles.

Without releasing his hand, I add, "As soon as Pete left, she fell to her knees and spat out blood. Her heart was racing, as she needed to stand up quickly before someone saw her down, not working. However, Nathan, you know how our mom is, always vain about her looks. She kneeled in front of a small puddle of water, trying to see how much of that gruesome mud had splashed on her beautiful face and cleansing it off with rainwater. It was her without a doubt. Her reflection on the puddle. Her face was bruised, and she looks almost like a skeleton, but it was her! Our mom is inside that camp. I have no doubt about it."

Nathan's expression is not of mistrust, but he seems filled with contradicting thoughts. He knows I would never lie about something so important to us, but he has no idea of my abilities yet. He releases my hand and turns around to face us, finally in control of his powers. Silver stands as well to my right. I notice she is tense, expectant, in case she needs to restrain Nathan if he loses control. He starts pacing slowly back and forth, with his right hand covering his mouth as he usually does while thinking deeply.

To help him understand, I explain, "Brother, since I was caught at Cold's camp, I have developed some sort of ability to sense other people's feelings and think other people's thoughts without them knowing. Silver, when you were forced to do that horrible but needed act to spare the child from Ex's torture, I could feel all your emotions as if they were my own. Your pain, your indecision, your anger, your desire to destroy Ex turning into the decision that broke your soul, all of it was within me. When it happened, I didn't even have to look to know it was done; your hollow sense of despair told me it was done."

Come on, I need them to believe me. I start biting my left thumb's fingernail, trying to cope with how difficult this is to understand. Their gazes are a mix between disbelief and attention. *I should have thought this out.*

Got it! I must tell them about thoughts they never shared. I point at Nathan; he stops pacing, and I explain, "Nathan, when you were standing out in the woods still trying to figure out how to save us, I sensed your curiosity about who the helmet guy was. The curiosity about who that was walking with such a sense of superiority and commanding the archers. You felt sorry for the guy being kicked and humiliated by Ex. Then you felt extremely interested about who that guy was as his features started to feel familiar. Even a second before you recognized me, I felt the full extent of your wrath-induced power surging through your limbs and shooting upward into the night sky. I swear, brother, I feel what other people close to me feel, I think what they think, and now I see what they see past and present."

Nathan looks straight at me, then gives a questioning look to Silver, biting his lip. She looks at me, then gives Nathan a questioning look. Do they believe me yet, or are they thinking about how to treat my craziness without therapists around?

"An empathic connection." Nathan speaks those strange words while biting his left thumb's knuckle and with his eyes now searching for something invisible on the floor.

Confused, I stare at him. "What do you mean?"

He elaborates, "If all of this is true, and I am not questioning the veracity of what you feel and think, then it means you establish an empathic connection with those close to you. It is not a means of communication, because you are not and probably will not ever be able to send thoughts, emotions, or images to the other person. It is a one-way street, to make it simpler. Our mom has it too, though she'd never admitted before The Day changed everything. When we were children, she always knew how we felt and could see right through our mischiefs as if we told her what we were about to do. This story, this connection you can develop, clarifies it to me. I had no idea it could be inherited or even developed, but I guess you have some of it in you."

Those words make perfect sense! An empathic connection must be what I developed with Silver, with Nathan, and now with Mom. A bunch of memories from our childhood rush through my mind. Certainly, she had it. We used to think it was a "mom's power," but it was past natural intuition. We were never able to lie to her—she always knew what happened far beyond what someone could guess. She just stood in front of us, with her eyes set on the culprit, and waited until we tattled.

Silver has been completely silent and motionless beside us. She lays her gaze on Nathan while nibbling on her own cheek. "Hmm. That is interesting, Nathan. Wouldn't have ever believed that type of nonsense, but what you do with fire has shifted everything I believe in. This world is far more complex and mysterious than what I thought it could be. But, why now? Why didn't Jay connect with your mom until now?"

Those words sum up the doubt we are all feeling right now. A moment before he speaks, I sense Nathan's clarity of mind with a possible explanation to Silver's question.

Instead of interrupting, I allow Nathan to explain to Silver what I just read in his mind, "Because of your story, Silver. Empathic connection is probably established only with people very close to you, and not with every thought, feeling, or memory. At least not at first, not until you are able to strengthen the bond for it to be enduring. When you started to describe White Tower so precisely, the name Jay seems to have discovered, his imagination aligned closely to our mom's memories, establishing the bond for the first time."

Now all three of us feel the same clarity Nathan feels.

Silver is still having trouble believing our theory blindly. She crosses her arms in front of her, and answers, "It still feels strange, discomforting. Don't get me wrong as I believe both of you, but what does this mean for us?"

Silver is hiding what she really thinks, hiding the fear filling her and killing the dream of safety she was starting to build. All of us are feeling the same clash between hope, doubt, and a hint of fear.

Before her thoughts wander farther, I clarify, "You know what it means, Silver. Nathan and I will have to go and find our mother. She is alive but suffering, and her days are numbered." As I start to feel tired, I disconnect from my brother and Silver. My head is dizzy, and I feel nauseous. I walk backward with difficulty, trying to avoid falling, and sit down on the individual couch to our left.

Nathan turns to me smiling, with something different in his eyes as he says, "Are you all right, little brother? I am proud of who you have become—a true warrior. Silver, you don't have to come with us. You can stay here while we go on this probably suicidal mission. Thanks to you I have my brother back, so all of this is yours as a sign of gratitude."

Nathan points all around the living room, meaning our house is hers if she chooses to stay.

He continues, "Now my brother has brought the possibility of our mom back, and just as there wasn't a second of hesitation to save Jay, we will not waste a minute pondering whether or not to save Mom."

Silver's lopsided smirk answers Nathan's offering loud and clear.

Nathan laughs and, faking disappointment, says, "I knew we wouldn't be able to get rid of you."

The three of us share a laugh, and I extend my left arm with my fist closed. Silver steps forward and places her closed fist on top of mine. Nathan looks at both of us and rolls his eyes at our cheesiness. Then he walks slowly toward us and places his fist, stacking all our fists one on top another. This is the moment when we decide to fight for something worth fighting for.

***

For the next three days, we work tirelessly to build up our weapon and food inventory, especially long-lasting food. We sharpen our few knifes and arrows, check our bows, and pack up everything we want to take with us. Most of our time we spend practicing for everything we can think of that we might encounter. What to do if attacked alone, to get the other two's aid. What to do if attacked together. What to do if surrounded. What to do if victorious in each situation, whether to chase our enemies or not. What to do and what not to do. This mission seems insurmountable, but hey, anyone would do the impossible to save their mother.

Nathan and I work for hours on our focus and ability to control our powers. During our sessions, we sit in our backyard beside each other, and without telling me, he bursts into flames or shoots a fireball up in the sky. I am supposed to predict them a second before. If focused and connected with him, I can feel his wrath build before exploding into flames. Silver and I practice the same way I used to with Nathan, using our obstacle courses. The difference now is that I must focus on what is in front of me and on what I can't see, so I can foresee what she will do based on what she thinks and feels. So far, I have not been able to.

My failures anger me. Success could mean an advantage on the battlefield. Foreseeing my allies' movements could help us attack united, organized. Besides, if I ever manage to control when and who I connect with, maybe my foresight could even work on our enemies. Predict their plans, their moves, their attacks, and avoid confrontation.

Nate has told me to try to channel strong memories into my powers. His rage fuels his fire, his desire to avenge those he loves, to bring benevolence back into this world, to amend what humanity has turned into. Without it, he alleges he wouldn't be able to produce even a spark. However, none of my memories or thoughts have managed to heighten my empathic connection.

Nonetheless, my failure has not stopped us from undertaking this mission. We have sat for hours thinking and planning what to do, where to go, and how to rescue our mom. Today is the last day for planning as three days was the limit, we set on waiting to depart. Mom's life depends on us. During my connection, as Pete The Perpetual attacked her, her frailness felt extremely real. Her body is close to buckling under the workload. Her breathing didn't feel right, and her body is extremely undernourished. She will not suffer a day longer than the best we can offer her.

For now, we only have two details clear. First, we must walk northward for about two months, and second, we must walk far around Cold's camp, as they must still be searching for us. This time they will be even more relentless. Tonight, we will dine well and sleep long hours, as tomorrow we start the mission of our lifetime.

Mom, here we come.

17
THE ELDER
TURBID WATERS

"MAY OUR SENSES BE ADVERTENT, and our aim be unerring," I say, kneeling with my eyes closed at our house's front gate, about to embark on an impossible journey. I hear nothing but the wind rushing through our empty neighborhood, forcing the overgrown grass of empty lots to dance and sing.

Even the slightest possibility of our mom being alive is more than enough to justify this quest. Jay has become an amazing young man, and I will give my life if necessary, to make sure he will still have the chance to become an adult.

For the last time in a long time to come, I open our secondary exit. Silver goes out first and scouts around to spot any visible or hidden dangers. She signals Jay to come out when everything seems clear. I follow, then secure the exit again, hiding it under the rubble for our improbable return, the four of us.

Jay is crouching and staring around carefully while holding his bow ready. Silver is doing the same, watching the opposite direction from Jay. This simple scene reassures me.

Not a word has escaped from me about Dad, but the fact that he wasn't in any of Jay's visions hints that he is not with her. My heart silently whimpers that he was not able to survive this hell.

They were together when everything got fucked up, on a business trip in another country that no longer exists. And to end up at the camp north of us, Mom and possibly Dad must have tried to come back to Jay and me but failed. How long since they were caught and separated or maybe killed? Many thoughts cross my mind about the hell they must have gone through, building my anger up within me, but it feels under control, useful, and deadly at my command.

We are going past the house where I had the pleasure of meeting Silver. She glares at me, wanting me to remember our first encounter. I allow her a small smile after making sure Jay isn't looking. He is walking steadily with his head down as if counting steps. He looks weird walking like that, but it means he is focused. The correct way to be.

To break the silence, I burst out a small fire in front of them. Both jump back and punch me playfully. "Both of you are just too boring."

They laugh as I'd intended.

The burden of what we have set out to accomplish should not rest so heavily upon their shoulders. My intention is to carry the bulk of that load by myself, for them to be alert, focused, and rested physically and emotionally.

We know Cold's camp is about seven days north. He seems like a grudge-keeping man, so we decide to walk northeast toward the coast for about fifteen days to reach the ocean, then walk parallel to it. Not along the beach, though. That would be the worst mistake, walking completely exposed against an immovable barrier.

After that we will venture northward when we're sure we have gone far enough around Cold's camp. At that point, we will stop and redesign our plan, since we have no idea of the landscape, the people or towns, the routes, or the enemies we may encounter from there on. As with everything, if we don't evolve and adapt, we will perish.

***

We are closing in on the ocean, walking east straight to it. You can smell the salt water on the breeze characteristic of the sea. Not even the heat of summer can mess this up. The sea has something special that warms the heart, at least for those who don't live on the coast. This feeling must be surging in Silver and Jay, as they are not as quiet as before and their long faces are smiling now. Their pace seems lighter, more joyous and hopeful.

And this is when I need to heighten my awareness, while theirs is lower. Especially Jay's, who is not as experienced as Silver and me. What has me confused is the fact that we have not encountered enemies all the way here—fifteen days walking undisturbed does not feel right. We spotted some broken branches, a few footsteps almost erased by wind and rain, but nothing more.

Both are walking together a couple of meters ahead of me. I speak out loud, "Remember, guys, be careful and attentive as we might not be alone."

Both nod. Jay keeps going, but Silver lingers for a second to let me catch up.

She whispers, "You are thinking the same as I am, Nate. Fifteen days without unpleasant encounters does not fit the equation."

I see the discomfort in her eyes and am thankful she's not worrying Jay right now. "Yes, Sil, I was just pondering on that. Two possible explanations: one, we are falling straight into a trap and have missed any hint of it, and maybe we are even being followed; or two, something bigger has caught their attention, which cannot be any good for us either."

Her face changes from the calm manner she had just a few moments ago into her battle face, focused, strong, even frightening. "Agreed, Nathan. Let's get to work trying to see if we are falling into a trap. If we don't find any clue, I believe your second idea must be true. Maybe they are battling another faction, ravaging a close-by town, or even migrating their forces back to the walled city. I've wondered about that since Pete was in Jay's vision. We don't know if that was now or before we dealt with him at the smaller satellite camp."

We continue walking behind Jay, my attention split between making sure he does not go too far ahead and paying attention to Silver who walks beside me.

She must be right but leaving their satellite camp unattended does not make sense. I voice my concerns, "Why would they migrate their forces back to the walled city? Both of you said there's mining and a foundry, very valuable assets to be left behind." Her scenarios are truly worrying. If they are battling or scavenging, their complete forces must be together, out of their camp. If by misfortune we bump into them, we could be surrounded in minutes.

Silver is just as doubtful, her gaze scouting every meter of the dense jungle we walk, "Just sharing my ideas, but their walled city is their most valuable asset. Trust me, if there is any type of threat to it, they would concentrate as many men and women as they can assemble to protect it. Maybe they have vast oil or potable water reserves there, or even larger mines at their disposal."

Silver makes a point, so I nod slightly. "Let's get to work." Jay stops six meters in front of us and watches our surroundings for any threat, using his training to avoid falling into a trap.

She sprints about ten meters away to my left and crouches, searching the ground for clues.

"Jay, what to do you see?"

He walks back, silently toward me looking confused. "Where is Silver?"

I look at him, sorry for taking him abruptly out of his joyfulness, and elaborate, "Something is not right, Jay. So many days without running into enemies worries Silver and me. We need to inspect the area to be sure we are not falling blindly into a trap. Need you to take up the center front. Silver is inspecting our left flank, and I'll take the right flank. Look for footsteps, wires, broken branches, anything that seems amiss."

He snaps out of his confusion and assumes a more serious look, eyebrows furrowed. He is in game mode once more.

I run twenty meters away to the right of Jay, and start advancing straight toward the ocean, but still with a clear view toward my brother's position. We go on and on, almost in a single file, trying to either find the trap or spring it once and for all, but nothing happens. Nothing seems misplaced, nothing moves, and nothing jumps out at us. Every second going by tries to convince me we are not in danger—not immediate danger, at least—but that is the exact thought that has always given me the worst anxiety. Silence is nerve-wracking.

Even before being able to see it, the ocean's relaxing sounds break the silence. The sound of waves crashing on the sand is enough to disconnect anyone from their woes.

About two hundred meters away, through the jungle, the blue transparent sea peeks as if curious but vigilant. The wind blows mildly, and the smell of salt water and sand takes control of my senses. We stand up straight and continue walking the last meters before reaching the coast. Our first checkpoint.

The three of us emerge from the jungle almost at the same time; I'm twenty meters apart from Jay and Silver is even farther away to my left. We stand still, looking out over the beach, seeing the waves and foam splashing on the white sands covered with broken shells and shade from palm trees. A long time has gone by since the last time we saw the sea, and yet it still conserves its power to soothe. The sun seems brighter, stronger, and steadier than anywhere else we've been since The Day.

Closing my eyes, I embrace the beauty that has been preserved here. The humid breeze moistens my skin, the sun warms my body, and the tranquilizing song of the ocean caresses my mind. How peaceful it feels, so that even my fiery powers seem to step back and allow this tranquility to lead the way. Oh, how have I missed this feeling, the sense that nature around us is in equilibrium and ready to help us recharge and go on with our hectic lifestyles. Trips to the beach used to be a way to escape our stressed-out lives, to leave everything momentarily behind, forgotten. Its magic is still here as if preserved in a time capsule, but the fact that no one else is here signals it is not a safe place.

Slowly opening my eyes, I see Jay and Silver having the same moment as I just experienced. Long overdue. The magnificent view of a never-ending horizon reminds me of how fleeting our lives are and how much we must value every second. The world is not what it used to be, and it will probably never be again, so we must embrace and cherish every second we are granted. Silver walks toward Jay, so I start getting closer to be together.

They are now together laughing at something, and I feel true joy. Next time, we will share this experience with Mom and, hopefully, Dad, and we will live every second of it to the fullest.

"What is that on the sea, Nathan?" Jay points out at something peeking out of the sea about one hundred meters into the water and to our left.

"I don't know, but we need to make sure it is not a threat. Let's get going." We start heading toward the odd hump coming out of the water, as it slowly floats toward the shore.

When we are about fifty meters away from the first hump, I notice several more humps floating behind it. Awestricken by this unexplained phenomenon, we trot toward the sea. As we get closer, my heart beats faster at the possibility of their being what I believe them to be. *Please don't be.*

I stop and grab Jay by his arm. "Stay here and don't move. I need you to be alert and be our scout. Nothing comes out of the jungle before you spot it. Don't give your back to it. Silver and I will go ahead to see what's going on. Understood?"

Even if he does not understand my command, he nods and answers, "Yes, Nathan. I will not disappoint you."

Half of it is true. We really need someone to serve as scout, but I need Jay to do it, so I can protect him from seeing what's in front of us.

Silver and I run as quickly as we can across the white beach. The closer we get to the edge of the waves, we can see it is starting to turn red. This cannot be happening—not now, not at this moment of peace and well-being. Destiny seems to be making fun of us, making us feel at peace just before sending us down a nightmare with no end.

We grab the first body that is face down in the water and drag it out of the sea. Three wooden arrows are sticking out of his back, probably the cause of death. The wet clothes and hanging limbs make it difficult. Dead, this man is dead, and there is a horrible open wound across the middle of his face. Silver's eyes are filled with sorrow and disbelief.

All the humps are dead bodies floating in the ocean. As we stand facing the sea, a dozen humps dance disturbingly toward us on the rhythm of the waves. Silver is trembling, and I am frozen in place, unable to move or stop staring at this horror. This world never ceases to amaze and horrify. Bloody water tainting our clothes, our hands dripping red, and the view of nightmares in front of us.

"Fuck." Silver expresses exactly what we both feel.

18
THE YOUTH
EVIL RESURGES

NATHAN AND SILVER COME BACK from the beach with their heads down.

"What happened, Nathan?" I ask.

"This world never ceases its cruel intent to destroy all the beauty that's left," Nathan remarks darkly, shaken and worried about something.

Silver just nods back to the beach where a bloody dead body lies.

Then I can see the reddish tint to the wet sand the waves have been kissing. Looking farther, I realize there are about a dozen bodies floating in the ocean. Being unable to do something, to save them, I start crying. How could this happen? Who did it? Where are all those poor bodies coming from?

"Get yourself together, Jay. If you don't, we could be next to join them," Nathan points out while glaring into the jungle and clenching his fists.

"Don't be so hard on him Nathan." Silver says.

My pulse rises and my nerves tense; Nathan hates to be contradicted in serious matters.

He turns and stares at her, half-angry and half understanding, clearly battling against his urge to argue with her. Fire starts pouring out of his fingertips, and Silver steps back in fear. Her green eyes are wide open, and her body is preparing to flee. I step quickly between them to avoid this getting out of hand.

Nathan looks at me in disbelief, and then sets his eyes on Silver, who stands behind me. He says, "Sil, you don't have to fear me. Neither do you, Jay. You are right. I was harsh. But let us be honest, harsh is the way our world has been molded. I trust both of you with my life, and both of you better be one hundred percent sure I will give my life to protect you without hesitation. However, to succeed in our mission and not all die trying, we must embrace the unforgiving world we live in. What angers me is the fact that there will never be a second of tranquility. There is no true safety left anywhere." His voice weakens as sadness takes control.

Nathan's eyes are as dull as I've ever seen them, and he has a tense jaw and sad frown. He stares at the dead body lying on the sand and continues, "Reliance is exclusive within us three, and with no one else. We cannot forgive our enemies, we cannot let our guards down for a second, and we cannot lose sight of our objective. Just as you did, I felt the old world once more inside the ocean breeze and music of the waves, but this massacre has shown us it was just an oasis, an imaginary relief in the middle of a desert of pain."

Silver comes forward, pushing me to walk with her toward Nathan, as the three of us embrace. Nathan voice lowers into a whisper, saying during our embrace, "Please, don't get me wrong. I have faith that good men and women still live out there, hidden from the horrors surrounding us. Probably those goddamn bodies belonged to some of them. I will use every single breath and ounce of strength my body can gather to protect them from men like Cold. This journey to rescue our mom has shifted. We will save her, of that I am sure, and we will work together to ensure others have the slightest chance to survive. When saving you, Jay, I felt that urge. Now, it is my fucking life mission."

I step back, and they continue hugging, with their foreheads together, speaking softly and inaudibly. Behind them, the jungle is moving gently with the ocean breeze, nothing odd about it. To my right, the beach goes on for about a kilometer until it reaches a mountain. The white sand reflects the sun strongly and blinds me momentarily. I turn around and see how the floating bodies are reaching the shore. Where do these bodies come from?

Inspecting the horizon over the ocean I see nothing but waves. There is no shipwreck or any hint about a possible origin for the dead. I gaze to my left, fighting against the sun's intense glare and spot something atop the cliff. Smoke is still rising behind the tree line. These bodies must come from a place on top of that cliff due north from here!

"Nathan, Silver, look!" I whisper urgently while pointing toward the cliff. They release each other from their embrace and turn their heads quickly toward the cliff. Silver covers her face with both hands in disbelief. Nathan stares silently, his features turning from sorrow into rage.

Nathan says each word with fierce conviction, "Do you remember we thought our five-day peaceful march was either a trap or a consequence of Cold facing a larger threat? Well, it must have been that second theory. He must be responsible for this, and he will definitely pay for it."

"Sorry I doubted you, Nathan," Silver says, embarrassed by her half step away from him. I have never seen Silver like this, with hunched-up shoulders, looking up to my slightly taller brother, her eyes filled with regret.

He steps to her and gives her a hug, kisses her cheek, and then grabs her face and stares deeply at her eyes as if speaking without words.

Both nod before separating and starting to walk back to the beach. It must be true that actions speak louder than words.

I grab our binoculars, while Nathan and Silver go back to the bodies, as they might give us a heads-up as to what we will face on top of the cliff. Trees at the border of the cliff cover my view. I inspect from the cliff's right edge, along its border, inland into the forest. Only smoke peaks on top of the forest line, and nothing else can be seen from here. I continue searching away from the ocean and see what looks to be a pathway leading to the top of the cliff.

Silver and Nathan come back to me, so I share what I have seen, "I cannot see past the forest on the cliff, but the smoke is definitely coming from behind it. Something must be burning still or have been burnt recently. There is a path within the trees to our left that seems to lead up to the cliff. Should we go?" Nathan's eyes are amber now; he is not willing to allow anyone else to die today. Without a word he starts walking toward the place where I pointed when showing them the pathway. Silver and I join him and walk in a single file.

Without looking at us, Nathan says, "None of the bodies have armor, and simple handmade weapons float with the dead. Shivs, wood batons and lances, barely sharpened swords, and clubs with nails pointing out of them. They were not a battling clan, village, or family, just regular men, women, and even children fighting for survival." I can feel the heat coming out of his body. Both Silver and I step a couple of meters away from him and continue our march.

He does not notice, as he is set on reaching the top of the cliff. He adds, "Of the twelve floating bodies, one was wearing Cold's clan armor. Our suspicion is valid; Cold attacked these villagers. After their murderous assault, they must have tossed them off the cliff. What is worrisome is that most bodies sink before floating days after they decompose. Those bodies were not decomposed yet, so they must be a small percentage of the massacred people."

I feel sick at the notion of more bodies left underwater, so I question to divert my attention, "Do you believe he attacked them for some specific purpose, or were they just in his way?" My question seems to be what both Nathan and Silver are wondering about as they look at me with the same thoughtful expressions. Either way, we are at immeasurable risk way beyond our capabilities this close to a force large enough to destroy an entire village.

Silver breaks her silence, "I believe they are marching somewhere, Jay. This place is about twelve days away from Cold's camp and wasn't a threat to his dominion. Maybe they were a faction paying tribute to him. Killing them must not be an act of war or a way to subdue a possible threat, but just a sacking to take resources they will use at their destination."

Nathan and I nod our agreement.

Nathan points out our next step, "We will proceed cautiously northward, toward their village. Maybe some are still alive and need to be saved from Cold's brutality, but we must be careful because this army probably outnumbers and outpowers us."

I sense we are all thinking the same thing. They viciously killed men, women, and children, and we will never be able to turn back time but can fight for those who managed to survive the first wave.

I feel Nathan's body heating up, radiating the rising temperature outward as his body is swelling. His steps are heavier and leaving burnt marks on the jungle soil. Silver has her bow ready, and her steps are slow, careful, lightweight. The time has come to face them once more, but this time together.

The three of us march along the border between the forest and the white sand, right where we must be to have clear visibility of the rising smoke and yet be invisible from the cliff. Scouts may still be around, even though the army has moved on.

Each step is a challenge for me; a misstep could be death to all of us. My nerves are on high alert, and every little noise startles me. Sil and Nate seem to be calm, walking in their attack stances, stealthily advancing. Occasionally, either one sprints ahead for recon, so in case they are spotted, the enemy will mistake our numbers. At least that surprise could give us the upper hand against scouts. Our biggest risk is to walk right up to the army accidentally, tripping into our deaths. This tactic was one we practiced and spoke of thoroughly when planning our mother's rescue. So different, theory from practice in the field.

They are fierce and focused on what we must do; I am scared. At their side I feel safe, but at the same time, unprepared. What if I fail them? In the end, an army is as strong as its weakest link.

Both are the most amazing warriors I have ever seen, and I am not even mediocre at fighting or hunting. They aren't even panting after sprinting several times, and my breathing is heavy, my legs aching, and my back hunched in tiredness. The battle has not even commenced, and my body and mind seem to be already defeated with fatigue.

A steep hill towers in front of us as we approach the walkway up to the village. The steps are carved into the soil and small canals of water are flowing down the steps and finding a way around our feet. Interesting how water resembles human nature in that manner—any obstacle that arises must be either broken through or avoided.

Nathan is leading our rise, followed by me and then Silver. Unmistakably, this is the best formation as the most skilled protect the weakest. My brother has his bow at the ready. I have a shiv in my right hand and a small metallic shield we molded back home protects my left flank. Silver is behind me with her bow and arrow at the ready too.

Nathan halts for a second and signals us to stop and wait. He crawls up the final steps to peek over the hilltop. He lies still for several moments, watching something in front of him, awestruck with the scene. Joining him slowly, we see why he fell silent and motionless. An entire village is burning. How many lives destroyed? How many hours of effort to build up this place lost?

No wail can be heard, and there are no bodies. This was not a battling village; they don't even have a protective wall. To the right, some farming lots have been scavenged. At the left, about thirty small cabins made of wood with thatched roofs are still burning. The fire must have been started not long ago. Cooking pans, food, clothes, rakes, plows, chairs, wooden table parts, and gardening cans are strewn around the area, discarded and broken. Cold's army left all of it behind while fleeing from their crimes. This village was not a threat to Cold. He just wanted to spread evil around this world; Satan in flesh and blood.

Nathan walks toward the town center where a small adobe church stands surrounded by burning homes. Almost all the buildings are burning, with some in the far left still standing without damage. We try to follow him but are repelled by the heat.

"Nathan, be careful!" I yell as he walks right in the middle of the burning horror. Silver covers my mouth and signals me to be quiet with her index finger. Enemies could still be around.

He barely looks back over his shoulder, his eyes glowing red with hate, and nods while signaling me with his left hand to stay back. Giving us his back, he stands with his legs slightly open and extends both his arms into the sky. His muscles flex and ripple, seeming to grow larger. Smoke and fire start pulling toward him, circling from the church and houses, reaching his hands and disappearing, seemingly absorbed by him. His body grows marginally larger while he grunts in anger.

Finally, the village is quiet. No more fire crackling, just the silence left behind by the deceased. Nathan walks toward us with a mean gaze, fumes still coming out of his body and his eyes gradually turning back to their normal amber green. "Let's go see if these sons of bitches left any survivors," are his only words, and probably the only ones he will mutter until we find a survivor or leave this ghost town.

We walk on the center path toward the unaffected houses to the far left and enter the first one. The soldiers broke all the houses' doors; they hacked and slashed their way into families hiding from the attacking army. Inside, everything is a mess; they toyed with them, destroying their homes inside out, before leaving with their belongings and tossing them all around the main pathway.

We exit and walk in the middle of the pathway through the remaining houses. *Oh, God, please let us find at least one survivor.*

Suddenly, we hear a moan close by, coming from behind us. Running, I follow the faint sound of a human sob. Six houses down and to the right, the source seems to be coming from behind a burnt-up shed, one of the smallest in the town. I see a woman surrounded by the burnt-up structure, lying on the ground and peeking inside a hatch she is holding open.

Her complete body and clothes are burnt up, but her pain is not physical. She does not even notice me behind her, or that Silver and Nathan have just run toward me. Leisurely walking toward the woman shows me the extent of her wounds. She is closer to death than to life, her skin destroyed.

I kneel down and say, "What has happened here? We are here to help."

With a soft voice, she replies, "The devil has come and gone."

Through the hatch, surrounded by debris, two small bodies lay, maybe four and six years old, curled together hugging each other…dead.

I drop to the floor, my vision blackening.

My brother kneels beside me. "Be strong, Jay. We need you to man up to the occasion."

Adrenaline rushes through me, fighting the blackness away. He is right; this is no time to be a foolish, frightened, useless child.

The woman is cowering beside the hatch where her children passed away in the most horrifying way imaginable. This is true hell, what these people suffered at the hand of the devil. Her pain starts to become mine and the burnt-up house starts to fade away, but this time it does not feel like fainting. Blurry images start to mix with my reality.

I am at the village, but it is not burning anymore. I am the woman shouting in panic at the hordes of men running toward her house. The men are waving swords, clubs, torches, and knives as they rush toward her. Her fear feels extremely real. She is uncertain what to do, where to go.

She runs back to her house and screams, "Phillip, Billy, get in here quick!" The two children are crying as she pushes them into the hatch, and she shuts it quickly behind them. Through the cracks, she whispers, "Hold each other. Together you are the strongest kids in the world. Nothing will hurt you down there. Don't come out until I say so." Her voice is strong with conviction, but at the same time broken with fear of the dreadful sounds coming from the village.

She runs outside but is pushed back inside by two men with black teeth and scars on their faces, wearing armor. She falls heavily to the floor and hits her head on a chair's armrest. One of them enters the kitchen and searches, tossing anything he isn't interested in to the floor or across the small room. The other one trashes the rest of the house, throwing her few possessions to the ground and tossing her furniture over.

"There is nothing here. She is poorer than my slaves," one says to the other.

They laugh and then leave as quickly as they'd entered.

The blow on the woman's head is making her dizzy, slowing her motions. She is sobbing at the mess they left, her heart racing like a drumroll in fear of what is happening to her neighbors. Her friends shriek and wail as they are slaughtered. She pulls a knife out of the back of her dress and walks confidently toward her door. A bald, bearded man is walking slowly up her steps, and she charges unafraid with all her strength and rage at him.

He smiles an evil smirk and pushes her violently back inside. She crashes into the wall, fearful of this inhuman. She meets his light blue piercing eyes as she tries to stand up on a broken leg. She feels no pain. Her mother's instinct has kicked in, and she will give her life to protect her children if needed. This man will not hurt her babies.

The man spills gasoline all around from a bottle he is holding and lights a match. She screams for him to stop and offers to do whatever he wants if he will just stop. His eyes fall on the hatch, and she feels the deepest dread—he knows the children are hiding there. As he turns back toward the front door, he drops the match into the pool of gasoline.

"Weakness is not welcome at White Tower," Cold says as he walks down the wooden steps.

Suddenly all the horrific sounds come back to her. Most of her village must have died by now, as there are fewer screams. The flames are spreading quickly across her wooden floor. The woman crawls toward the fire, fighting the pain in her leg and planning to throw herself on it to put it out before the whole house burns down and her children with it. She is about to roll over the fire when a gust of wind enters the front door and stokes the fire. She hits her head in a panic, confused, and falls unconscious.

My eyes open sluggishly, as if waking from a dream, and I am back at the burnt-up house. The woman of my vision lies dead beside the hatch, and Silver and Nathan are kneeling beside me. "I have seen what Cold did to this woman, to this village. He just did it for the sake of killing; they were outnumbered and outpowered. They took their food and water and still burned down their whole village, a farming village that could not have done any harm. Before leaving, he even made fun of the woman, saying, 'Weakness is not welcome at White Tower.' He burned this house knowing these poor innocent children were in there."

Anger and sorrow send tears running down my cheeks, the mixture of the woman's pain and my own more than my heart can stand. I pound my fists angrily on the burnt wooden beams around me, bloodying my knuckles.

Nathan moves toward the dead woman and her two children, pulls the small bodies out of their hideout, and lays them gently beside their mother. He pulls a blanket out of his backpack and covers them, his face full of pain and grief and his teeth clenching as he fights back his tears and fury. Both hands rest lightly on their foreheads, making small crosses over them.

It is the first time I have ever seen my brother act in the faith I am quickly losing to all this hatred and evil. He rises and walks back toward the central path, not looking back. Silver runs behind him. As I stand up and walk feebly behind them, my mind is dumbstruck by what happened in this peaceful, undeserving village. Nothing makes sense. Hard work and peace are now a sign of weakness?

My brother is standing about five meters away, giving me his back, with his head on Silver's shoulder as she hugs him. He is not crying, just staring down at the ground as if searching for hope where none is to be found. Silver backs slowly from him, and he shakes his head in disbelief.

19
THE ELDER
STRENGTH IN OUR NUMBERS

EVERYTHING HAPPENED IN A RUSH; Jay seems to have connected with the deceased mother of those poor, innocent children and confirmed Cold's men are marching to White Tower. He lost the connection as soon as she passed away, and now an entire family lies on the ground because of Cold's evil. How many families have succumbed to that same fate? How many more?

Silver understands me even without words. She knows when to speak, when to embrace me, when to give me space, and when to support me. She is hugging me, and her body heat comforts me while I am struggling to comprehend the full extent of our enemy's tyranny. The notion of death becomes more understandable when you experience it close at hand, with a few people, than when you see many dead bodies. That family did not deserve this fate. That family could have been us.

Silver ends the embrace, and we both walk back to Jay, who is standing a couple of meters away from us, lost in his thoughts. Under our feet, the rubble of burnt houses creaks and taints our shoes with ashes. We continue walking together, the three of us, toward the burnt church, to finish searching this ghost town.

Silver speaks without looking at either of us, "Nathan, Jay, this a terrible news. White Tower is a massive fort and strategic center, and now includes Cold's forces too. Our mission is beyond impossible. During my travels, a few people mentioned the myth of White Tower. Allegedly, the tower in the middle of that place is white with small red dashes painted with the blood of the slaves sacrificed. Every single dash represents a day their rule has been unchallenged. Above the White Tower, a never-ending fire illuminates the sky as a beacon of their challenge to any God who desires to interfere with their rule." Silver's voice trembles with fear as she starts to believe, and the myth turns to reality.

My body starts to feel empty again, but now with the fear of being unable to fulfill our mission. If our mom is inside that stronghold and the White Tower story is true, she might be dead. If she is alive, she is captive within a city where a large army will soon arrive to strengthen their numbers.

Jay is silently staring at the ground, and Sil is staring at me with a serious gaze, waiting for me to answer. Their silence convinces me I must think of an alternate plan; they depend on me, but I am afraid and hopeless. After all, I am a survivor, not a strategist. This mission is overwhelming, and nothing comes to mind to overcome the impossible. What to do when everything crumbles under your feet and even in that chaos others depend on you?

We walk past the burnt church and walk toward the cliff's edge. At this place, Cold's men must have disposed of the bodies of the defeated. Men, women, children who passed away trying to defend what was rightfully theirs. Silver is staring at the horizon, standing to my right, with the wind blowing on her face, washing her tears away.

Jay is standing at my right, inspecting the sea beneath us, probably searching for more bodies. How can a fourteen-year-old cope with all we have seen in this town? How can I help him stay strong when my strength is faltering?

The waves crash against the rocks beneath us, and no more bodies can be seen. The wind howls at us, and the spray on my face makes me feel cold and in despair. I stand beside Jay and place a hand on his shoulder, gently pulling him away from the cliff. He does not need to search for more pain.

I speak strongly, "We are about fifty to fifty-five days away from White Tower. Trying to outrun Cold's army to save our mother before they arrive is extremely risky. They might be spread out or walk in random directions while raiding villages and scavenging. That approach just seems too unpredictable, too risky. When Cold's army arrives, as large as it seems to be, this mission becomes impossible. Entering a walled city leaves us enclosed—we would be walking into the enemy's den with no possibility of escaping. Besides, Mom's condition might not be suitable for a quick escape."

My cheeks inflate as I expel air in discontent at my inability to devise a plan.

Jay speaks with a broken voice, "What about Mom, Nate? We cannot just accept defeat and leave her to die, can we? She deserves better. She deserves our best try even if we die doing it!" Jay is breathing heavily, angered by the situation.

He is challenging me but means no harm; it is just his reaction to being powerless to save a loved one. This world has taught fighters like Sil and me that success is a blurry synonym to survival. Sometimes plans crumble, hope is shattered, and living a day longer outweighs your desire to go beyond simple survival. Hands behind my back, I to stare at the ocean and think.

Maybe within those waves and the sound of water crashing against the cliffside, an answer to this dilemma waits for me. We must stand against a vast power and somehow rescue the innocent victims of the evil empire and survive. I know destiny works in mysterious ways and the impossible becomes possible and the powerless become gods, but will destiny be in our favor?

As the soothing sound of the sea guides me in an ocean of ideas and fears, a horse's hooves clomping toward us brings me back to reality. I turn, finding Silver is holding her bow at the ready, waiting for the equestrian to come into view, and Jay is crouched behind nearby debris from a burnt-down building a couple of meters to my right. My focus turns to the sound of the approaching gallop as blazing power dances at my fingertips, ready to sear whatever dares to attack us. I walk in front of them, ready to protect them from whomever dares to attack us. Seconds turn to minutes as the heavy jungle obscures the oncoming danger. Only a courageous enemy would charge in this world, or an idiot. Too much risk in losing the element of surprise.

I watch a horse emerge from the jungle line carrying a man with a sword and leather body armor. It halts abruptly at his command forty meters in front of us, partially covered by the burnt church. The man walks his horse from side to side, staring dumbfounded at the destroyed village, tears streaming down his cheeks, then dismounts.

I signal Jay and Silver to walk with me toward the man, trying to stay hidden behind the church ten meters in front of us. Around it, I can see the horse is unattended and the idea of stealing it crosses my mind. It could really help us to outrun Cold's army before they reach White Tower. Damn it, but it would leave this man alone and incapable of outrunning Cold's men should they return. *Am I capable of harming others for our own sake?*

Before I answer my own question, the sound of the man's desperate run brings me back to caution. He is dashing toward the group of burnt-down sheds, painfully, as if each step hurts. This man, broken by the horror laid out on the cliff top, does not even acknowledge our presence or the threat we could be to him. He runs as quickly as his feet carry him and turns left close to the place where the woman rests with her children. We run to keep up, with our weapons ready to strike in case he is fooling us.

As soon as we turn left toward the woman's burnt house, we see him again. His hand touches the scorched remains of the shed where we found the burnt woman who died saving her children. A devastating and heartbreaking wail comes from the man as he falls to his knees. His entire body quakes with violent sobs he is unable to control. Sil, Jay, and I approach cautiously. None of us wishes to speak, to interrupt this man's agony—not because we are heartless but because we understand his need to release what has broken him.

As I lay my hand gently on his shoulder, his blue eyes meet mine and a tortured soul gazes up at me. This man has lost everything, his family, his village, his present, past, and future. Cold has sentenced this man to lifelong misery.

"What has happened?" His words are like a distant echo brought by the wind.

He turns toward the bodies covered with my blanket. I explain, "An evil man who goes by the name Cold attacked this village, your village, I suppose. He leads a large army with no morals, no conscience, and no goodness left in their long-lost hearts. We recently discovered he is heading to White Tower, the walled city due north, and seems to be raiding villages along the way." My hand is still on his shoulder, unable to protect him from the truth just spoken.

Jay asks, "Sir, was this your house?"

He nods, unable to raise his head or speak.

Silver kneels down and puts a hand on his other shoulder as she says, "Your wife fought valiantly. She did everything she could to protect your children, but the devil himself entered your house and took fate into his own hands. He will pay for this. All the evil he has committed will crush him in time, and we will make sure of it. Our roads have crossed his several times and will once more for revenge."

He stands up sluggishly, both hands holding his head as he looks all around at the devastation. The three of us step back to give him room as he is still shocked.

Jay speaks, and the man turns toward him with deep regret in his eyes, "Your family is resting now. We have laid them together and covered them. We are deeply sorry for your loss, and please trust that we are here to help. You are not alone, and if you wish, you will not ever be alone again," Jay offers, hoping he'll be open to the possibility of a life beyond the one lost at Cold's hands.

Even though adding this unknown man into our plans seems risky, this situation changes everything. However, I feel deep empathy for this man as fate barely allowed me to escape his same destiny when I miraculously saved Jay from Cold's camp. His life could have been mine. Solitude makes life unsurmountable.

Walking painfully like an old man with pain-stricken joints and frail bones, he fights the urge to surrender and forces himself closer to the bodies of his deceased family. He kneels beside them, crosses himself, and starts to pray on the day his life was lost.

The three of us walk back toward the cliff, allowing him to give his final farewell in peace and privacy. None of us can speak yet, so we walk silently crestfallen, listening to the waves and the man's inconsolable wail. As we approach the cliff, the sound of the crashing waves blocks the man's suffering.

We sit at the edge, feeling the wind moisten our faces with the ocean spray. I finally muster the courage to speak, "What that man suffered is what could have happened to me, to us, if I failed at rescuing you both." Jay frowns slightly and then nods, while Silver looks at me dolefully.

She shares a piece of her heart with us, "I have been in that same place, kneeling beside deceased loved ones. He must believe he is partly responsible for this by not being around when the attack happened. That is how I felt, and that is something I have never forgiven myself about." Silver stops speaking abruptly as she starts sobbing. I place my right arm around her shoulders and bring her closer to me. She rests her head on my chest and cries almost silently.

Jay looks at me with a pale face, searching for my strength and guidance, but I am as lost as he is. He blurts out his concerns, "Nate, what are we going to do?" He is desperate to find an answer, to hear a master plan I have been devising, but there is nothing thought out. I stroke Silver's head softly with my left hand, feeling how she is calming down as her sobs slow down.

How confusing to have such an amazing sight in front of us in such a harrowing moment.

Unable to answer Jay right away, I say, "Let me sleep on it. Maybe the world of dreams has something for us. We have experienced too many heartbreaking emotions today and my thoughts elude me. I promise we will find a solution to this, but let's rest." Jay nods with his eyes wide and his mouth tensed shut.

The three of us stand up and walk to our left, entering the forest line close to the cliff's south wall. Silver and I work on preparing the places where we will sleep tonight, while Jay preps a small fire to cook us supper. Our chores manage to distract us from all the evil surrounding us for a while, forcing us to concentrate on something else than death and suffering. Tomorrow must be a better day, as we will not be able to withstand so much pain again. Poor man.

***

A day has gone, and the man has not left the side of his family, giving a last goodbye.

Today we must march on. Cold's army has enough of a head start for us to continue our journey without much risk of stumbling into them. We sit around our campfire on this cold, damp morning, with the wind whistling and the sea striking the cliff violently. We have been silent for a while, and I have been pondering on what to do next with no success. Silver is sitting beside me on top of a fallen tree, and Jay is still lying down beside the fire, tossing a rock up and catching it without moving. Through the trees I see the man walking toward us, slowly treading the center path between the burnt sheds.

He comes into the forest and stands in front of us with bloodshot eyes and puffed cheekbones, and says, "Thank you. Thank you all for leaving me in peace to say goodbye to my family." His voice is trembling. He is slightly taller than I am, closing in on forty years old, with a larger, muscular build. His hair is black as night, and he has a stubbly beard. A long pink scar on his neck contrasts with his white skin.

The three of us nod once, acknowledging his gratitude. He is struggling to say something, and Jay is staring at him intently, probably trying to connect empathically but failing. Finally, he blurts with a broken voice, "I hope not to trouble you, but I need to give my family a proper burial. However, I am not able to even touch their bodies without further shattering my already broken heart. Could you help me?" He is hunched and unable to stare at us directly, standing still awaiting our response.

I stand up and walk beside this shattered man. Placing my right hand gently on his shoulder, I signal Sil and Jay to follow me with my left hand. Before walking past him, I whisper, "You are not alone, friend." He turns around and walks with us out of the forest, in front of the burnt church that is tearing down as time goes on. Its south wall is about to collapse, and the whole building will fall soon. No one dares speak as we walk on the center path. We turn left toward the man's destroyed house and see how the three bodies are still in the same place we left them.

The four of us carry the bodies of his family. The four of us cry as we dig two miniscule graves and a large one with our hands. And the four of us cry as we lay them gently in their final resting places. Each thrust of dirt falling on their pale, innocent faces crush our hearts. The sight brands our memories while we give them a last farewell.

The man soldiers on, heartbroken but unwilling to give up, his calm demeanor contrasting with his desolate tears. "We were farming families, living in peace. Cold's men used to come once a month to collect tribute, a wagon full of our crops. In exchange, they didn't kill us or abduct any of us. It was not the best deal, but at least we didn't have to build walls around our home. Now, I regret the moment I trusted those bastards to respect our agreement. My villagers, my family, my children have paid the price for my naivete," he says, tears streaming down his face. He turns to Silver. "You spoke of revenge. Count me in."

Sil and Jay nod in approval as their eyes glint with hope again. One more in our ranks means a greater chance of success. Yet he must still earn my trust both as a man and as a warrior. If we fight together, side by side, he must be worthy of holding the fate of my family in his hands. We finish burying his family and stand beside their graves.

We share a couple of minutes of silence, each giving a final farewell to them. I think about what this man must be feeling, about how to help him without exposing my family to any threat, and about the courage of the woman who gave her life trying to save her children. This encourages me to strive on and save my mother. She would have given her life for Jay's and mine without a doubt, and I will not surrender and give up on her.

The man crosses himself, finishing his silent prayer. While still staring at the dirt mounds in front of him, he mutters, "What is your plan?" He uses a determined voice, clenching both fists at his side hard.

Without thinking too much, I share our mission with him, hoping this is not a terrible mistake, "We are headed to White Tower to save our mother; my name is Nathan, he is James or Jay, and she is Silver, whom we met in this hellish world. Cold's army is heading in the same direction. Honestly, we haven't yet devised a plan to infiltrate such a stronghold with an army as vast as the one he leads."

The man answers quickly, "I am sorry, I did not introduce myself. My name is Rick Porter. Strength in our numbers is what we need. My travels have led me very close to White Tower, and I can assure you there is no way to enter or exit safely, at least not alive. Saving a captive is an impossible task. Few have tried it, but absolutely none have succeeded." His comments feel like cold water running down my back. We turn around and start walking back to our camp.

He continues, "Suspecting Cold would eventually betray our agreement, I have been traveling in search of fellow villages being repressed by him, willing to join forces and face him head on.

Fifteen days ahead on foot, a small village has agreed to help us. They are a small town, just like mine, but they have had enough of Cold's reign. They largely compensate for their lack of military skills with never-ending courage. Their leader agreeing to join forces against Cold may have been ill-timed for my village, but not for you, my friends."

The three of us stop walking abruptly. He stops walking a couple of steps in front of us and turns around, smiling at our surprise. Jay looks at me wide-eyed with a large smile on his face. Silver is staring at me, judging my reaction, while grinning excitedly at the news. *Life is such a puzzle*. When I felt lost and incapable to devise a plan, this man comes into our life and lays an opportunity at our feet. Maybe we cannot save my mom alone, but maybe we can save her and others by growing our numbers.

Since no one else speaks, I say, "Please go on, Rick." He gives me a lopsided smile, turns around and continues walking toward our camp. We follow him, expectant for what he is about to share.

He goes on, "Their leader also spoke of a place existing between myth and reality. He alleged that four days from his village, a town three times larger than my own hides from the rest of humanity. They know about Cold, but he does not know about them. They have lived deep within the jungle, ensuring no one they don't wish to know about them lives to tell the tale. These people are warriors, trained to kill, to attack quickly and retreat into the jungle. Just as the Russians did in World War II, they attack swiftly, unpredictably, with enormous force. Our only hope resides in getting these men and women, both villages, to join forces with us. The four of us alone are no match against White Tower."

Rick's confidence gives me a sense of peace at the sight of a clearer path in front of us, like a lost vessel on the ocean spotting a lighthouse's beam. I say, "Rick, if you are willing to help us, you should go on ahead without us, ride as quick as the wind and alert them about Cold's army. Let us not allow what happened here to be a lesson not learned."

Sil and Jay nod agreement.

Rick concludes, "Do not worry, Nathan. Thank you for worrying if I am ready to leave my village behind, but there is no sense in binding myself to the cruel reality. Now, you give me a chance to avenge my family and to protect others from evil. I will do as you say, friend." Rick pulls a piece of parchment out of his satchel and starts drawing a map with directions for us to reach the village.

We reach the burnt church that collapsed during the burial. Rick walks toward his horse, which we tied to a tree along the forest line. He hops on his horse, and I release the rope holding it. He nods to us and gallops away.

This will be the last village Cold will attack without retreating in fear, confronted by humanity's joined courage.

20
THE YOUTH
ABANDONED

RICK HAS GONE AHEAD TO Valor; the name Nate gave to the first town we will visit about uniting against White Tower. We have packed all our stuff in our large backpacks and started our journey behind Rick. Our best scenario is if Rick manages to reach Valor before Cold to ensure they are not attacked and destroyed. Our worst scenario is anything else.

We leave Rick's village, and the wind carries the smoky smell along with us through the dense jungle we enter. Our road has no road, and we are to keep as close to the shoreline as possible and walk due north. Eventually, we will reach a turbulent river, impossible to go through. There we are to turn west and walk along its border for a couple of kilometers until we reach a rope that was tied from side to side, allowing people to risk their lives crossing on top of slippery rocks on top of the riverbed.

Even if that idea scares me, I know it is the right thing to do. Nathan is walking in front of me with a steady pace, focused on what is in front of him, with his right hand grasping his bow in case we need it. Silver walks to my left, our footsteps coordinated, and she looks around constantly trying to spot any threat. I cannot concentrate, as images from Rick's village, his wife's death, and his family's burial pop in my mind constantly.

Even though I was not able to connect empathically to Rick, I can feel his sorrow. His resilience is admirable, as he was capable of riding away alone, willing to risk his life to avenge those he lost.

Nathan speaks without turning, "We must start thinking about strategy. We based our plans back home on stealth and only three of us going to White Tower; now, we will possibly have a slightly larger group of followers. This first place, Valor, needs our guidance, our skills, and our leadership to be useful. Otherwise, they will be sitting ducks, marching into a trained, bloodthirsty army and certain death. No one should die of unpreparedness because of our mission." Nathan speaks quietly while we walk through the jungle. There is no way to know if Cold has left scouts behind to alert him of possible dangers coming from behind his army.

Silver says, "I agree, Nate. It is time to start planning. Our march is going to be fifteen days long, so time is in our favor to strategize. Do you know *The Art of War* by Sun Tzu?" Sil asks both of us.

I shake my head no, but Nathan smiles as if he were thinking about the same thing.

The jungle feels cold and humid, with wind dancing around the trees. The approaching clouds start pouring rain on us, but we continue our walk. There is no time to be lost. Nathan waits for us to catch up as the heavy raindrops crashing against the foliage hinder our hearing.

Silver looks at me with a tender look and explains, "Jay, *The Art of War* is an ancient book written by a Chinese military general and strategist called Sun Tzu. Cold does not seem to be a strategist, but a violent, full-frontal-assault type of leader. Maybe if we attack based on a plan built upon strategic choices and train our forces accordingly, his force can be overcome by intellect."

I feel reassured by her comment. Cold's forces will outnumber us, even if we manage to obtain both Valor and the second village to join us but outsmarting him doesn't seem like much of a reach.

Nathan keeps his gaze up front, listening to what Silver adds,

"We must lead by example, fight as equals to those who join our cause. Your power, Nathan, with your skills, Jay, are going to be of utmost necessity."

I speak out, "Couldn't there be more people with powers? Maybe some are as powerful as Nate, and they could turn the tide in our favor." Nathan does not even blink at my comment, and Silver stares at the ground, thinking about my doubt.

Nathan shares his reservation, "We cannot suppose more people have powers, Jay. I mean, we cannot plan based on suppositions but on hard evidence. For seven long years I have survived facing countless enemies and meeting very few fellow survivors who have not been corrupted by this world, and none have shown or commented about anyone having powers. Have you ever met or known of someone with powers, Sil?"

Silver shakes her head, staring at Nathan while sharing, "No, you two are the only ones. You know how far I've come from and I have seen and met countless people, but no one is like the two of you. It would be naive to plan our strategy expecting others to have any type of supernatural abilities." They shatter my hypothesis and hope. We are really supposed to save Mom with strategy and luck, not with a mutant army.

Nathan stares at me for the first time in a while with a sorry look in his face. He tries to comfort me, "Do not worry, Jay. We got this! You will see that strategy will outweigh our powers to succeed." He looks at Silver, his hazel eyes wide and bright over his lopsided smile, teeth barely visible. He is excited, ready to act.

Silver continues explaining, "Next, we must set a meeting point to gather all the forces who agree to join us. A place close enough to White Tower that we can attack from it in a couple of hours' march, but far enough to chase and kill any scout who finds us. I know no place like this, but maybe one of the leaders we will meet can help us. By the way, Nathan, how do you want to address those leaders to ensure their support?" Silver turns her gaze toward Nathan with the question lingering.

That question has bothered me since Rick suggested we must

convince entire towns of people to fight against such a horrid threat as Cold, his army, and whatever lies within White Tower.

Nathan walks forward and holds a couple of long branches for us to go through. The rain keeps falling heavily, the mud under our feet getting slippery as the forest grows denser. He answers Sil, "Leave that to me. People will live under a tyrant's gruesome rule when hopeless, suppressed. That is what Cold does, destroy dreams of safety and peace. If he raids, attacks, enslaves, kills, and demands tribute from surrounding villages, they will live under his rule. When death seems to hover over you every day, people will heartbreakingly let go of the possibility of change. But hope never vanishes completely. Thoughts and feelings deep within our minds and souls hang on, in solitude, to the notion of life without restraints and violence. That hope works just like a gasoline-soaked rag, seemingly useless until someone adds a spark."

He is walking confidently, clenching both fists as his words excite the three of us. Nate proceeds, "All those men and women have had their hopes shattered by Cold and his men. We will ignite it, feed it with the tangible possibility of fighting for those they love, those they have lost, and those to be born who they won't want to have to live in this world." Nathan's voice rumbles through the night, dismissing and challenging the darkness around us, ready to bring light to those who have lost their way and their lives.

My heart races and goose bumps run over me at the prospect of really raising an army that could end evil's reign.

***

Day two. It feels awry to think we will soon be headed to war. My heart is working on a higher gear, constantly pounding my chest as I fear what the future may hold. The idea of saving Mom is the only thing making me go on. We had to sleep inside a tiny cave, lying atop our thin blankets that failed to soften the feeling of rugged rocks under them. While Silver and I slept, Nathan stayed awake to heat us with his powers. He was stubborn about it, alleging we should sleep dry to avoid falling sick so soon in our journey.

The rain ceased almost as soon as the sunlight started advancing shyly through the canopy. We had some apples as breakfast and continued walking north, searching for the turbulent river. The soil is damp, and I have slipped and fallen twice now. At least my clumsiness has lightened the mood, and both Nate and Silver laugh at my dirty clothes and face. Silver is walking by my side again, while Nathan walks about ten steps ahead clearing our way with his swords.

Silver speaks aloud to me while holding a small red mushroom on her hands. "Do you see this? Would you eat it, Jay?" Since I trust Sil, I walk toward her and grab it. The color reminds me of cherry-flavored candy, strong, bright red. Before eating this magnificent 'shroom, she alerts me, "Wait! Look ahead, Jay. Do you see that boar? What do you notice?" This is starting to confuse me, and Nathan halts, turns around, and watches the scene intently, mute and with half-shut eyes, carefully assessing the situation.

Without completely understanding what is going on, I answer, "I don't know, Sil. It is eating grass." Suddenly it hits me, the boar is eating grass carefully, not aggressively as you would expect them to do. The reason seems to be it is avoiding the red mushrooms peeking out of the grass. They must be poisonous, so I toss the red mushroom resting on my palm. A second before lashing out at Silver for bullying me, Nathan joins us and places his hand on my shoulder. He is restraining me; his eyes tell me there is more to this than a joke.

Silver explains before I lose my temper, "That is another strategy we will use, we must appear weak even if our numbers manage to give us strength enough to face Cold up front. A defenseless mushroom from the outside could be deadly from the inside. He is an egotistic man, and his pride will be his doom. Along the way of my travels, never have I seen a force remotely as large as Cold's army. His shortsightedness will become recklessness.

"His recklessness should allow us to divide his forces and attack simultaneously by all fronts. This way, their arrogance becomes one of our advantages. Our extreme caution will grant us the chance to appear where he expects resistance the least, and attack where he is less prepared to confront us." Now I see, Silver and Nathan are continuously planning, readying themselves to lead whoever joins us. My naivete clouded my judgement; this is no game; there are no jokes left to be said until Mom is saved and Cold is defeated.

***

We finally reach the turbulent river after thirteen days of walking north. Rain has fallen every single day, and the journey has been exhausting. Slipping and standing back up, avoiding the numerous fallen branches, and sleeping on top of rocks and trunks is no fun at all. The whistling wind hushes our voices constantly, so every time we talk, we must stand very close together and walk in synchrony.

Nathan and Silver have thought out most of our strategy, leaving some wiggle room to adapt it based on whoever joins us. Their plan seems to be the best possible, yet every time they discuss it, some new change is done. I think they are being overly cautious, but now again, they are far more experienced and wiser than I will ever be.

We walk west along the river's edge, deafened by its roaring current. Nathan walks in front of the group staring up front, I walk behind him and am supposed to keep looking south to ensure no enemy comes at us from the jungle, and Silver walks behind me while she searches for any possible danger at the other side of the river.

The river's strength sends a constant mist at us, refreshing our bodies as we walk upstream on top of sticky mud and slippery rocks. I am being as careful as possible, walking three meters away from the river to avoid falling to my death. My legs ache horribly, and I am panting, trying to keep Nathan's unrelenting pace.

Nathan halts suddenly and points ahead without turning. My heart skips a beat, panic taking control of my entire body. My only reaction is to grab my bow as quickly as possible and follow Nathan's index finger to see the threat we are facing. Why can't I see what he is seeing? The north edge has nothing weird about it, the south edge is free of dangers, and the river's current is crashing against a path of rocks crossing from side to side. *A path of rocks!*

On top of the path of rocks, a thick rope becomes visible. We have finally reached the crossing point! Nathan signals us to continue walking, advancing the last one hundred meters. He inspects the rope, pulling on it to ensure it is well strapped and tightened. Silver washes her face with water from the river's edge, while I inspect how slippery the rocks are. They are as slippery as it gets.

Nathan turns toward us and alerts us, "The rocks are slippery. We must be extremely careful not to get into the current, as it would thrust us downstream to our deaths. If you can, I would advise you to hang from the rope instead of walking on top of the rocks while holding the rope as a handrail. I will go first, then both of you are to cross together. Understood?" He shouts to surpass the thundering scream from the river's current.

Silver and I nod.

He ties the rope around a tree on our river edge and skillfully hangs himself from the rope, his body about half a meter above the rocks and current. He moves easily along the rope, his hands and feet moving in synchrony and advancing unhesitantly. Finally, he reaches the north edge, having crossed the forty-meter-wide river. Before we start crossing, he secures the rope's knot on the north edge and gestures us to cross.

Silver goes first, hanging herself the same way Nathan did.

I grab the rope strongly with both hands and swing both feet on top of it. My shoulders are sore and holding myself is painful. We start working our way across the rope together. Silver stares ahead to see how far we have left, and then looks back at me to ensure I am holding tight. The river's current is impressive, close to my head, threatening me should I fall.

My hands are getting tired, and we are only halfway across. My biceps and shoulders are screaming in pain, I am not going to be able to go all the way. I can sense Nathan's fear as he notices I am losing my grip. *Come on, Jay, hold the fuck on!* His thought sounds clear in my mind, desperate and afraid.

Without noticing, my legs slip, I barely hold to the rope, and I feel how my muscles on both shoulders are about to be shattered. Nathan screams something unintelligible, my terror blending with his. The river's current is crashing menacingly against the rock where my legs are dancing around, trying to stand up.

Silver lowers her legs and wraps them around me, holding tightly. I can feel her strong muscles pressing against my hip as she lifts me slightly above ground. The binoculars around my neck slip and fall heavily on the rock, slipping slowly into the current, making fun of my inability to save them. The river takes them away, disappearing forever in the white rapids downstream.

Silver hangs herself from her legs and right arm while helping move my legs back on top of the rope with her free hand. Within the moist disaster around me, I notice how a couple of tears are falling down my cheeks, so pathetic. She screams, slightly audible on top of the resounding river, "Are you okay? Can you go on?" I nod, ashamed of how useless I feel.

We continue advancing quickly, but she does not lose sight of me now. We reach the north edge, and she swiftly dismounts. Before I get off the rope, Nathan grabs hold of my shirt collar and tosses me heavily against the damp ground. His hands are trembling uncontrollably, and I have never seen my brother as scared as he is right now.

***

Today is our fifteenth day since we left the destroyed village to walk toward Valor. For the first time in our travels, we see the destruction Cold's army causes to nature. A large section of the jungle has been cut down and left behind. They did not even deforest for wood, they just did it because they wanted to. Amongst the shattered trunks and branches, we find a couple of bodies. They are dressed in Cold's armor, and they seem to have been killed in a swordfight.

I leave as Nathan inspects the bodies to understand what happened here. He must be worried, as I am, that Cold's army could have faced Valor and killed them all, losing only two men. However, we have not reached Valor; we have not seen the village. I think it would be very stupid to try to face Cold's army up front in the middle of the jungle.

Silver is walking around the destroyed jungled, searching for clues as well. Nathan comes back toward me and calls on Silver. As soon as the three of us are next to each other, he says, "I do not think this is the result of any confrontation between Cold's army and another faction. There are no signs of enemies, no blood stains, no more bodies and no arrow holes. This must have been a nonsensical fight amongst Cold's army to show who was stronger and braver, cutting down trees and fighting like gladiators to death." I cannot believe human beings could be such inhumane, so animal, but Nathan must be right because Silver does not contradict him.

Silver says, "However, we must be very close to Valor. We should double our pace to ensure they are still standing, and that Rick is still alive." Nathan agrees, and we continue walking north, away from the destroyed jungle and into the trees spared by Cold's stupidity. As we leave the destruction behind, I start reminiscing about our journey, in case Valor is still standing and we need to explain to them about our plans.

Our entire journey has been a planning session with

discussions, drawings in the dirt, simulations with twigs and rocks, thinking about possible scenarios, plans A, B, C, D, and all the way to Z. My brother and Silver have dedicated every second of their waking hours to this endeavor. I have mostly listened silently, reviewed our tactics, learned them, and readied myself for the moment when I'll have to teach others at Valor.

Filled with regret, with fear, with sadness, I'm terrified at the thought of our failing because of my lack of skill. Nathan looks so confident, with his mind set on doing such an enormous deed for humanity, and here I am, feeble and petrified like a child asked to overcome bed-wetting.

The jungle is dense once more and we are walking again in our triangular formation with Nathan in the lead. There are no uncommon sounds within the jungle, only wind, branches crashing against each other, and our footsteps splashing on top of water puddles.

According to what Silver and Nathan have explained, our strategy starts with the three of us. We are to train whoever joins us, teach them about our grand plan and show them our commitment by marching side by side every step of the way. This frightens me as it means people will look up to us. No longer a follower, but a leader, even though I feel terribly underqualified.

We keep advancing and there is no sign of Valor yet. This relaxes me since the farther away from the destroyed jungle without reaching Valor means there is still a chance that Cold did not visit and destroy them. A light rain starts fighting its way through the canopy, obscuring our view with the mist.

After training our followers and marching to White Tower, we must group all our forces. Our hope is to find people from several villages who will march alongside. I am still unclear about how Nathan expects to convince them, but he seems confident, and I have never seen him fail at achieving something he is committed to fulfill. His stride reflects this, walking farther north without really knowing where Valor is, willing to risk his integrity by leading our march.

The only detail he has shared about convincing people to follow us is the need to make every man and woman believe in himself or herself. He calls it sparking hope from within, as external forces cannot extinguish true inner fire. What does he mean? He avoids thinking about it when we are together, since he must know I am trying to read his thoughts and emotions. As soon as I connect with him, he shifts his thoughts to show his self-assurance about our mission.

Now, the destroyed jungle is far behind us. I turn around and see how deep the jungle goes; to my left and right only trees, branches, moss, and roots can be seen. The sun is trying to raise the day's temperature, fighting against the damp soil beneath the trees and the changing winds coming from the ocean to our right. We are too far into the forest to be able to hear to the waves, but I can smell we are close to the beach. Nathan is striving on, doubling our pace, feeling anxious about reaching Valor as soon as possible. Silver taps my shoulder to start walking faster, and we go on.

When the time comes to attack Cold's stronghold, we will be outnumbered, so Nathan and Silver have thought of ways to avoid being surrounded or overpowered quickly. They say we must appear weak at first. Cold has constantly showed his arrogance, exposing his true weakness. He believes he can destroy whomever he faces and never stops to think about his enemies' numbers or strategies. We call this the Red 'Shroom.

Curiously, as I am thinking about this, I notice how a cluster of those mushrooms grows on the left side of a couple of trees ahead. Their color is vivid and inviting, appearing to be harmless and delicious. Nature knows how to do things the right way, and it is truly beautiful. Silver looks at me deviously, noticing how I am looking at the mushrooms as we go past them. I can sense within her mind pride and curiosity, knowing I am going over everything they have taught me so far. Before I connect completely with her thoughts, she stares away and looks at Nathan. For a split second I can feel how she is blushing, and I laugh out loud at her, receiving a playful and painful punch to my right arm.

Once the battle starts, our strategy to appear weak could be successful for a short while, until Cold's forces regroup and attack in a more orderly fashion. That is the time to divide them, a Divide-and-Conquer scheme according to Nathan's explanations. Silver tried to explain it by saying that the sum of constituent parts is never the same as the total. Honestly, when she said that I only nodded to please them, but I still have trouble understanding that concept. I am the sum of a lot of organs and stuff within me, so why would I be more than that? *Do they mean my soul?*

Well, I guess I will eventually understand that scheme better as time goes on and we explain it to others. After Cold's forces regroup, maybe behind White Tower's wall or maybe in front of us at the battlefield, we are going to take a huge risk. We are going to become obvious and do whatever they would expect us to. Nathan says we must seem predictable to force their arrogance up once again, moving in a foreseeable pattern to ensure their reaction is one we can expect and counter. He explains it using boxing terms, saying that throwing ten consecutive right jabs will make your opponent raise his or her left defense and lower his or her right; that is when you change your game again and try the left hook knockout.

That is our last step, the left hook knockout. We will strike back where he presumes it is improbable, and strike swiftly to take advantage of the opening. My fear is what to do if by the time we execute our last step, we are still outnumbered, surrounded, or losing the battle? Silver said we would have to adapt, and try again with the same tactic of regrouping, becoming obvious, and then surprising our enemy; but how probable is it that Cold will fall twice or more into the same trap? How stupid would that be?

However, even though I am doubtful, I understand our sevenfold strategy is our only hope since we will never outnumber our enemies. Now we must teach it to all who follow, all willing to fight against the man who represents all the evil ruling our world. I will understand all those who don't join us, overcome by fear.

The jungle starts to become less dense, and the sunlight's glare becomes more intense. Nathan stops at the jungle's edge ten meters in front of us. We catch up with him, keeping our cover behind trees, and look ahead.

Finally, Valor peeks over a hilltop in front of us, one hundred meters more to go. For a couple of minutes, we stay hidden, looking from right to left, listening to the silence around us for clues. No one can be heard, and my fears of being too late flash back to my mind and make my heart pound heavily. Silver looks at Nathan, who has a fierce look, his jaw clenched, his frown tense, and his eyes turned into amber.

He starts walking toward the town, up the hill, and we follow him. I am walking backward, staring back at the jungle to our left to make sure no one surprises us. Silver walks backward the same way, protecting our right flank, while Nathan is walking dead on toward the town.

As we enter the town from the south, its similarity to Rick's town, or at least what it must have looked like before Cold ravished it, is amazing. Same wooden homes with thatched roofs, gardens, and a central road leading to a monastery of some sort. The only difference I can see as we get closer is in a field behind a barn where a fence is unfinished, the dirt freshly scattered.

As we walk further into the town, something feels amiss. Our footsteps echo through the silent village, and there is no sign of damage or fleeing inhabitants. Cold's army left a mess not far away from here, so we know they came close. Nathan stops and crouches to inspect horse hooves marked on the road leading to the monastery at the far end of Valor. Could these be marks from Rick's horse, from the inhabitants of the town, or from Cold's scouts?

Nathan finishes inspecting the hoofmarks and whispers, "Let's split up, but beware of your surroundings. Silence is usually a clue about unsuspected danger."

Fuck, this is the real deal. We walk in different directions, spreading out to look for clues in the village. Nathan walks toward the homes at our left, Silver heads toward the monastery at the far end, following the road, and I go to inspect the barn and farm area to our right. The gardens are plotted by crop, with clear rectangular lots each with a different produce. A large wooden barn built at the left side of the farming area is projecting its shadow on top of the field of tomatoes.

This first lot is full of ripe, red tomatoes hanging from vines tightly wrapped to stakes. Their color, like that of the poisonous mushrooms, is an irony of nature's game. How to trust it when it uses the same colors for delicious food and lethal mushrooms? I walk on a groove dividing the tomato plants. How I wish I had a bit of salt on me to taste those exquisite fruits.

Halfway across the tomato lot I see carrots are peeking out of the ground on the next plot, partially harvested or in small piles between the rows as if forgotten there. Not rotten, the vegetables have not been long on the ground. I turn left toward the barn to inspect its inside.

An uncomfortable feeling gets ahold of me. The barn is wide open, and the horses have either fled, been led away, or been stolen. The hoofmarks are recent; I can feel the soil between my fingers moist and loose, so not enough time has passed for it to dry out and harden. Still, I don't hear a sound from anywhere. I walk into the barn's back door and notice how inside each of the six stalls is a bucket of clean, moss-free water and freshly cut hay. The tall wooden barn creaks gently as the wind blows against its walls.

As I head back out the front door, the heavy wooden doors rock gently in the wind, the only sound for miles. The field to my left looks like an archery range or a fighting field. The soil is heavily trodden. At the end of the field stand three white sacs with small lashes and holes in them. It does seem like these people were training for something before fleeing their town.

As I step outside the barn, someone grabs me in a choke hold and sticks a knife to my neck. There is no way to escape or to call for Nate's or Sil's help. I am once again in trouble of my own making. A thousand ideas cross my mind, but none feel right for escaping this hold. As my vision fades and blackness closes in on me, I hear a familiar voice use a demanding tone. Heat waves burn my face as they emanate from his body.

"Let go of him if you wish to see tomorrow," Nate says.

21
THE ELDER
PHOENIX

"Let go of him if you wish to see tomorrow," I say menacingly, feeling the full extent of my powers embrace my body.

Silver goes around the man holding Jay, points her arrow at his back, and waits for my command to shoot. He is holding Jay right outside the large barn to my right, ten meters in front of me. Jay is losing consciousness and even though his life is in danger, he is not struggling to break free. He trusts we have this under control.

The man is shaking in fear. He is no assassin. I gaze deeply into his eyes, trying to make him see this does not have to end in his death. We are not enemies, at least not yet. Jay is calm and still, understanding the situation perfectly and ready to do his part if needed. The attacker slowly lowers his knife and releases Jay, who falls to the ground and catches his breath back, then the man holds his hands up in surrender. His knees are barely managing to hold him up.

"Don't!" A familiar voice says from behind me.

I turn to see Rick approaching from behind me, gesturing with his hands for us to stop. My pulse is steady but ready to spike in case he has betrayed us.

I order him to explain, without losing sight of the man standing beside my brother, who is coughing loudly. "You better have an explanation for this, right now!"

Silver points her bow at Rick, and I can hear how he is getting closer to me, slowly and carefully. I see over my shoulder how he is going around me, three meters away with both hands up. He says, "He is one of the villagers here. I arrived in time to alert them about Cold's army, and we have been hiding since. This man came back to see if everything is safe and must have stumbled into Jay. He didn't know he wasn't a scout from Cold's army. A forgivable mistake."

Against all my training, I believe him. His voice, his gestures, and his eyes, most importantly, are truthful. The moment I nod, Silver lowers her bow gradually and walks toward Jay to see how he is holding up. He has stopped coughing, and Silver is crouched to his right, signaling me he is okay.

Rick says, "May the rest of the men and women of Valor come so you trust me?" My gaze is set on his eyes, as I ignite my right hand and cover it with fire. "You better not be lying to me, Rick." His eyes go from my flaming hand, back to my face, lowering one of his hands to whistle loudly. The high pitch goes across the town behind me, calling the men and women of Valor back to their homes.

I turn around and see people start coming from behind the jungle past the monastery. They start walking down the central road and heading toward us, walking in small groups that I suppose are families. There are about thirty strong men and women and ten or more children. My tension slowly turns into relief and joy, as I order the flames to extinguish before they come any closer. Their walk is a sight to behold, returning to their homes and welcoming us with their smiles and claps. Their presence fuels my hope once more. Now to do something with that hope, we must convince this first town to join our cause. The hardest step is always the first.

Our road to save Mom is becoming clearer ahead of us.

***

The leader of Valor is an old man called Dan; his balding head still holds a few messy white hairs. His tan skin contrasts with his green-grayish eyes, giving him a look of wisdom and experience. He must have been close to one meter and ninety centimeters tall, but old age has brought him down almost to my height. Still, his build is broad, reminiscent of a fierce youth, but his attitude is that of a leader, a man of words and compromise, of knowledge and eagerness to learn and teach simultaneously.

After the men and women from Valor settled back in their homes, and nightfall soothed the town, Dan summoned Rick and me to his shed, the smallest one in town located right next to the monastery. A simple home for a simple man. He serves us tea of some sort. Hints of vanilla, lavender, and cherry aromas fill the room, opening my appetite and setting a friendly ambiance. He walks slowly with two trembling cups in his hands, refusing our help, before sitting in front of us on his rugged and stained red couch.

He speaks first, "Drink, friends. We have a lot to talk about and little time to do it." His voice is as soothing as his personality. Rick and I sit on a green couch in front of him, with a small tea table separating us.

I answer him, "Thank you, sir." It feels right; I am talking to a man who is my elder in age and wisdom.

He inspects me with a glance from head to toe, then sips his tea.

I take a sip too, enjoying the blend of flavors washing down my throat and warming me inside out, then look at Dan and say, "As Rick told you, Cold is marching with a large army to White Tower. His malevolence has no limits, and he will destroy all villages, men, women, and children wherever he goes, threat or no threat, just because he enjoys hurting people. Rick's hometown was not a threat, was not threatening to stand against him or stop paying tribute, yet he destroyed all of it and killed everyone."

Rick chimes in, "I told Nathan and his crew about your promise to help us, but now there is no town to aid. However, there is still something to stand for, Dan, hope. We intend to harness and train a large force to stand up against evil, against whoever has participated in the decline of humanity."

Dan stares deeply into Rick's eyes, sadness reflecting from his wise eyes as he understands how much Rick has lost. Without speaking, he turns to see me, understanding I have more to say.

I continue, "We have been calling your town Valor. Rick explained that you were willing to fight even without proper training. We can offer two things you did not have before. First, we offer you a plan where you will not be alone, where men and women will battle side by side with your townsfolk. Second, we offer hope for you and your people." My eyes did not stop gazing into Dan's inquisitive eyes for a second.

Rick elaborates my thoughts, knowing Dan better than I do, "Nathan is speaking of strength in numbers, Dan. You spoke to me about another village ahead, hidden from this world but ready to fight for it if called upon. They must not be the only ones who want to have a world of peace, a world where people can live without having to fight for survival to no end." Rick's voice fills with grief as he continues, "A place where a man can love his wife and raise his children and see them grow into adults with a future."

Dan's eyes fill with pain and empathy at Rick's suffering voice. I feel it too, the need to do something, the need to eradicate all that stands in the way of happiness, of families, and of life. Cold is everything against which I stand, and every ounce of strength within me and every breath I take will be for the sole purpose of destroying him.

Finally, Dan shares his thoughts, "Your words come to ready ears, my friends. A long time ago, I convinced myself that the moment of rising would come. Time has weakened my body and aged my bones, but my will and desire to fight are untouched. The time has come to do something. Only action can change the fate of the world, not ideas, not plans, and definitely not watching hell rain upon earth without reacting." Dan stands up, goes around the tea table and places a heavy hand on each of our shoulders. "Now we must convey this to my people. The choice is not mine, but theirs."

He calls out for someone standing outside his shed. A young white kid about Jay's age enters, illuminated by the candlelight all around Dan's shed. He stands with both hands behind his back, listening as Dan says, "I need everyone to come here; they must listen to Nathan's and Rick's plea." The boy runs out quickly to fulfill his orders.

While we wait, Dan pours a second cup of tea for Rick and me and refills his cup before sitting back on his red couch. He is lost in his thoughts while blowing on his tea cup. Rick is looking around the shed, before standing up and pacing around, inspecting everything around us. I sit back, tasting the delicious tea with my eyes closed, thinking how to convince an entire town to follow us. I am ready for this; we have worked hard up to this point. Let's write history.

About fifteen minutes after the boy ran off to gather the entire town, he enters back into Dan's shed, panting. He says, "It's done, sir." Dan stands up, places his cup on the tea table, and points toward the exit. "It is time, my friends." The kid holds the front door open as Rick exits hurriedly, followed by Dan and me.

As the three of us walk outside of his shed, I see all his people conglomerated on the central road. Their eyes are eager, as they wish to hear about the road ahead. Some of them have worried grins and watery eyes. A few are standing straight, proud to be in this moment. Some are angry, maybe at the possibility of having to deal with something they wish to avoid. I see Silver and Jay standing in front of the crowd and call them with my hand to stand beside me.

Dan exclaims loudly, "People, my lovely people, this is Nathan, Silver, and Jay. You all know Rick by now. This respectable group of individuals has suffered as much or even more than we have suffered under Cold's rule. Their families have been torn apart, they have been humiliated and enslaved, and, despite such harshness, they have come here as a guiding light for us all." Every single man, woman, and child in the crowd looks at Dan with a deep sense of respect in their eyes. I feel it as well inside of me; this man charms with his authority.

He continues, "Rick's town, where most of us had friends and relatives, has been destroyed." The crowd reacts, whispering in unison, some people shaking their heads, others staring at each other with desperation, and most cannot hide their fear. "There is nothing stopping Cold from doing the same to us, and we have all known this for a long time. Rick might have saved us once by alerting us to an incoming army, but we cannot depend on that working again. We must choose a different path."

A young man steps forward, with a child on his shoulders, and asks "What path is there besides hiding, dear leader?"

Dan smiles at him as a grandfather does when about to teach a grandson, and answers, "We may join our friends against Cold and his army. We have trained for this, but the moment to decide if training will turn into action has come. No one is obliged to join us, and no one will be left behind against his or her will. We will leave horses and crops behind for those who decide to stay. Your future will be here; though while Cold lives, your future could come to an end soon. You have all made me extremely proud so far, and your choice will not change that."

Another man, hiding within the crowd, shouts angrily, "You are only four, a child, a young woman, a young man, and Rick. We are barely thirty men and women. What chance do we have to beat them?"

Rick speaks loudly and confidently, looking straight at the man who tried to hide behind his fellow villagers, "You are not the only town under Cold's reign. My town was the same, and you know it. He killed every single one of us, leaving not a child alive. You say we are only four, but that means you are four soldiers stronger now. If you *don't* act, what will prevent Cold from doing to your village what he did to mine?"

I intervene before the man answers, strengthening Rick's point by saying, "The other towns Rick mentioned will join us too. We will march ahead, alone, to convince them to fight alongside us. Before we go, we'll train and prepare you, so we can fight as one army and outsmart Cold's brute force. They've been taking advantage of your good hearts, your fear, your morally based survival instincts, and they won't be expecting an army of people willing to end his evil reign. Cold will never stop ravishing, destroying, and killing. Do you really want to live this way? Do you want your fellow men, women, and children to have this life forever?" I can see that my words begin to sway some, but there is still resistance on several faces and too many heads shaking in the negative.

A woman holding a small child against her chest expresses her fear, "It still feels like walking into the lion's den. Buying an early ticket to all of our graves!"

Rick looks at her with watery eyes and answers, understanding her fears, "Lady, I had two children as beautiful as yours. They were full of laughter and life. Their mother, the love of my life, was a blessing to me and to this world. She was the strongest person I have ever met, willing to die for what she loved." Rick's voice starts to crumble under his pain, but he keeps going on the sheer strength of his will. "She did die for what she loved. Cold burned down my house, and all the other homes in my village, making sure she and my two babies burned to death inside." He raises his voice as he goes on. "You don't understand what he is capable of. He and his men slaughtered everyone, either letting them burn in their homes or throwing them off the cliff like trash. There is no single town capable of standing up against him, and the day when his armies march here and do the same to your town will come."

It looks like Rick's speech managed to turn more doubtful faces into supporters.

A young man around eighteen asks, "What if no one joins us?"

His words have been revolving inside my head for a while. The four of us plus this town's force is not enough. Cold's army would destroy us in the blink of an eye without breaking a sweat.

Silver grabs my left arm and smiles at me. She knows what to do to get their support. She whispers into my ear, "Ignite their hope."

I smile back at her. She is right; we are not just four people willing to lead this battle. We are a force by ourselves, willing to do whatever it takes to save this world. I close my eyes and look up at the sky. The moonlight illuminates me as memories of all the suffering Cold has caused builds up my anger. The voices of the crowd fade away. My nose wrinkles and my teeth clench as I bring my wrists closer to my torso, hunching up to harness all the strength of my body so I can ignite their hope.

I am ready and before showing them our true power, I say, "You say we are just four. You say what if no one joins us. Well, we will have to surprise him with something else." My changed voice silences the crowd and fixes their attention on me. The moment my eyes open, my fire explodes upward and encircles me.

"Phoenix," says the young man, his eyes dancing with reflections of fire and the beginnings of hope.

22
THE YOUTH
TIME TO GO ON

Cunning as always, Silver must have told Nate to show his true power to gain the town's support. Dan, Silver, Rick, and I step back a couple of meters as a fire tornado spins around Nathan and up into the night sky. He is lighting up the entire town, chasing the darkness of night away. I can feel my arm hairs rise, excited at this amazing fire spectacle, and all this coming from my brother! How exciting to be part of this, and everyone on the road is staring amazed at his power. None of them must doubt we are in this to win. Cold has nothing on us. I laugh silently at their naivete when questioning Nathan a few moments ago.

Though I've seen this before, I stare intently at him through the flames. Nathan is looking at me with a large smile on his face and winks joyously. I stick my tongue out to him, taunting him for his display of strength.

"Phoenix! Phoenix! Phoenix!" The entire town joins the chant of the young man who doubted our cause just a minute ago. I feel goose bumps running up my back as things seem to have turned in our favor.

Nate's red gaze captivates all of us. His smile soothes while the rest of his body amazes and even frightens. He says, "Will you join us? Will you fight against evil alongside us? Will you fight for your brothers and sisters, friends and family? Will you fight for what is right, for humanity?" Nate's words cut like a scalpel, incisive, deep, and clean.

Everyone reacts differently. Goose bumps, nods, fists clenching, arms shooting upwards, screams, and hurrahs.

Nathan starts to flame down, probably becoming exhausted with such a huge effort, when Dan grabs Nate's hand and pulls it in front of them. Rick places his hand on top of theirs. The moment it lands there, Nathan orders fire to revolve around the three strong hands as laces tying a present. It does not burn them, as all people seem to understand right away. This power is at their disposal and is good and benevolent.

Dan speaks out, with a commanding voice, "Under this fire, let us make a pact to always protect each other. May this be known as the day humanity decided to fight together against the evil corroding our world. With God as my witness, I will fight to the death beside you, Phoenix."

All the crowd stares, watching history being written. They start chanting, screaming in celebration, excited at the incomprehensible sight we have all shared. The mood can be felt, hope and a desire to fight together is almost tangible. We are finally together under Nathan's leadership.

***

Today is the last day of training before some of us go to the next town, the hidden town, to see if they will join our fight. We have trained day and night for three days after Nathan won the town over. At the break of dawn, the day after Nathan showed his powers, we started working to make sure their excitement turned into actions.

Training has been rough, Silver and I focused on teaching them how Cold's men fight, how they coordinate their attacks, and what their weaknesses are as an army. Nate and Rick taught them weapon building, retreat strategies, and strike-evade-repeat fighting. Rick, Dan, Silver, Nate, and I have constantly met to decide our next steps.

Almost all the villagers have trained, including the five who will stay behind to take care of the youngest and the frailest. We will leave the horses behind, so they can keep the farm going and escape if it comes to that. The twenty-five men and women who have agreed to fight with us will stay at Valor, training with Rick and Dan, as the rest of us head out to the hidden town. If everything works out, the two forces will meet up at Valor soon. The effort of these twenty-five brave soldiers has been amazing. They are tired, beaten up, and sore, but their inner strength seems to be never-ending. We are proud to have them with us.

Three men and three women went ahead to the hidden town to alert them about our arrival. We need their strength. If no one else joins us, all this training will only be useful for defending Valor when Cold comes to destroy it. None of us has forgotten these men and women have less than a month's worth of training. Together we can do it, but we need a "together" large enough to beat Cold's army. If we succeed at defeating his first assault, all our hearts will be fueled to fight on, to do everything it takes to get our lives back.

I am sitting down with my back against the barn's front wall, staring at the twenty soldiers as they train under Silver's lead. Some are practicing their archery, others are training for melee attacks, and three couples are having a swordfight sparring. The sun is high above, raising the temperature as midday is coming close.

Dan walks past the barn and looks back at me. "Come with me, our last meeting is about to start." I call out to Silver, and she nods, acknowledging she will join us. Dan walks beside me with both hands behind his back, and a slight smile illuminates his face. I want to ask why he is so happy but am unable to overcome my shyness. It is weird how even an inviting and gentle man can be so imposing and impressive.

Silver joins us, sweating with a reddened face at the effort and heat. Dan welcomes her with a happy gaze and continues walking firmly toward his shed. Valor's sounds are interesting to me. As we walk away from the training ground, the effortful shouts and the horses' neighs fade, giving way to the laughs and loud conversations occurring at the small plaza beside the houses. Kids scream as they run around, chasing each other, playing tag or hide and seek.

The monastery has its front doors wide open though no one is inside it. For the first time I notice how beautiful it is. The doors are painted dark brown with large bronze knobs. The windows are colorful, depicting scenes from the Bible and giving its interior an amazing light show. Inside, I can see how wooden benches are lined in two columns leading to an altar that is hard to distinguish from here. *Why haven't I gone in the monastery yet?*

Nathan and Rick are standing in front of Dan's house, waiting for us as we walk toward them. They were having a friendly conversation that stops as soon as we reach them. We go inside Dan's house after he opens and holds the door for us.

He places a hand on my shoulder and, staring at the +3 branded on my forehead, says, "I can see you have suffered Cold's evil. Thank you for guiding us."

He made me feel like I am a leader in his eyes, not simply a soldier. My past experiences and pain have made me a better man, ready to help others, and I vow never to be ashamed of the scars from my past.

A sweet scent fills my nose as I enter Dan's home. Dan is standing to our right by a small table where a teapot is being heated on top of a small kitchen stove. Rick is standing in front of us beside a tea table, and Silver sits beside him on a green worn-down couch facing away from me. Nathan goes to help Dan pour the tea.

As I walk toward the green couch, reluctant to sit on its dirty coat, I pay attention to how small Dan's shed is. A couple of meters past a red couch that faces the green couch, his bed is pushed horizontally against the wall, its covers tightly placed on top of it. He has a small bedside table where seven books are stacked one on top of another. Farther right, three meters away, he has a small counter separating his kitchen from the rest of his house. Nathan's room back home is almost as big as Dan's entire house. This amuses me.

Dan walks back to the red couch and sits, placing two tea cups on the table in front of him. Nathan sets the remaining three cups down and stands at Rick's side. I stand next to the couch, facing my brother and Rick, ready to listen to Dan. He says, "Welcome all. This will be the last time we shall all sit together before the moment to fight comes. All our effort has been a gift to my soul, as hope and a sense of meaning illuminates all my townsfolks' faces. Thank you for being here." Dan always starts our meetings with soothing and exciting comments, a contradiction of perfection, as Nate describes this man.

Nate asserts confidently, "Today is the last day we will all be together here, and I just want to go over our plan one last time. Rick, I believe you should stay here and continue Valor's training alongside Dan. Your combined strength and leadership will give us the best chance of their being as prepared as we can make them. These people are the most courageous I have met in my life, and they will follow you to their deaths if you ask them to. Are you two willing to stay here and lead this valiant town?"

Dan and Rick nod in unison, while I smile widely, feeling animated at their agreement. Silver claps and laughs softly, excited by Valor's luck by having both on board.

Rick says, as his eyes fill with tears of joy, "It's my honor to lead alongside Dan."

He must be feeling the moment to avenge his loved ones closing in. Nate seems to understand as he nods at both men. Some words are stronger when left unsaid.

Silver continues, "We must define when and where we will meet with all our forces before marching to White Tower for our final fight."

Dan stares at the ground in front of him, thinking deeply

about Silver's suggestion. Finally, he says, "About a month from here, there is a waterfall. A dense forest hides it, and Cold's men rarely visit it because of the harsh terrain surrounding it. The waterfall is barely six hours away from White Tower's main entrance, so I suggest we establish that as our meeting point."

Nathan looks at Silver, and they share a laugh. They must have known Dan was the one who would solve the only part of the plan they were unable to define. Rick pats Dan on the back, saying, "You are too wise, old man." We share a laugh, and Dan's deep, guttural giggle resounds across his shed above our cackles.

I blurt out as soon as our laughter recedes, "Now we have defined where, but when will we meet?" Time already feels stretched too far with our mother suffering, and it takes months to get anywhere. If all of this succeeds but she fails to live long enough for us to reach her, our efforts will feel hollow.

Nate answers, "Forty-five days from now. This will allow Rick to train Valor for fifteen more days before marching to war. If we manage to quickly convince the hidden village to join us, we could use the spare time to find more villages and try to convince them to join us as well. Cold's reign goes far beyond Rick's village, Valor, and the hidden village. More men and women must wish this horror to end, and it is our duty to find them and offer them an option, a possible solution to their nightmares. We are going to offer the opportunity to face off against Cold once and for all."

Dan stands up slowly, fighting against his tired muscles, and hugs Nathan as a proud father hugs his son. Silver stands up and starts clapping at the idea of finding more villages. Dan releases Nathan from his embrace, and both start clapping. Rick and I join in, and I start cheering. Silver howls, and we share another warm laugh.

Dan names the hidden village by saying, "Strength. My village is Valor owing to its inner courage and desire to fight for freedom, for life, for our future. The name you have given us represents all the men and women living under my guidance, and it will lead our efforts and decisions from now on. Strength must be the name of the village the three of you will visit. They live to fight and have trained all their lives for this moment. Their endurance and resilience will fuel all of us to go on, to fight without mercy or doubt. They are the strength that complements our valor." He speaks softly but clearly, staring down at the tea table while his wise words resonate.

Rick says, "We will use these fifteen days wisely to fine-tune our training, our tactics, and to be able to easily join efforts with all the towns we manage to convince to join us. Valor is the lighthouse guiding all villages toward a safe future—let's make it shine as brightly as the sun."

Rick is the right choice to lead Valor, and evidently, Nate knew it long before the rest of us. By the look he's giving me, he knows I just came to understand that decision.

Dan brings out a map where he has intricately drawn all the pathways, roads, and hidden trails around his town and explains where Strength hides from the world. "Proceed carefully. Cold and his men constantly patrol through these areas. And don't go far away from the road, as the forest is treacherous in these areas. People have entered it to never come back. Beware, my friends."

Nate says, "Soon the time comes for the five of us to meet again and start the siege for humanity, for a history where men and women won security for their future and grasped it violently from the reigns of evil."

As the time to part ways has come, I step around the tea table and hug Dan. He surrounds me with his long arms and the warmest hug I have ever felt. Silver kisses Rick goodbye, and Nathan shakes his hand while patting his back with his left hand. They share a smile, while Silver hugs Dan strongly, making him gasp for air and laugh. I extend my hand to Rick, who pulls me to him and hugs me with one arm, while messing my hair. The five of us nod at each other, as Nathan, Silver, and I walk toward the front door.

When we exit Dan's shed, the entire town has gathered under the moonlight, holding flowers and torches. The smells of smoke and damp grass and the forest fill the air. They are humming a song unknown to us. Dan and Rick stand right outside the door's frame and wish us farewell. A young man about my age has our backpacks ready by the door, and he bows as we approach him. Nathan places his right hand on his shoulder, pushes him up, and shakes his head, while saying, "You will never bow to anyone again, my friend. We are in this together." The kid blushes and wishes us luck as we grab our backpacks.

Dan and Rick catch up with us, and as the five of us walk down the main road, many of the villagers walk with us to the edge of the forest. They hug us, kiss our cheeks, and give food, weapons, and clothes to Nathan, Silver, and me, to help us during our journey. We nod and smile and thank them. Their faces are full of hope, eyes glittering with tears of joy and expectation. The light they shine from within is far brighter than the one their torches or even Nate can create. For this and for Mom we fight, and for this and for Mom we will not fail.

Where the road ventures into the forest, Dan hugs each of us and whispers something. To me he says, "Your heart is true. Don't fear to use it, as empathy is far more powerful than what you may imagine."

We walk into the woods, illuminated only by the torches we hold because the moonlight cannot reach through the forest's dense canopy. This is exactly what all of this is about: fighting darkness despite how deep it seems to go. The hum of the townsfolk fades in the distance behind us, but it has been branded into our memories.

"May our senses be advertent, and our aim be unerring," Nate says aloud.

For the first time, Sil and I truly understand the meaning of his adage.

***

The night is darker tonight and, once again, my fears are creeping back. This sense of not knowing what lurks in front or behind is nerve-wracking. Nate and Sil look confident, and I don't understand how they managed to become like this. Do they even fear the uncertain?

The only thing keeping all my terror at bay is the concentration needed to avoid tripping over roots, vines, and fallen branches as we tread deep into the forest, searching for Strength. According to Nate, using Dan's map, we should have arrived by now. Of course, there are no points of reference, but the distance we have covered and the time that has gone by since we left Valor indicates we should have found it.

The torches flicker and dancing shadows confuse the way ahead. How are we going to find this town? How will we spend the night here if we don't with no open space for setting up camp? I trust Nate, but sometimes he is too stubborn to accomplish his objectives. No rest until success, he says. And—

I swoosh upward, light and darkness revolving around me at a dizzying pace. Nate and Sil scream, impotent against whatever the hell just happened. Something stops me abruptly and then I am rocking back and forth. Though painless I am in panic, unable to understand the blurry forest dancing in front of me as I am upside down.

It's a trap! Stupid me walked into a trap. Of course, I had to fuck this up. Instead of thinking about my fears and Nate's judgement, I should have simply stared down while walking. Now what will we do?

Nate and Sil look around the nearby trees for the mechanism holding me. They seem to find the correct tree and get ready to climb, but an arrow stops them, scraping Silver's shoulder. She falls to the ground in pain. Nate searches the darkness, unable to see where it came from or how many enemies are around. Then his eyes turn red, but he is containing his fire, waiting to spot whoever hurt Silver.

An arrow flies out of the darkness, and I fall hard to the ground. Air rushes out of my lungs as I hit the hard earth, leaving me almost unconscious. I squeeze my eyes shut and moan in pain.

A bright light fills the dark forest. Nate has lost it.

"Wait! Phoenix, we know you," says a female voice.

I roll to my side, trying to catch my breath, and see him positioned to lunge with both arms outstretched, ready to attack. "You better explain yourself quickly, ma'am," he commands, giving them a second to convince him not to burn this forest to the ground.

The voice moves closer, saying, "We were visited not long ago by a man from Dan's town, now named Valor. He explained about your mission to face off against White Tower and Cold and about how you have trained them." The woman steps out of the darkness just a few meters from us. "We want in."

She looks to be about forty years old. Her black garment crisscrosses her body. She has brown hair and is taller than Nate, with soft features that clash with the large scar on her right cheek, going down her neck and into her outfit. She is a beautiful warrior. Behind her, ten or more soldiers emerge. All of them are equipped with a quiver filled with dark arrows and a shiny bow, long swords, a small golden shield, and a rope tied across their torso. They surround us, walking toward us from all directions.

She says, with both arms up, "I am sorry for attacking you. We could not be sure if you were allies or enemies. Our secrecy is our advantage. Consider we did not attack to kill." A hoarse laughter that does not correspond with her sweet appearance follows the woman's voice.

We stand up slowly, Silver holding her hand over her bleeding shoulder and Nate leading us closer to the woman. She is smiling widely as the soldiers move slowly behind her, standing to either of her sides, holding their bows up to show they mean no harm. Nathan stands two meters in front of her, with both arms at his sides and flames revolving around his open hands. Silver and I stand behind him, and I see her wound is only a scrape. She is angrily facing the woman in the dark robe, her right nostril trembling.

One of the soldiers steps in front of the woman. We know

this man, he is one of the men sent from Valor. He explains, "Of the six who came from Valor to this village, only I survived." She limps toward us and tells us about an ambush. "Cold's men are dead now, along with five of our own; they were savages. This is no game." The three of us were extremely lucky to have met no enemies in our way.

We say some words for them and share several minutes of silence. The fact that traveling from town to town is a deadly task reinvigorates our endurance, strengthening our desire to succeed. Life is not meant to be like this. Humanity is supposed to be free, to be safe to explore and civilize and grow in a healthy environment. Anything less is not right.

Their leader, the woman in black, says "If you are willing to trust us, I can take you back to our village. There we can talk things out, plan together, and give you a place to rest and dine." Nathan orders the fire to extinguish around his hands, and nods once.

The soldiers lead the way, walking about ten meters in front of us. The woman in black, Valor's soldier, and the three of us walk in a single file. Nathan does not lose sight of the woman, while Silver helps the injured woman as she limps on her weakened left leg. I keep track of the soldiers in front of us, making sure no one disappears into the night.

Twenty minutes after meeting this crew, the soldiers stop at the edge of a cliff. To the right a wooden palisade blocks our path, and to the left the dense tree line from behind us circles around to the cliff's edge. A dead end? The woman pulls out what seems to be a whistle from around her neck and sends three slow bursts and one long high-pitched screech into the night.

Out from the darkness in front of us comes a wooden box large enough to fit all of us, tied with ropes to a pulley system. The ropes allow it to be pulled to and from the cliff's edge and from somewhere beyond our sight into the darkness. Its base is wooden, about three meters long and two meters wide. Around it, wooden boards enclose the base so the people who ride in it can avoid falling into the cliff to their death. On the side closest to us, there is an opening on the box's enclosure covered with a black net tied to the sides with hooks. It works as a door to the box.

The woman in black pulls the box closer to the edge and releases the net. The soldiers step in, followed by Valor's survivor. Their leader turns toward the three of us.

"Get on, friends. I promise our Skybox is as safe as they come," the woman says, gesturing with her hand toward the wooden structure. After we walk onto the base, she whistles once more, this time two long bursts. As the last one ends, the Skybox starts moving. "Welcome to our home. I am Mary Beth, by the way, but call me Em. All three of you, Silver, Nathan, and James are welcome." She hooks the black net once again, closing the Skybox.

I grab the handrailing tightly, afraid of this Skybox failing and all of us falling to our deaths. The darkness below us is disheartening, making it impossible to see how deep the cliff goes. The invisible descent seems to howl beneath us. The box advances through the blackness of night for about twenty meters, the ropes tensing and making the wooden boards creak scarily.

The cold wind of the night gives me goose bumps. Silver and Nathan stand at my sides, Sil looking behind us toward the forest we just left behind, and Nate looks toward the place we are being towed to. Em looks at the three of us blissfully, excited about having us with her or happy because we just fell into her trap. I cannot trust this woman; she is too silent and judging.

I can finally see land again in front of us. The Skybox made a curved path over the cliff toward the right from the place we left behind. It comes to a stop, and Em releases the black net before she steps out.

More men and women receive us with silent glances, all standing ready to defend their home. This is Strength.

We walk between them, as they move away to either of our sides as we walk on. They are all wearing dark robes, like those

Em uses, and dark makeup covering their faces. The torches they hold illuminate their faces and make it difficult to look behind them. Thirty meters ahead, dark green tents stand almost three meters tall.

The soldiers accompanying us step aside and join their fellow villagers, who are forming a path toward the tents. Em tells the woman from Valor, "Go to the medical tent. You should be taken care of." She nods and walks into the first tent to our right. The tents are set up in an orderly fashion, at either side of a two-meter-wide path and about a meter and a half from each other.

After the fourth tent at either side, a larger opening is left before the fifth tent. A campfire is set in the middle, surrounded by large, light brown trunks. Em sits down on the one closest to us and invites us to sit on any of the other three trunks. Nathan sits right in front of her, across the fire. Silver and I sit to her right and wait for Nathan to speak out.

He says, "Thank you for receiving us, Em. I am sorry for doubting you, but you must give us credit. People do not usually react well to being trapped in a spider web and being shot at." He smirks at her, and she laughs at his smugness.

She makes fun by saying, "Well, in that case you should be more forgiving, considering you had menacing flames surrounding both hands as I introduced myself." The four of us share a laugh, imagining how fearful it must be to meet someone with flaming hands in the middle of the night at the deepest part of an unknown forest.

Em continues, "Would you like to see the rest of the town?" The three of us nod and stand up. She says, "Your tent is that one over there." She points at the first tent to our right, after the campfire. "You will find three cots, each with a pillow and a blanket, a basin with water for you to drink and wash yourselves, and a small plate with some fruits. We've been expecting you for a while now." Four more tents go past us, before a campfire exactly as the one we came from is set.

Em walks two steps in front of the three of us. She turns her head and tells us, "Each tent holds three to four people. They are set in groups of eight, each with a campfire as the one we just saw. People sleep in them and work together to make sure their quarter, made of eight tents, is clean and the campfire is always lit. This way, in case we are ever attacked, our sight will not be compromised by darkness."

After the fourth set of eight tents, the path meets a perpendicular dirt road. To the right it leads toward a training ground about twenty meters away. Em grabs a torch from a small base and walks toward the training camp. She stands by its surrounding wooden wall, about sixty centimeters high. "Here we practice every day. We practice archery twice a week, hand-to-hand combat twice a week, sword skills three times a week, stamina and conditioning every other day, and strategy and battle tactics three times a week. Every single man, woman, or child living here must train. We are very conscious about the perils living beyond our wooden palisade." Nathan and Silver agree by nodding, so I emulate them to avoid looking lost.

Em walks past us, going back toward the path leading to the sleeping tents. Instead of turning left toward them, she points to her right while explaining, "If you go right, you will find a large wooden building about forty meters in that direction. There we share our meals, meet when important decisions have to be made, celebrate birthdays and training successes, and hold a weekly meeting to talk about possible improvements to our defenses, tactics, work, and living standards."

She walks forward on the dirt road. Her torch illuminates the path in front, fighting against the darkness ahead. Here we walk in a single file, since the road becomes narrow with thick bushes and vines to either side. I fear a snake might pop out and try to bite me, so I walk right in the middle of the dirt path. Nathan is walking close to Em and Silver is walking close behind me, as usual.

After walking for about fifty meters, out of the dark night, I can see a metal door standing in front of Em and Nathan, who have stopped walking. The door is closed shut and to either side I can see a two-meter-high stone wall. It goes as far as my sight can distinguish. Em explains, "We have cleared a path beyond this door as an escape route. If we are ever attacked and our enemies' siege manages to open a gap in our front defenses, my men and women can escape through here. If they walk due south, to our right, they will eventually walk to the cliff's edge again. There, three Skyboxes were built to help them reach the forest again. Dan has agreed that if my village is to fall, my followers can escape to his town. It is part of a treaty we have had for a long time." She is looking intently at Nathan, expecting his reaction.

Nate understands her approach and comments, "Thank you for trusting us with such a confidential strategy. I know you have shared it to show you are truly committed to our plan and trust us completely. Tomorrow, we will talk again to clarify how your village, which we have called Strength, fits into our plans, and how you can improve them with your experience and knowledge. Now, can you lead us back to our tents? We are exhausted."

Em smiles and places a friendly hand on Nathan's shoulder. "Let's go," she says, while handing her torch to Nathan for him to give it to Silver, who will lead the way back. We walk back to the crossroad, turn right and walk between the tents again.

Em stops in front of the second tent to our right and wishes us a good night as she enters what must be her sleeping quarters.

Nathan says farewell with his right hand and continues walking ahead of us. Silver and I catch up with him. He looks at Silver and me and remarks, "Let's have a nice rest tonight, since tomorrow we are to see how strong they really are before convincing Em to join our cause. Are you okay, Silver?"

She nods, blushing slightly at Nathan's worry about her small cut. We reach our tent and walk into it. The three small beds are set up side by side, and the plate of fruits is illuminated by two flickering candles. Time to eat and sleep.

***

A day has gone by, and we are mesmerized by this close-to-mythical town. The fog of the cliff and the wooden palisade hide a large town with almost one hundred villagers who work as an assembly line. Everything is in order, everything is done for a purpose, and everyone is committed to defending and improving his or her home. Part of their daily routine, at least as far as we have seen, includes heavy training. They are a warring faction with heavy defenses on the front line and extremely well-polished soldiers behind them. Since the moment they heard about our endeavor, they doubled efforts to build up their weapons and ready their tactics.

We have told them all about our training at Valor and the strategies we have set for battle. Em has agreed to have her experienced and well-trained soldiers teach Valor's soldiers about their tactics. Their strength lies in teamwork, so Valor's volume of people must be used to support their organized method of attacking. When the time of battle comes, we will form mixed battalions with soldiers from both towns, led by Em, Dan, Rick, Nathan, Silver, or me. Our attack methods will be those of Strength but adapted to the numbers Valor adds to our squads.

I am lying on my cot, while Silver is helping Nathan cook our supper. I'm thinking about how different our mission has become since the day we left our house. This world is so different than the one I imagined we lived in. There is so much horror and cruelty, but also so much hope and human kindness. I really do not understand how people can be so different, some good and some evil, some selfish and some selfless. Just comparing Nathan and Cold makes me think they are not even from the same species.

Nathan enters our tent and walks toward me. He sits down beside me and starts playing with the candle's fire on my bedside, passing his index finger through the flame. Without looking at me, he speaks, "Brother, we have not spoken for a while now, and I want to know if you feel lonely or unappreciated in this quest." His preoccupation surprises me, as I did not expect this conversation.

"Nate, I understand you have too much on your plate right now. Saving Mom, leading people, training, strategizing, finding more people to join our cause, and Silver." I grin at that last piece of worry. He looks at me without completely turning his head and grabs my head under his armpit while messing my hair with his knuckles. He laughs and comments, "You should be more attentive to my moves. There is much to learn, you little prick." We laugh loudly, and he tells me to shush with his index finger on his lips, as we need to avoid catching Silver's attention while she cooks outside.

Nathan asks, "How are you coping with your powers, Jay?" I am grateful to him and to destiny, as my brother is the only one with whom I'd talk about this, and he is the only one who understands me, having experienced the same. I open up, "I am afraid. In part I am afraid that these powers are useless to our cause. Your powers are amazing; they can help us defeat Cold by convincing people to join us, but also by using them in the battlefield. You can kill as many as you like. On the other hand, I am afraid my powers are misleading us. What if Mom is not alive, and I have convinced you to risk all our lives for nothing?" My voice cracks with fear.

Nathan sits staring at the candle, and says, "My powers are a great weapon to be used in our journey, but they have physical limits, as I can only use them for a specific period of time and within a specific range. Your powers do not have such limitations, as you were able to connect with Mom who is far away and with Rick wife's memories, which were in the past. Without your powers there would be no journey, there would be no hope for us, and we would still be sitting back home uninterested in or ignoring a larger reality." He stands up and starts pacing in front of my bed, as I sit on the edge and stare at him.

He adds, "You also have to understand that my powers cause pain, both physical and emotional. I have killed people, Jay;

some may have been innocent, working under orders, and yet they are dead. That makes my powers both a blessing and a curse. For every life I have taken, a little piece of me dies inside. I am not the one to decide when another human being lives or dies, and yet I have had to take such a decision numerous times for the survival of both of us. Your powers are only a blessing, used for good, so do not dare to undervalue them." Nathan's voice sounds shaky as he speaks, pointing at me excitedly, trying to make me understand his point.

Nathan squats in front of me and places a hand on my knee, while saying, "Last, do not fear the possibility of not being right about Mom's whereabouts. If she is there and if she is alive, we have taken the best decision possible. We have been brave enough to take our powers and use them to save who we love the most. If your powers are misleading us, they have accidentally led us to a mission larger than either one of us. We are igniting hope in dozens of families who have lost it, fighting against something evil that has taken away happiness from this world and demanded fear in return. One way or the other, your powers have opened a path toward a better future." Nathan stands up, pats me in the back and turns around, walking outside our tent.

I tell him, "Thank you, Nathan. I admire you for your courage and decisiveness." He answers without turning around, "I admire you, Jay." The moment he exits our tent, I lie back on my bed, thinking about what we just said. My brother sees everything with a positive attitude, past the difficulties in the way with his mind set on an end goal. He wants to help Silver and me, but also help anyone else who he can. He is the most selfless person I have ever known, and I am proud to be his brother.

Silver calls for me from outside the tent as the supper is about ready. I stand up and walk out of the tent to see both my brother and Silver sitting on the trunks around the campfire to the left of our tent. They are cooking together, sharing a laugh while the flames illuminate their happiness.

I sit down on the trunk, as we are about to eat our supper. The dancing fire creates shadows around us. Tomorrow morning, we will leave to find more allies. Em is walking toward us, coming from the tents beyond ours and into the village, accompanied by two men and a woman, all wearing their armor. She sits down with us around the campfire where a stew is boiling and filling the air with the smell of cooking meat and spices. The bubbling water sounds off into the night, and the fumes rising from the casserole dance in the stale air. A treat to the senses.

Em sits beside me, while Nathan and Silver are sitting together on the trunk to my right, tending our supper as it cooks. The three soldiers stand in front of us, waiting for Em to speak. She says, "My friends, tomorrow you shall go on and recruit as many more allies as you can. While you try to recruit more people to our cause, I will take sixty-five of my soldiers to Valor two days from today. We will train with them and head together to the waterfall where all our allies are to meet before battle. We should arrive at Valor a day before they plan to leave, so we should be able to join forces with no problem. If we arrive at the waterfall before you do, we can secure the place together and set up defenses."

Nathan starts pouring the stew into the wooden bowls Silver hands to him, using a long metallic spoon, while listening to Em's explanation. She continues, "Before you leave, I have been thinking about where you should go from here. We know of a town about nine days on foot, north from here. Their attitude toward strangers may be a problem, though. We have never been able to establish a healthy relationship, if that is what it should be called, with them. They are cunning and always look after themselves before thinking about others. Nonetheless, you represent a once-in-a-lifetime opportunity to eradicate oppression and fear for them as much as the rest of us. Given that, they should join us and be loyal until the end. We should not expect them to be allies forever. Once Cold is defeated, they will retreat to their town and continue their selfish ways."

Nathan nods, handing the first bowl of stew to Em. He continues serving more bowls, giving the second to me, and the following three to the soldiers accompanying Em, who sit together at one of the remaining trunks. Finally, he gives a bowl to Silver and serves the remaining stew into his bowl. I notice his bowl is half empty, as the stew ran out from sharing with our unexpected guests. He notices I have seen his bowl and shakes his head, alerting me not to say a thing about it.

Em takes a sip of stew and gasps with delight at the delicious flavor. She smiles at Nathan and continues speaking, "We call them Stealth, as they are masters in the arts of furtiveness. This is Lisbeth and two of my bodyguards, Chester and Khan." Lisbeth bows her head slightly without getting up, while Chester and Khan stand up and give each of us a playful fist pound. Chester spills his stew when trying to sit down, and Khan laughs loudly at his clumsiness.

Em shrugs and continues, "They will accompany you for safety but also for efficiency as they know the way to Stealth. Take care of them, and I assure you they will take the best care of you three, my leaders."

Lisbeth punches Khan playfully to make him shut up and says, "Trust me, the three of us will protect you with our lives. Em is our leader, and she has commanded us to ensure you get safely to the waterfall, and we will succeed." She stands up and walks toward our tent and goes past it. We see that she goes into a tent beyond the next campfire. After a minute or two she comes out, carrying something wrapped with a dark blue blanket.

She stands next to Nathan, who is finishing his stew, and starts unwrapping whatever is within the blanket. Three shiny swords, one on top of another, can be seen. Each has a special hilt designed to our hold. She tosses the blanket to the floor and hands Nathan his sword. He stands up, grabs the sword by its hilt, and bows to Lisbeth, thanking her for the gift. Nate's sword has red vines shining on its edge, a large hilt made of black rock, and two sharpened points upwards at its edge.

Then, Lisbeth hands Silver her sword. It is the shiniest of all, reflecting the light from the campfire, as if covered with glitter and varnish. Silver grabs it without standing up, thanks Lisbeth, and inspects it in detail, rotating it with both hands. Finally,

Lisbeth walks toward me and gives me my sword. It has my name inscribed on the blade. It is shorter, closer to a knife than a sword. It has a black, bumpy grip made from leather and a sharp, shiny, silver blade with a three-pronged point at the end. A gift of kings to the three of us.

Nathan thrusts his sword's point on the ground and rests both hands on its hilt. He says, "Thank you for such an amazing gift. We will use these swords to lead beyond the battlefield. You will see how these will become a beacon of hope where there is none. As we march north from Strength to recruit more followers, knowing you are protecting the weak at Valor relaxes me. Strength is a blessing to our cause, and we are going to fight with all our forces, all our resilience, and all our cunning to ensure your village prevails and lives on in a world without subjugation."

Lisbeth sits in between Chester and Khan, who are still sitting on the trunk in front of Em and me. Nathan walks around them and places a gentle hand on each of the men's shoulders. He continues, "Lisbeth, Chester, and Khan, welcome to our family. As you know, James is my brother, and I will kill anyone who dares to hurt him or Silver, as you might remember from the moment we met."

Em chuckles as the rest of us laugh at the memory of our first impression.

Nathan goes around their trunk, and stands next to the campfire, extending his right arm toward Em. He says, "Now, join us, Em, in the Fire Pact that we sealed with Dan, and will seal with all who march side by side with us."

Em embraces Nate's calloused hand and fire encircles both, unharmful fire, a Fire Pact. Silver, Chester, Khan, and Lisbeth cheer and applaud, while I stare at the fire surrounding their hands in awe. Ninety soldiers between Valor and Strength, and a leader filled with an eternal, raging fire ready to burn all who stand in our way. Cold will never be prepared for the fiery justice coming.

23
THE ELDER
SEPARATE PATHS

JUST AS EM PREDICTED, AFTER nine days we can almost see the village ahead. It blends in well enough with the surroundings to be hidden from plain view if you don't know to look. We are about two hundred meters away from what looks like a hut, but if our companions hadn't seen it, we might have gone by without recognizing it.

Khan, Chester, and Lisbeth have shown us how much more advanced Strength is when it comes to survival. They never let their guard down, are constantly thinking about what to do and how to overcome any threat, and they move and work in unison, the consequence of years of training.

Our talks during the journey have shown us their fighting methods. Fighting is never simply a reaction; it is always planned. They draw up their plans and implement and adjust them based on the changing environment, then assess and improve continuously.

The only thing I resent is their detachment from the world, how they've lived hidden without helping others. Sure, they've stood up to fight for humanity now, but a long time has gone by without their help. I have not spoken about it, but I sense Silver and Jay feel the same blend of excitement and amusement at their abilities and teamwork, and resentment, judgement, and doubt about why they have not used them for good. I feel a vacuum inside, resulting from the clash of those emotions. My silence is the sign of this internal struggle. Jay can probably sense it.

Khan, Chester, and Lisbeth signal us to stop with closed fists held high. Their torchlight flickers as the six of us stand in the middle of the forest at night. There is a construction in front of us; it looks like a watch station. Thirty meters ahead, more camouflaged buildings stand, almost invisible. The three of them go past the watch station, which is surrounded with flora, and we stand next to it looking around its corner, Jay holding one torch to illuminate us. They walk toward the camouflaged buildings. I can see two buildings in the same line as this watch station, and a smaller and taller outpost toward the right.

Khan goes to inspect the outpost by himself, as Chester and Lisbeth walk each on one side of the buildings ahead. They are crouching, moving forward silently. They inspect the buildings through their windows before continuing. Khan catches up with them, deciding the outpost did not pose a threat to us. As they go further, I lose sight of them and there is no sound other than our breathing.

Minutes go by and Silver, Jay, and I are in a circle, looking back to the place we just came from, to have a complete view of our surroundings. Our arrows are at the ready to shoot at any threat. I tell Jay to throw the torch a couple of meters to our left to avoid attracting attention to our location.

My eyes grow accustomed to the darkness in front of us and the torch's light coming from our left. I see a couple of bushes move slightly twenty meters in front of us, stronger than the current wind could move them. There is something hidden in the jungle. "We are being watched." I stare intently, trying to distinguish something, as Silver and Jay start moving anxiously, having noticed the bushes moving as well. I decide to take a chance, knowing my inner fire can be summoned if necessary. With my arms raised, I holler, "We have come to seek your aid. Em sent us." I see both are surprised at my decision, their eyes wide and their hands shaking as they hold their bows, but soon they will understand.

I walk toward the bushes, knowing someone is hidden around here. Ten meters in front of the watch station a shadow tackles me and both of us land in a fighting stance. The man is slightly shorter than me and covered in plants and paints the color of the dense flora around us. Sil and Jay rush toward us, but four similarly dressed individuals appear on either side of them. Two grab Jay by his arms and toss him to the ground, the other two try to contain Silver as she throws vicious punches at them. They walk back a couple of steps away from her as she takes a fighting stance. Three more come from behind her and pin her down. Jay and Silver look up at me, desperate, so I try to calm them down, showing them both palms up.

Jay squeals in terror, "Please, we are allies. We have come as friends."

More and more potential enemies come out of the dense forest from all directions. There must be almost two dozen of them. *Where is Lisbeth, Chester, and Khan?* Silver is fighting back with all her strength, trying to get free and help my brother, but fails. I am still standing ready to confront my assailant, and the way out of this mess is clear to me.

The camouflaged men and women surround me and my attacker, blocking Silver and my brother from my view. No one attacks, and my heart is racing, excited to confront whomever dares to try to hurt us. Time to show them who I am.

Before exposing my powers, I notice disappointedly how Lisbeth, Khan, and Chester are brought beside Silver and Jay. They make them kneel and cover their mouths with what look to be black cloths. *Okay, time to show them not to mess with us.* For a split second I see Silver's eyes through the crowd, and they show no fear or anger as she stares at me.

I remove my backpack and place all weapons on the ground, trying to hold back a smirk. The man darts toward me, but I dodge him effortlessly. He rolls and jumps back into a wide stance. The attacker comes again, throwing wild punches at my body and face. I protect myself efficiently, landing my own precise punches without receiving any.

Time to go on the offense. I charge at him, dodge a punch by lowering my head and moving to the right, grab the man from the waist with my left arm, and throw him violently to the ground, knocking the breath out of him. I remove my shirt and use it to tie his hands and feet together like calf-roping. This face-off is done; he was no match for me.

Before I can stand up, another man grabs me from behind while a woman rolls in front of me and kicks me in the abdomen. My muscles enlarge at the same pace that I'm building up my wrath. I feel confident as I am getting angrier every second, and these people have no idea who they are facing. Each strike empowers me.

I flip backward over the man holding me and kick him in the back, sending him crashing against the woman and both to the ground. I leap on top of them and land a punch to each of their faces, knocking them out.

"Who else wants to test me?" My voice is challenging and aggressive, my arms spread wide and my eyes red as blood.

About a dozen of them step forward. It is time to show them who I truly am. My body is ready. Silver looks at me and I nod to reassure her that everything is under control.

As the twelve enemies run straight toward me, I open my arms wide and engulf my body in a flaming, spiraling sphere. My body is completely enlarged, the pain from the blows I received fading. The only clear part of my body through the flames is my red, incandescent eyes. All enemies step back in fear.

"I am Phoenix. We have come for your aid, for your allegiance to our cause. Cold and White Tower are a menace to humanity, to our survival, and to our future. This will stop; this will not be our lives. If we don't stand against him, he will stand above us for all time."

I finally understand who these people are, so I speak with

my deepest voice, "You are the village of Stealth. You are a proud people who should not be forced to live in the shadows."

I notice how they start looking at each other, afraid to continue their attack, listening to what I am about to say, "Will Stealth march with us? Or will you hide in the obscurity of fear despicably?" I challenge all of them fearlessly.

An old woman comes out from behind the observation shed, walking feebly toward me. She is not stopping or halting her advance even if the fire is about to consume her. I open the fire sphere and let her inside, enclosing both of us within. The soldiers tense up, retreating at the extreme heat surge. She places a loving hand on my cheek, just the way grandmothers do. She is smiling with love and hope in her expression.

"Welcome, our hope bearer," she says in an old voice, cracked by a lifetime of use and sweet as maple.

"We know about your mission, about who you are, about what you have done, and what you hope to achieve. Marching against Cold is an immense risk, as we might all perish against him. His forces are vast, and their entirety could be unknown to us. We could march with all our allies up to White Tower's high walls just to find we are outnumbered, outpowered, and doomed," says the elderly woman.

I order the fire to recede, and she stands in front of me, looking deeply into my eyes as she expresses her concerns. Her fear is sincere as she looks around her people. She raises her left arm and closes her fist. As soon as she does, her soldiers remove the mouth covers and release my crew. They all stand up, ten meters in front of me, and walk toward me.

I introduce them, "Madame, this is Jay, my younger brother. She is Silver, and she has been with the two of us since this journey began back home, a long way from here. And these brave men and woman are Lisbeth, Khan, and Chester. They come from Em's village, which I believe you know." The elder nods and greets each one of them with a frail handshake and a smile.

She says, "My name is Madame Claire, and I lead this town.

I think I heard you call it Stealth, right? It was well about time to give it a proper name." She laughs, and I join her. Some of her soldiers start going back toward the watch station and walking past it deeper into the forest. About a dozen stay behind, surrounding us, protecting their leader in case we try something against her.

I say, "Madame Claire, we know our mission is full of perils, we know we are asking you to march with us to an uncertain end, and we know we do not seem to be much of an army. Nonetheless, you need to understand two things." She raises her eyebrows to listen to my plea.

I continue, "We know Cold and his methods. Silver and Jay, as you can see from their painful scars, have survived enslavement under his control, and here they stand ready to face him again. If someone escapes death and is willing to face it again head on, it must be because the tide has turned and there is hope of a different end." Madame Claire holds her hands together, crossing her fingers while thinking about my words.

Before she answers, I add, "Second, we would not have come here without a plan and without an offer. Em told us you are very cautious with your decisions and how you relate with others. I understand why you do it, I have lived hidden from this world, forbidding my brother to come out of our house for all this time. The most important thing I learned is that hiding only postpones the inevitable. Hiding only makes you grow weaker, while evil grows stronger. Allow us to explain this further and what we offer to your people." She nods and points toward the watch station.

Madame Claire comments as she starts leading the way, "Let's go to a place where we can sit and speak freely, my friend."

We walk past the watch station and beside the two buildings I was able to see before. As we advance, and the torches held by the soldiers and ourselves light up the way, I start seeing the village of Stealth. They have been very careful not to let their pathways be too obvious on the ground by walking in a disorganized way, zigzagging as we go further. Their buildings are all covered with branches and foliage, and they have painted them with mud to make sure they are almost undiscernible from the forest surrounding them.

To my right I see three or four more buildings and one outpost. To my left I see four or five buildings and at least two outposts. Every twenty or thirty meters, Madame Claire points at the ground showing us a thin thread we are to skip over. She explains, "Those threads are attached to bells around our village. That way, we can know where an enemy is when attacking us." I am amazed at their cunning, and Silver and Jay, walking at my right, look at each other, surprised by such a smart invention.

We are almost one hundred and fifty meters away from the watch station where we met Madame Claire. In front of us, small wooden walls, about a meter and a half high and two meters wide, stand dispersed through the jungle. Madame Claire says, "This is one of our last lines of defense. Our tactics are based on stealth, just the way your name to our village makes obvious, so we are ready to confront anyone attacking us by hiding in the shadows, in our buildings, on the canopy, and strike them from all directions. However, if we are overpowered, we are to retreat here and take a final stand using these barriers as cover." She really has everything thought out.

These wooden walls are all over the forest, to our right and left and up front. We walk almost fifty meters past the first wall until we reach the last one. Here, a large oval part of the forest has been cleared, left without trees. It must be four meters wide and twelve meters long. She introduces the area, saying, "This is our training ground. We usually practice our stealth tactics in the forest, deep undercover with trees and mud and branches and moss, but sometimes we train here for a more common type of confrontation. One where we would not be able to hide from our enemies." Silver, Jay, and I smile, probably thinking the same thing. They have been training for the type of battle we are going to ask them to join. Now, we must be able to show them this and convince them the time has come to exit the shadows. Chester,

Khan, and Lisbeth stare intently at the training ground, probably analyzing it and comparing it to their own back in Strength.

Madame Claire walks slowly, dragging her feet as she is getting tired from our long walk. Right after the training ground, the largest building I have seen in this village stands. It has the same construction type, wooden walls with openings where windows should be placed, covered with nature as camouflage, and the door is never in the front face, probably to make it easier to escape an attack without walking straight into the enemy.

A soldier opens the door and allows us to enter. Madame Claire goes in first, and the six of us follow her. She sits down on a wicker chair in front of a three-meter-long table and invites us to sit in the chairs placed around the table. Chester and Khan sit beside her, Lisbeth and Silver sit to my left, and Jay and I sit in front of Madame Claire. The soldier holding the door walks in, ignites the torches held by metal bases across the room's walls, and leaves, shutting the door behind him.

I stare at Madame Claire as she looks back at me. I think she wishes she did not have to question our effort, hoping desperately for our success. Her sadness at this contradiction is palpable to me from her gaze and worrying to the rest of us, as it could lead her to decide not to join us.

I try to convince her, "Madame Claire, life sums up to the key moments. You have led your people successfully to endure all the atrocities this world has experienced since The Day. Now, we offer you the opportunity to go a step farther and ensure a life worth living for your people and their descendants." She moves anxiously in her chair. Jay is tapping his right foot against the floor, and Silver, Chester, Khan, and Lisbeth look from Madame Claire to me, and back again.

I proceed, "Our world will not be fixed, at least not soon enough. And it isn't fair—we are not willing to accept Cold living as a king at the expense of humanity's well-being. What makes him worthy of corroding everything around him, destroying, killing, and devastating entire villages?" I say, hoping to convince Madame Claire.

Madame Claire looks around the room, with doleful eyes as she notices we are desperate for her help. She comments, "Don't misinterpret my words, youngsters. My hope goes with you, and my people's future is of the utmost priority to me. Our enemy is poison to the world, quickly spreading its noxiousness without a cure. We do know what he did to the village standing atop the cliff and know that nothing stops him from coming here and doing the same to us, or to any other town, for that matter. We know our secrecy is not eternal. However, we have seen his armies. We have unsuccessfully tried to make a stand when we thought a stand could be made and lost brothers, sisters, mothers, fathers, sons, and daughters for our efforts." Her voice seems unaltered, but something convinces me she is speaking from her heart.

"Nate don't look at me. It's me, Jay, speaking to you through our empathic connection. Madame Claire's heart feels shattered, and I've seen why. Please allow me to show you."

Jay's words come into my mind at the perfect moment. I think back to him, *"Yes, show me."* All of a sudden, a torrent of images floods my mind. Her people are making a stand against Cold's army, close to the watch station where we first met. They were courageous, fighting desperately to protect their village, but outnumbered. Cold's men are running at them from every direction, like a wild stampede. They massacre most of the menfolk, who die valiantly while each try to fight two or more enemies at a time.

The survivors are captured, stripped naked, whipped, and chained. Madame Claire was younger back then. She saw the bloodshed first hand. Cold's men viciously attacked and even raped the few women who dared to run toward their husbands, toward the fathers of their children or their surviving sons.

Madame Claire was one of them. She must have been five years younger than now, and she used her frail body to fight against two men who struck her with disdain while she tried to give her son a last hug. They kicked her and punched her until she fell to her knees. Her son desperately tried to get free of the chains holding him, to aid his grieving mother.

Cold walked silently toward the scene and ordered the soldiers to halt. He stared down at her with contempt. In a heartbeat, he slashed at Madame Claire's son and gutted his throat. His light blue menacing and evil eyes still stared into her sobbing eyes. "Don't ever fight back," he mumbled in his deep and terrible voice at her.

Jay's voice sounds again inside of my head. "*That is the reason they hide. They fear his power, and they cannot conceive of exposing themselves again.*" The memory blurs and fades away as Jay ends our connection and his voice escapes my mind.

Jay stands up from his chair and speaks out, "Madame Claire, I am sorry for your husband's and son's loss. I understand why you fear making another stand. We know we are asking for your lives in exchange for the possibility of a new tomorrow. Is that not why your family gave their lives? So, the future of your people would not lie in slavery and senseless death?" Lisbeth, Khan, Chester, and Silver look at each other and then stare at Jay, surprised by his intervention. I stare at Madame Claire as he speaks, listening to every word intently, understanding he is taking control of the situation. Madame Claire squints her eyes and smiles. We are on the right track.

She sighs, her shoulders slumping in defeat. "You are able to see my memories?"

Jay opens his eyes wide and sits back on his chair, his face getting pale as he covers it with both hands. Through his hands, a semi-muted voice says, "I am so sorry to intrude, Madame Claire. I did not mean to disrespect your privacy." Madame Claire looks at me and winks, letting me know no harm was done.

She comforts my brother by saying, "Don't be sorry, James. You are right, my loving Chris and valiant Anthony would have jumped onboard with you the moment Nathan showed us his true power. They are the ones who keep me willing to live for our people and safeguard their present and future. There will never be an opportunity like this again. I have led selfishly, prioritizing my people over anyone else, but the time to see my people as part of a larger picture has come. We will fight alongside you, and we will make Chris and Anthony proud. Thank you, James, for reminding me for whom I truly live."

I place my right hand on Jay's shoulder. I feel proud of him, taking such a bold and dire move, leading.

Madame Claire elaborates, "We can offer thirty more soldiers to your cause. We won't leave our home unattended, but you will be amazed at what we can offer you. I offer our village as a training ground for anyone else who joins our cause. We are expert at hiding and working in the shadows, so our enemy won't know what is coming until it is knocking on his front door." Jay's jaw drops as he looks at Madame Claire in awe. I laugh and slap his head playfully, while Lisbeth, Chester, and Khan cheer at Madame Claire's decision to join us. Silver stares silently at Jay, her eyes showing how proud she feels.

Madame Claire smiles and lets us celebrate for a minute, then she continues, "Nearby, there are seven more villages living under Cold's reign. They are mostly farmers, hunters, and gatherers in small groups, and their military expertise may be null, but their numbers could prove essential. You should recruit them, bring them here, and we will train them to survive and be useful in the battlefield." Her eyes are set on me as she shares such valuable information. I feel excited at the possibility of new recruits and nod at her slowly in gratitude.

She stands up slowly and walks around the table toward me. I stand and extend my hand to thank her for her decision, but she slaps my hand away and hugs me lovingly. I feel the loving hug of a grandmother combined with the strong embrace of a leader. I whisper to her, "Thank you." And she cackles softly before answering, "Thank *you,* Nathan, for fighting the fight no one has dared to embark on."

The rest of my crew stands up and speaks loudly, celebrating

Stealth's decision to join our cause. Each one hugs Madame Claire whose eyes have a glint you only see when someone is hopeful.

The six of us exit our meeting satisfied and excited at the success. I grab Jay by his shoulders as he walks in front of me and shake him strongly, kissing his head for making this happen. Lisbeth, Chester, and Khan are walking in a single file, with their arms on each other's shoulders and skipping as they advance, laughing and cheering. Silver catches up with me and stands to my left, staring at me and raising an eyebrow. I smile widely, hug her, and raise her from the ground. As Jay tries to reach us to join our hug, I create a small fire in front of him, making him fall back, as the six of us share roaring laughter.

He stands up and the six of us hug excitedly. Stealth is a key village owing to their location close to the waterfall as much as their stealth abilities. Without them, we would be a two-legged stool, but with them alongside Strength and Valor, we are complete.

A soldier comes out from our right, surprising us as we were unable to see or hear him before he speaks, "That is the building you six will share." He points at the camouflaged building six meters diagonally to our left. He goes away silently into the night.

Lisbeth, Chester, and Khan walk toward our sleeping quarters. I say, "We will catch up with you later, friends. Have a great night's sleep." They raise their hands in farewell and enter the building speaking excitedly, their laughs resounding inside as they close the door.

I tell Jay and Silver, "Come here." We enter a tent two meters to our right. Here they store food. Entering, we see raw meat hanging from the ceiling, vegetables loaded in small crates, and spices stacked on a counter. "I need to talk with both of you." My tone of voice is different than the one I used during our celebration, and it does not appease them. Jay looks at me silently, while Silver crosses her arms. Something is troubling me, and I need to share it with them. Once more, I am forced to do something that discomforts me and will enrage both.

I share, "Remember how Em advised us about Stealth's selfishness and how they look only after themselves?"

Jay and Silver nod.

I sigh and say, "I am not yet completely convinced they will join us. Their commitment could be temporary, just for show, and we could get to the waterfall just to find out they have bailed on us. We cannot allow that to happen. I need both of you to stay here while I go on to meet with leaders of the other villagers."

Silver turns around and shakes her head angrily. Jay steps closer to me and stares at me with watery eyes.

I speak again, "Yes, I am suggesting parting ways, which we have never done voluntarily since The Day. My heart feels shattered at the suggestion, and I'm afraid of what could happen while I'm away, but our success rests on Stealth as much as on Valor and Strength. Sil storms out of the tent, angrily arguing with my idea."

I stay with Jay, grab him by both shoulders, and stare into his eyes.

He says, "Why, brother? Why now?" Jay's voice sounds defeated.

My strength has been his strength, and our closeness his safety. Without me, his world seems to turn into an obscure and frightful place that he lacks the tools to fight against. He does not understand he is becoming powerful and skilled at survival and no longer needs me.

I try to explain my decision, "Dan spoke to me of another town. They live the closest to White Tower and are the ones who know Cold's tactics and White Tower's layout as no one else does. In the past, they even cooperated with Cold, but their tie broke when a new leader killed their old one. He seems to dislike Cold with a venomous hate, but he seems to dislike everyone else as well. No one has managed to have any communication with him. They live their own lives and are content when left alone. Cold does not even bother to attack them, as the losses would be high in return for no loot, since they live simple lives with few resources and no aspiration to grandeur. Nonetheless, their knowledge and their abilities would be key to saving Mom and humanity." I am grieving as the words leave my mouth. Once more, my decision goes against my heart.

Jay's watery eyes break my heart, even though he nods, supporting my decision against his will. He is trying to understand why we must part ways, while figuring out how to convince me to stay. He tries to speak but decides not to, waiting for me to explain myself better.

The light coming from the torch behind me shows me he is shivering slowly, fighting against his desire to cry. I continue, "You two will stay behind to train with Stealth, to receive anyone I manage to convince to join us. Build up our forces. I need you and Silver to lead our soldiers up to the waterfall. My mission will take about seven days and you must leave here even if I have not returned. In eleven days, you will march to the waterfall. I need you to lead the same way you showed me today you are capable of."

He nods with his head down, so I pat his left arm.

I need to make him understand, so I add, "I am proud of who you are and who you are becoming for this mission. Remember, we are saving our mom alongside hundreds of mothers and fathers from ever having to lose their children. We are also saving hundreds of children from losing their parents as we have. Our fight is for us—us, not just Nate and Jay. Cold is a bad weed, and if we don't tear it apart from the root, it will grow back stronger and larger than before." A small, silent tear rolls down my cheek.

Jay looks up at me, taking control of himself, and speaks softly through a broken voice, "You will always have my support, brother. The world has been the most unfair to you, forcing the harshest decisions into your hands. Go on, deal with Silver and rest assured we will go through with what you ask us to do."

We hug each other, and I feel his warm and skinny body gasping for air as tears roll down his cheeks and onto my chest. He cleans his tears off with his right sleeve and separates from my embrace. Before I leave, he nods toward the tent's entrance, telling me to go and deal with Silver before it is too late. He smiles sadly, and I kiss his head, saying, "I am proud of you, little brother." He sighs and answers playfully, "Shut up, BB."

I laugh and rush out of the tent in search of Silver.

I enter our sleeping quarters, but she is nowhere to be seen. Lisbeth, Chester, and Khan are already sleeping, so I exit silently to avoid waking them up. I walk back toward the building where we met with Madame Claire, searching for her right and left. As soon as I reach it, I see her standing silently in the middle of the training field, staring at the sky in search of answers. I join her, standing silently beside her. We stare at the night sky for a couple of seconds, before I say, "I am sorry, Sil."

She lowers her head and pushes me strongly, making me stumble and take a couple of steps back, "You bastard! How dare you leave us behind? For once, I believed I'd found a family, a second family. Now you risk all of it to be a hero. You know I lost everything last time my family was torn apart. How dare you embrace me in your family just to break it apart!" Silver lashes out, raising her voice.

I walk back toward her with both arms stretched wide open. She is glaring at me, with one foot in front of the other, as if ready to attack me. As I walk a meter away from her, she charges at me furiously. I step to my right a split second before getting tackled, grab her from her waist with my left arm, and pulling her toward me strongly. I wrap my right arm across her chest and hold her firmly with my stance wide open.

She is struggling to get free, but I fight back. I feel the same fear she does. I speak softly to her, "Sil, my soul is shattered by the decisions I have to make and the wrongdoings this world has forced me to do. Every step I take seems to lead me in the direction I fear the most. You say I am leaving you behind, betraying the family we have created, but how wrong you are."

Her fighting recedes, so I release her. She turns around and looks at me, dolefully waiting for me to speak again.

I share a fear I have with her, "Besides making sure Stealth keeps true to their word, I need to be sure both you and Jay are safe. I am going on into an unknown territory where I could lose both of you forever. Death could be waiting for us ahead." My inner fear blends with my wrath and impotence at the crossroad where I stand.

Silver is sobbing heavily, her face red and moist with tears, her lips tight and trembling at the sight of me.

I look at her beautiful eyes and place my hands at either side of her gorgeous face. "You are the only one I trust enough to take care of that which I value the most. Sil, you are my safety net, my strength, and the reason I have lived with less of a burden since the day you joined us. There is nothing I value more than Jay's life, not even my own. Besides my direct family, you are the only person in this world I would die for. You have brought to my life something beyond survival and James's security. You have brought peace, happiness, excitement, adventure, and love to my life. You shout at me while the only thing I want to hear from your beautiful lips is the same that I will tell you now. I love you, Silver, because you are a reason to live for and to die for." My voice cracks, stumbles, shouts, and lowers as my words are genuine, loving and filled with pain.

Sil walks toward me with a look I have never seen before. Her heart is wide open, no fear or anger left. She places a soft hand on my neck and pulls me toward her. Our kiss under the night sky reflects the situation in which we are living. Love is the only light against Cold's relentless evil. What a cliché.

24
THE YOUTH
UNITY

NATHAN LEFT THREE DAYS AGO with Chester and Lisbeth; Khan stayed behind with Silver and me to ensure Stealth will join our fight. They train constantly at their skillful art of deception and slyness, with the goal to become invisible. We have learned a lot from them, the ways to use nature to your advantage. After all, the surprise element in any attack is key to overcoming an enemy that overpowers you.

My hope, all our hope, goes with Nathan. We are not yet enough of a force to face Cold. The hordes I saw rushing toward Rick's town through the deceased woman's memory were barely a sample of all his numbers, and they were dozens. The brutality and quickness with which they destroyed the town are unmeasurable.

What if all this effort is useless? What if Cold's armies are unbeatable? Are we convincing people to march to their death? These questions have stolen my sleep, and I find myself constantly inattentive to those around me. They deserve better; they deserve Nathan.

He placed on me so much responsibility to ensure Stealth joins us in this endeavor. I feel unable to succeed at this. Silver has done exactly what he asked us to do. She has met with Madame Claire daily to draw up plans and speculate about scenarios. Her angle is to make them feel a part of the planning and not just an invitee to the event.

Inside Madame Claire, I still feel doubt and confusion, but her intention to join us is true. The memory of her family binds her allegiance to us, and she has managed to convince those she leads. I know so, since these days have allowed me to practice my empathic connection.

With some people, those with the strongest emotions, I have managed to connect for brief spurts of time. Some are extremely attached to our cause and some are extremely afraid. I am somewhere in between, to be honest. We must save Mom and I understand why our mission grew exponentially to save the most people possible, but it frightens me.

By now, we are one hundred and twenty people ready to march to White Tower. Rick, Dan, and Em must be training together, amassing our largest force. Why is my power an emotional one and not a psychic one? How much do I desire to see the future and know if we will die soon? Useless.

Sometimes, in secret, I still wish Nate and I were back home before the rifle, before Silver, and before Cold caught me and transformed me. Life seemed much simpler back then, behind the walls of ingenuity. After all, ignorance is bliss, is it not? That saying sounds familiar, but I cannot remember where I heard or read it. It does not matter. When living behind a veil everything seems natural, until the curtain falls, the truth behind a trick is shown and the magic is lost.

Without Nathan, I wander too much away from our goal, from our mindset and from our planned future. I wish I could connect with him from this far away, but no matter how much I try, I fail. If I could feel his wrath again, his raw power and determination, all these doubts and hesitations would vanish once more.

This angers me. Why do I depend on his feelings to erase fear? How feeble am I? It does not feel right to be so dependent on another person, even if he is my brother and protector. In this world full of peril, it is the riskiest way to live, at the mercy of another's life.

Someone is coming toward me; branches crack as they are broken under the weight of someone or something. I am guarding Stealth from the outpost, the one we saw the first time we came here. I crouch and try to find the source of this noise through the forest. Even with daylight I am not able to see anything, just hear it. My companion, one of their soldiers, places a finger on his mouth, signaling me to be dead silent. My heart races again, and some of those trained instincts get in gear.

My hand grasps my three-pronged knife, a beautiful gift and a needed one in this world. I am trembling half in fear and half from adrenaline shooting throughout my body. The man beside me grabs his bow, prepares an arrow, and exits the watch post through its backdoor. He vanishes into the forest toward the source of the sound, crouching silently. Should I stay, or should I face the threat?

That sound seems familiar to me. It sounds just the way Dad's knife sounded when slashing at undergrowth when we camped. More branches break as something is getting closer to us. I believe there is more than one person coming toward us, as the sound is no longer concentrated in the same spot.

A voice comes from the woods, "Come on, everybody, this town has to be somewhere around. That flame-guy said it was called Stealth, but this is being excessively cautious. We have been wandering for hours now." *What the hell is happening? Flame-guy?* I am certain now that a group of people is coming toward us, but are they friendly or foes? Flame-guy must be Nathan, right?

The source of the voice appears ahead, coming out of the bushes in my direction, thirty meters away. A tall, blond man, wearing cargo pants and a green shirt, is slashing at the jungle leaves with a machete. He is walking straight toward our outpost. I leave the outpost to greet them and spot the man who was accompanying me in the lookout come down from a tree closer to the speaker. I catch up with him, and both of us march toward the unknown man. He raises his bow to be cautious, and I grab my knife as well. You can never be too cautious in this world.

I address the man and notice how he is being followed by three more people. They stop their advance and listen to me, as I say, "Hello, friend. We heard you are looking for Stealth, sent by a flame-guy. Who sent you really?" I use the deepest voice my throat can create and try to look menacing. The man beside me is succeeding at this far more than I am. His skin is colored just as the forest, dark shades of brown and green, with small splotches of mustard and black on his face. His bow is tensed to its maximum, pointing his arrow at the blond man.

The blond man raises both hands and tosses the machete away before answering, "Phoenix sent us after our Fire Pact. He said in Stealth we should ask for Madame Claire, Jay, or Silver. Please tell us we have arrived at the correct place. My name is Thomas, and these are my neighbors." His voice is stumbling on each word, as his inner thoughts show me fear. He is pondering whether he mistakenly walked straight toward an enemy, or if he has arrived at his destination. After all, he just met two men in the middle of the forest after being lost for hours.

My companion says, "You have arrived at your destination. Welcome." His voice is unfitting for his appearance, too high-pitched for a mean-looking man. The blond man looks at me, questioning who I am, probably finding me like the description Nathan shared with him. I say, "I am James or Jay, as my brother told you. Please follow us; we must go to Madame Claire immediately." As I turn, Thomas stays behind, still holding both hands up. Behind him, two men and a woman are holding their hands up as well, staring intently at us.

He says, "Wait, before I follow you, I must trust you. Phoenix told us to look for Jay first, even before Silver or Madame Claire." He stops and feels ashamed to say his next words. "He said you could read our thoughts. And that is the only way we should trust you," he asserts with a hint of disbelief, and I feel a frenzy of horror at the test set upon me. Nathan is forcing me to use my power to connect empathically with a man I have never met, who might not have any strong emotions for me to grab ahold of.

I look at him wide-eyed, at his three companions, and at the camouflaged man. The sounds of the forest become unbearable, the wind through the bushes, the rain falling somewhere deep in the jungle, the man's breathing, and my continuously moving foot pushing the soil away from my shoes. I cannot concentrate with so many distractions around me. *Why did you do this to me, Nate?*

A voice inside my head says, "Because I believe in you." For a second, my fear managed to arouse my connection with Nathan and hear his reassuring voice. "Now, make me proud, little brother." I smile, confusing all those staring at me, who are staring at me as if waiting for me to do some sort of magic trick. *Nate will always be with me; I should not ever be afraid.*

Staring at the man, all becomes clear to me. His ideas, his thoughts, and his personality flash by me. Thomas is really his name, and he is thinking about what to do if I am an enemy instead of an ally. He is figuring how he could grab his machete and attack before my companion shoots him with his arrow. He thinks about the others they left behind to scout ahead, and how to make sure they escape in case we are foes.

I have read his mind enough to convince him I am James, so I share, "You four are scouts. This is an act, and you were loud to ensure someone found you quickly. It was Nathan's idea, since he knew finding Stealth was a challenging task unless someone in Stealth found you first." Thomas turns his head and winks at the woman behind him. He looks back at me and waits for me to continue. The other two men smile expectantly.

I continue, "About eight more people are with you, hidden to avoid any threat you encounter first. Nathan wants you to join us, to train with us, to march with us to White Tower and fight. You have sworn to aid us, and you did do the Fire Pact before coming here." Thomas and his three companions lower their arms. He extends his hand, and we shake excitedly. His three companions go back into the jungle to bring out the missing people. Thomas smiles in incredulity at this experience.

He says, "Jay, it is an honor to meet you. Please guide us to Stealth and Madame Claire to start our training as soon as possible. Nathan sparked hope in every one of us, but you have just strengthened it, my friend."

Finally, through the trees and fallen brown and green leaves I see the eight people being led by Thomas's three mates. They are twelve in total, and each one greets me and my companion with a handshake, a hug, or a kiss on the cheek. They are excited about finding Stealth and eager to start their training.

We walk together toward the watch station, where my companion stays behind to stand guard. I lead them into Stealth, following the same path Madame Claire showed us, making them hop over the threads attached to bells, and feeling extremely hopeful with this first omen of success sent by Nathan. More are to come, and we will be ready.

***

I am reclining on one of the small wooden walls close to the training ground. Silver and Khan are teaching a large group of men and women, about forty of the new recruits and ten or fifteen soldiers from Stealth. They are working together, trying new tactics out and practicing combat. Their moves raise dust clouds and I cough occasionally, staring intently to see if there are any improvement opportunities in their skills. At the same time, I am listening intently to how Silver and Khan lead, as I must learn to order others during battle.

As the class progresses, I lose myself in deep thinking. Nate left Stealth seven days ago in search of another town to join us. The twelve whom I met four days ago were the first ones to arrive. Since then, thirty-three more men and women have come to our call. Some had basic survival training; others came with some battle experience, but most were simple men and women marching under the banner of hope. They want to give their towns, their families, and their friends a future worth living for. All of them are tired of Cold's domination, enslavement, and fright. Their resentment and hatred are widespread, and it has fueled our desire to train harder, to work faster, and to give all that it takes to succeed.

All of them say Nathan's as a bold leader who speaks from his heart, who listened to them, took time to comprehend their fears, and gave them the opportunity of a lifetime. They say he is never demanding or imposing, but warm and understanding. Of course, all of them tell amazing stories about Phoenix's astonishing powers, with their eyes glinting with excitement. Their hopes and dreams are the reason why we make all this effort, and the reason why Nathan will not stop until he manages to rescue Mom and defeat Cold for good.

However, one specific case has become our war banner. A small child arrived a day after the initial twelve, and he has become the fuel to our scorching desire to end Cold. He walked with his head down and did not lift it to celebrate his arrival in Stealth with all those walking with him. I spotted him within the crowd and his depression touched my heart. No kid his age should carry burdens as heavy as his.

He is the sole survivor of his town. Cold sacked it less than half a month ago, since bruises and cuts still cover his arms, legs, and face. He managed to hide while Cold's men attacked viciously and insatiably all that he knew in the world. From the few words he has managed to say, we know he lost his mother, his father, and two sisters.

At night, he cries, muffled by his pillow, trying to be the valiant little boy his father taught him to be. In the morning, he has been the first to wake and walk to the training field. He wants to avenge his family, and his tiny arms, holding an unsharpened sword, swinging it with all his strength, has moved every single man, woman, and child in Stealth.

No kid will ever suffer what Little R suffered. He chose that name, with the R standing for revenge. How soul-shattering to see him, but at the same time how strengthening and inspiring to see him dedicate his young life to such an honorable mission. For him, for his family, and for all humanity.

Khan has taught us battling skills, Silver and I have trained everyone on tactics in the battlefield and adaptability, the soldiers from Stealth have shown how to become invisible and use our surroundings in our favor. Now, Little R has given us the missing piece to the puzzle... a clear reason to use all this training. He has given us the destination on the road we are building together.

25
THE ELDER
PERSUASIVE VIOLENCE

LISBETH AND CHESTER HAVE BEEN key allies in this journey, even though we have not encountered severe perils on our way to the last town. We have been able to find scattered travelers and small villages across the forest. Most of them listen to our plea but decide not to join us. I understand their fear of facing Cold and his massive army. They decide based on their present, trying to avoid exposing their families to Cold's revenge in case we lose. It hurts me to see them turn down our offer and hinder our chance at success, but I must respect their decisions.

However, a few have seen in us a beacon of hope, an opportunity to avenge those who have died under Cold's disgusting empire, or a chance to give their kids a better future. These men and women remember life before The Day, and they wish to give their descendants a chance at such a life. More than forty have agreed to march to Stealth and train with us. I am certain that at least the first twelve arrived safely as I managed to connect empathically with Jay for a short time when he met them. I hope they are safe and training together, building the foundation for our future.

We are walking through the shadows of a moonless night. The wind is howling against the moving branches of tall trees around us. As we move north, the flora changes and becomes taller, and the weather is less humid. It increases the range of our view, and at the same time makes us more vulnerable to surprise attacks. Lisbeth and Chester walk silently, watching carefully where to step to avoid breaking twigs or walking on dry leaves that may alert our enemies.

We see three enemies ahead, one to our right and two to our left. We fan out and I take the center front, advancing slowly to see if there are more enemies ahead. A man is taking a piss about forty meters to my right. Suddenly, Chester inaudibly murders him, the sound of his urine stream muted as a silent rush of blood spurts from his neck. Even though I try to follow Chester with my sight, his movements close to the forest floor make him nearly invisible. Soon after he kills our first enemy, he vanishes from sight.

To my left, two men are walking together. I can see a campfire ahead, almost fifty meters in front of me. Those two must be guarding it. Their paths are random, which heightens the difficulty of a stealth kill; no pattern is discernible to surprise them. Nonetheless, suddenly, Lisbeth falls on top of one of them from a tall cedar tree, killing him instantly with her knife, breaking a thin slice through his chest. An awful way to go if you ask me.

Before the second man turns around at the inexplicable sound behind him, he is down. A precisely thrown shiv is protruding from his throat. Their abilities amaze me. They just killed three enemies before I even managed to get close to one of them. This mission together has taught me the basics of their training. Stealth is far more than avoiding being spotted; it is an art of deception, of skill, of patience, and of luck. They have trained for many years to be the best warriors, and yet they avoid direct confrontation. Before overpowering an enemy, they try to outsmart him. They are not flawless in the execution but are in their result every single time.

The remaining eight men are sitting around a creaking fire.

Chester and Lisbeth join me, and we crouch silently toward them. When we are twenty meters away from them, Chester goes farther to my right and Lisbeth to my left. We will try to surround them before attacking.

Their conversation is grotesque, gloating about massacring a town of farmers who were unable to make a stand. They have no idea a historic stand by farmers, gatherers, hunters, travelers, moms, fathers, daughters, and sons will soon end their reign of tyranny.

They will never know about this stand, not from the place where we will send them. A direct fight between the three of us and the eight of them is unfair, as we are much more powerful. As soon as I am ten meters away from this hoard of disgusting henchmen, I stand up casually in the middle of the night. The one sitting down, staring straight at my direction, opens his eyes wide and says, "Who the fuck are y..." His voice is shattered by the arrow trespassing his gut. He blabbers blood and falls face first into the campfire.

The remaining enemies stand up shouting obscenities and reaching for their weapons. I send an arrow flying at the enemy closest to me as he is turning to aim an arrow at me. He falls with my arrow deep in his right shoulder, and before his body hits the ground, I shoot a precise arrow into the back of his head.

They try desperately to attack me, but before any manages to shoot an arrow they are all killed by our constant volleys. Their bodies thump loudly as they hit the ground to never stand up again. When the last enemy falls, we walk toward them and search them to see if they carry any valuable weaponry, foods, or beverages. I will never grow accustomed to sacking an enemy's body of valuables, but it is the way this world is built.

We pull their bodies away, stacking them side by side forty meters away, and walk back toward their campfire. We sit on the same trunks they sat on before dying, and decide to stay here for the night, taking turns as watchers to avoid being victims to the same tactic we just used.

I say, "Lisbeth, Chester, go ahead and sleep first. I will take the first turn since I am wide awake." They nod at me and spread their blanket right next to one of the trunks on the side of the campfire. This way they are concealed from enemy fire in case we are attacked, and the fire heats them up through the night. They start wiggling until each finds a comfortable position to sleep in.

I stare at the night sky, enjoying the amazing view of constellations. Back before The Day, only in the wild could you manage to see so many bright stars at night. Now, you have this astounding night show every single day. While identifying Orion's belt, the Big Dipper, and the Small Dipper, the only constellations I know, I get lost in my thoughts.

Is life ever fair? As far as I am concerned, it has not been fair for at least seven years. Loving someone with a true heart and no selfishness has led to suffering and seemingly unsurmountable trials. Chrissy did not deserve what happened to her, but no one other than me cares. Being good has led all of us to an early grave or to a bending path toward evil.

These days have brought back Chrissy's memory. Together with the feelings I have for Silver, they are pulling my heart apart. Seven years may seem enough to mend a broken heart, but they are not, as wounds as deep as the one this world inflicted upon me never heal. You learn to live with the pain and deal with the moments when your mind plays tricks on you and brings back all the memories and enjoyable times just to hurt you.

A shooting star crosses the night sky from left to right over the purple-black canvas of the universe.

What troubles me is if my feelings for my past love are unfair to Silver. However, my feelings for her are just as strong as those I felt long ago, and at the same time completely different. I loved Chrissy for her persona, for how she made me think and live, and how she inspired me to find the best version of myself. On the other hand, I love Silver for being a light in a mist of darkness, a reason to fight for, to live for, and even to die for without hesitation.

Life is never as simple as it seems and plans rarely pan out as they are supposed to in the first place. The wind is blowing slowly now, whistling lightly as it advances through the forest. How I wish this peacefulness was real and perdurable. However, I know this is an illusion, an oasis in the middle of the dangers of a desert.

A bright spurt of light illuminates to my left, going deeper into the forest, following the direction we were headed in before bumping into Cold's men. Another one bursts to the right of the first and another larger one right behind it. Something is on fire. Fire in the horizon, in the direction of the last town.

I scream, "Lisbeth, Chester, get up! Something is going on, and we need to go now!" They open their eyes, looking wildly around, getting their belongings back in their satchels, and tying their shoes hurriedly. I start running toward the fires ahead, pacing myself to allow them to catch up and avoid tiring myself before time. Those fires must be about two kilometers away.

Lisbeth and Chester catch up with me, and we trot toward the fires. Another bright light can be seen through the forest, closer to us, maybe a kilometer away. We start running as fast as our legs can carry us. Once again, plans never work as drawn in the back office.

If Cold destroyed the town and the men and women are killed or enslaved, our mission has taken a serious blow. Their knowledge about White Tower is crucial to our operation. None of us has a clear understanding about Cold's defenses, numbers, and layout within the city walls. We would be walking into the lion's den without the slightest idea of direction.

Their debacle could mean we have to turn back and halt our mission. I will not lead a death march, especially when all those men and women will stand up against hatred with hope in their hearts. Their future, for which I am willing to fight, must be of safety and liberty, not of death and suffering as slaves. The end of the tunnel must be light, not a cliff leaving them to rot in darkness.

With every step, my eyes show me more clearly how the fire is consuming a town, the town I hoped to convince to join us. My fear mixes with anger, and fire starts erupting from my limbs. My rage is fueled by the same force destroying my hopes ahead. This is not how it is supposed to go down, it is not fair to be so close, with our destiny at hand, just to have our dreams scorched down. We were on the verge of building the vessel to escape our castaway existence, just to see it collapse before touching the sea. How fucking ironic, fire.

The forest flashes by us, twigs slashing against our skin painfully and roots constantly trying to make us trip. Chester falls at my right and stands up immediately to continue with our sprint. Lisbeth does not even flinch at his accident and runs untiringly with me toward the source of the luminescent destruction. Her gaze is set on the fire, worried and enraged. My powers help me accelerate past her.

After more than ten minutes running through the forest, we arrive at a small town burning up; all houses and communal edifices are torched. At a wooden stable in front of us, a horse whines hysterically at the destruction surrounding it. I run toward it and fight against the burning front gate to set it free. Chester and Lisbeth are unable to aid me, as fire has raised the temperature to mortal levels. No human shouts can be heard; something is amiss.

This time, I will not be using my powers to retain the raging fire since I suspect Cold's men are around, waiting to attack us when tired and hurt by the destruction they caused. A window to my right breaks as the wooden frame collapses, allowing me to enter the stable. Falling debris, wooden trusses, and beams are collapsing everywhere.

The wooden plank holding the door closed is heavy and releasing it takes most of the strength left in my body after the tiring sprint. The horse dashes beside me to freedom, safe and sound. The whole structure collapses, and I barely escape from the creaking, burning death trap.

As I crawl away from the destruction, a dozen arrows fall around me, halting my advance in all directions. Raising my head slightly shows me Lisbeth and Chester are lowering their weapons and raising their hands, surrounded by arrows as well. I tell them, "Don't move. We are surrounded." Chester and Lisbeth nod. We are surrounded, but we are not defeated yet.

A tower of a man emerges from the forest, standing two meters tall, with black skin; he's bald with piercing brown eyes filled with hatred, illuminated by the massive fire surrounding us. He is wearing a cutoff khaki pant and an immense bow across his wide chest, proportional to his body but massive to anyone else who tries to wield it. His steps trample the ground floor, leaving a gigantic footprint behind.

He does not even notice Chester and Lisbeth as he strides past them. Could this be Ex's replacement? Is this Cold's right-hand man? If he is, I am up for a challenge. Using both of my arms I bolt myself up and stand in a fighting stance, ready to face this threat. He charges without hesitation, a bull about to tackle me.

I dodge and roll to my right, evading his left foot by millimeters. He knew I would react that way and almost sent me to an early sleep with a massive knockout. He throws a lightning right jab that I stop with my left forearm, aching terribly at the blow. He has left my left arm unusable for a moment, as the pain sears up to my shoulder and a bone might have snapped.

Another massive strike comes from his left fist, and I duck as fast as possible before it lands straight on my right ear. He grabs me from my shoulders and tosses me in the air, using all his body to catapult me three meters high in the air. I crash hard on the ground, being able to turn my body slightly to cushion the fall with my left shoulder. Now my left arm is completely numb, hanging beside me as if not a part of my body.

I stand up with trembling legs, afraid of an enemy for the first time in my life. He charges again with unforeseeable speed for a man his size, but this time I stand my ground. He kicks with his right leg, trying to foresee my evasive roll and losing balance, allowing me to shove him with all my strength and make him fall. A tower falling to the ground.

Using all my speed and reflexes, I jump on him, landing kicks with all my strength on his torso and face. He grabs ahold of my right foot before it inflicts more damage on his body and twists my knee violently, making me fall and leaving me at his mercy. Fuck me.

He lands on top of me, both knees beside my torso, and throws hammering punches at my face. My arms are receiving a destructive beating, trying to cover my face from this man's deadly attack. Fear starts to escape from me, as my inner power prompts me to remember who I truly am. Hello, old ally.

"Get off me!" All my power and anger bursts from within and sends the massive mountain of a man flying high into the sky. He crashes into a tree, just like two cars crashing head-on, breaking its trunk in half. The tree falls before the man gets up, and he pushes his arm on his knee to try to stand up.

His body is failing him even if his mind is still set on attacking me again. His first step is feeble, and his second step useless. His train-like build smashes into the ground, gasping for the air the tree swiftly stole away from him. Pushing himself with both fists on the ground, he gets himself up to his knees, resting on his shins and watching me with hate.

The massive man says, "I know who you are. A messenger came here and requested our aid in your enterprise. He was weak and did not live to tell the tale of the trials I set him to do. His inability to convince me about the possibility of joining you troubled me." He is gasping for air and looking straight at me. I stand up and walk toward him in my transformed self, with fire revolving around my legs and forearms.

He continues, "For days, I have thought about your arrival, about your quest and your offer to my people. I would never follow a frail, pathetic match-boy in a quest to fight the strongest force in this world. Now, you have shown me the true leader of the undertaking set upon me. Behind your banner, I will march." The deepest voice I have heard in my life emits from the man's swollen mouth. His head lowers almost imperceptibly, recognizing me as an equal.

For the first time I notice the dozens of soldiers behind him, holding their bows on me as I speak to their leader. They lower their bows and set them on the ground, just as they bow at me.

My body aching with cuts, bruises, and inflammation manages to take me to this man. Both of us are agitated, gasping for air and recovering from the strenuous fight we had. I extend my arm, and he grabs it and stands to face me. I say, "Dan told me about you, about how you have dared to stand against Cold and held him back." My voice sounds ridiculous compared to his. He nods, and his eyes widen slightly.

He squints his eyes, remembering Dan, as he says, "Dan is a man of wisdom. He is the only one who could come to my people and receive an amicable welcome. Once more, he has proven this by sending you straight to me. No one else would have a chance against me in a one-on-one confrontation. You are a warrior, not from skill, but from the heart. Never surrendering is the only way to succeed at this legendary crossing."

I nod at his comment and grit my teeth as severe pain shoots across most of my limbs. I laugh at how frail I must look, and say, "We came directly from Madame Claire's village, from Stealth. Alongside Dan's village Valor and Em's Strength, we have convinced several wanderers, survivors, and hopeful men and women along the way to join us. We amass about one hundred and sixty soldiers."

He is standing tall in front of me, the receding flames of the village shining brightly on his dark skin. He looks down at me fiercely, with a menacing glare.

I continue, "We have trained in the art of courage, of battle, of stealth, and of war tactics for almost two months now. All of us will march to the waterfall hidden close to White Tower. We came here for your knowledge; you are the only one who knows about Cold's city enough to plan an assault with a bare chance of success. Even if plans never work, we need your guidance to have clear first steps in our encounter." He listens to me with a serious stare, unmovable and concentrated on every word.

He raises his sight and looks at the burning town before saying, "You are right, plans never work out, but they are needed nonetheless. That waterfall is about ten days away from here. We will join you, but these ten days will be crucial to our success. We need to use our forces efficiently as we are still outnumbered. Your army of one hundred and sixty along with my forty soldiers is still inferior in numbers to Cold's vast army. Each one of us will have to kill two of them to succeed."

Lisbeth and Chester join me, walking slowly to avoid angering the massive man.

He continues speaking without even acknowledging their presence, "My village has specialized in long-range attack; you can call us Range in your jargon. Let us get away from here swiftly, as we burnt up our village to bring out some of Cold's men and kill them. The horse you saved was part of the bait. This way, we start reducing their numbers. After doing so, we will meet formally and define our next steps." He turns around and starts his heavy stride into the forest, followed by his forty soldiers. He seems fully recovered, even though I still feel close to having been beaten to death.

Without looking back at me he comments, "By the way, I will not be calling you by that stupid-ass name Phoenix or making a ridiculous Fire Pact. Nathan it is."

For a split second he looks over his shoulder and says, "My name is Bull." He smiles slightly at the irony and continues delving into the forest. Sick bastard.

We wait hidden in the shadows about two hundred meters away from the burning village. We are all scattered around, silent, waiting for our enemies to come inspect the fire. Bull is reclining on a tree, his massive body completely rested after our encounter and ready for his next battle. I am sore from his blows and my left arm is still completely numb. I cannot understand how he was able to recover so quickly. He stares at me silently, with no emotion in his eyes. Lisbeth and Chester were ordered to stay close to Bull's second in command, far away from me.

Finally, after almost thirty minutes of silent waiting, we see about three dozen of Cold's men marching toward the town to inspect the fire hazard, coming from the north, to our left. The hold their formation until they enter the town and their leader orders them to scatter around.

They run around town, trying to find something to save from the fire and take for themselves. We walk slowly toward them, hidden by the trees. Bull's men get ready, with their bows stretched and their arrows held with their fingertips. Each is aiming at a different enemy and awaiting Bull's command. He stands beside me, watching how Cold's men run around his burning town, waiting for the perfect moment to strike.

He raises his right hand. As soon as he closes his fist, every single one of his men shoot an arrow at our enemies. They fly from all directions, causing chaos and death without a possibility for escape. Cold's men barely scream before they are muted forever, with one, two, or even three arrows precisely shot at them. Their precision is Swiss-clockwork level; even when everyone was running wildly in search of cover, I did not manage to see a missed arrow.

The fire starts to fade away, and the night's darkness falls back. Bull's men go into the town and search for any survivors. Bull walks heavily behind them and waits in the middle of an open space for them to finish their search. Lisbeth and Chester join us as we wait. After a couple of minutes, they come back to him, gather around, and shake their heads, signaling no survivors were left.

Bull nods and starts walking back into the forest without speaking. I say, "Bull, where are we going?" He looks at me with unexpressive eyes and mutters with his deep voice, "Away from here." He continues walking and his men follow him silently. I stay behind and ponder whether to follow this mysterious man or to try to go ahead and find more followers. However, Dan was very insistent on how important it is to get Bull's support in our endeavor. Against my judgement, I tell Lisbeth and Chester, "Let's go. We need this man's allegiance and it is not safe to stay here." They nod and walk each at one of my sides, looking at Bull's soldiers, attentive to any change that could threaten our safety. I walk with my sight set on Bull, making sure he does not order his men to do something stupid against us.

While we delve deeper into the forest, going northward toward White Tower, I analyze what we just saw. A detail I did recognize was Cold's men's formation when marching toward the flaming town. They were not walking in a block formation or in a disorganized manner; they were marching in a wedge formation with two accompanying circular formations on each side. These men were meant to spot any hazard coming from any flank, while the main formation marched toward their main objective.

This bothers me as Cold's men have trained on a tactical level. Someone has already replaced Ex and has dedicated these past months to improving their battle mentality and preparation. Before this, Cold's men were numbers; now they could be an adaptable specialized army. I catch up with Bull, who is walking in front of his men, and ask, "Have you ever seen Cold's men walk in the same formation they had when entering your town?" He looks down at me, turning his head slightly, and shakes his head. "It is not a common formation during their attacks. They usually charge head on with disregard for their possible losses." His answer troubles me as it confirms my suspicions.

He stares straight up front as he walks, looking ahead through the dark forest, and adds, "Cold has around three hundred and fifty men at his disposal. I believe he has summoned all of them to White Tower these past months, since the influx of soldiers has increased steadily. There have been rumors about an attack on a town of his, far south of here. A man covered in fire killed one of his main supporters and burnt large sections of his stronghold.

Do you know anything about this?" Bull stares straight into me with a sly expression.

I smile and say, "A man named Phoenix did it to save his brother." He grunts, annoyed at my nickname. I explain the truth, "Cold kidnapped my brother and forced him to become one of his soldiers. He fought valiantly every day against torture and humiliation. It took me a long time to track him down and rescue him. In so doing, I was forced to torch several sites at Cold's stronghold. I guess he decided to leave for White Tower with all his men before being victim of a second attack."

He continues walking silently, grabbing his neck with his massive right hand as he thinks. Finally, after a couple of seconds, he comments, "That attack must have alerted him to his weaknesses. The way his men formed up today is unusual. Their style has always been full frontal assault, but now they seem more alert, better trained and adaptable." *Fuck.*

It is time to explain our strategy and make sure he is on board with our mission. I explain, "We have used a Seven-Fold Strategy to train all the villages joining our mission. First, we will lead by example, marching alongside our soldiers. They must feel accompanied during fighting since most have never faced such a challenge. Second, we will group all forces at the waterfall close to White Tower. We must understand the full extent of our forces and our capabilities and align all leaders with our final strategy." He nods, approving the first two points.

I continue, "Third, we have tried untiringly to spark hope. People must believe in our endeavor to stand their ground when faced with adversity. This battle is for our freedom and for that of our relatives, our loved ones, and for the future of humanity. Cold is a plague; he will spread and infect further territories unless we cut it from the root." Bull rolls his eyes and cackles, as he says, "Too literary for my taste, but okay."

I make my eyes turn glaring red and stare at him. He laughs at my unsuccessful try at looking menacing, and I smirk. I continue explaining our strategy, "Fourth, we must appear weak at first. Cold is a proud man who believes himself to be invincible and the best suited man to rule everyone else. We must take advantage of this flaw. Show him a small force, untrained, unprepared, marching to his front door. Our idea is to lure him out of White Tower first; make him believe he is about to viciously destroy those who dared face him up front. Force him to forget formations and training at first; back to his old assault methods." Bull stops and looks at me, finally interested in our strategy. He is silent, looking sideways and in deep thought.

His men halt their advance, and he orders them, "Set up camps!" His voice echoes strongly through the forest, and his soldiers start working immediately in an organized way, setting up tents, building campfires with wood they find scattered around, and searching our perimeter. I am amazed at their incredible preparation, and both Lisbeth and Chester help them work on the camp. Before ten minutes go by, our camp is set up, and our perimeter inspected thoroughly.

In the middle, four piles of wood are spread out, ready to be ignited into campfires. Bull's men grab stones and start crashing them to spark the fires. I sit with Bull in front of the central pile and wink at him. At that precise moment, all four piles ignite, and his men gasp in awe and laugh at my creation. Bull looks at me and shares a deep, guttural laugh. Lisbeth and Chester volunteer as scouts to defend our perimeter first, and I stay behind with Bull to continue explaining our strategy.

He says, "Taking advantage of Cold's ego to make him attack outside his walls sounds clever. Within those walls he is near untouchable, but if we go knocking on his gate with a pathetic army to bait him out, all of this could work. He is more egocentric than a strategist."

I nod as goose bumps race across my body at the possibility of having Bull's support. I continue, "Fifth, once we manage to face a large part of his army outside of his walls, we will divide it. Attack from all fronts, break his center formation, force them to flee in opposite directions and into a trap. Chase them off with a bee swarm right into the lion's den, our full forces attacking together and getting into White Tower. In the best scenario, this should cause a massive blow to his numbers. In the worst case, we will kill a handful of his men and expose ourselves to the largest portion of his army." He sniggers at my cynicism, and the few men who are within earshot laugh at how smoothly I comment on our possible deaths.

I laugh with them and continue, "Don't worry, men, we are one step ahead of our friends and ten thousand steps in front of Cold. Even if a proud man, he is also an intelligent and cautious man, so we have planned how to react as well. Today's formations showed us something changed, and his alertness is at a high level. He is becoming vigilant at the possibility of being confronted by a force that could cause him harm. Probably he will not send all his forces to face us, and he will stay behind his walls with another supporting battalion." Bull's men come closer, no longer pretending not to hear our conversation.

Now that I have their attention, I go on explaining how we intend to finally defeat Cold, "When we face this second threat led by him or his trusted leaders, our sixth step comes to hand. We must seem predictable and take the risk to do what he expects us to do. He might not take the bait, but we deem it necessary to cloud his judgement with enough doubt to believe our initial success was fortuitous and not a consequence of preparation." I get several dozen nods from Bull's men, and he stands up and paces around the fire, grabbing his neck again while thinking.

Finally, I finish my speech, "If he falls into our trap, we execute the seventh and last step of our Seven-Fold Strategy. At that moment in which he fails to value our strategic capacity, we turn back to the unpredictable and unexpected. At that moment we must be extremely adjustable to the battlefield conditions, both geographic and circumstantial. Based on what happens, our armies should react the least expected way to avoid falling head-on into his strike." Bull stops pacing around, having listened to our Seven-Fold Strategy. He looks at me unflinching and unresponsive for a minute or so.

He says with his deep, commanding voice, "We might have a chance." The goose bumps on his forearms give away what his expression is trying to hide, excitement. "There is only one thing stopping me from truly trusting this plan. You." His comment freezes me with fear. I thought we trusted each other after our confrontation and the conversations we have had. Dread takes ahold, as I have shared all our strategies with a man who mistrusts me. Wild thoughts run through my mind about how to take down all these men if they betray us. I stand up and walk closer to him. We stand and glare at each other.

Bull understands my reaction and says serenely, before I do something impulsive, "Don't misunderstand me. You are a leader and an exceptional strategist based on what you shared with us. Besides, you have used your powers and persuasion to raise hope in men and women who have lost everything. The dawn of a new era is becoming tangible, clearer as each day goes on and your forces become larger and better prepared." He manages to calm me down, but I am still confused about his mistrust.

Before I ask, he says, "Nonetheless, I don't trust you to be such a Samaritan. Risking everything, even your brother who you saved back from deep within hell's walls, does not add up for a man such as yourself. Now tell me, what is truly moving you? Where does your determination come from?" His eyes lock dead on with mine, his eyebrows frown, and his lips seal tight. No way of hiding myself from him. Time to lay truth on the open.

I open up to him and his soldiers, "My mother. For seven years I have lived my life to ensure my brother's safety, all by myself. Both of our parents were away when all hell broke loose, and we have not seen or heard a thing about them so far. You might not believe me, but my brother has the power of empathic connection, a sort of mental connectivity." Bull's men make fun of my comment, untrusting, but he stays silent and pays attention.

I disregard his men's reaction and continue, "He has seen how

Cold enslaved our mother. She is dying, and we are not going to stand back and wait for her death. Cold tried to take away my brother from me, and now he is trying to take my mother away forever. As almost everyone has, I have lost a loved one to this world. A piece of my heart was ripped away to never mend. I will not lose anyone else, not before I die fighting." My eyes tear up.

I feel ashamed of sharing my feelings and becoming frail in front of so many people, but I continue, "He will die in a swirl of embers, and I will die with him if necessary. I give you my word, all this is to heal the world from the evil he represents. No one should ever feel again what I felt when my heart was torn out of my chest." Unnoticing, my arms are in flames with my fists clenched at the hatred I feel toward Cold and all he represents. Bull's dark eyes glow with the blue and red dancing flames.

He looks at me unflinchingly and utters, "Do not fail."

***

Five days have gone by since we arrived at Range. Bull has unknowingly taught me about fierceness and resilience as a leader. His men and women are the most enduring I have ever met, walking long distances with no exhaustion. Their precision is also inhuman, achieved by extensive hours of practicing and evaluating their surroundings and the environment's impact on their shots.

I am lying on my blanket, about to get a good night's sleep as today I do not have lookout responsibilities. Lisbeth and Chester are sleeping close to me, and the campfire to my right warms me tenderly. The night is silent, without wind singing through the forest. Through a small hole between the branches above me, I can see the night sky with its blinking stars. Before the world of dreams takes control, I reminisce about our journey up to this point.

Since we started this quest, the world has grown exponentially for me. Meeting hundreds of men and women who have survived hell and adapted to new lifestyles. The only common ground between all the people I have met is fear and hatred toward Cold's evil. He is a widespread and growing disease in the world.

During our march toward the waterfall, we have met numerous towns enslaved or destroyed by Cold. His armies are devastating all that stands in their way, even if harmless. If they don't believe you to be of any worth to them, you and your family will be slaughtered or forced to live under his filthy rule. Such a disgraceful black-and-white mentality.

Everyone we have met on our journey has shared a gruesome story about Cold or his followers. They pillage, rape, destroy, burn, and humiliate those who are not cruelly assassinated. I was honest with Bull; my mother is the driving force in my persistence; but everyone we have met has branded into me the need to eliminate the source of all this suffering.

In the end, how much would my life be worth if I led it selfishly to save one person when I had the chance to save hundreds, maybe thousands? Destiny has granted me powers, and now it has laid in my hands the opportunity to use them for the greater good or hide and disappear into forgetfulness. When I die, hopefully not soon, I wish to be remembered. I wish for Jay to remember me as a man willing to give everything away for the greater good.

Why am I going to risk my life for others? Of course, it is not because I am a benevolent and selfless man. No; the reason is that no one else is going to do it. Bull, Madame Claire, Dan, and Em are all wiser than me and better leaders. They have managed to keep their villagers safe during all these years; yet their mindset is centered on survival and not on resolution. Only I seem to believe a better future can be obtained through sacrifice.

If no one else does it, then maybe I am meant to do so. And if I am not meant to do so, and destiny is a hoax, then why the hell not act, if in the end we will die anyway? People have joined us because we are a dim light in a world of darkness; so, no matter how dim we truly are, they see us as a resplendent alternative to their future.

During these five days we have been joined by seventeen men and women. Their courage comes from their desire for liberty and the memory of those lost under Cold's evil rule. All of them will not witness more suffering without acting; they will not allow anyone else to suffer what they have suffered.

The men and women from Rick's village who were slaughtered taught me what life has unfairly taught our followers: if you don't solve the disease from the root cause, more and more people will fall to it and suffering will occur. This is it. This is the time when we solve the issue or fall ill and die from it, but we will not become sand grains at the beach, forgotten in the immensity of the oceans.

When my thoughts start to blur between consciousness and subconsciousness, I feel a gentle tug on my left arm. A woman from Bull's army looks at me and says with a blushing face, "I am sorry to wake you, Nathan, but Bull needs to talk with you." I smile and nod at her as I get up slowly, trying to wake up. I stand up quickly and get dizzy, missing a step and almost falling on top of this woman. She holds me and laughs, blushing even more at my clumsiness. I apologize and signal her to lead the way.

We walk about twenty meters, and she points at Bull's tent. She holds the entrance for me and I walk in, seeing Bull sitting on a trunk expecting me. I greet him with a raised hand and stand in front of him, on the floor. We are five days away from the waterfall and sixteen days ahead of our schedule. Our plan is to reach it first and secure the surroundings for all our forces. We cannot be found before the time of the assault, as much of our success depends on surprise and unexpectedness. I believe he wants to talk with me about our plans.

He speaks out, "Nathan, please sit down, my friend." He points at a trunk in front of him, and goes on, "Your Seven-Fold Strategy is the only possible road to success. I have dedicated long hours of thought and cannot find an alternative. This does not mean it is flawless; it only means our plan is the least bad possible." He lets an almost silent snort out while keeping a worried look in his face.

I sit down, attentive to what he is about to share. He lights a candle set on a small wooden octagonal table in front of him, and as the flames illuminate his face, he says "To convince Cold to send part of his army to eliminate us outside White Tower's walls we must march to his front gate. However, this frontal assault will not only be a ruse; our front battalion should have a chance to open the gate and continue their progress in case they defeat whoever Cold sends to fight them."

I stare at the dancing flame on the candle while I analyze his comment. He is right. Our frontal assault should not be thought of only as a façade to lure Cold's army out. It should be capable of opening the gate in case they defeat Cold's first assault, quick enough before he sends a second wave. Bull explains, "To do so, we need a ram. A large wooden structure to hammer down his front gate and open his defenses. A doorway to flush all our forces into White Tower. Both you and I know a second battalion will be waiting, hidden in the shadows of the forest, to surprise attack Cold's men when they chase our front battalion during their simulated retreat. Nonetheless, if they succeed and don't retreat, we must ride the tide of battle and rush to the gate, destroy it, and continue our frontal assault."

Bull is smiling, imagining our initial success at the gates of White Tower. His massive fists are closed tightly, and he smirks at the candlelight. I say, "Let's polish our plans, right here, right now." He laughs, stands up, and walks toward a small satchel hanging from one of the tent's columns. He grabs a small roll of old and yellow parchment, an ink pot, and a pen. While raising my right eyebrow I make fun of him, "Did not imagine you're being a fifteenth-century notary." He grunts and laughs at my joke. Bull sets the parchment, inkpot, and pen on the table in front of me and points at the pot saying, "Write, secretary." We laugh and continue planning. I kneel beside the octagonal table and start drawing.

As I draw White Tower's gate and walls extending horizontally on the parchment, he says, "At the same time, whatever the result, two more battalions will be climbing White Tower's walls, one southward from the wall and one northward from it, to cleanse them from archers and open the gates in case the ram fails. Besides, their ladders have to be left ready for the rest of our soldiers to climb if we definitely fail at opening the gates." Bull's idea is genius; we must be ready to do so under unexpected success. I finish drawing our first battalion attacking the front gate with the ram, and our second battalion hidden on the forest behind. He snaps his fingers, wanting me to go faster; I roll my eyes and hold my hand up to make him wait.

I draw our third battalion divided in two groups, one to the left of the front gate and one to the right of the front gate. They go atop White Tower's wall with ladders. I draw without too much detail. I say, finally, pointing at my drawing as I explain each part, "I agree with all that you propose. A frontal assault with Battalion 1 carrying the ram. A simulated retreat into the forest where Battalion 2 will join Battalion 1 to eradicate whatever threat Cold sends to face us. Battalion 1 should be formed up by men from Strength and Valor and led by Em and myself. Battalion 2 will be your men and women, Bull." Bull tries to touch the map with his index finger, but I slap it away as he would make a splotch.

He grabs his hand as a reaction, and we laugh at how weak he looked tending to his index finger. I continue explaining and drawing simultaneously, adding details to the battle map, "Battalion 3, made from men from Stealth and the sixty-two men and women who have joined us from all the other villages, will be hiding in the forests with large ladders. Based on how well we manage to defeat Cold's first wave, they will climb up and rush to the front gate. The north force will be led by Silver and Jay, the south force by Rick." As soon as I say her name in my story he whistles playfully, so I command the candlelight toward his face, making him step back and rumble.

I have told Bull who each one of my co-leaders is. He knows about Rick's village and those he has lost. He knows Jay is my brother and that he was enslaved by Cold, and that Silver helped him survive and has been an amazing support during all this journey. I smirk and continue explaining without looking at him, "If your battalion and my battalion succeed swiftly, we will rush as well toward the front gate with the ram. Either they will open the front gate, or we will smash it to smithereens. Bull, this seems plausible." My heartbeat races at the notion of defeating the largest threat on Earth, as far as we know at least. While repeating our strategy to Bull, I look at our parchment proudly.

I notice I have not drawn a thing beyond White Tower's walls and gate. I ask, "How far is White Tower from the front gate?" Bull narrows his eyes as he tries to remember. A long time has gone by since the last time he entered White Tower as a subordinate to the man he overthrew. That moment in his life was the key to our present. He decided to lead his fellow men and women away from Cold's subjugation. Maybe he will tell me his story one day.

Finally, he answers, "About six hundred meters. As I told you before, Cold will stay close to that filthy tower with his best soldiers. He is not brave hearted, so he will test us out before facing us directly." Bull's words resonate with hatred and a desire to avenge all the suffering Cold caused to him and his followers. He sits heavily back on the trunk, looking as I add White Tower and the distance from the gate.

I turn it around for him to see and add, "After opening the gates, we will march with all of our forces toward White Tower then. At that moment, our battalions will merge to ensure each one has soldiers from Strength, Valor, and Stealth, and archers from Range, with a commanding leader. Our march will be steady but controlled to catch our breaths before our final confrontation. Right there, we will decide how to be unexpected. Only the terrain and battle situation will tell." The last details to the parchment show our final strategy. May our senses be advertent, and all our aims be unerring on that fateful day.

Bull sits silently and grins, looking at me across the candlelight. He has something more to say, I guess. I squint my eyes, trying to guess what this mountain of a man has hidden, and he exposes, "Cold has a sawmill close to here, maybe two days away from our road toward the waterfall. We will assault it to build the ram and both ladders. That is the only place where wood and tools to work it are readily available. The risk of being defeated there is real; maybe Cold has strengthened its defenses, but we must be valiant." Bull's knowledge once more proves essential, and a new challenge arises in our future. Here is where I feel more comfortable, when there is something to overcome.

I smile and make fun of him, "Let's go, carpenter." This time I walk away from him, going back to sleep, having bullied the Bull.

26
THE YOUTH
MARCH

TODAY IS THE DAY WE march to the waterfall, to the beginning of the end. We are a group of more than seventy-five men and women, eager and nervous at the same time. We decide to start our journey in the middle of the night to avoid raising any suspicion from anyone we cross roads with. As we walk past the training grounds, I see the people from Stealth who are staying behind holding torches and humming. *Triumph, triumph, triumph.* They are saying it almost under their breaths, humming from their torsos and making an amazing melody that makes my arm hair tingle.

Some of them are sitting on top of the wooden walls used as defenses, some are peeking out of their camouflaged buildings, and others are standing in front of us, making a light path with their torches. The scene is beautiful and scary. These people could be sending us away to victory or to our deaths. Their lights dance on the forest ground, and shadows are projected on the trees around us. I am walking in front of the group, beside Madame Claire, hand in hand. On her other side, Silver walks wordlessly with Khan beside her. People come forward and smear our faces with dark green and brown paint, each coloring a part of our exposed skin.

As we go past the watch station where we met the people from Stealth, darkness creeps ahead as no more villagers stand ahead of us. Madame Claire whistles softly and sweetly, and those we designated as torch bearers in our battalion ignite their torches. We spread out to walk in three large blocks made of roughly twenty-five people each, one in the back and two in the front. I take the lead of the right block, Silver takes the lead of the left block, while Khan stays behind to lead the back block.

Madame Claire stays behind as her age and health could be a nuisance for everyone, according to her. As the three large groups of people stand silently in the middle of the forest, with our torches dancing the darkness away, she says, "Fellows, I am honored with your courage and willingness to fight against tyranny, against evil, and against the tide. Your fight is not for today, it is to mend the pain from the past and to build a future worth living. I will wait for your return right here, patiently, anxiously, and lovingly. Go make me proud, sons and daughters, friends and family." We all stare at her, my heart racing and goose bumps running across my arms, listening to their leader, our leader, motivate us. *We will make you proud, Madame Claire.*

Silver, Khan, and I go back to our blocks, and start walking in synchrony. As we go northward toward the waterfall, my thoughts take me away from this reality.

Our next seventeen days will be of rough terrain, and we will travel with extreme caution to avoid meeting people and arousing suspicion. We cannot travel heavy, and all horses are left behind, as the road is impossible to ride on. We have trained for thirteen days based on our Seven-Fold Strategy, but the final details of our plan are still unknown to us. Nathan is the one responsible for defining our battle plan, and I am certain he is being extremely cautious and thorough designing it. Some days I have managed to read his thoughts, when he gets excited about our strategy or angered by our enemies, but the images and thoughts are short and sporadic, making it impossible for me to understand what he is doing or where he is.

I have not yet understood how people, including Nate, are able to walk in the forest and avoid getting lost. All trees are similar; there are few path marks and no road signs. Our walk is as silent as seventy-five people can make it. Some branches crunch under the weight of our soldiers, some branches sway against the wind, and some small talk done under breaths can be heard.

Silver and I stayed close to Madame Claire during our training to ensure Stealth's allegiance will not falter when faced with a real threat. Their nature is evident in their actions. The men and women from Stealth are usually silent, walking suspiciously in the shadows with alert eyes, and vanishing every now and then from view. Their attitude and lifestyle feel awry and make me uncomfortable. Are they enemies or friends or something in between?

Of course, it is all in my mind, and probably Silver's. Their actions are based on their survival method, and it does not necessarily have to be a conspiracy theory about treason. Nonetheless, Nathan asked us to stay alert and work constantly to get Stealth to march to the waterfall and fight by our side. He must have a key task for them in the battle. How I wish I could see our future. I am even afraid that we will not meet again.

Nathan must be traveling a similar road to ours. I believe he is accompanied by some new followers whom he did not send back to Stealth because of a time constraint. He must be walking north to the waterfall by now, planning to get there first and greet us as soon as we arrive. I can imagine him smiling with his eyes narrowed because of the mist coming from the waterfall. Nate will have figured out the final details of our plans, and hundreds of men and women will join us there. It will all work out. It had better be that way, or we are all doomed.

As we march, I remember the first days after Nathan's departure from Stealth. They were the most difficult. We constantly heard comments, some meant to be heard and others that reached our ears casually, doubting our endeavor. Why should we face an undefeatable enemy when it does not even know where we are? Why join forces with people who have no idea who we are? One man's power is not enough, no matter how great, to face the largest army in our known world.

Madame Claire, Silver, Khan, and I worked hard to convince those naysayers. There is no undefeatable enemy as there is no undefeatable hero, we said. The reason why Stealth must march, even if it still enjoys anonymity, is that as Cold's claws widen their reach, everything will perish, including them. And when that occurs, they will be the last left, with no one to turn to for aid.

The reason why they must join forces with people who don't know about their existence is that humanity is at risk, not Stealth or Valor or Strength alone. When you donate you don't do it because you personally know every single recipient, but because you wish to act selflessly for the betterment of others and, directly or indirectly, yourself. Well, that last thought was Silver's, and I repeated it constantly since it was very convincing.

Last, their allegation about one man's power and its unlikeliness to overcome an entire army is bullshit. Nathan is not the source of our power, and his fire is just the tip of the iceberg. Our power is built on hope, on the possibility to fight and succeed at eradicating evil from our world. We are walking toward a door, through which lies a better, safer, more prosperous future without a constant death threat. Why wouldn't we open it?

I do not know why I am fighting with them in my mind, since they are already marching. I guess I resent they were not on board and fully committed to our cause before. They could have also helped other people, but they decided to hide and survive themselves instead. I do not like their selfishness, but they did march in the end and are going to be key to our possible victory.

I know what was the straw that broke the camel's back to make them join our cause. It was because of Nathan. As he sent men and women back to Stealth to train with us, people from Stealth comprehended we have a slight chance of winning. The mood in their town shifted drastically. Before their appearance, Stealth had to trust our word about other villages and people who had joined us. With them, they saw it to be true, and they experienced how hurtful Cold is through all their stories of survival. From that day on, everything changed for the better. A painful light.

From then on, training went extremely well. The soldiers from Stealth are professionals and easily understood our plans and tactics. They even trained us in their arts of subtlety and cunning. The forty-five men and women who joined us, sent back by Nathan, though unskilled and lacking battle knowledge, have worked untiringly and incessantly to improve, to learn, to adapt, and to become valuable.

Even after the soldiers from Stealth finished their training, The 45, as we named them, asked Silver and me to train them further. In return, both of us had to train the hardest we have ever trained, even harder than under Ex's cruelty. Endurance training, strength training, stealth training, melee training, even retreating correctly from battles. With each minute of these workouts, our self-confidence and trust in each other solidified.

Today, we march in search of a new tomorrow, into an unwritten history. The ending might be unknown, but God dammit, I feel optimistic. For too long I felt lost, and now I feel my faith coming back. Our footsteps sound like a drumroll of hope. Here we come, Nathan!

***

The road has been treacherous, and our seventy-plus force almost impossible to hide. Stealth is deep inside the jungle, so our advances have been slow. Vines grapple with your feet, roots and mud constantly make you trip and slip, and the heavy mist disorients everyone. We have walked with our three-block formation when the terrain allowed it and spread out when needed.

For thirteen days we have walked and ran and climbed and

descended. For thirteen days my body has suffered aches it has never felt, but we are persevering to reach the waterfall on time and well. We have decided to camp for the night, as the rainfall has stopped, and we are well covered by bushes and trees. We build three campsites about thirty meters away from each other, one for each block of twenty-five soldiers. This way, in case of attack, we are not all together to be surprised and killed quickly; instead, we have two blocks as backup.

I sit next to the campfire, drinking warm coconut water before going to bed. I can see Silver giving orders, probably telling her soldiers who will be working as watchmen during the night. Khan is helping his men set up their campfire, pulling large trunks around for them to sit on and use as cover in case of attack. My camp is already set as my block is extremely efficient, and we have devised a team method to do it quickly. It is sort of a competition between blocks, so we do not share how we do it.

As I see them organizing their blocks, I think about how Silver and Khan have guided us as if reading a map, even though the entire forest looks the same to me. The only changing scenario occurs when we must cross a river. The first one was easy, as Stealth had a tight manila hemp rope crossing from side to side, like the one we crossed with Nathan days ago. The current was strong because of heavy rainfall up the mountain, but all of us managed to cross by holding on to the rope and helping each other. This time I was not close to drowning, so I consider it a success.

The next two rivers were true challenges to all of us. The first of these two rivers we crossed was shallow and about ten meters wide with a moderate current. Nonetheless, the rocks were extremely slippery with sharp edges. Under our feet, the rocks were dispersed, creating small holes where you could easily break a bone. We managed to go through without serious injuries, but twelve of us, including me, slipped and cut ourselves on the edges. Two men had to get stitches as they were losing too much blood from their wounds.

The second of these rivers taught us something key to our mission. Danger is unexpected. The river had a moderate to heavy current and was about twice as wide as the first one, but with rocks peeking out of the water, allowing us to cross safely. We crossed in groups of fifteen, to be able to help each other while having a strong force covering our backs in case of attack. I led the first group and crossed easily. Each group used our same route and managed to cross without mishaps.

The current started to turn darker, tainted with brown dirt. The current was constant and there was a thundering sound coming from upstream, which I did not understand. Silver led the last group. As she started to cross, the water got even darker, and the current started to rise. I screamed for them to hurry, to run across, as something was wrong. She hopped skillfully from rock to rock, followed by fourteen soldiers.

The last one of the group, a skinny lady from The 45, slipped and fell. Silver was already on the shore and went back to help her. I looked upstream as she skipped across to the fallen woman and saw a massive flash flood coming toward us, one hundred meters away. I ordered all our men to run away from the shore and stayed behind screaming at Silver, "Run! Run! Run!" Silver did not even look back at me; she pulled the lady back up on the rocks and started hopping back to our shore. The water, carrying branches and moss, raced toward them, forty meters away. Silver jumped out of the river's way, followed closely by the lady, who had a serious injury on her ankle.

She fell as soon as she touched the ground. I ran as quickly as I could toward them, so Silver and I grabbed the lady and dragged her out of harm's way. By a split second they were able to survive, as the flash flood covered all the stones we had used to cross, and the riverbed widened a couple of meters on each side. It was a close call, and one we have learned from. Sometimes, everything seems normal and safe, but you never know what dangers wait around the corner.

Besides the rivers, we have had to climb steep walls covered in moss and falling water, carefully climb down curving cliffs and through heavy bushes covered in thorns and burning substances. The few of us who left Stealth looking the way men and women looked back before The Day are unrecognizable by now. Mud, blood, sweat, and rags, rather than clothes, cover our bodies. My arms and legs are scraped and bruised, constantly bleeding and aching, but no one ever said changing the world was going to be easy.

The unending rain seems to clean everything around but us. A seventeen-day march through the forest is no child's play, especially when you delve deep to avoid any contact with other human beings. We have had to eat weird birds with funny tasting meat and about two dozen brown mountain rabbits who, unfortunately for them, crossed paths with us.

Yesterday, we saw a mountain lion. A majestic creature walking elegantly through the trees as if it owned them. It barely turned its head to see us before continuing its way, dismissing our presence as if unworthy of its royal gaze. What an amazing creature. If we ever survive this mess we got into, I want to travel around and explore nature. I want to do it with my family. The way that mountain lion walked, freely and securely, is the same way we want people to live. Walking into the forest should not be a risk, but an adventure.

Memory of our mom has given me a strength I did not know. In every slip, cut, fall, bruise, and painful strike, her image has come to mind and made me endure. I know we are doing this for everyone else and seeking for a better future for humanity, but how difficult it is to truly care for those whom you don't know. In my heart, all my effort is for my mother. She is the guiding light in my journey, and all others are worthy, respectable, and enjoyable companions.

This I have shared with no one. I am supposed to be one of the leaders, and yet I don't feel attached to the main cause. How could someone risk their lives for others, even for people who are not even born? I am afraid of death, of entering that eternal dim room were nothing makes a sound or can be seen. A place of no return is as haunting as the evil I witnessed from Cold.

Time to go to bed. I spread my blanket next to the fire, roll my towel to use as a pillow, and cover myself with my heavy sweater. The burning twigs of the fire creak and soothe me out of thinking about death. *Good night, big brother. See you soon!*

***

We have arrived at the waterfall a couple of hours before dawn, right on schedule. The waterfall is about six hours away from White Tower's main gate. It is the best place to hide, but the worst place to be. We walk from the south toward what looks like a cliff. As we reach the edge, I notice that the waterfall is deep down a steep downhill terrain, about a hundred meters down from where we stand, hidden by a dense forest, and surrounded by slippery rocks and moss-covered dead branches.

We start walking down the hill, holding hands in three lines, stepping carefully with our feet sideways, trying to avoid slipping. Khan, Silver, and I lead each line, walking in parallel without uttering a word. As we approach it, the thundering water deafens us, and the mist becomes blinding. The humidity is extreme here, as the water raises a constant mist. About ten meters behind me, a man slips but is caught by the woman in front of him. His loud scream seemed a muted whisper from my position. We all laugh at him, lightening the mood.

I understand why this is our meeting point. The steep terrain and dense forest are the best cover for our forces. The heavy sound of water crashing violently against the dark blue pond mutes all the noise we cause. Last, the waterfall has at least four ways to be reached or escaped from. We are going down its south entrance, but it also has a steeper entrance behind it, due north, and two bending exits to our right and left that go into the forest. In case we are found, we can run away from peril or try to surround it before it alerts others. Of course, it also means we can be surprise attacked from any of our four flanks.

We have arrived on the day we agreed with Nathan, Dan, Em, and Rick, yet no one has arrived. We finally reach the bottom of the hill and start searching around to ensure we are alone. We are alone.

Our men and women from Stealth are getting nervous, anxious, and even angry. Some are speaking loudly to each other, some are throwing their stuff on the ground angrily, and others are glaring at Silver, Khan, and me. We are gathered right at the edge of the pond, looking back at them.

A couple of men approach us, and one starts demanding answers, "Was it all a ruse? Are we the only ones who are fighting against Cold?" The other one steps closer to Khan, confronting him and saying, "We are leaving right now before we are found and slaughtered!" Khan steps closer to him and faces him with hatred in his eyes. "Step down, boy, or you will be the first death to be mourned." The two men look at each other, deciding whether to attack or stand down.

I step between them in a hurry, as Silver steps closer in case we need to intervene. I try to calm them down, "Look, men. We established today as the day to meet with all our forces. The day ends at midnight, so if after that no one has arrived, you are welcome to leave. We will stay and wait for the army we have assembled, the army of brave men and women who are not scared of facing Cold. If you are afraid, leave, but do it after midnight." Both men look at me and blush, Khan grins, and Silver places a reassuring hand on my right shoulder. After a couple of tense seconds, they walk away to talk with the rest of Stealth's soldiers. The 45 seem to be on board with us, ignoring Stealth's possible betrayal.

As soon as they leave, Khan taps my back and says heatedly, "You know they are right. What if we were left alone by your brother? What if Dan's forces were unable to survive the journey? What if my fellow villagers died because of this desperate attempt?" Silver frowns, and I ask her empathically, *"Do you think our doubts are true?"* Khan had long, private talks with Madame Claire before she appointed him in command. Silver and I are doubtful if he shifted his allegiance.

Silver pulls him by his shirt to make him turn toward her, as she answers, "Shut the fuck up. You are a coward if you are not willing to believe in our mission. You are invited to leave as well at midnight." Before he answers, Silver grabs my arm and pulls me away from him. He looks at us angrily, his nostrils flaring and his gaze menacing.

Silver and I walk toward a large stone on the other side of the pond and sit down, staring at the waterfall. She pulls me closer to her, and we sit silently, looking up and down the flowing water.

What happened to everyone? We are only seventy-five strong, while Strength and Valor together sum up ninety soldiers. Without them we are sitting ducks; we are like fish in a barrel with a waterfall to muffle any sound. Silver seems to be under control, expecting everyone to arrive soon. I am the opposite; my anxiety is killing me.

Where is Nathan? Our mission's success depends heavily on his leadership and power. He has been able to ignite hope in all our followers, but it will not burn forever. If he does not arrive soon, we will soon suffer desertions and maybe uprisings. The harsh place where we wait will only quicken the collapse of our initiative.

I stand up and start pacing by the pond, feeling the dew from the waterfall in my face. Silver stands and walks back to a tent our soldiers are setting up. She is taking the lead to listen to them and reassure them we have hours left before we must start growing worried. It relaxes me to watch the waterfall, smell the humidity, and feel the mist wash my body. This is the only soothing moment before I go back to worrying. The condensed drops are sliding down my nose, over my lips, and into my shirt, tickling me. Behind me, people start screaming wildly, and my nerves shoot back to their maximum.

Arrows start to fall on the men and women who are twenty meters behind me. Enemies must have found us! Running as quickly as my feet carry me, I grab my shield and bow and arrows that are lying next to the tent. All the missiles seem to be coming from the same direction, the same hill we came from. I can see them.

A group of about thirty armored soldiers are spread out, walking halfway down the pathway to the waterfall. Some of our men and women manage to fight back with their arrows and spears, hurting several of our attackers. Our problem is they have the higher ground and the surprise factor. One arrow, two arrows, three arrows, and only one hit. My aim is off, my trembling limbs and blurry vision screwing up my chances.

Silver gathers about a dozen of our soldiers and starts running deep into the forest to my left. She will try to go behind our attackers and end their attempt to defeat us. They vanish through the trees, but her advance will take far too long before she manages to encircle our foes. Her attempt reduces targets for our enemies and increases the arrows raining down on me and those closest to me.

Ahead of us, Khan is leading a frontal assault with about thirty men with their shields up, but their advance is slow as the steep hill is slippery and treacherous. Their feet slip and sink in the deep mud. One of them trips on a root and slides a couple of meters behind the group. An arrow trespasses his thigh, and his desperate scream alerts us this is no drill.

Another arrow pierces his chest, and one cuts deep into his throat. Blood comes gushing out of both wounds, and his scream is forever silent. Khan watches him fall and orders his men to continue. Everything seems to be in slow motion now, my heartbeat hammering in my eardrums. Even the waterfall seems to have fallen silent, and the rainfall creates a backdrop effect.

What are we doing? Men and women dying because of our attempt to save our mother. People are suffering and scared. The soldiers from Stealth are acting professionally as usual, fighting back with all their skill and strength. They are leading the soldiers who joined us to ensure our numbers don't break because of chaos and fear.

This makes me aware of my place in the battle. So far, I have been afraid and immovable under this attack. My inactivity is only going to cause further deaths. It is time for me to act and lead; it is now or never.

I order, "Come to me, archers. Form up a line; soldiers, protect the archers. Shield wall!" My scream sounds more commanding than I imagined it would be. About eight archers rush toward me and the rest of our soldiers form a circular protectory shield wall. We start shooting back at them, managing to inflict damage and forcing them to retreat. This allows Khan and his men to advance faster, as the aerial threat diminishes.

Khan orders his men to break their shield wall as soon as they are about thirty meters away from our enemies, and all our soldiers run toward them. We shoot a volley of arrows to halt their retreat. The few remaining enemies try to run back uphill or into the forest. They have a head start on Khan's men, who are fighting strongly to keep their run going on the harsh terrain. Some of them are going to escape, and I fear they are going to blow our cover.

Silver and her Stealth group appear behind them coming out of the shadowy forests, blocking their retreat. Their attack is swift on our enemies; I can see their swords slashing down on the running enemies. Some of them try to go back downhill and are met by Khan's group. The mist makes it difficult to distinguish clearly, but it seems likes most of our foes perish. Only one or two survived, standing down and lowering their weapons.

We have defeated them! However, we have fallen men and women. I order my soldiers to find the injured and stand beside them with one raised arm, so that our medics can tend to them quickly. I walk toward the hill and see we have soldiers down, either dead or severely injured by arrows. Their moans are heartbreaking, as they ask for forgiveness or help. One, two, three soldiers raise their hands beside fallen soldiers. About fifteen in total stand in my way asking for help.

The few with medical expertise or knowledge run around the battlefield, breaking arrows, using tweezers and nippers while trying to extract metal heads from their wounds. All around me I see pain, but at the same time I see love and caring for those down. As I walk, I see a man lying to my right, unattended. I stand beside him, raise my hand, and help him sit up with my left hand. He reclines against a large rock and holds me tightly. I say, "I am here for you, friend," and he stares at me and nods slowly, frowning with pain and breathing unevenly.

Silver and Khan walk down the pathway toward us. They are each holding an arm of a surviving enemy. He has an arrow sticking out of his right side, just under his armpit. The rest of our soldiers walk behind them, picking up the arrows and bows of our fallen enemies, and carrying all bodies down toward the waterfall. One is leading a horse and ties it down at the end of the path; it must have been the horse of whomever led our enemies.

Silver and Khan toss the man in front of me. Silver grabs him by his vest and pulls violently while demanding answers, "Who are you and why have you attacked us?" Her voice sounds menacing and unforgiving. Her fist strikes the man's jaw, and her foot pushes his chest, making him fall on his back. The man's eyes look around nervously, knowing his death is soon to come. He is no general or commanding officer, he is a simple soldier. A medic finally comes to attend our fallen soldier.

The enemy mutters under painful gasps, "I am just a soldier. We were on a regular scouting mission, checking the surroundings of our city. We usually come down here for a swim, to relax for a while before going back to report. We happened to spot you, and our officer ordered us to fan out and start shooting arrows. I am truly sorry! Please, don't kill me! I was just following orde—" His voice breaks before ending the sentence, and large tear drops fall down his cheeks and blend with the muddy water beneath his resting head.

Khan shouts, "Fuck you!" while raising his sword. Silver stands in front of him and stops him. "You know, he could be of importance for our plans. He will soon die for his misdoings, but not yet." Khan stares at Silver and then walks away. She stares at me and nods the way she always does to calm me down.

She uses her more subtle and conniving voice. "Now, let's have a talk," she says, pulling him by the arrow in his side. His scream breaks the silence of the night as he is forced to a stand. He limps beside her slowly, until they reach a low cot. She makes him lie down, face up, and wait for medical help. She will interrogate him further while I continue helping our injured soldiers. A bad start for our mission. We need Nathan. We need an army.

***

It must be close to midnight, and no one has arrived. We have been here seven or eight hours, and the only fucking thing happening was an attack that left nine dead soldiers and a captured asshole. Our men and women have been busy tending to our injured, but their restlessness is growing again, and I fear they will soon defect. The captured man has been of almost no help to us. He answers with evasive comments and grunts at his arrow wound. We have tended to his wounds to postpone his death, but he seems resolved to die without ratting out Cold.

His initial fear and spectacle were a scam. As soon as we got the arrow out of him, cleansed his wound, and sewed it closed, he stopped talking. He used us to get cured and then stopped, caring only for his well-being. The man seems to understand we are not a warring faction, or a violent group of people willing to torture him or kill him painfully for information. His constant inspection of everyone frightens me; he must be counting how many of us there are, how strong our forces, and where and how to escape. My powers have been of no use, as his mind is shut.

I am exhausted and afraid. Nothing has gone as planned. Silver walks toward me, where I sit illuminated by the fire light next to the pond. She says, "Go to sleep, Jay. I will stay awake for a while, until Khan comes to change the watching shift with me." Her voice is interrupted by a loud shout, "He is getting away!" I stand up hurriedly, making my head dizzy. The moonlight illuminates the man running sluggishly toward the hill.

He grabs the horse, releases his noose, and painfully manages to get on top of him. The gallop uphill is impossible to catch up for us. Silver and I run desperately, readying our bows in case we manage to stop him. He is getting away from us, with all the intel about where we are, how many we amass, and our armory. This man has fooled us since the beginning; he was the captain of the attacking group. Our arrows fall embarrassingly short. Fools.

Silver and I run as quickly as possible uphill, watching him outrun us easily. Arrows swoosh above us and fail to strike him. His silhouette, riding under the moon, dimmed by the forest shadows, rushes away from us, escaping back to his master. He reaches the top of the hill and vanishes from our view. We have failed, and now Cold will come here with all his forces to pursue us, as we flee back to our hometowns defeated.

Silver and I run exhausted to the top of the hill, our enemy already running away far ahead, barely a silhouette. Once more, as our hope fades away into obscurity, a light illuminates the night sky. A volley of flaming arrows illuminates a parabolic path. The night lights shine on our eyes. A miracle of some sort is happening. Could it really be an ally attacking the fleeing man? Or is it another attacking group?

Fear and hope clash within me, and I grab my arrow and bow just in case. I walk toward the source of the flaming arrows, almost three hundred meters ahead, holding the arrow resting on my fully elongated bow. A silhouette, taller than the one escaping, walks through the night toward us. I point my bow at him and jog alongside Silver. The silhouette seems to be pulling something. I scream, "Show yourself or we will shoot!" He continues walking toward us, ignoring my command. We jog faster, ready to attack in case it is the escapee. His hand is outstretched and pulling something heavy with a handful of lights protruding from what he is pulling. They look like burning arrows on a body.

Each step closer shows Silver and me a tranquilizing image. Nathan is walking to us, holding the dead man with two piercing, ignited arrows on his back. He releases the dead body as soon as he spots us in front of him. I lower my bow and arrow, running excitedly toward him. It's a miracle. I cry happily, and Silver runs past me toward my brother.

Nate says, "Did you lose something?" His grin illuminates more than the moonlight.

27
THE ELDER
ONE

PERFECT TIMING. ONLY SILVER, MY brother, and Stealth have arrived, and they were victims of a surprise attack. Thankfully, we were able to catch the fleeing enemy. If our cover were blown, all our plans would have to be thrown away and redrawn from scratch. Maybe we would be forced to retreat and live to fight another day. The moonlight was an ally tonight, as spotting him in the darkness could have been nearly impossible.

Bull and I and our forty-two companions were delayed because of our carpentry needs. Cold's sawmill was heavily guarded, and the battle was brutal. We lost fifteen men during our attack; this mission turns more real and more heartbreaking as we advance. We buried them and gave them a proper ceremony. Jay told me we lost soldiers to the surprise assault. Courageous men and women should not be the ones lost in this endeavor; Cold should be the only one to suffer. He will, soon enough.

Every one of them will be remembered. This is not a saying, it is real. The moment we saw those floating, massacred bodies back at the beach, I understood the road ahead of us would be filled with suffering. Since then, I have insisted that every single one of our soldiers must build bonds of friendship and unity with the others. This includes getting to know who your fellow men and women were before The Day, who they are now, and who they want to be once we succeed.

Everyone who has fallen is lovingly branded in the memory of our surviving members. Their deaths will only boost our desire to go on and to create a world that allows all those visions of a better future to be true. I will not play the magnanimous, legendary leader here. I suffer within and constantly feel ashamed and afraid of having led these people to their death.

In my mind, turning around and fleeing is always an uncomfortable possibility that will not fade. However, on the outside I project all the confidence, power, resilience, and trust I can muster. They constantly look up to me to find guidance and hope. Finally, I understand those amazing leaders from history and what it truly means to be an icon. I wish I studied them more before this moment, to learn from them, and to be a better leader.

As a leader, you are not perfect, you are probably the most afraid and doubtful, but you walk with your head up high and speak about a future at arm's reach. You show a brick façade even though behind it a weak base feebly holds your inner strength. No one would understand. Death because of your own actions changes you deep down. It's a responsibility tainting your heart with pain, forever.

The surviving members of Sil's and Jay's army change their expressions as soon as we walk downhill toward their camp. They cheer silently to avoid being heard, and their eyes glitter with hope once more. Bull marches heavily behind me, ordering his men how to go downhill with our equipment. The battering ram and both enormous ladders spark hope in our mission. Jay's soldiers run uphill to help them, working together. A unison of helping hands.

A plan laid in front of them was all they needed to be fully committed. I am sorry for taking so long to get here and for being unable to devise this plan sooner, but now we are ready. We must wait for Strength and Valor, and the time to execute has arrived. Silver, Jay, and I walk toward the campfire set next to the pond.

Our soldiers set the battering ram and ladders down and walk toward me, while the ones closer to me start waking others up to gather around.

I command the campfire to grow and illuminate us better. I say, "For now, we are going to bury and celebrate the lives of the fallen men and women. We will not light up fires as a precaution; however, praying, chants, and speeches are encouraged. All of us need to feel safe to be ourselves in this world, since this fight is destined to allow us to be ourselves once more." Men and women nod, while others gasp through their cries.

As the medics scatter around to bring the corpses closer, dozens of soldiers start digging the nine graves. Jay, Silver, Khan, Bull, and I help them, dirtying our hands to honor those who gave their lives. The burial also serves another purpose. Bull and the soldiers from Range need to interact with Khan and Stealth's soldiers. Cohesion is a key to success. A fight led by leaders who don't know each other, who don't work together, and who don't respect each other is doomed to fail, becoming like Cerberus, a three-headed mess.

Sharing this pain works to solder our bonds. Our efforts point at the same direction, and all those who have died are watching us from wherever they are, chanting for our perseverance and victory. We work hard, sweating, sharing the pain on our hands as we dig deeper together.

Finally, we set the bodies inside their resting grounds, and cover them, working together. As I stand and see all our soldiers covering the bodies, I notice how beautiful this place is. The waterfall to our left, the forest to our right, and the northern entrance ahead.

The slow, muffled chants blend with the whispered prayers and the waterfall's resilient splash, creating an ambiance of tranquility. The moonlight reflects off the pond and the rising mist moistens our weary faces. Beauty covering pain, and resilience built through cohesion.

***

The sunrise is creeping on the horizon and nothing preoccupying happened at night. Most of our men and women managed to rest after our ceremony. None decided to leave, as I pleaded with them to wait just one more day. The few who wake up and rise with me grant me a welcome surprise. Villagers from Range and Stealth cook and eat together, as if they had known each other for a long time. Teamwork, humor, friendship, and selflessness are a welcome sight to my spirit.

The sun rises further, and its warmth showers all of us. The mist crashes with the sunrays and small rainbows can be seen all around us. Smiles become frequent on our soldiers; even Bull seems to be less uptight than his usual self. He is cooking some fish on a casserole next to the pond, and Silver and Jay are eating together on a small table next to him, laughing the way they are meant to. I walk toward them with that breathtaking feeling of awe and excitement.

I kiss my beautiful Silver and give her a good morning hug with all the love I share with her. I bump Jay's hanging fist and mess with his hair, which is desperately needing a wash. The breakfast is amazingly delicious, refreshing, and strengthening. The mood all around could not be better. The sun heats us as the mist cools us down.

A man, one of our scouts, comes rushing down the hill right next to the waterfall, the one opposite from the one where I arrived last night. Most of the heads turn to see what is happening, and some worry comes back to their gazes. People stand up and run to get their shields, swords, bows, and arrows ready. Small groups start forming up with their shields raised and arrows ready. Silver runs back to one of the groups to our right and stands behind the shield wall. Jay goes hurriedly to get his bow from his belongings. Bull stands in front of me, protecting me, and waiting to see what is happening.

The man slips and falls heavily on the mud but gets himself

up and continues his race. He is looking for me, so I stand up on the log where I was sitting for him to find me more quickly. He dashes through the people readying for battle, even jumping over the few sleepy heads who have not woken up. He says, "Sir! Good news, they have arrived!" The man's comment confuses me, as I had expected bad news.

I don't understand, so I ask, "Who?" He smiles and breathes heavily, trying to catch his breath. He was instructed to give me any news, before communicating it to anyone else. How he managed to run without shouting enthusiastically the news he has brought, escapes me. As he mumbles, "The rest of our forces have arrived!" I scream at the top of my lungs, using my most comprehensible voice to be heard by everyone, "Our army is complete!"

Everyone lowers their shields and cheers, deservedly. No need to mute our enthusiasm. The time has finally come, and joy can be felt from body to body, from eye to eye, and from smile to smile. What an amazing day. It must be written down in history, since days like this when hundreds of people join in a common cause and a common feeling rarely occur. I lead the run toward the northern entrance and stand at the edge of the hill, waiting for our soldiers to arrive.

As if coming straight out of the sun that is still rising over the mountaintop, dozens of singing men and women start their descent toward us. They are marching in formed up lines, with their faces illuminated with cheerfulness. They sing in synchrony, "The day to change the world has come; ahoy, ahoy, ahoy; all who stand shall fear our stride; ahoy, ahoy, ahoy; the night will end, and light arrive; ahoy, ahoy, ahoy." Their song leaves me petrified in ecstasy.

Valor, the village with the least battle preparation, marching organized and chanting a war cry sends a couple of tears streaming down my cheeks. Strength joined them and their unison, both marching and singing, is the most welcome sight I have ever seen in my life.

I send a fury fire burst toward the waterfall, breaking the stream and causing steam to rise. The fumes blend with the mist and cover our allies' stride in a fortuitous beautiful scene. The time to change the world has come. They walk down to us, Rick, Dan, and Em leading them.

Bull, Silver, and Jay stand beside me to greet them. As soon as they reach us, everyone scatters around, and we hug and celebrate. I can hear laughter all around and cheers excite me. I hug Rick and Dan amicably, smiling widely at them. Silver and Jay are talking hurriedly with Em, who is probably telling them about their journey. Behind us, soldiers from all villages are getting acquainted, laughing, shaking hands, hugging, and conversating loudly.

Bull stands silently beside me, as if protecting me, but his eyes are glinting with excitement. He walks toward Dan and hugs him softly while speaking in his ear. Dan looks at me proudly and then nods while staring at Bull. I walk toward them, and Dan places an arm on each of our soldiers. He says, "Let's change the world, my boys."

As our initial excitement passes, we walk back toward our camps. Our new arrivals find places to set their cots and weapons to rest after a long walk. We are finally assembled, our complete army ready to march on our enemies and change the world. Watching our entire force has fueled our hope, my hope particularly. During our journey, at times I have doubted myself and the probability of success. Now, feeling the mood, looking at everyone's gaze, smiles, and energy has me convinced. It is now or never.

Rick, Em, Khan, and Bull will be frontline leaders. Silver, Jay, and I will be leading alongside them, focusing on strategic cohesion and soldier morale. Dan preoccupies me as his health might not withstand the batter of battle. The trip has taken a toll on his body, but his stubbornness would never allow him to sit this one out. For now, before we part to our destiny, we must polish our plan, communicate it to all of them, and allow the information to trickle down to our entire army.

When the battle erupts, I know plans and drawings will be fiction. The reality of conflict will allow us to use them as guidelines but believing everything will stick to a plan written during peacetime is believing you will not drown by learning to swim from a book. I ask them to join me inside our main tent, located twenty-five meters away from the pond.

They sit down on the logs we have set around a small table and look at me as I stand up behind them. I say, "Welcome, everyone. I am joyful at the sight of all our men and women gathered, bonding and preparing to fight for humanity. Our march will be one written in history books if we succeed. If we fail, Cold will bury our memories in his deepest resentment and hide it from the world. You see, hope works like ashes, it can be fed and strengthened by an almost imperceptible wind blow. Let us succeed." They applaud, Silver winks at me playfully, and Jay closes his fist at me.

I smile and continue, "Bull and I have devised a plan, and now we ask for your wisdom to polish it and have it ready to execute. Our Seven-Fold Strategy is based on leading by example, grouping all our forces, and believing in ourselves. Those first three points are our responsibility, those gathered here today. The fourth point consists of appearing to be weak and arousing our enemy's self-confidence to divide his forces, our fifth point. Once the first hammer strike hits the anvil, Cold will regroup his forces and become wary. At that moment, our sixth step is to change tactics and seem predictable once more." All of them nod, acknowledging their understanding. After all, it is not the first time they are hearing our strategy.

Bull looks at me, expectant for the moment when I share our new details. I proceed, "By doing so, Cold will make the mistake, once more, to believe we are not a threat to him. His poise will be his doom, as at that moment our seventh and last step will end him: become unexpected. He is not a talented tactician, barely a consequential one, and his success has relied exclusively on extreme force and fear. We need to expose him by being clever and adaptable." My introduction seems to touch each one of our leaders in different ways.

Dan stares at me with sure and supporting eyes, as if he could nod without moving his head. Rick is barely controlling his urge to avenge his loved ones, tapping his right foot incessantly on the ground. Em's jaw is clenched shut with raging eyes riled up with hatred and excitement to go to war. Khan is listening closely, mysteriously, and hiding most of his thoughts behind a poker face. Bull stands menacing beside me, supporting every word with grunts, nods, and approving comments. Silver is thoughtful, trying to find any loose end to our plan. And last, Jay, my brother, seems to have understood his role. He is staring straight at me, unmovable, repeating key aspects of the plan to himself to memorize them.

Jay asks, "How are we going to do all of this, exactly? Your words are still abstract, aren't they?" Showing once more his age in his words. That need to know everything as soon as possible. There is no way of convincing him to stay behind, even if my heart is on the verge of shredding at the possibility of losing him. Jay wants to fight for mother and for humanity, finally embracing his place.

I say calmly, "Patience, Jay. At the battlefield, sometimes being patient and analyzing context will allow us to adapt and overcome the continuously changing challenges ahead." He lowers his head, slightly embarrassed, but quickly raises it to continue paying attention. A childish reaction followed by a mature decision. I take the yellow rag with our devised plan out of my satchel and place it on the table. All of them lean forward to look at it.

I start explaining while pointing the map, "Step one. Battalion 1 led by Em and me will march toward the front gate with our battering ram. This is when we should seem unprepared and weak to lure Cold's army away from White Tower. Our formation will be an inverted U shape, covering the ram; we will look disorganized and unprepared to fuel our enemy's misplaced confidence. We will be a mix of front assault soldiers from Valor and Strength, and archers from Range.

"Cold will probably order a large first wave of soldiers to eliminate us swiftly. At that moment, we simulate a retreat to the forest, leaving our ram behind. Bull and Battalion 2, or B2, composed of archers from Range and whoever boasts of being a good shot, will rain an incessant attack on our pursuing enemies. We need you to start crafting those arrows tonight, Bull. Let's cover the sky with a swarm of death." Bull nods subtly.

I continue pointing to the right and left of my map, "Simultaneous to our surprise attack, Battalion 3, or B3, will initiate a climbing attack on White Tower's walls. All the soldiers from Stealth, and the sixty-two men and women from all the other villages, will be hiding in the forest with the large ladders we built. The north force will be led by Silver and Jay, and the south force will be led by Rick and Khan. Same strategy executed in two places at the same time. We need precision here." Rick, Silver, and Jay look at each other and smile. They are pleased to know their role. Khan seems uncomfortable but keeps his doubts to himself.

Dan comments, "You should not worry about me, Nate.", His soothing voice sends shivers down my back; he knows. "You are trying to keep me safe by leaving me behind, but that is not your responsibility or your decision, my friend. I will go to war and remind this old body of its golden youth days. I will die holding a sword, or shooting an arrow if necessary, with a leer on my face and optimism in my heart. Thank you for your valiant try, but sorry for your pitiful failure." He laughs with a warm tone and a gaze filled with decision, giving that belly laugh only old, large men have.

Laughing at how easily he saw through my plan, I accept his role and say, "You read me as clear as a stale summer lake, Dan. For days I have pondered on your role because of your health, but as you say, it was never my decision. Please join Em and me at B1. Marching alongside you will be a pleasure and an honor, my friend." Still feeling dread at the possibility of losing such a wise and genuine man, I agree to his wishes. The world needs more men like him, not to lose them. I push Bull with my elbow, as it is time for him to finish laying out our plan.

He slaps my head teasingly and continues with his imposing voice, "B3 will climb the walls, north and south from the front gate, and rush toward it. Your utmost responsibility is to eliminate all archers standing on top of the walls who could attack B1 and B2. By the time you succeed and arrive back at the front gate, turn your bows inward toward White Tower. Avoid their second wave that will try to reach the gate in time to protect it again. B1 and B2 will have defeated the first wave and advanced to destroy the gate with the battering ram." Rick speaks to Khan inaudibly and he nods. Jay seems more relaxed now that he knows he will be leading alongside Silver.

Bull adds, "If they destroyed the ram we left behind in our initial retreat, you will have to open the gates. The mechanism is unknown to all of us, but in that scenario our success rests on your hands. Work together, be extremely cautious of the perils on top of the wall and run as quickly as your enemies allow you to without unnecessary risks." The plan is laid on the table, both in words and on the yellowish rag I have been carrying.

No opposition is heard from the destiny-picked leaders around me. Seconds turn into minutes while I'm waiting for a word to be muttered, doubt to be expressed, or an improved plan to be devised. This is what we will do and succeed at. Silence turns into laughter and hope-filled delight. We are at the threshold of destruction or freedom for humanity. The pages of history are waiting to be written.

Rick speaks out, "Once we enter, what then?" His question is inspiring as he assumes we are going to succeed. I answer, "We only know White Tower stands close to six hundred meters from the front gate. We suspect Cold will have stayed behind with his best and largest force. Bull has not entered White Tower in years, so the exact layout beyond the front gate is unknown." All sit back to listen intently.

I continue, "Before marching to our final confrontation, our battalions will merge. Each leader will have men and women from Strength, Valor, Stealth, Range, and free villages under his or her command. First, we catch our breaths and reignite hope in our men, then we march straight to that filth of a man." Rick seems dubious of my answer; however, that is the only one he will be receiving today. No one has managed to enter White Tower and leave, so our eyes will decide what to do next at that moment, and not a second sooner. No previous planning will work, as it would be like drawing on a black cloth with a black marker.

I conclude our meeting by saying, "May our senses be advertent, and our aims be unerring on that fateful day, my friends." I extend my right hand palm down, and one after the other, they place one hand on top of another. Bull rolls his eyes and places his massive hand last. Fire covers them in a binding swirl, the final Fire Pact. All our eyes sparkle at the luminescent flames, and our hearts fill with rage and readiness. Bull, although displeased at the cliché, laughs at being finally forced to do what he menaced me to avoid. Each one joins in laughter.

The day after tomorrow, a new beginning will be written. The day to change the world has come; ahoy, ahoy, ahoy.

28
THE YOUTH
THE REALITY OF WAR

THE SOUND OF TWO HUNDRED men and women walking through the forest is unreal, as if the world of dreams becomes reality. The leaves crumbling at the weight of footsteps, the mud sounding squishy, the branches being broken, and the heavy breathing. Oh, the heavy breathing gets my nerves up. Some of our soldiers are excited, ready for war, while some others are nervous, crying silently, trembling, with goose bumps on their forearms and grieving faces. I feel more like the second type than the first. A void in my stomach and cold shivers on my neck and back. Silver leads the group, and I walk at the back of our battalion.

We could easily be marching to all our deaths. Swift, violent, and irreversible deaths. Cold will not forgive anyone who dares stand in his way. He kills with complete disregard for human life, just as he did to the old man who was not chosen by his henchmen back when I lived inside hell. The brand on my forehead and Silver's will always remind us of what waits ahead if we fail. We could all be treated like trash, disposed of once Cold overpowers us. That is what those heavy breaths and gasps represent and hiding them has proven impossible for some of us.

We packed everything early in the morning and worked

together to raise the ram and ladders and take them uphill. The sunny morning dried the mud just enough for us to walk without sliding. So many men and women marching in the same direction, ready to do what it takes. I guess we will not be completely sure about our commitment to this cause until we reach White Tower. The moment one of us dies, this will become real. I only hope I am not the first to die. I know it is selfish to think so, but I cannot shake that idea off.

Instead of allowing all my nerves to poison my heart, I am trying to consciously grasp my responsibility here. When we were attacked by surprise, my actions might have saved several of our men and women. The moment I took the reins, no one else died around me. We fought together and succeeded as a unit. When we work as individuals, we die; that's the simple and heartbreaking truth.

We have walked for two hours now, always going west toward White Tower. Four more hours to go and my nerves are sky high and doubtfulness constantly clouds my judgement and resolve, but outside I project confidence. Some of those eyes moving quickly from person to person, seeking assurance, land on my own in despair. At that moment, I cannot fail these people, least of all at this moment when their life rests at the edge of the abyss. A place of no return.

I walk toward a man twice my age whose entire body shivers as tears fall down his cheeks. He is holding a sword feebly with a white hand lacking blood because of his tight grasp. His other hand is dragging a wooden, decadent shield, barely strong enough to protect him from one single arrow. He looks at me and blushes at his fear, trying to hide his face under his ragged clothes and drying his tears desperately with his shirt collar.

I pull on his shirt and say, "Why do you think it is shameful to be afraid, sir?" A dozen heads turn around, others are listening without turning, and the man trying to hide his true feelings looks at me. I continue, "Fear is human, and we are marching to save humanity, so why should you, or I, or any of us, hide our humanity?" More heads turn around, and all the unit marching with Silver and me halts.

The man mumbles, "Are you afraid, my young leader?", He no longer cries but sobs every now and then. I give him a trembling smile and answer, "To be honest with you, I believe I am the most afraid in all of our battalion. Hell, in all of our army!" Some laughs lighten up the mood, including the man, who no longer exudes fear. He stares directly at my forehead brand. I take advantage of this and share, "Yes, as you can all see, I was captured by Cold along with Silver. We know how scary he is, we know what waits ahead if we fail. But we won't." Silver walks back toward me and stands beside me, listening and looking around at our soldiers.

I blush and continue, "We are marching to war, even if soldiers have not existed for so long. However, are soldiers made from a training lifestyle? Or are soldiers truly made from adversity demanding common men and women, with or without training, to stand up for themselves and those who they love?" Silence surrounds me, accompanied by nodding heads and reassuring glances. Silver winks at me and pats me on the back to go on.

I raise my voice to its loudest, "We are Battalion 3, and we will be marching with an enormous ladder, directly into the, probably, tallest wall in the world. Our task is to climb it and run toward a gate to be opened. God dammit, it sounds fucking scary!" The numerous people holding the ladder start moving it up and down, celebrating my comments.

The large man who no longer cries raises me on his shoulders for everyone to see me. I shout, "Sure, we can be scared, we can doubt if it is possible and have a second thought regarding the correctness of what we are marching to do. No one in this army is expected to be incorruptible and fearless. If you were that type of being, you wouldn't be fighting for those you love, because you wouldn't even care if they live or die. Being corruptible and being fearful has everything to do with loving someone so much that you have second thoughts, nerves, doubts, and terror building inside." I see how the battalions next to ours have stopped as well.

Almost a hundred heads are staring at me, and I feel butterflies in my stomach. Before I choke on my own words, I proceed, "What we need is to channel those fears into anger, use our humanity as our driving force to succeed at this impossible task. Each one of us has the ability and the drive to overcome fear. How are we to defeat ourselves, before defeating the threat that stands behind that damn wall? Well, the answer is right in front of us." Some people frown at this last comment, while others smile, knowing I am soon to answer their doubts.

The large man takes me to the center of our battalion for more people to listen. He stands on top of a small boulder, allowing me to see all our army coming closer to us. I shout to the top of my lungs, "The only way to do it is together. We are two hundred hearts beating in unison, marching to the same destination, dreaming the same dream, and willing to fight for the same purpose. Without us, this whole enterprise would be a death wish. Without us, my brother could torch the wall down and perish in exhaustion before even being able to face a single enemy. Without us, all would die as Cold's threat spreads like a disease through the world." Men and women start raising their voices, screaming, cheering, and humming once again. Some even start singing Strength and Valor's tune.

I conclude, "Don't forget that standing here today is the result of deciding to face the inevitable head on, instead of running away with our backs wide open to death. Sure, you could turn around and go back to your home towns, to your families, to that fake tranquility, but how long would it take before Cold reaches there and torches everything down, destroying everything and killing everyone you love?" Silver is staring at me, not in disbelief but with the proudest gaze I have ever seen from her green eyes. Massive cheers erupt and through the crowd I see Nate too far away to distinguish, but I feel within me his congratulations and pride.

Battalion 3 is ready. Our army is ready. I am ready.

***

The last three and a half hours were uneventful. We walked under the morning sun, the humidity rising and making me feel sticky and breathless, the ground getting harder as time went on and it dried up, and our army walking at a steady pace. The terrain has been easier than expected, probably hardened by the numerous people who have walked toward White Tower. So many steps from enslaved people walking toward that hellhole. It angers me deeply to know my mom is one of them. *We are coming!*

Nathan ordered us to stop about a half hour away from White Tower's entrance. All battalions have sent scouts around to ensure no one finds us, killing anyone necessary or alerting us in case a large group of enemies came close to us. All our army is together for one last time before our final showdown. The time has come; there is no turning back now. Our last tally came to two hundred and one soldiers, plus Dan, Em, Khan, Bull, Rick, Nathan, Silver, and me. A man short of two-ten strong. Nathan summons all the leaders to the center of the army for a final meeting.

I walk with Silver, going toward the center of this massive multitude. Our soldiers pat our backs, cheer, smile, fist bump, and congratulate us. This feels so exciting that words to adequately describe it escape me. I can see the rest of the leaders are already gathered twenty meters ahead, waiting for us. We stand one next to the other in a circle. Nathan is standing surrounded by all of us, the seven leaders, and around us the remaining two hundred and one men and women willing to die for humanity. We are ready, both physically and mentally.

The memories of days when Nate hunted and gathered to bring back food to our well-protected house, to train me to survive against perils I could not quite understand, are blurry. After all that has happened to us, and all that life has violently taught us, our former life feels more a dream than truth. The man standing in front of me is a legend.

Nate looks at Bull, who nods and says with the voice of his transformed self, deeply and loudly, "Men and women, ahead of us awaits the war to change history. Cold is waiting cowardly behind those towering walls with three hundred and fifty soldiers. He believes he has us controlled, dominated us with his fear tactics, and destroyed our hopes, but guess what? Hope cannot be controlled! Hope cannot be dominated! And hope cannot be destroyed!" His voice is covered with massive cheers that resound through the forest. We are no longer afraid of being found. We want to be found.

He continues, "Let's go, men and women! Let's march to his doorstep and break it down! Let's run into his hellhole and send a clear message to anyone who dares stand against kindness, love, family, and loyalty! Let's go!" Nathan points in White Tower's direction as he screams excitedly, transforming into Phoenix with fire around his arms, his red eyes glaring at each of us, and his body enlarged with massive muscles marked against his shirt. All of us take a step back and yell at the top of our lungs, cheering at him, at us, and at our future.

As Nathan comes back to normal, we start hugging each other and wishing each other luck. Dan comes first to me and hugs me tenderly while saying, "You are the future, Jay. Take care of it since us oldies will not be here for long to see how amazing it will be." I hug him tightly, feeling his heartbeat against my cheek. Em and Khan come together to me. Khan grabs my head while Em messes my hair and they laugh. She says, "Go kill them, boy!" Khan adds, "Bet I defeat more enemies than you do," as he winks. I answer, "You will swallow those filthy words, old man." We laugh and pat each other on the back.

Someone taps my back, and as soon as I turn, Rick embraces me lovingly. Under his breath he mutters, "Take care, Jay. You represent the future I wish for this world, and I know my wife and son are watching us proudly from above. Let's make them even prouder." I answer against his chest, "We will avenge them and build a great world where no one will suffer like you or your family." He grabs my neck and slaps me teasingly as he concludes, "You better, punk." His laugh and his gaze are so comforting.

Bull strides heavily in my direction; he is truly massive and imposing. He says with his deep voice and dark eyes, "Do not worry, kid, I will keep your brother safe. You take care of yourself." I nod, mildly scared of the mountain of a man in front of me, while feeling extremely relaxed at the thought that he is loyal to Nathan. I sense in him the willingness to give his life for Nathan's.

As I stand alone while the other leaders embrace each other and give their farewells, a wall of fire emerges surrounding me. I laugh and see that Nathan crosses it in front of me. He is his normal self, easily controlling the fire around us without looking any different than when we played back home. He says, "Jay, the time has come to become bigger than ourselves. Mom waits for us, and humanity hopes for us. Let's give all of them a reason to dream and ensure Mom lives a long life beside us to enjoy this world." I lose control of myself and tears run wildly down my cheeks as I run to him. I hug Nathan, my brother, the one I owe my life to, and sob heavily. He kisses my forehead and finally says, "I got you, brother. You are not and will not ever be alone in this world." I nod quickly, unable to say a word.

The fire around us extinguishes, and Nathan holds me tightly. Silver comes to us and whispers, "It is time, boys." Nathan releases me and messes my hair one last time before he turns around and says, "See you two soon. Be careful."

We walk back to our battalions, and I see everyone around us is doing the same, wishing luck, hugging, kissing, crossing others, and smiling. Those smiles warm my heart as Silver and I walk together, her arm around my neck. Some soldiers bow as we walk toward the center of our battalion. When we reach it, everyone huddles up as close as possible.

Silver says loudly, "Men and women, there are few words left to say. I only want to say I am already proud of each one of you for being here. You are risking your lives for your friends, your family, and your loved ones. We will make all of them proud today, don't forget that." All our soldiers are holding hands and nodding eagerly. All those I can see turn toward me, waiting for my final words.

I say, "Oh, come on! I already said way too much!" They all laugh and hoot loudly before I conclude, "Remember, it is okay to be afraid, but let's make sure those assholes behind White Tower are terrified and horrified far more than we were ever. It is our time to make the world what it should be!" I howl as loudly as I can, and all our battalion howls with me, raising their arms to the sky and jumping enthusiastically.

Silver and I start walking to the front of our battalion and lead them north since we are to climb White Tower's wall north of its main gate. Our men and women follow us, with their bows and swords held and ready to use. Our entire army starts walking toward their designated places in Nate's final plan, and once again the march sounds incredible. A stampede of hope from men and women courageous enough to try to change the world.

Two months ago, I was not capable of leading myself, and now all these souls are following me. Funny how life's road is twisting, confusing, and unpredictable. There is still a small thorn inside of my chest pressing and making me feel uncomfortable with the idea I am not ready for this. I guess no one in my position is truly ready. When life gives you lemons, you better take them and do something with them. Don't pass them on, don't throw them away or wait for someone else to do it for you. Probably the saying was not like that, but who cares?

Silver walks in front of our group, and I walk around seeing them eye to eye, reassuring them everything will be all right. I am also in charge of ordering men and women to rotate while carrying the massive ladder, to ensure all our soldiers are well rested when we reach the wall. We go farther north, and I can barely see our other battalions behind us. Only the dirt rising from their heavy footsteps.

Finally, I feel the courage to speak to Nathan, so I walk into his mind and say, "Brother, thank you for showing me everything I know, for making me a better man, and for showing me there is hope for this world. You have been a brother, a father, a mother, and a friend all these years. We are going to finally reunite our family in a world far better than the current one, for you to finally rest and be who you want to be." I can sense his joyful tears listening to my comment. Now he is unable to speak, but we walk together with our minds connected, sharing our hope and excitement.

After about fifteen minutes marching, Silver signals everyone to halt and starts our final meeting, while everyone gathers around in a circle, taking a knee, sitting on the hard forest floor, or leaning against a tree. "We are Battalion 3b. You all know our main goal is to climb White Tower's wall due north of the main gate. Our first step is to secure the area, try to snipe any watchmen on top of the wall. The longer we manage to stay a secret, the better. Stealth buys us time to penetrate the enemy's city and get closer to the front gate to reunite will all our forces. If we are spotted before reaching the gate, we are only fifty-two, if we are spotted at the front gate, we are two hundred and nine. Understood?" Silver speaks loudly, and all our soldiers listen intently, barely reacting to her.

She continues, "However, we are all brothers and sisters in this unit, and honesty is a need. I honestly doubt we will be able to reach the front gate without confrontation, so, every step must be together, whether being attacked or not. No unnecessary risks are to be taken. While some of us climb the ladder, others must keep watch in case we are attacked by archers on top, behind, or in front of the wall. The first waves that reach the top of the wall are to secure it for the rest to climb. Hold strong and together against all enemies who attack. And remember, inside enemy walls we are subject to an attack from any direction. Therefore, please remember and brand this into your minds, those who are at the edge of any group of soldiers hold their shields high." She shows the correct position, crouching slightly with her shield up, covering from her knee up to her head.

She explains, "Imagine a cocoon and those at the edge are the shell. We have practiced this, but in the heat of the battle you must remember these words. No more surprise attacks will manage to hurt any of us. We have learnt this the harsh way, and none of you will perish because of our unpreparedness ever again. Your lives are as valuable as my own to me; please defend yourselves and others with the same love." Our soldiers nod and copy Silver's position, practicing one last time.

Silver smiles and goes on, "Another key aspect to our success is the status of our inventories and weapons. Pick up anything and everything you consider valuable to our war. Knives, swords, bows, and shields in better shape than yours are to be taken, even replacing your old ones. Arrows, canteens with water, and any supplies found are to be taken, period. We don't know how long this effort will take until victory, so we plan for the worst scenario possible and wish for the best." I must accept embarrassingly that I had not thought about this.

She continues explaining our plan, "Once all manage to climb the wall, we rush southward toward the main gate in the cocoon formation, that is, to our left. When faced with enemies, the front or back shield holders may open to allow a frontal melee assault. As soon as any threat is eradicated, we are to form back up as quickly as possible. Any slit in our shell is a place through which an enemy arrow could kill or injure one of us. No slits, or I will personally slit your stupid-ass throats!" Silver's comment gets a short but genuine laugh from our soldiers. They are silently concentrating on each of her words, reassuring both of us of their readiness for this endeavor.

Finally, she remarks, "Last, when we reach the front gate, everything could be resolved, or hell could have broken loose. Nate's or Rick's battalion could have opened the gates and defeated Cold's initial wave. Away from fairy land, Cold's initial wave could be so massive that we reach just in time to aid Battalions 1 and 2 in the battle. We could arrive at the same time as Rick, or he could reach the gate after us, or be defeated before we manage to come to his aid. In any scenario where the gate is still closed, we must use all our strengths, our cunning, our teamwork to destroy that fucking gate. If we must tear it apart using our fingernails, so be it. Manicure for all of you after succeeding, but I want you to give blood, sweat, and tears until that gate stands no more. I want to hear it crumble into rubble and never stand again. Opening that gate is our main task, and if we succeed, we will be opening much more than a gate. We will be clearing the way for the future we are fighting for." Silver's speech leaves me speechless, ironically.

Funny, inspiring, vibrant, and clear at the same time. Her hand gestures and gaze are imposing, her voice is demanding and reassuring, and her words are piercing. It is an honor to fight with her and for her.

We have about two and a half hours to rest before the time for our attack comes, so our soldiers lay their weapons down and get comfortable. Some find a place to sleep, others untie their shoes and massage their tired feet, while others start chatting with others. This time is needed both physically and mentally. I walk toward Silver who is sitting right where she gave her amazing speech.

I sit right next to her and rest my head on her shoulder. She rests her head on top of mine, and I can feel both our breathing slowing down. Time for a final nap before marching against evil.

***

Silver moves and wakes me up. It is time to get ready and march to White Tower. Our success depends heavily on our coordination with Rick's and Khan's battalion, so we must be punctual. I concentrate with my eyes closed for a couple of minutes, trying to connect empathically with Rick as we planned. I feel how my consciousness leaves my body, travels across the forest, and looks for Rick's. Finally, I find him standing up, staring at his soldiers who are gathered, taking turns speaking motivational words. I say into his mind, "Time to go." He feels nervous at the intrusion, even though he expected it. He laughs and tells me back, "Good luck, kid. Make us proud!" Time to go.

Our soldiers are doing their final rituals and preparations. I see a man about ten meters to my right, kneeling and praying with closed eyes and both hands up to the sky. He mutters his prayers and stands up while crossing himself. To my left, about a dozen men and women are huddled up, with their arms around each other's shoulders. One woman is speaking unintelligibly, heatedly, with her closed fist pumping in front of her, pointing to the others and motivating them. In front of me, I see how large our battalion is as they start approaching Silver and me, silently and with readiness in their glares. I have never seen so many people with the same mentality and determination; it gives me shivers.

I stand up alongside Silver and she says, "We got this, men and women. Let's make humanity proud. Let's make ourselves proud." Our forces nod, patting others' backs, holding hands, and sharing winks and smiles. We are truly ready. A large group raises the ladder over their shoulders, and we start marching the last fifteen minutes up to White Tower. Now I understand what feeling butterflies in your stomach means. The fluttering sensation, the void, the nervousness, and the slight need to puke.

I try to connect with Nathan one last time before the battle erupts and he needs to concentrate. This time I keep my eyes open, searching for my brother's mind as we walk west in the forest. I find it easily as it is familiar to me, and he shares his emotion and happiness at this connection. I notice his last thoughts before speaking to me are prayers. He was searching for guidance and protection from above, even though I thought he was a nonbeliever. His relationship with God seems to be close and personal, and I feel ashamed of interrupting.

He says, unbothered, "Hello, little brother. How are you doing?" His voice echoing inside my mind soothes me. I answer, "Our forces are ready, marching toward the wall, highly motivated and concentrated." He smiles lopsidedly and answers back, "Great, but that is not what I asked." We share a nervous laugh, both staring at the ground in front of us, avoiding branches and leaves as best as possible.

The best thing to do here is to be honest, so I share, "I am extremely nervous. My stomach is a mess, and I am afraid of failing. Mom is so close, and it excites me, but these men and women depend on us. We cannot fail them." I can hear my trembling voice inside his mind; my body shivers as it feels colder with every word. Nathan listens calmly, thinking thoroughly about his answer. I cannot feel him nervous or preoccupied, and I am not able to understand how he does it.

Finally, his words come to me, "Little brother, in life you will always have two ways to see the same situation. In front of adversity you may believe you will fall defeated and, trust me, you will succumb to difficulty. The other way to see it is believing you will fly past it, learn, become a better person, and share your learning with those around you. Two sides to the same coin and, yet, extreme opposites." His words confuse and calm me at the same time. I do not answer, knowing Nate's explanation is far from over.

He pauses for a couple of seconds before continuing, "You are fearful of failure and that is perfectly natural, but it is one of the ways to see our endeavor. The other way is to see it as a challenge waiting to be overcome. There will never be a better chance to change the world than this, there will never be such a motivated army fueled by hope and the desire to build a better future for our friends and families. Therefore, you can be afraid of confronting our present and be ready to run away, or you can face failure staring straight at its eyes and say, bring it on. I do not fear failure because I know we are undefeatable together. We are going to succeed at saving Mom and saving humanity. We are ready." I can feel him frowning, his inner fire building steadily, his gaze set on the path in front of him, and his readiness to do whatever it takes.

I nod and feel part of his wrath, his resilience, and his desire to succeed in my body. Nate says into my mind, "May your senses be advertent, and your aim be unerring, little brother." The cold shivers and void in my stomach turn to a rising temperature in my body and my muscles tensing. My nostrils flare up; I frown and clench my teeth. Finally, he adds, "And may God be with you." His power is so massive, my body barely manages to maintain the connection with his mind. I feel his support and best wishes, so I say "Bring it on! And may God be with…" as I lose the connection.

As we walk closer to White Tower, about five minutes away from our final showdown, I think about Dad. My entire body feels cold once more. I believe that my vision did not show him because he is not with Mom. This saddens me, as it may mean he has passed away. Before this sensation throws the positive ones away, I think about Nathan's words. He is right, I can see this as proof that Dad will not come back to us or see it as the possibility to save him once Mom is safe and tells us what she knows about him. I cackle at Nathan's wit. How has he become such a wise man without our parents or school to teach him?

Silver has been walking next to me all this time, lost in her thoughts. She turns to me and says, "You were talking with Nate, right?" I smile and wink at her, as she lays an arm around my shoulders, saying, "You did right. Bring it on!" I stare curiously and laugh at how similar she is to Nathan, saying the same exact words.

Our steps fall heavily and deeply into the dirt, leaving dark footprints. Rain has started pouring, wetting the ground under us and refreshing our forces as we stride. Destiny has decided to cover us with gray clouds and rainfall. The smell of fresh moist grass appears and disappears as the wind howls from all directions. The group of soldiers carrying the massive ladder to White Tower's wall changes with other, more rested men and women.

The sound of the few metal armor plates we have rings and tingles as we walk. Every step closer to the wall, unexpectedly, seems to vanish our fears. If hope and excitement had a smell, it would be this blend of grass, metal, wind, rain, and joy. The sound? The sound is a beauty branded in our memories from now on. In the end, I believe no one would rather be elsewhere than here.

Yes, death could wait ahead, creeping the shadows to take more than one of us, but we are taking this risk for all those we love, the fallen we loved, and all those unborn who we will love. Nathan has sparked this in all of us; he has fed us with hope and nurtured us with clarity about our purpose and our goal. Fear and doubt seem a thing of the past.

I know the time to face real men and women trying to kill us is close, and everything might change. The romanticism of battle becomes a lie, and the truth paints a whole different picture. None of us here has lived war, not in our country or what used to be our country. We are all amateurs, and our roughness is a consequence of this world's adversity, cruel and unforgiving.

We are arriving at our last stop before our assault. White Tower's wall stands high, about four hundred and fifty meters ahead. We are walking in deep forest, covered by the canopy from any scout standing on top of the wall. We gather one last time before charging. We have about ten minutes before executing our plan; no turning back and no second doubts.

Silver asks, "I need five volunteers to scout ahead, and four volunteers to scout north and south before we attack. Who will go?" Everyone stares at her in silence with deep respect. Almost all hands in our battalion raise up as volunteers, and my heart rushes in excitement. Everyone is ready to do their job, and their hearts and minds are set on our mission.

Sil chooses the volunteers, and they fan out to do their job.

The comradery here is unexplainable, as if a family reunited after a long time of no contact. Smiles are gifted, pats on backs, hushed jokes are widespread, and all their eyes glitter with happiness. These men and women understand they are here for themselves and for those they love, and for those they want to give a decent world to.

Time goes by and our moods swing from joy to concentration and anger. Every second transforms each face from happiness into a war grin. Swords are held, shields are grasped, and bows are tested. We are ready. A minute is left before we advance. The scouts from north and south come back and join our forces, each raising their hands to their foreheads indicating no threats ahead. Silver nods and our forces form up in a wedge formation. The front and outside men and women hold their shields up, the middle men and women raise the ladder, and behind them, the remaining soldiers ready their bows and arrows.

Our front-line scouts appear out of the shadows. Each one raises one of their hands, indicating the number of enemy soldiers spotted ahead on top of the wall. Straight ahead, two men are patrolling; to the right or north, four enemies; and to the left or south, three enemies. We can do this, we have some of the best archers and nine static or slowly moving targets. An easy catch.

The archers join in and stand in their designated positions within the wedge formation. Silver commands, "Go!", so we march in sync. A slow and deep hum rumbles from deep within our loins, the rhythm of our attack. The sound of mud squished under our shoes, the rain tingling against our armor, and our heavy breathing are the sounds of war. Most of us have a hand on the ladder.

Each step brings the wall closer, and through the dense forest its base clears up. Gray stone bricks hold the wall's base together. On top of them a plain white wall, covered in putty, builds up to six meters. In the uppermost section, a brick layer with slits and openings covers the soldiers up to half their torsos. As soon as we walk into the clearing, created by ten meters of chopped trees in front of the wall, we will have a linear distance of about twelve meters from our enemies.

I share my insight, "Men and women. As soon as we walk into the clear, kill every single one of them. The longer we manage to keep a secret, the better for our safety. They will be twelve meters away in a straight direction; please don't miss!" Our soldiers clatter their weapons against a part of their armor. Our signal of understanding. Time to attack. Silver shouts, "For us!", as we run out of the forest.

Our heavy steps, the branches crushing, the rocks tumbling, and the armor clanking alert those on top of the wall. Arrows fly past our ears, swooshing quickly and striking their targets. All the enemies fall almost simultaneously. One hundred percent efficacy in our first attack, no injuries, no enemies alerting others, and no missed shots. This is too good to be true. Our wide smiles and joyful nods reaffirm our unexpected success.

The man beside me is from a free village. He is smiling the widest smile I have ever seen; his eyes are full of confidence at our endeavor. I cannot quite recall his name, but he is a proud father of two, fighting for them and their future. His heart is pure, and his motive is the reason why we are risking everything now, instead of postponing the inevitable. He lowers his head slightly at me, as if in slow motion. An arrow pierces his throat.

Blood spurts from the deep wound, and speckles moisten my cheeks and lips. The taste of death. Happiness turns to screams, and our formation raises its shields again. I crouch more by intuition than by thought, to protect myself in case any other attack comes. My eyes are wide and my hands trembling without control, while the man's body lies a half a meter away from me. He is dead. This is real. This is no game.

Silver points to our right and screams, "There he is!" A frail enemy, with an arrow sticking out of his clavicle and blood-tainted clothes and armor, is leaning against the wall's front edge and readying his bow again. His grin is evil and dreadful. Silver strings an arrow and pierces his forehead violently. The inanimate body falls from the wall, crashing against the moist grass. Thud.

This is war. This is it. We were so stupid to feel excited for one small step, as if celebrating a great opening in a marathon. Stupid, stupid, damn stupid. Before lowering our shields, the front men make a quick visual scout. No more enemy soldiers standing or peeking on top of the wall. The formation opens, and we place the ladder, digging its anchors deep into the mud.

While two men stay, hammering the ladders' support, we start climbing. Silver goes first with Lucas, our best fighter by a mile. Rough, violent, vicious melee attacker, and an immaculate shot with his longbow. Two by two we go up the slippery ladder and up the wall. I stay behind to protect the last of our men, and secretly to ensure no one runs away.

I start climbing, feeling the slippery wooden boards of the ladder under my feet, the rain wetting my body and making my clothes heavier by the minute. As I get up, our formation is made again on top of the wall, this time a square. I get in the middle of the formation with my bow ready. On each side we have raised shields to ensure no arrow pierces our defense from any direction; four men are walking backward to shield us from behind. We advance slowly, avoiding a break that might be caused by rushing. Each step increases my anxiety, and apparently everyone's. My voice breaks the silence, "Breathe, men, breathe!" I need to ensure they regulate their breathing and use it to relax.

Nothing has changed; we are walking and walking, and nothing happens. Our breach point, where we scaled the wall, was about a kilometer away from the front gate. We decided to go far north, as well as Rick's force marching far south, to avoid facing a strong force early on. At least they will not expect us to attack the front gate from the top of the wall. We must be about halfway there by now. In the distance, faint sounds indicate war has erupted elsewhere. Nathan.

A bell tolls, ringing loudly from inside the city. Loud thumps start hammering against our shields as arrows fly from within

White Tower. I cannot see much past our shield formation into White Tower, only some old, shabby, wooden buildings close to the wall. We hold our formation and continue our stride. The only way we are stopping is to face enemies on top of the wall. Through the miniscule slits between our shields I manage to see about fifty archers lined up, attacking us from inside White Tower. Far behind them, an abomination.

The White Tower is on the horizon, with a terrible flame on top of it illuminating all the way to the wall. The fire's light sends a blinding glare in our direction. It illuminates the front gate menacingly.

A shadow surrounds the dreaded construction; our enemy's main force is still waiting. We are facing their first wave, and it seems to be bait compared to the main banquet waiting to be served. My heartbeat accelerates violently at the thought of having erred. What if we are not capable of winning this, what if our men are not strong enough, or simply not enough to face this threat waiting for us patiently?

Before my thoughts wander further, our front men yell aggressively, and Silver's voice howls, "For tomorrow!" Finally, enemies have climbed the wall and are rushing toward us, stopping the arrow volleys coming from inside White Tower momentarily as we are forced to fight face to face. Silver's agility proves impossible for our enemies, as they slash, push, pull, and poke unsuccessfully. She dances around their weak efforts and sends them to an early grave. Her face shows me she is not enjoying this. She kills by need, but she still wishes to be the woman who had never done so.

I run through our men to join Silver; my place is in front of those I lead, not behind. A man with terrible teeth and an unwashed beard runs at me with his black sword held up high. He strikes down heavily, and I roll to the right to dodge his attempt. Before he turns, I cut his left knee from behind and stab his lower back with my three-pronged knife. It trespasses him, while his legs fail him, and he falls to the ground. Dead.

I have killed a man. I feel ashamed and scared. What have I done? Is this really the right decision to make? All that I believe challenges the reason why I fight. Death is no game, and it is not my choice to make for someone else. A metal crash sounds loudly right behind my head. I turn around quickly, while ducking, to see Silver's sword holding off an enemy's attack directed at my neck. She says menacingly, "Big mistake, pal.", Her eyes are as wide open as they go.

She sends his sword flying, and before it hits the ground his neck is cut deeply. She yells, "Jay, keep your head in the game. If you doubt, you die." Her command brings me back to the reality of where I stand. She runs forward into the enemy line, leaving me behind. No time to lose, no time to take care of children here.

I take a quick glance around and see the violence and hatred around me. Bodies fall, blood flows, metal cringes, and the rain is incapable of cleansing the death left behind. We are winning, by far, for now. Our men and women look undefeatable, their faces filled with anger and resilience. They are willing to put their lives on the line for those they love.

They teach me without even looking at me. We are all in this for a reason. Cold's men are fighting for him, either brainwashed or by their own decision. They are far away from him, sent to die against a force larger than theirs, and still they fight. They attack without even protecting themselves, their stances are wild, and their strikes unpredictable and violent. Humanity has long left their hearts and a more primitive desire to kill has taken hold.

Our men and women are fighting for the future, for those they love and those who have not yet arrived. Their stances are calculated, their blows thought out, their defenses high, and their decisions two steps ahead of their time. No one is willing to die; they are willing to live to fight another enemy and to cure the world from this disease. And I am one of them.

I stand up and tackle an enemy attacking one of our female soldiers. He falls to the ground, spitting at me, throwing wild punches, trying to bite me as I hold him down. His eyes are crazy and his teeth rotten, with pus coming out of some of his cavities. His insults blend with his desperate breathing as my companion drills her sword deep into his left side. Even in death, his gaze is not human, his dark eyes without compassion in them. He is something else, something worse. Corroded by evil.

We are defeating this wave of enemies. I stand and see my fellow men and women are fiercely advancing, even if our enemies will not retreat. They die fighting, giving every ounce of their strength and every drop of sweat and blood for Cold's cause. This war will not be easy; every centimeter of ground will be fought to death for, and our men must be extremely motivated to go on. Our duty, beyond leading, is to ensure they remember why they are here and why they cannot retreat and fail. Tomorrow's peace is built with today's fierceness.

The front gate is about one hundred meters away. We seem to have a minute's peace before more enemies come toward us. The few encounters still happening come to their conclusion. Our soldiers are tired, gasping for air, tending to their wounds and those closest to them. One by one, the survivors turn their gaze toward Silver and me. This is the moment to lead.

I raise my voice above the sounds of war, "Everyone, form up. Help those in need, and make sure they stand in the middle of our wedge formation. Shields up and march!" They rush to form up, carrying the wounded and helping them stand in the middle of our formation as shields rise to protect us. Our steps are heavy and coordinated, advancing once again toward our main objective.

The few enemies who climb the wall and run toward us are quickly and easily defeated. The front shields open; a couple of our soldiers swiftly execute them and join back in formation. A well-oiled machinery, working in unison. Through the small slits between our protective cover, I manage to see the main confrontation outside of White Tower, Nathan's battle for the front gate.

Soon we will be able to aid them. One hundred of our men

are down there, giving their lives to break down more than a gate, an enemy. For now, I must focus on our path, our battle, and our condition. We started as a fifty-strong force, plus Silver and me; but now we must be down to thirty-five strong plus Silver, five wounded soldiers, and me. Ten have fallen. This saddens me deeply and enrages me at the same time.

Even though it feels awry, I keep thinking that I hope they managed to kill at least two or three enemies before being defeated. If they failed to do so, our remaining men and women must kill three or four enemies. My anxiety increases at those numbers, as we are not unerring soldiers; we are simple people fighting from the heart. Their breathing starts to stabilize, and their fierce faces relax me. Their minds are set on accomplishing everything needed to succeed.

Sweat is the only sign betraying their exhaustion. Some feet slide or trip as we advance, and blood in their bodies reminds them of past encounters; however, their faces show their commitment to our cause. No one seems to be afraid anymore. Their physical effort has been strenuous, and yet no one has his or her face down or their shoulders hunched. Mind over body.

The enemies who dare face us keep failing. We are unstoppable, as even the tens of arrows clanking against our outmost shields fail. The sound never ceases to scare me. Metal against metal, people trying untiringly to kill at least one of us. I hear the screams of those running toward us and their last gasps of breath before dying. Walking over their bodies, getting our shoes wet and dirty with their blood, is depressing. Why has the world come to this?

Hundreds of different paths could have been taken, leading to better places than this, but people decided to follow Cold, to stop fighting for what they loved and succumb to his malevolence. Fear is an illness. The way they fight against us, how they scream and fight to the death are convincing about their allegiance. They are not slaves, but aides. If we don't take them down, they will overrun us by sheer numbers. No time to think about possibilities beyond our reality.

The front gate's towers are twenty meters away. At our left, in front of the gate, a massive battle is held. The ram has not reached its destination, and it lies unattended as hundreds of men and women clash swords, tackle each other, hit and bite and shout ferociously. Without counting, it is evident Cold sent a larger force than we expected. Our one hundred men don't outnumber their opposition. Our aid is needed.

As a dozen of us stand closer to the ledge watching over the battle, the remaining walk with Silver toward the opposite side. Silver commands, "String, aim, release!", attacking the enemies standing close to the wall within the city. The strings releasing arrows resound behind us, as enemies groan and gurgle while perishing. Silver wants to kill all of them before opening the gate; she is clever. This way, our success will mean our soldiers from Battalion 1 and Battalion 2 will not have to face more and more enemies exiting the city.

I order those around me, "Let's aid Nathan!" My dozen companions ready their bows and start sniping the unexpecting enemies. They are so focused on what stands in front of them that none has noticed arrows are killing them from behind. I find my brother, fighting menacingly less than a hundred meters away from me. He is fearful, using quick bursts of fire waves and tornadoes to burn the multiple enemies trying to defeat him. They know his death would mean a crippling blow to all our enterprise, so about a dozen enemies are trying to surround him.

My instincts try to convince me to abort our mission and run to his aid, but my mind and training manage to control me. My assistance to his effort would be deplorable, compared to what I can do here.

Bull is fighting close to Nate. His massive size goes hand in hand with his relentless force. He tackles the enemies trying to face him and kills them with an impressive speed. His method is unforgiving. Swords are sent flying from his enemies' hands, shields are bent and broken against his blows, and enemy after enemy succumb to his anger.

Constantly, he stares Nathan's way. He has his back, and it tranquilizes me, seeing he is keeping his promise to me. Both men are amazing fighters and have developed an evident mutual respect. Nothing will stop them, and there is no force strong enough in this world to face them together. He continues his frenzied killstreak and enemies start avoiding his battle area, fear impregnating their souls. An outstanding warrior we have found in him. I command, "Attack! String, aim, release!", as our men continue raining arrows on our enemies down below.

Closer to us, Dan is fighting an enemy. He dodges a fierce blow to his head and impales the man trying to kill him. Another enemy runs toward him from his back. My eyes grow wide and desperate, incapable of alerting him. He is too far away for my arrows to protect him. Oh, no, oh, no, I cannot witness his death. Panicked, I shout at the top of my lungs, and it proves as useless as watering plants during a rainfall.

A second before the running enemy manages to cut deeply into Dan's body, Dan turns around and cuts his hand off. The sword falls and is instantly covered by the gushing blood. Dan walks toward the aching man, his suffering visible even from this distance. Dan kneels beside him, whispers something, and sticks his sword quickly into his neck. He stands up slowly, supporting himself up from one knee, moving slowly, like the old man I met.

His body remembers all it learned throughout the years, but it is still feeble and tired by age. Once again, he proves to me that our mind is stronger than our body, capable of overcoming limitations under distress. However, we have limits, and his body is failing. His motions are casual, even in the turmoil of battle, walking toward more enemies with a peaceful face.

Two more enemies, two women, hurry toward him. His steps don't hasten or falter at this assault. He stumbles and barely manages to keep up walking to them. Something within me convinces me he is ready to die. His passiveness and demeanor are not that of a warrior, but of an elder. He must be convinced there is nothing else he can add to our battle. The deathly swords are raised in coordination, waiting to fall heavily upon this serene man.

As they violently fly toward him, they crash against another sword protecting him. Em jumps from behind him and blocks the attack. She circles her sword and sends both enemy swords to the ground. Before they hit the soil, the two enemies fall to their knees dead. She pats Dan on his shoulder, points out toward the forest, and smiles at him before going on. He starts walking slowly back to the forest, with his unsure steps and tired body.

Em is a titan. She goes through our enemies as a hot knife through butter. None survives past two blows. She uses the force of their attacks to her advantage, sending their swords flying or their arms bouncing back, leaving their guards wide open. She ducks, rolls, runs, jumps, and evades as a ballerina, while striking, shouting, defending, and impaling as a Greek deity. Her stride, unlike Dan's, is untiring and graceful and intimidating at the same time.

Behind us, more soldiers start climbing the wall, running toward us from all sides. Arrows have stopped flying in our direction as Silver's attack seems to have either killed all their archers or forced them to retreat. Behind us, deep inside the city, the massive black beast still waits, unmovable, around White Tower. Our efforts have not altered their strategy, and they will wait for us. Maybe they still hope for us to be unable to breach the walls, or maybe they just don't care if we do.

Our soldiers form up once more. Enemies crash against our shield wall and fall pierced by arrows, swords, and even pikes. Their agony is a terrible sound, blending grieving shrieks with gurgled blood. More and more come our way, and this might be too much for us. We are about thirty left standing, and as more and more enemies run toward us, our arms weaken, and our defenses may falter soon.

Heavy breathing followed by tired exhales worry me. I say,

"Silver, as soon as we have a second to spare, we must change our front shields." She nods, and everyone seems ready. The moment occurs, and a split second between two waves of enemies allows us to switch. The soldiers behind the front men and women place their shields in front of them. The front soldiers lower their shields, turn sideways, and walk past the new front soldiers. It works precisely as we trained, working as a team, as a finely tuned car switching gears. At least I remember those in video games, since I did not learn to drive.

Enemies crash against the new shield wall and push, and we hold our ground, our feet heavily on the ground. Enemies are all around us; we are in a square formation with a shield wall along all our perimeter. I am in the front line now, closest to the gate, feeling the immense force coming our way. Down, in front of the gate, the battle seems to be slowing down; we must be winning or losing, but up here, the fight seems never-ending. We need for some miracle to happen just about now. We will not be able to withstand this constant, unnerving assault.

Those behind us are trying to rest for another switch in the front shield line, but they are done for. Their arms hanging heavily by their sides, only a few are capable of stringing and shooting arrows through our formation's slits. I am tired. I feel my shoulders burning, my arms trembling, and my sight seems to be getting blurry. My teeth are grinding, as if strength could come from them. Silver's screams and orders fade as my body starts to faint. Please, Jay, don't give up, but my body will not listen. My shield starts to lower, and I fight desperately against my weakness. If I faint, our shield wall will have a deathly opening.

Suddenly, a loud boom wakes me back up and fills my ears with a screeching sound. The wall trembles, but it still stands strong. Our enemies halt for a second, and then continue their assault. The peril seems to have missed its mark. Have we failed? Was that explosion meant to open the gate? There is no time to ponder as we are back to our last stand, fighting for our lives, using every single weapon and method necessary to succeed.

The explosion accelerated my heartbeat and gave me a second strength, standing again in the shield wall, holding against a wave of enemies crashing against us.

An explosion twice as strong and loud as the first erupts in front of us. The enemies in front of us, standing closer to the gate, fall to the force. With my ears buzzing and my head hurting, I order loudly, "Charge!" We attack the fallen enemies who are unable to stand up. It is a bloodbath. Those behind us run away in panic, and our soldiers gather their remaining strength to shoot arrows at them. They hit their targets consistently, and the enemies are falling to the ground one by one. The tide has turned. The miracle has happened.

I walk toward the ledge and stare down at Nathan's battlefield. Rick exits the gate's debris and smiles up at me. He yells to the top of his lungs for me to hear, "Guess we had an ace up our sleeve, Jay." His smile is contagious, and we start to cheer in celebration. A large dust cloud starts covering us. Rick turns around toward his battalion; they are down to about twenty soldiers. Rick walks back into White Tower, leading the way.

The surviving enemies fighting Nathan are still plenty, probably forty or more. They start running back toward the city's entrance, deciding it's better to face Rick's men than Nathan's. His force is diminished, and the fleeing men outnumber him. He orders his battalion to retreat into the city and find shelter. Their attack is to be guerilla-like. Silver and I order our men to ready their bows to kill as many enemies as possible before they enter the city, but our arrow supply is low and our bowmen weak. Their trembling arms are missing their marks.

God dammit! The explosion has blocked our way down. I order desperately, "Run! Find the closest way down to help Rick!" My scream is frantic, and our soldiers rush back, away from the gate, seeking for a ladder, a door, a stairway to aid them. The enemies' quick steps sound louder and louder. The situation is desperate, we have no way to help our fellow men and women adequately. I see Rick's forces running toward a block of buildings deeper into White Tower. They must be as tired as we are; this will be a massacre! I run with our soldiers and Silver, feeling all my muscles aching and failing me. We need to get into White Tower as soon as possible.

As I turn west, I see that a large force of Cold's army starts running toward the front gate. They will try to surround Rick's force as they are rushing into the city looking for shelter. Rick orders them to stop and forms a two-line formation, one looking west toward White Tower and one looking east toward us. He is ready for a final stand, and we are about to witness it impotently.

Rick salutes me from afar, but it is a goodbye. My jaw shivers as two teardrops fall from my eyes. This cannot be the end to Rick's story. He still has so much path to travel. He should live the life Cold took away from him, rebuild his destiny, and enjoy hundreds of better days to come. He is one reason why we started all of this. We don't need a martyr; we have plenty of those.

The soldiers coming from White Tower are about three hundred meters from Rick, and those fleeing from Nathan have entered the fallen front gate, about a hundred meters away from Rick's stand. Suddenly, a massive heatwave hits my back. I order loudly, "Everyone, lie on the ground!" I turn around and see an enormous fire wave crashing against the wall, as high as the wall itself. It rages wildly, blowing hot wind at us, the wall fighting against the massive force.

It vanishes as quickly as it appeared. I stand up and walk toward the east edge of the wall, toward Nathan's army. I see across the battlefield and see Nathan twenty meters in front of the fallen gate, with both arms stretched in front of him, fully transformed, with a ring of ashes around him. He is breathing heavily, unmovable, with his red piercing eyes visible from this far away.

I run to the other edge and see how Nathan has eradicated the entire force of enemies fleeing from him. Rick's men raise their shields and weapons celebrating. Immediately after they turn around to face the army coming from the west, they hold their shield wall up and start retreating toward the gate. Cold's men halt their advance and wait for a couple of seconds before hastily retreating toward White Tower.

As Rick's battalion retreats slowly toward us, we find a ladder attached to the wall. One by one, we descend into White Tower and walk toward the fallen gate. Nathan has saved us once more. The time to regroup and rest has come. Now, our hope rests on Cold's arrogance. We need him to wait for us at White Tower, to believe he will defeat us easily, for him to grant us time enough to rest. The first battle has been victorious, but at what cost?

29

THE ELDER

THE DAY TO CHANGE THE WORLD

GOD BLESS RICK. WHEN THE battle's tide seemed to be turning against us, he somehow managed to blow up the front gate and send those giving us hell in a frenzied retreat. I had been saving my powers for later, but after seeing his resilience, his ingeniousness, and his leadership, there was no way I was about to let him part. Those hordes of men running toward him from the east and west were menacing; he was doomed.

I transform back to my normal self and start feeling the consequences to my attack. I feel exhausted, both physically and mentally. The overuse of my inner fire makes me feel heavy, nauseated, and disoriented; this probably sounds like a hangover, but it is worse. Water will not quench my thirst and reboot me; it seems to evaporate within me. Only time manages to strengthen me back to my normal self. This was not the moment to use it. This is way too soon.

Don't get me wrong, saving Rick is encouraging. Even if he was leading maybe two dozen soldiers, their input to our army is invaluable. They managed to overcome the enemies facing them on top of the wall, devise a plan to break through, and stand their ground against an insurmountable force about to annihilate them. In this war we don't need more martyrs, we need leaders who men and women are willing to follow to the end.

Around me the battle has ended, and reality crashes in on all of us. I see dead bodies with terrible wounds, blood taints the ground, and moans and painful screams are widespread. The sounds and the smell are sickening. Each gust sends a fragrance of blood, sweat, dirt, metal, and human excrement at me. I walk around our men, patting their backs, nodding, trying to raise their spirits up again, almost unsuccessfully. They look up at me as they tend to the wounded, inspecting their own wounds, or lying on the ground while catching their breath.

We are exhausted and weakened. Bull comes to me and we walk around together, inspecting our forces, their status, our weaponry, and our fallen. Em and Dan are standing way back looking at the battlefield and speaking with sorrow on their faces. Behind us, Jay and Silver lead their forces out of White Tower, going over the debris of the fallen gate. Bull and I walk toward the ram to wait for them. I call Dan and Em with my left arm to come over.

I am extremely exhausted, so I recline on the ram's wall and wait, breathing deeply to control my racing heartbeat. Bull places a heavy hand on my right shoulder, so I nod to reassure him I will be fine. Silver and Jay join us; they are covered in dust, with deep gashes in their faces and arms, breathing with difficulty, coughing dryly. Their battalion goes to aid our injured men and women.

Dan and Em get to the ram silently. We are waiting for Rick and Khan to come out of White Tower. Finally, I see Rick walking over the front gate's debris, leading his soldiers. Their battalion takes their injured soldiers toward a wide opening behind us where everyone is gathering the people who need assistance.

Rick limps toward us crestfallen. Proportionally, his battalion suffered the most during this first encounter. More than half their forces died to ensure we were able to enter White Tower. The survivors must have their hearts both shattered and strengthened by the experience. They will need strong support from all of us to go on in this tough road.

Khan has not reported back. He led Battalion 3a with Rick, and he must be either exhausted or injured. Rick finally reaches us painfully, his arms rest at each side, his eyes red and puffed by tears. His battered body seems to be holding up against the multiple cuts and bruises, but his mind is broken. I walk to aid him in his stride, since he moves as an old man. I say, preoccupied, "How can we help you, Rick?"

Rick speaks staring at the ground, sobbing, "The battle in the south side of the wall was brutal. The forces we met were stronger, larger, and better prepared than expected. They had several small nests built along the way, covering them with sandbags while they showered arrows on us. At first our shield formation held strong, but they started alternating between melee assaults and arrow fire, forcing us to open our shields and become vulnerable. They did not care if their arrows killed one of ours or one of theirs." His memories come to life in his eyes as he stares into the nothingness and reminisces about the pain. All of us gasp and come closer to Rick. Bull and I place a comforting hand on each of his shoulders, while Silver, Jay, Dan, and Em stand in front of him with doleful eyes.

Silver says sadly, "Rick, we did not know. If we had, we would have sent more soldiers with you. The north wall was not that heavily guarded." She apologizes for something she did not commit, a righteous woman. Rick answers, "I know, Sil. Don't think I am complaining or seeking a culprit. The plan was ours, and so is the responsibility for its consequences. My pain is from what we lived through and from those we lost, but the mission was fulfilled, though abated." He clarifies himself, showing his virtuousness through red suffering eyes.

I add, "We will give our brothers and sisters the farewell they deserve. Tonight, let's hope for Cold's arrogance to halt him from attacking, and share a moment to say goodbye to those who we owe our lives to." My words come from deep within my heart, my fist holds my anger back, while my words spill out my suffering. We all knew this war would have casualties but knowing is far different from living through this.

A soldier comes running toward us; he comes to my side and whispers our fallen count. My heart breaks at the number, so I share, "We have lost a total of sixty-six brave men and women. Each and every one of them is a bastion to our army now. Let's find those closest to them and have them share a eulogy for each tonight." My suggestion is followed by reassuring nods and hums. The mood is harrowing, but within pain there is hope. If we don't suffer for those who fought beside us, we will not be able to overcome the toughest parts of our journey waiting ahead.

Even though I wish we could rest more and give them a better farewell, I must be responsible, so I order, "For now, let's send some of our forces as scouts and lookouts. We need people inside White Tower's walls, some on top of the wall, and some deep into the forest north, south, and east of our current position. We cannot be surrounded or surprised during our ceremony. Ensure everyone is ready in case we need them to fight." My carefulness does not allow me to lower our guards, even if my heart dearly hopes for a peaceful evening. The truth is we are at war, and the tides may turn unexpectedly if we become sloppy.

Jay's voice breaks my train of thought as he asks, "Where is Khan?" I feel embarrassed. Blushing, I recognize I have not asked for him. Rick's agony added to my planning has made me forget about my responsibility and respect for one of our leaders. Rick lowers his head and looks wearily at Jay. Those words seem to have stung deeply as he starts crying uncontrollably.

I look at him wide-eyed, as he says, "Khan did not make it. He gave his life to protect us when we found the explosives to blow the front gate. It was destiny that made us hide in a house where, unexpectedly, they stored them. He told us this was fate, this was the only way to turn our perils into opportunities. The gate had to fall for our forces to unite and overcome the numerous army sent by Cold." Dan lowers his head and holds his hands together in prayer. Em frowns in anger at our loss. Jay hugs Rick and cries together with him. Silver comes to me and embraces me, weeping into my chest. I feel devastated.

Rick continues without letting Jay go, "When we started our push toward the gate, losing men and women from the frontline who tried to carry the explosives, he led the way. He constantly faced numerous enemies at once, dodging, running, tackling, evading, and striking with an impressive speed, almost impossible to follow by eye. We were all exhausted, but his perseverance reinvigorated all of us." I feel so proud of Khan and so grieved about losing such an amazing soldier. Such an amazing man.

Rick lets go of Jay and looks at each of us, sharing, "The path toward the gate's base was clear for an instant. He yelled for our men to run and ignite the explosives. We ran together, covering them to ensure they reached their destination. A wave of enemies came hollering through the houses just beyond the walls. They outnumbered us, and we were defeated, but Khan gave us the opportunity to defeat Cold once and for all. He grabbed one of the explosives off one of our men. Using one of our torches, he ignited the wick, turned around, and winked at me. Before any of us could persuade him otherwise, he ran into our enemies fearlessly. The first explosion you heard was Khan giving his life to create the opening for us to destroy the front gate without enemies on us." Rick finishes his story and all of us share a group hug, remembering Khan and wishing him a final farewell silently.

Finally, I say, "Khan is the reason we succeeded, and he is the reason we are going to destroy Cold and all the filth standing beside him. The world deserves a future where men like Khan lead, instead of sacrifice." Rick falls to his knees and starts crying desperately. We try to console him. He says, "Thank you, Khan, thank you for the gift of tomorrow."

After a couple of minutes of silent cries and sadness, Rick stands up and says, "I will go ahead and coordinate with our men and women tonight's ceremony. It will help me clear my mind and give closure to my pain." I nod as he leaves our group and heads back toward our army.

The rest of us stay behind. I look around at them and think how all proved to be far more menacing than I believed them to be. It saddens me deeply to have lost Khan, and I wish none of these amazing leaders would fall. The world needs their resilience, their intelligence, their leadership, and their commitment to our future.

Bull was a destructive force in the battlefield, an amazing force. He is the only one who seems to be as good as new and ready for round two. Em was unstoppable, wrathful, a lighting striker; even though that word puzzle seems uncomprehending, it is the only way to describe her. Her moves are both elegant and extremely violent, as if a ballerina could wreck a car with her dance moves. Her grace is only equaled by her fierceness. She is standing beside me, waiting for our next step, both eager and at peace, though her body is not completely ready to fight again.

Dan is either asleep or meditating in our circle, held by Bull and Em with his eyes closed. The decision, even if it never was mine to make, to allow him into battle was one of the best I have made lately. He is still an impressive fighter, predicting his enemy's moves well ahead of time, striking calmly but effectively. However, his biggest contribution to our effort is his leadership. Soldiers around him seem to fight twice as resiliently as those around any other one of us. His presence is an amulet to them, the past enduring the present to build our future.

Silver and Jay are an amazing duo. They were able to reach the front gate in time, aid our forces with their arrow fire, defend themselves, and have minimal losses. I am extremely grateful to Silver for keeping my brother safe, but I know it was not completely her merit. I am proud of Jay and grateful for his effort.

It is time to go back and lead our forces; our bodies may not be fully rested and our injuries far from healed, but our responsibilities are far more important than our wellbeing at this time. I tell them, "I believe it is time to go and be with our battalions, listen to their traumas and fears, tend to their injuries, give them clarity about our next steps, and lead the ceremony. They need us far more than our bodies need our care. I'm sorry for this, but we are the chosen ones."

Dan opens his eyes and smiles caringly at me. Bull and Em nod and walk with him toward their battalions, walking away from the ram and White Tower. Silver and Jay walk with me, and I ask, "How are you two?" Jay looks down and answers softly, "War is war. The issue is that none of us had ever experienced it, so even if we talked about it and prepped for it, the reality is far more traumatic than expected." I agree with him. The three of us are different people now, even though it is unnoticeable. The memories of what each one experienced will be forever branded into us, and the pain will not ameliorate.

Silver hugs me by my waist as we walk, and I kiss her head. I inspect her to see how she truly is. She is covered in dirt, dried-up blood, and bruises. Her hair is a mess, and her skin is sticky from the dried-up sweat. Her lower lip is swollen, and a small cut over her right eye forces her to squint slightly. She is battered down, in pain, and exhausted without a doubt, yet she strides by me confident and committed to our cause. She is so beautiful and so amazing, I wish I could protect her every second of this war, but I cannot.

I wish I could be beside her and Jay every second of this to ensure they are well protected, away from danger and hurt. How I wish I could do so much more than my body and mind are capable of. However, life is not like that. Not in this world, not in the past world, and not in the one we are fighting to build. Sometimes coming to that conclusion makes us feel desperate with impotence. There is nothing to do more than accept it and go on. I must not allow my emotions to take control during the battle, as I could make a mistake and risk many innocent lives. How difficult.

Silver and Jay say goodbye and walk to my right toward the forest line, calling their battalion for a meeting. I look around and see Dan and Em about thirty meters to my left, giving instructions to our battalion. I walk toward Bull, who is straight up front, gathered with Battalion 2. As soon as I reach him, his soldiers cheer me. I hold my hands up embarrassed, asking them not to greet me so effusively. As the cheering fades, I say, "Soldiers, I need some volunteers to ensure we will not be surrounded. I come to you because I need marksmen capable of shooting down an enemy far away and with scarce light." Almost all of Bull's soldiers raise their hands as volunteers. It amazes me how loyal and courageous they are.

I pick two couples and four trios of soldiers and start assigning them to their tasks. I say, "You two will go on top of White Tower's wall, north of the fallen gate. You two will go south of the fallen gate. You are to stand guard; while one sleeps, the other must stay alert. Cold's army will probably stay around White Tower, waiting for us and setting up traps. That is okay, if they stay there, we will be fine. Any movement toward us, you will come to me as quickly as possible and alert me. Look for any rope or ladder or anything that will allow you to scale down outside White Tower quickly, in case you need to flee or come to me. Rest for a while, because I will need you up there in thirty minutes." The three men and the woman nod once and start prepping their weapons immediately.

I turn to the four remaining trios and command them, "You three will go north through the forest. Walk a kilometer in that direction and patrol walking east and west. Use random patterns, do not be obvious in your patrols. Try to always have another one of you in sight to avoid a surprise attack." They nod and stay listening while I give the remaining trios their orders. I point at one of the trios and say, "You three will do the same but going west, behind our army. We do not know if White Tower has other exits close by, and they might try to surround us." I point to another trio and say, "Same thing but to the east."

The last trio looks at me baffled as there are no more cardinal directions to protect, unless I want them to go into White Tower toward Cold's army. I smile at them and their fearful stares and share the last order, "You will not go into White Tower, so stop sweating." We all laugh, and I continue, "You three will oversee surveillance around our ceremony. As simple as that." They say "aye" in unison, and the four trios go to prep their weapons, equipment, and supplies.

I turn around and see how our army is congregating around the ram. I guess our leaders have chosen that place as the location for our ceremony. Bull pushes me with his shoulder and looks at me teasingly over his shoulder. His battalion follows him, and I walk behind them toward the ram. I feel sadness creeping inside of me, as I did not want this moment to come, and at the same time I need it to happen. Closure is sometimes one of the most difficult steps of any relation, event, or decision. Nonetheless, without it nothing would work out.

Everyone gathers around the ram. The ambiance is a mixture of sorrow and respect. The only sound comes from the scrape of shoes on the wall's debris from our scouts. We will honor those fallen today and all of those who have fallen to Cold's reign. Tonight, is the last night before all this comes to an end, and I am worried and encouraged at the same time. It feels as if I am being torn apart by two forces pulling in the same direction; very confusing.

We are down to one hundred thirty-plus men and women, facing a force that doubles our numbers. They have far more experience than us and are relentless in battle. However, retreating to regroup and strengthen for a future attack is unassailable. Where will we find more allies if we have traversed our known world? Besides, if we step back, Cold's forces will step forward, rebuild their stronghold, and attack each one of our villages one by one, until there are none. Now or never.

My duty tonight is to convince everyone that tomorrow is the start of a new day, of a new life, and of a new world. My task is to convince everyone of something I am not yet convinced of; how unnerving. The memory of Valor's men marching downhill toward the waterfall flashes quickly in my memory. I feel as if the mist and the excitement of that moment come back to me, caressing my face and heart simultaneously. Their chant.

I stand on top of the ram and take one last look at the crowd surrounding me. These men and women are my brothers and sisters, and I am ready to die for them. I speak out loudly, "The day to change the world has come. We stand here tonight on the verge of history and eternity. Not because we are going to die, but because what we do tomorrow will change the course of humanity. Cold, his men, his White Tower, everything and everyone he represents are an ignominious threat to what we all represent as human beings. Throughout history, humanity has pillaged, fought, destroyed, and moved on, to extents no one is capable of comprehending. We have been a parasite on this world." Some look at me expectantly; others are confused at my words, and I see Dan nodding a couple of meters in front of the ram, understanding where I am going.

I continue, "The world, nature, stepped up and said no more. It took back what was rightfully hers and sent us deep down the food chain. It sent us back to the basics of survival, and we have failed. No more! It is time to show the world we deserve to live in it, by eradicating the true evil that lives within humanity, and starting again. We must respect each other and that which surrounds us." Now I am getting more cheers, more applause, and more nods from my people.

I look at them for a couple seconds, imagining what I am about to share, "Don't you agree the waterfall was one of the most beautiful places ever seen? And yet, we had to go there only to hide from evil, instead of going there to pay our respects to nature and the permission it granted us to live. Now, most of you must be pondering about my intention, speaking about nature instead of against Cold. Let me clarify myself." My crowd laughs and some yell out, saying, "What have you done to Nathan?", "Are you drunk?", and "Invite us to try that liquor!" I laugh and feel comforted by their cleverness.

I hold both arms up to calm them down, and continue, "Nature decided to rewrite our wrongdoings, giving us a blank slate to live a better life, one more according to our place in this world. However, we were never allowed to live in peace and prosperity, to take advantage of our second chance, because of him. He took what was not his, he transformed peace into horror, stability into chaos, families into orphans, and humanity into a disease." I see my soldiers frowning, looking toward White Tower in discontent and screaming obscenities, releasing their anger.

I raise my voice even higher, "Some of you know, and some don't. My first motivation here was to save my mother. She is one of the tortured souls within White Tower, enslaved, humiliated, and broken down every single day. My mission was to save her, and only her; it was enough to fuel my anger, my desire for revenge. However, when Jay, Silver, and I saw what Cold did to Rick's town, we understood two things." My voice sounds menacing, and my body is heating up with the wrath I am feeling.

I raise two fingers up and say, "First, we were selfish to think Cold had only done damage to my brother and me. It was shortsighted to believe we could save her, and everything would be fine. Covering the sun with a finger. Saving her, if even possible, would change absolutely nothing. His forces could easily come back to us someday, when we had our guards down, enjoying a lie as a life, and send us back to this endless pit of grief. Second, we learned we were not alone. For seven years, my brother and I chose hiding as the best method to survive. It worked for our objective, but at the same time it worked toward a wrong objective. What good is it to survive in this world? What good is it to eat when others cannot even open their mouths because of the inhumane beatings they suffer as slaves? I will answer for you, my brothers and sisters. It is not worth it to live if you are not willing to grant the best possible quality of life to yourself and those around you."

More than a hundred pairs of eyes look at me intently, with tight lips and clenched jaws, closed fists and angered gazes. I assert, "In our hands lies the chance to be worthy of living or the decision to retreat and wait for the inevitable pain. Are we that pathetic? Are we that selfish? Think about those you are fighting for. Think about sons and daughters, fathers, mothers, brothers, and friends. Think about those born and those unborn. Think about all those kind souls who will not see tomorrow's dawn, not because they did not deserve to live, but because Cold judged and executed with no right." People start shouting hurray, pumping their fists up, yelling with unhappiness and anger.

I lower my voice slightly as a powerful and sad memory comes to mind. My voice cracks, "Think about Khan. He gave us his life and deserves our perseverance to end the fucked-up mess that worthless piece of shit has created. Khan sacrificed his life, but it was not to open the front gate. He sacrificed to open an opportunity for us, a once-in-a-lifetime chance to redeem ourselves and grant those behind us the world they deserve." My words stumble in my knotted throat, filled with emotion and wet by my tears.

A group of six soldiers bring Khan's remains toward me. He is wrapped on a brown linen, covered completely. Our army opens a path for them to bring the body closer to the ram and place it on top of it, beside my feet. I place a hand on his remains, grief inside of me, stomach void and my mouth trembling. I mutter the only words that can come out of me, "From dust we come, and to dust we shall return." Even if my body is not quite ready for it, I use my powers to light a pyre around Khan's body. The numerous doleful eyes staring at me are heartbreaking. People hug each other, cry on each other's shoulders, and speak softly. Others are praying on their knees or standing up and holding their hands together. My fellow leaders are looking straight at me, making sure I am fine and holding strong.

As the fire burns Khan's body to ashes, one by one, the closest friends or relatives of the sixty-six fallen soldiers share an emotive eulogy. Their words echo through the night, making me feel stronger and more motivated. All those soldiers were willing to give their lives for those they love, so why wouldn't we commit ourselves to fulfill their wish for a better future? As their words end, I light up pyres just like Khan's to accompany the dead in their journey to the afterlife. Prayer and meditation take a hold of the ceremony, and an almost imperceptible hum fills the entire field.

The fires dance through the night as the moon shares its light with us. Midnight is coming closer and our army disperses, walking away from White Tower's gate and setting up their sleeping quarters in the clearing in front of the fallen gate. Tonight, we rest and pray for a better tomorrow. I feel the burden of each one of those deaths on my shoulders; my body is weak and exhausted, but my mind is restless. Please guide me, please make me a better man, a better soldier, and a better leader.

***

Against all odds, the night was uneventful. Our forces managed to rest without any surprise attacks. Our scouts patrolled our surroundings all night, taking turns to rest, and did not spot a single threat or a mischievous movement in Cold's army. They have decided to stay behind and protect their White Tower, confident that we will not be able to defeat their massive numbers. I sit on my cot and see how our forces are getting ready, packing their belongings and prepping their weapons and armor.

Silver wakes up beside me, squinting her eyes at the bright sunlight, while covering her face with both hands. I bend over her and kiss her tenderly. She says, "Hello, handsome," and I answer, "Hello, beautiful." I hope deep inside this could be the way we start every day of our lives in better conditions. I imagine us lying in my bed back home, cuddling through the night, and waking up to singing birds and the pastel colors of a stunning dawn. While my mind wanders, I stare at her, enamored by her beauty. She blushes and looks at me playfully, making fun of me, "You should try to be less obvious with your crush if you want to avoid scaring her away." I glare at her and push her back on the cot, while she laughs, and I tickle her toned abdomen.

We stand up and look around the field. Bull and Em are far away to the west, close to the gate, and speaking with our scouts, who are on top of the wall. Dan is still resting in his cot a couple of dozen meters to the north. Rick is kneeling in front of the ram, praying. I say, "Do you see Jay?" Silver shakes her head while looking around. She says, "Maybe he is cleaning up. There is a river close by, we should go and rinse ourselves. Especially you, Nate, you smell." She laughs, grabs a small satchel with her clothes and towel, and runs away toward the forest away from White Tower. I grab my satchel, roll her cot over, and run behind her, chuckling and threatening her.

She runs around a couple of men who are packing a couple of pots and pans with a towel, then she rolls around an unused cot and continues sprinting. Occasionally, she turns around and her smile makes me ecstatic. I jump over the cot and run quickly; three soldiers are carrying a log and I almost crash against them. I slide on the ground to a halt and nod at them while walking around to my right. Silver is farther away; these twenty meters of a head start will be hard to reduce.

I command a fire wall in front of her, making her dive to her left, roll, and stand up again running. She looks back at me and grins, as she continues running into the forest. I use the power within me to boost my strength, accelerate, and run inhumanly fast. Her footsteps in the forest are heavy and easy to track, so I continue toward her direction hurriedly. I stop running for a second to listen intently, but there are no more footsteps. She must be hiding.

I ignite both arms on fire and start walking tauntingly through the forest in case she sees me. Three meters in front of me I see her shoe coming out of a tree. It is a trap; she left her shoe to make me believe she is hiding unsuccessfully. I decide to trigger it to find her, so I walk toward the shoe, crawling slowly. My right arm extends toward the shoe, and I listen to the slightest sound behind me of a dry leaf being stepped on. With a wide smile on my face, I roll around on my back and turn to find her cursing at her failure.

Sil jumps on me and punches my right arm, shaking her head. She smirks and says, "Shut up, idiot!" Immediately she lays her soft lips on mine, with a hand on my hip and the other on my neck. I place both hands on her lovely face, caressing her while tasting her, enjoying our lives and daydreaming. I grab her by her leg and roll over, lying on top of her.

The wind blows her hair softly on her face, and I get lost deeply in her green eyes. She smiles at me, as words escape from me, "I love you, Silver. This may be my last day alive, as it could be the first day of the rest of our lives, so I need to tell you I love you. You are a blessing in my life. Promise me you will be safe today. Promise me we will be together tomorrow." She blinks slowly, looking straight into my eyes and caressing my left cheek. She says firmly, "Nate, do not worry about me. I will be fine, and I will look after Jay. You must focus on the battle, on leading us, and on giving everything you've got to defeat Cold's empire. We will be safe today. We will be together tomorrow. And I love you like I have never loved a single soul outside of my family."

I kiss her once again, feeling our love through our dancing lips and tender caresses. I wish I could stay here forever with her, and at the same time, this strengthens my desire to succeed against our enemies. If we defeat them, the world we will build will allow us to enjoy, to love, to travel the world and share a life. This is a mirage of what we could build, and it inspires me.

A voice comes from somewhere deeper into the forest, "That is absolutely disgusting. You two should be leading our soldiers, not doing that!" I look up and see Jay standing with a disgusted face pointing at us. Sil and I laugh as I say, "Shut up, ugly pigmy. Only because you are too ugly to be loved, does not mean I should stay single!" The three of us share a laugh as I stand up and help Silver get up as well. We swat the dirt away from our clothes and walk toward Jay.

Sil says, "Ugly pigmy, where is the river?" I cackle as Jay looks at Silver in discontent; he has recently bathed and has even combed his hair. Jay points northeast and answers, "About three hundred meters in that direction. Hurry up." He walks past us and gives me a shove with his shoulder, barely making me move. My brother grins at me, and I wink back.

Silver and I walk hurriedly toward the river since we must hurry. The trees shade us from the heating sun. The day to change the world is a beautiful one, with a bright sunlight and a pleasant breeze. We can hear the slow river flowing and the sound calms me. However, water taught us in the past that the world may seem benevolent and tranquilizing, but the truth is that we are never to let our guards down. Not until we have defeated the colossal challenge in front of us.

Silver takes her shoes, socks, pants, and shirt off quickly. I stare at her, mesmerized by how attractive she is. I have never seen her without her clothes, and I blush and get aroused by her beauty. She gets into the river's calm waters and starts rinsing her hair and face. She stands back up again and says, "You are too in love. I think I am going to get bored by those puppy eyes. Get in!" I laugh loudly and am embarrassed at being caught drooling over her. I take my clothes off, except my underwear, and run toward her, splashing her face on purpose. She laughs, and I interrupt her with a big kiss, while she wraps her legs around me and I raise both of us out of the water.

We must look like two lovebirds on their honeymoon, and that is exactly how it feels. We are newlyweds, not because we are married, but because we are about to embark upon an adventure together that will change our lives forever. Add the fact that one or both of us could be dead tomorrow, and it is impossible not to love Silver, to kiss her, to dream about being with her for the rest of my life. We walk a couple of meters away from each other to resist the temptation to continue kissing until the world ends and finish washing ourselves.

The cold water relaxes my body, but it does not cool me

down. Inside I feel my power building up, amassing an impressive force, waiting to be released. Just like a volcano getting ready to erupt, with magma rising slowly to the crust, withholding its massive energy for a final explosion. Silver walks outside of the river and dries herself under the sunlight. I wash my face once more, feeling the cold trickling water on my closed eyelids and my lips, concentrating on enjoying the moment. The birds sing, the sunlight heats my body, and the wind pushes on my hair gently.

I walk toward Silver, kiss her cheek, and start readying myself. This place is stunning, and we will come again once we have succeeded in our destiny. It does not make sense to have such beauty in the world and be unable to enjoy it and protect it. Humans have the biggest responsibility of all species, as we can destroy or improve our ecosystems. Why are we so vain and egocentric? Why do we make decisions that affect everything around us with complete disinterest and lack of responsibility? This is part of what we must change, and it all starts with defeating Cold.

Silver and I finish getting dressed and start walking back to camp. It must be around eight in the morning, the time to write history. Sil extends her left hand to her side and I grab it, feeling her warm skin in my hand as we walk together. Our footsteps are the only sound I notice, while my mind wanders to the future battlefield. Our plan is set, our men and women are ready, our enemy is expectant, and the time to face our biggest fears has come. There is no turning back, no surrender, and no place for fear.

Silver looks at me, and I give her a supporting wink. She says, "Are you really okay?" I guess she is worried about my crumbling under all this pressure, as her frown reveals her concern. She is amazing and having her here allows me to have an anchor to reality. I look ahead and answer, "We will be fine, Sil. The responsibility laid upon me, upon us, upon all our leaders is massive and the consequence of fate. I believe we are ready, and I am convinced we will succeed. Nonetheless, I am fighting against the dread of losing one of you and of people dying for our cause. Even if it is possible and a normal consequence of the decisions we have made, I cannot accept it as a reality. I promise you I am focusing on using that dismay to our advantage, to lead better and to fight fiercer."

Silver smiles widely and presses her grip on my hand, excited at my words. She kisses my hand and adds, "I am proud of you, Nate. We are tremendously honored to have you in our ranks, as our leader." I blush immediately and feel goose bumps running on my arms and butterflies in my stomach, caught by surprise at her comment. I am lucky to have such an amazing woman walking together with me toward a nearly impossible mission.

We exit the forest and see all our forces are assembled in a massive square formation in front of the ram. All our supplies and cots are neatly organized behind them, waiting for our return. Silver and I walk among our ranks, who open a path for us toward the ram. Our men and women smile, bow, nod, and cheer as we walk by. I laugh as it feels like walking down to the altar. Silver rolls her eyes at me and giggles. Bull and Dan are straight ahead, waiting for us in front of the ram.

Silver releases my hand and walks to Jay who is right next to Dan. Em and Rick are looking at me excitedly from behind Bull. I climb on a couple of boxes and logs they have set up beside the burnt ram. I look at our army, at the last hope for humanity, and feel honored and riled up. This is it!

I extend my arms and say at the top of my lungs, "Men and women, we have prepared for this day. Not for days, not for weeks or for months, but for our entire lives. The world sent us back to our roots and, as always, two forces have emerged. Evil, horror, tyranny, slavery, and pain took the reins of humanity and built this godforsaken place. Family, love, tenderness, respect, and kindness were stepped on, humiliated, and killed. Today it all ends! Today we fight to change the world! Today we will enter history as those willing to give their lives for those who have lived subjugated for far too long. This is it, men and women!"

Our army stares at me excitedly, gritting their teeth, clenching their jaws, pumping their arms, clattering their armor, and patting each other. I conclude, "Let's make the earth rumble under our feet as we march into a better tomorrow. For us, for our families, and for our future!" A massive roar erupts as every single soul cheer and screams as loudly as they can. I turn around to look at White Tower, surrounded by the large enemy army. They must be hearing us, they must know we are coming, and they must be panicked.

I climb down the wooden boxes and hug each one of our leaders. We are ready; their gazes are focused and filled with hate. Bull hands me my bow and quiver, Dan gives me my sword elegantly, and I prepare myself for battle. We march toward the crumbled gate, as the drum of footsteps behind us really does make the earth rumble.

For the first time, I enter the walled city of White Tower. The crumbled wall under my feet reassures me we are on the right path. Cold's army has stayed deep inside the city, surrounding the tower erected in front of us. A dark shadowy mass, silent, unmovable, waiting for us. Uncertainty and fear try to creep inside of me, but it will not be able to defeat that which moves me to lead my people.

Rick leads our army into the city, while the rest of us are to meet one last time on top of the wall. The stairway up the wall is slippery with moss and the smell of humidity, that of a neglected pond. Silver and Jay lead the way, and behind me comes Em, Bull, and Dan. Dan's strides are slow and careful, curious since I saw him fight elegantly and swiftly with that same battered body. Khan's memory is still fresh, and it makes me think about these leaders with me. We cannot lose anyone else, not because we would be unable to be victorious, but because the world we are building needs people like these.

On top of the wall's uppermost section, we stand to gaze upon the massive army waiting for our move. Their armors reflecting the sunlight challenge us, and their shadows dance under White

Tower's fire. At least we were not in error when expecting Cold to hold his ground around his precious tower. Our task is to decide how to tackle this unbelievable obstacle in our way. Cold did send a large part of his army to face us, but what is still waiting to battle us is far larger. A sea of men poisonous to humanity staring back at us from the distance.

I ask my fellow commanders, "What do you see?", to break the silence and start planning. Jay takes the initiative, "A block formation," he replies, surprising me once more with his enthusiasm and maturity, yet he still fails to see more than two steps ahead in time. That is why Silver must always be by his side.

Dan adds, "Yes, my young friend, but look deeper. We know Cold's army is about three hundred and fifty units strong. Less about one hundred and thirty we defeated yesterday still leaves us with about two twenty. Do you see that many soldiers around White Tower?" Dan's passive and nurturing voice once more guides us with its wisdom. He does not condone wrong or hurried answers but uses them to lecture and teach. I am honored to have him as a master and friend.

Jay quickly amends his answer, "No. He is still withholding a part of his army, either as backup or to force us to engage directly and be surrounded.", a ready-witted comment. Dan smiles, places a hand on Jay's shoulder, and says, "Exactly. Now, we cannot be sure as to what those hidden forces are going to be used for; however, we must use this knowledge to our advantage. This is what will allow us to be unexpected as the Seven-Fold Strategy suggests." We all nod, and I look at all of them silently, reading their gestures to make sure we are all on the same page.

Dan continues, "Our forces will have to engage in a frontal assault to trick Cold into believing we fell into his trap. Before long, to avoid heavy casualties and succumbing into Cold's trap, our forces must adapt. How do you suggest we do this?" Dan sets the conversation's tone and direction, guiding our train of thought.

Bull suggests, "The frontal assault could work in the first

place. We have trained exhaustingly, and the first battle proved us right. Ninety enemies coming from White Tower, plus the soldiers both our north and south forces faced on top of the wall, were no match. Why should we march predisposed to fail in a frontal assault?" He is striding head on.

Silver mediates, "You are right, Bull. If the battle's tide favors us, we will ride the wave and push on. Given a favorable initial strike from our forces, the decision must be to go on, to fight through, and try to defeat Cold's main force before his trap springs into action. What we are suggesting is to be ready to react in case our initial strike fails to be dominant, before his con comes into action and defeats us." Sil is right, it is not a black-and-white decision, but a strategy that needs to contemplate adaptability.

Em points out, "I believe that as we approach White Tower, we should advance slowly, searching every building in the city, every crack and crevice to ensure this hidden force is not behind us. This way, if we need to retreat, we would all be certain which way to go. If we march straight on without ensuring the path behind, we could retreat straight into a tight spot. As a bear's trap, two iron jaws clenching and enclosing us." I am surprised by how wise she is and how none of us had thought about it. Dan and Bull nod; Silver and Jay look at each other.

All their faces turn toward me expectantly, as if I possess the answer to their dilemmas. The pressure is on me, but under pressure is when I usually work the best. Quickly weighing the pros and cons of the alternatives I have thought of during their conversation, and blending all their suggestions, I come up with an answer. At least a suggestion.

We huddle up to hear my plan. I slowly explain out how I believe we should approach Cold's army, with a team-based formation, inspecting the path ahead and behind us as Em suggested. Each step in my plan is supported by their nods, smiles, or sly grins. The ambiance begins to heat up, not with temperature, but with excitement. Dan stares at me with his deep gray eyes, making me feel x-rayed. The others notice it and turn their attention to him. Is he doubting my plan? Has he found a mistake dooming us?

Dan finally answers our silent doubts, "The day to change the world has come. Nathan, guide us into the future." No more words are needed; time to act.

Dan, Em, and Bull descend the stairway slowly, walking to the front of our army that stands organized within White Tower. I hold Silver and Jay back. I hug Jay and whisper to his ear, "Brother, you have made me the proudest man alive. Be careful, listen to Silver, remember your training and experiences. Mom awaits us, and we will succeed." Jay hugs me tightly and sobs at my words. Cleaning a couple of tears away, he stands in front of me, nods, and says, "Thank you, brother, for leading us. Thank you for allowing me to live." I kiss his head and pat his back as he goes down the stairs.

Silver looks at me with doleful and watery eyes. I grin and open my arms for her to rush into a hug. We hold each other in silence. I kiss her head, then her forehead, as she stares up at me. We lock eyes and kiss tenderly with our lips tasting our love. Her warm body against mine comforts me and relaxes the rush of emotions running through my mind. This is the place where we are supposed to be, there is no other place, no other path, no other present than this. I say once more, "I love you, Silver. We'll meet at the other side." She kisses me lightly once more and answers, "I will be waiting, my love."

We walk down the stairs holding hands and walk toward the front of our army. The sun is starting to heat up, and the moist soil hardens under our feet. Several towering clouds rest over our heads, promising a refreshing shadow during our confrontation, and possibly a relaxing light rain.

We have decided to ensemble three squads, instead of battalions, to avoid confusion. Squad 1 or S1 will be front and center, led by Rick, Bull, and myself with sixty-five soldiers. Most of them are melee fighters, skilled warriors who attack dead on without retreating. Squad 2 or S2 will march to our left, guided by Em and Dan, with thirty-five more. Squad 3 or S3 protects our right, led by Silver and Jay, and the rest of our thirty-five men and women. Behind their squads, our bowmen will walk protected by a shield wall held by some of our strongest.

Their task is to shower our enemies with a continuous rain of arrows, forcing them to engage S1 straight forward. As the battle progresses, S2 and S4 will disperse into a curve formation, semi-encircling our enemies, and guiding them deeper into S1's direction. They are the most vulnerable against Cold's hidden forces, since they will be spread out. We must be ready to retreat as soon as it becomes necessary to avoid heavy losses.

White Tower's light blinds us as we stand ready for war, failing to stop us. Swords crashing against shields, shouts of hope, hugs among friends, kisses between partners, whispers of good fortune, and enamored dreams about the future to come. We are ready to send Cold and his evil to a place of no return. Even though my body is still weary from yesterday's efforts, my heart and soul are fueled to their maximum, expectant of the moment to erupt all my power to aid these men and women who risk their lives for humanity.

And Mom. Her smiling face flashes constantly in my mind. A memory of one day, when she looked back at us from our house's garden, with the wind blowing her hair toward her face, and she was laughing at our resistance to help her by doing our chores. Making that memory come true again is the wind behind my sail.

S1 is ready; S2 and S3 are formed up. Walking in front of all these courageous fellows gives me that amazing feeling of emptiness in my stomach and eagerness in my spirit. There is no turning back now but doing so has never been part of the plan. Our future awaits behind White Tower, beyond Cold's destruction and on what we will build on top of this city's remains. Before turning toward our army, I look ahead, toward the towering white citadel and the black mass of enemies waiting for us. I smile threateningly.

I look at our soldiers and say my final words, "Men and women, brothers and sisters, we are here for something greater than any one of us, and far more transcendent than all of us together as well. One hundred and thirty-plus, ready to fight, to persevere, and to endure for all humanity. Your families and friends, of yesterday, today, and tomorrow, have laid upon us the responsibility to cleanse the lot where we shall build our well-deserved future." Our soldiers listen intently, holding their cheers and clatters for my speech.

I continue, "Remember our fallen brothers. Those who have succumbed in the past, and those who have given their lives during this endeavor. We owe them our lives, our last drop of sweat and thread of strength. One step back from us is one step forward for Cold, for his sickness to spread farther. See them ahead of us, all enclosed around White Tower, contained and certainly afraid. Do we want them to regain all the terrain we have grasped from their evil claws?"

Our army answers in unison, "No!" Their sound reaches our enemies. I add, "We want them to go into nonexistence. We want them to be a wicked memory of what humanity became and what it will never become again. For too long we have lived in darkness and fear, for too long we have secretly wished for someone to act upon our principles against theirs, and for too long we were self-absorbed by doubt clouding the obvious. We are those chosen to act, we are those chosen to shine light upon darkness, and hope upon fear. We are those chosen to change the world." I stop pacing in front of them and look straight to the heart of our army.

I conclude, "Are you ready?" My voice reaches its peak, and it is immediately followed by a shower of hollers and screams, of swords rising to the sky and shields crashing to the ground. Goose bumps on every single centimeter of my body and up to the back of my neck make me shiver. Destiny did not choose me, these men and women did, and trust my word, I will not let them down. My life is theirs, and if necessary, I will give it to ensure tomorrow is ours. Jay will have Mom, and they will have the world they deserve.

Bull's deep voice resounds across the plain, "March!" Bull and I lead Squad 1 as it starts walking first, leading the slow charge. Armors cling and slow breaths filled with emotion take control of the mood. No more words are spoken, but the connection between all of us is palpable. Jay must be having an uncontrollable and incomprehensive mountain of emotions swirling in his head. *Use it, brother, use it to your advantage.*

Once S1 has a twenty-meter lead, S2 and S3 simultaneously start their advance behind us. I can hear their heavy footsteps behind us, covering our backs and giving me a sense of invulnerability. This way, our archers are slightly behind, becoming a more difficult target for our enemies, and protected by our main frontal assault force. While our enemies focus on us, they will start encircling them and pushing them unknowingly into our clasps.

Our formations walk through the houses between the front gate and White Tower. These are well-built, painted houses destined probably for Cold's army. An orderly and clean neighborhood, with straight and clean pathways, advanced training grounds with courses and equipment to our right, a large common ground to our left, and the largest stable I have ever seen popping up about fifty meters in front and to our right.

We zigzag through this façade. We know this life is granted by Cold only to those willing to kill, rape, pillage, and humiliate at his command. This town is built on top of the hundreds of men and women who have died from slavery and unforgiving raids. This place is the reason why we are here, to mend the damage he has committed.

While we advance, our men and women walk into the houses to scan the premises. I can hear them breaking the doors down, rushing into the houses with their weapons ready for any confrontation. Around and under them we look for hatches, inside we look for hidden panels between walls and on rooftops.

Before we engage the large force waiting for us, every house must be inspected and rejected as a threat to our retreat. Encirclement is not going to happen to us; we will not be caught between two clenching enemy forces.

One by one, the houses are inspected and eliminated as possible threats. Their doors are left open to signal others they have been inspected already. No threat is found, and we continue our slow but steady advance toward White Tower. We leave the last house behind, walking like an ocean wave on the sand. Four hundred meters to go, wide in the open, no more houses between us and them. The sun shines brightly and clearly, showing us the way.

White Tower is erected high in front of us, higher than the myths, made with white blocks in a cylindrical formation. It has no moat around it, no arrow slits, no windows, and no strategic value. It is only a symbol, an edification of hatred and arrogance. At its uppermost section, where it turns into a triangular roof made with red bricks, an immense fire, framed with an arch, rages. The never-ending fire. The army in front of it looks expectant, and my heartbeat is racing as we approach them.

Close to the top, a scaffold protrudes from the tower. It is built about two meters below the fire, and it goes around the entire circumference. In it, a dark shadow of a man stands, leaning on a railing, contemplating the whole scene. That bastard must be Cold. He is not even amongst his forces, hidden away, staring as a spectator. Before the day ends, I will make him a participant. I will strike him down from his hideaway.

Each step bringing us closer to it proves the disgusting and angering myth. The tower is painted all around with small red dashes, counting the slaves sacrificed in this earthly hell. Silver's story about White Tower is true, and my wrath boils inside, desperate to erupt against that demon. I will not stop until he turns to ashes and the wind blows them away into oblivion.

Fire twirls around my arms and falls behind me as a king's coat. Our forces cheer in anticipation, "Phoenix! Phoenix!

Phoenix!" Their screams are high and loud, reaching our enemies, who start moving side to side, nervously. They are not as immovable as they try to look; they are afraid of us, of not knowing, for the first time, if they will succeed. This time, they are not facing unarmed, unprepared men and women. This time, they are facing the largest threat to their existence.

S1 halts its advance three hundred meters away from enemy lines, and S2 and S3 thin their formation to ready for our encircling maneuver. While waiting, I look around to analyze our surroundings. White Tower is imposing, with the sun shining strongly into its front face, showing the red dashes of evil. To the left, an old forest lies on the ground, cut down, burnt, and destroyed. The ground is dry, broken, and unamendable.

To our right and deep inside the city, a quarry peeks behind the tower. Around the quarry, hundreds of broken-down, unattended houses stand. With incomplete walls and fallen panels, those houses look closer to chicken barns than human premises. There is where they hold slaves, and there is where Mom is. Our formations are set, and we are ready to engage. Our move.

Before giving the order to strike, I look once more toward the quarry and the slaves' citadel. A mound of some sort is visible between White Tower and the houses. It confuses me; it is not homogenous as a mining mound, but irregular and shapeless. My body freezes, and not even the expectant gazes of our army get me out of the shock. That mound is made from human bodies; the irregular shapes are heads, and arms, and legs of dead bodies stacked one on top of the other.

My body shudders violently with vengeance, and the fire within me becomes uncontainable. My body enlarges the most it ever has, and my piercing red eyes shine back to me from my shield. A massive fire column shoots straight up from my body, reaching the clouds, illuminating as strongly as the sun, accompanied with my loudest scream. "Men and women, to us, to our future, and to all those lives depending on us. To war!"

Our march restarts steadily, hurried and contained at the same time. Our lines advance with heavy strides, aligned with our shields up and our swords at the ready. Our archers string their bows and pull back their arrows, waiting for the signal to engage. Screams of hope resound along swords crashing against shields, and blend with reassuring yells. This is it, what we have all worked for; this is what so many have passed on and deposited their hopes and dreams on us, for a world without evil.

Our enemies' first shower of arrows falls on us, but each leader manages to give the order to raise shields in time. No casualties, and hundreds of arrows wasted. Two hundred meters separate us from the army twice as large, but half as courageous. Their motivation is weak, ours is eternal. They start moving again expectantly, holding their ground and formations.

S1 will be easily surrounded by the long formation they have, we hope for it. As soon as they break their block formation and try to engage us all at the same time, our S2 and S3 will enclose them with arrow fire. We need them to try to eradicate S1 first, and it places Rick, Bull, and me in a tight spot. We must hold them back, fight two or three enemies at once, and give our archers the chance to skim forces from their backs before they notice their mistake.

One hundred meters and their arrow volleys have become continuous and disorganized. Our shields are held up, not lowered for even a second. Each hit resounds against the metal, and the slicing of our swords breaking the inlaid arrows is reassuring. Cold is silent on top of the tower, in his safe place; what a cowardly, useless piece of shit. His army starts advancing toward us, two massive human waves about to collide.

Thirty more meters and we are still marching in formation, orderly to avoid a break. They run at us, breaking their front line, opening clear marks for our archers. I scream to the top of my lungs, "Shoot!", and our archers skillfully trespass their irregularity with arrows digging deeply in their legs, their torsos, their necks, and even their heads. At least twenty enemies crash to the ground lifeless, and their fellows run on top of the deceased bodies to continue their stride forward. A complete disregard for human life, reassuring us about our motives.

Our forces stop as planned, ready to receive the enormous running mess of an army coming toward us. An instant before the clash of both forces, time seems to slow down. Rick is expectant, staring straight into our enemies with his shield up. Bull has his massive sword ready, with his strong legs in position to start tackling his way into enemy lines. Dan moves his sword elegantly, in circles and sways, calm, ready, and expecting his first enemy. Em has no shield, and is standing still, with a wide stance and one sword held in front of her and the other at her side. Fool the one who dares to attack her.

To my right, Jay is nervously tapping his front foot, desiring to run toward the enemy. Silver holds her sword in one hand and her shield in front covering both. I stare at my sword and decide to give it an edge, and a signal for our forces to see me. Fire surrounds the blade. Time.

A last yell from our forces and the battle begins. Swords clash all around us, shields push and crash against enemies, arrows fly over our heads, dust clouds start to rise around the entire field, and bodies start to fall. A man wearing a dark robe over his armor strikes heavily toward my head, but I dance around the blade and cut his calves. With a swift turn, my blade rips into his back and protrudes through his chest cavity.

Two more come my way. My sword crashes against one of theirs, while my shield protects my head from the other. I cross my left arm to stop the other's sword with my shield, while my sword goes toward my left assailant to prod with its point. His thigh rips open, and I turn, pushing the enemy at my right with my shield, while my sword circles around to end the fallen enemy who holds his bleeding leg. The other one slips to my shove, and I jump toward him, driving my sword deep into his abdomen.

Blood spurts, staining my face and blade, but the strong fire encircling it evaporates the blood immediately. To my left, Bull is striking enemies down with a ferocity unknown even to me. They crash against him, useless as wind trying to move a mountain. A giant against mice.

To my right, Rick is leading a handful of soldiers in a frontal assault, instructing them who to engage and warning them about enemies approaching; he is a team leader. Jay and Silver are protecting their squad from the few enemies who have decided not to engage S1. They fight in unison, covering each other's back, commanding their fellow soldiers to shoot arrows. To my left, Dan is fighting graciously through enemies, killing slowly but constantly. Em is a far more electric fighter; it's even difficult for me to follow her.

Around each one of us, our squads are engaging enemies with no rest. In most encounters we are outnumbered, facing at least two enemies at the same time. The battle is brutal, bodies piling up on top of each other, blood dripping from open wounds; screams of pain and terror across the field are widespread. A woman tries to cut my legs off, but I jump in time and kick her sword from her hand. Before she manages to run away, I slice her right arm and thrust my sword into her right side.

I command our men and women, "Come on, give your everything. Death to evil!" They must go on, stand their ground, fight with principles and skill. However, the number difference is proving significant. Around me, more and more bodies of our forces pile up. We are fighting audaciously against an insurmountable wave of nonstop enemies. For everyone we kill, we seem to lose one of our own. This way we will not be victorious.

I see how one of our soldiers fights an enemy with fierce blows landing from his sword and shield. He turns and twirls to find an opening, he works hard to defeat the enraged adversary. He ducks and rolls, he tackles forward and digs his feet deep into the ground to get a stronger stance. Twenty blows, and the fight is not over. He finally blocks a wide hit with his shield and manages to plunge his sword through the enemy's throat. I am almost beside him, running to his aid.

Three meters away from him. His exhausted body makes him rest his arms on his knees while panting; an enemy grabs him from behind and cuts his neck with a hand knife. I send a fire wave and calcinate the enemy. The moment I reach my soldier and turn him around, I see his unresponsive dead eyes. He worked his life off to kill one enemy, just to be backstabbed easily by an undeserving foe. Our excessive work is tiring us and making us vulnerable.

The other squads are facing similar destinies. Men and women of our own are dying, every time more quickly. Our strategy with archers is proving effective to direct the heavy load of attack from our enemies toward S1, killing their back forces before they reach us. However, the concentration of forces is taking heavy casualties from us. Time to start retreating into the soldiers' houses. Too soon.

Before giving the order, I see Dan deep into enemy lines about sixty meters away. He is holding an enemy by his hand while penetrating another's head with an upward thrust from his sword. He releases the other's hand, and a second before striking him down, Dan flies three meters high and crashes painfully on the ground. His frail old body takes a massive hit, and he is finding it hard to stand. Using his sword as a cane, he gets back up to face toward the enemy he just failed to execute.

Ten meters in front of him, Cold walks with a maniacal smirk on his face. Dan runs unstably toward him with his sword up. An instant before reaching his target, he is pushed back by an invisible force, managing to hold his ground by shoving the sword into the ground. Cold points his sword toward Dan, who is lunging six meters away. The sword starts to gravitate on its own, flies toward Dan, and quickly as a bullet trespasses his neck.

My eyes open wide, and my anger spikes. "Dan!" My words are mixed and lost with the chaos surrounding us. While running I strike enemy after enemy down, slicing them with my fiery sword, using my shield to cover and shove them away before burning them up. Cold is walking back toward White Tower, so I double my run.

More and more enemies try to engage me, halting my advance, but all to the same end. My sword crashes against theirs, my shield clangs against their futile attempts to hurt me, and at the slightest opening, I cut, trespass, or burn them to their graves. My anger is unending, and all those in my way toward Cold will perish. His death is the only way to make this massive army retreat. He walks arrogantly among them; they will continue their attack.

Five men start surrounding me. They have finally understood one or two of them are simply not enough against my wrath. This could be trouble. One strikes me from behind, and I barely manage to duck and crash my sword against another's shield, used to protect the first attacker. Two more enemies run toward me, so I duck and roll beneath their strikes and cut one's ankle. He stumbles but reassembles in their circle, supported by his uninjured leg.

They start walking toward me, attacking with their swords, spitting at me, trying to catch my attention and create a chance for those behind to kill me. I spin around with my sword extended to make them step back. One step back and two steps forward is what I get from them. A tight situation; there is no other way.

I release both my sword and shield, and before they hit the ground, I bring both arms together in a cross in front of my chest. The moment I extend them and raise my head to the skies, a swirl of fire erupts from my body and consumes the five enemies. The whipping flames engulfing them, twisting around their exposed bodies. Before they touch the ground, they are dead.

My body resents it, and I take an unwanted knee. Gasping, the fire around my sword starts to flicker as a candle left with almost no wick to spare. Bull sees me down and redirects his attack toward my direction. He shouts in his deep, commanding voice, "Protect Nate!" An enemy crashes against Bull's massive running body and falls back, receiving Bull's large sword through his abdomen.

More and more enemies crash and fall against his rampage, and our men and women take advantage to stab and kill them. He is close to me, while I fight off an enemy with my sword while kneeling. I stand up feebly and face him straight on. Each crash of our swords exhausts me. My vision is hazy, my arms are heavy, and I feel the fire within me dimming. Heavy breathing is not managing to bring me back to my senses, as the exhaustion is internal, but not physical.

Bull is ten meters away from me when an arrow digs deeply into his shoulder blade. He turns around and another arrow sticks into his abdomen. Two more hit his right thigh, and he falls, silently, staring toward the enemy lines and giving his back to me. I gaze up and see Cold with a quiver and no bow. I finally understand the hurricane that almost blew me down from my tree hideout when pursuing him while searching for Jay.

He is sending arrows flying toward Bull with his powers. He commands wind. That bastard will not take away more worthy men from this world. I kill my enemy with a quick slice of my sword to his neck. I turn toward Cold, gathering my remaining strength, and shoot both my arms in his direction, sending a flash flood of fire. He sends a whirlwind in my direction, sending the flames around him; an invisible shield protects him. My anger builds up and it fuels the flames further, making them larger and fiercer. He continues protecting himself against them, but they close in on him every second that passes.

Cold starts retreating into White Tower, entering a door behind him and disappearing in the shadows. The fire strikes the tower, as a wave crashing on a cliff. A coward. This allows me to limp toward Bull and instruct those around us to cover him with a shield wall. I scream, "Time to execute phase two!" Rick, Em, Silver, and Jay repeat my orders loudly.

All our front forces reconstruct the shield wall, and we start retreating slowly, still engaging our enemies, but walking back toward the soldiers' houses steadily. Rick appears beside me, and we start dragging Bull's heavy body. I am fainting with the effort, so another soldier grabs Bull's arm in my stead. They drag him along, as the enemy army continues its advance, engaging our frontal line, and showering arrows on those behind them.

Help. A known voice resounds in my head, as I turn to my right and see Jay and Silver surrounded, fighting almost ten enemies at once. Their squad is stripped down to the bone, with only fifteen men and women left, unable to protect their leaders. I order, "Come! Protect Bull, help Rick. I am needed elsewhere." My voice sounds commanding and desperate at the same time.

The few enemies left within our retreating shield wall go down one by one to my sword. The enemies outside are trying desperately to break it and failing. The flying arrows crash against my shield, held up high while running to my brother's aid. I create a wave of fire in front of me, burning three of the enemies surrounding Sil and Jay. I jump high over the fire and shove an enemy out of the way. "Let's go." I wink at Silver and pat Jay's shoulder.

The three of us engage the remaining seven enemies in synchrony. Sil ducks and I strike an enemy's helmet with a heavy blow, while she pushes her sword into his groin. Jay tangles himself in a quick sword fight with one of them, as I surround another with a flaming tornado.

Jay succeeds at overpowering his enemy and dodges another's strike. Silver pushes a woman in my direction, and I cut her neck with a swift slice. Three on three now. Each one of us pushes forward, and swords and shields try to block our attacks desperately, however uselessly. They die with no honor or glory. We walk toward the front wall to aid in our orderly retreat.

I speak into Jay's mind, *"Jay, listen to me. It is time for our plan. Run back toward the soldiers' town, turn left, and run as quickly as you can up north. Mom must be in the quarry peeking behind White Tower to the right. Find her, protect her, and bring her back toward us. I will lead phase three of our plan. When you hear it go off, start running your ass off. It will be your cover. Go!"*

Jay looks at me, nods, and vanishes behind us in a dash. Silver turns her head, sees him running, and smiles toward me. As we hold the shield wall against our enemies' pushing, walking slowly back toward the housings, she gives me a quick kiss. She understands our plan, and I love her for it. I say under my gasps, "Thank you for protecting him, Sil." She grunts and says, "Nothing to be thankful for. He is sort of my brother-in-law." She laughs beautifully, and I give her a small nudge.

Our shield wall starts reaching the first houses, and phase three is about to go off. Behind White Tower, a loud horn rumbles across the landscape. About fifty horses emerge and start galloping in our direction. Cold's backup has sprung, and at the worst time possible… They run quickly across the distance between our retreat and our enemies. Cold's army stops harassing our shield wall to allow for the cavalry to engage us.

We break the wall and start running back into the town and toward the front gate. I stop about ninety meters into the town, and stay behind; no one even looks back, except Sil. The horse hooves make the ground shake, the dust cloud behind them looks menacing, and the enemy forces decide to join their stride by running toward me. They start funneling straight in my direction; they know who I am and why they must kill me first. At least, I can buy time for my army in their retreat.

I raise both my hands and point them in their direction. I don't have enough energy left to calcinate the fifty horsed soldiers and the almost one hundred running men and women. Concentrating, staring toward Cold to build up my rage, fire starts sparking inside of me, restarting, using the last of my inner fuel. Time for phase three; time to change the tide of battle.

With all my remaining strength, I send a ray of fire from each one of my hands toward the houses lining the road on which I stand. The enemy advance halts momentarily. Since no enemy soldier is burnt by the first wave, they proceed their stampede against me. Another couple of rays of fire emerge from my hands, twice as powerful and long. Small fires start igniting on the front steps of the house. It has worked.

A massive explosion sends wood panels, dust, and debris toward Cold's army. Horses, men, and women are sent flying to every direction, crashing against the fallen houses, and flying back toward White Tower. Smoke quickly covers the landscape high and above, obscuring my entire vision. The fifty cavalrymen are dead, their bodies thrown all around the devastated road.

The survivors of Cold's army are getting up feebly, confused and deafened by the loud explosion. They are looking around for their weapons and shields, starting to feel the aches in their bodies caused by the unexplainable occurrence.

Khan found much more than one bomb. As we walked through the houses, making sure Cold's backup was not hiding within them, we planted the explosives for phase three. They have fallen into our trap, extremely naive of them to charge. Become unpredictable. That crazy Sun Tzu was right, but the war is not over.

The remaining commanding officers from Cold's army reorganize their soldiers and restart their advances. They understand we are still weak in our numbers, and the tide of the battle has not turned completely, it has simply leveled. They are walking more cautiously through the small cloud and destruction toward me. I try to stand up and fail. My body is done, every limb is drained from life energy. Fifty meters away, almost one hundred enemies are coming toward me. Time to die.

My hands try to reignite the fire, but only sparks appear. It reminds me of a lighter without fuel. Damn it, I wanted to die fighting, not be killed as a helpless man. As the smoke fades away, they see me and start running hastily. I smile. I have given my life to the world, and now my army has the chance to succeed finally. We are no longer outnumbered two or three to one; the two armies are almost equally large. My best wishes. I hope Jay saves Mom, and I am truly sorry for not being able to share the new world with them.

The smoke cloud rushes in my direction with amazing speed, even hurting my eyes. There's the sound of a hurricane blowing in my direction, throwing debris and dirt. The soldiers' houses are fighting to keep upright at the unexpected winds. The violent winds clear everything around me. I am left alone and unprotected against the enemies. Cold must have cleared the ground from his weakling hideout. What a disgrace of a human, and how cumbersome to believe so many people have followed him for so long. A leader not worth following.

Arrows start falling around me, failing to strike. I laugh at their uselessness. They are doomed. With my remaining strength, I sit up. An enemy archer points an arrow at me; he is dead on, the arrow of my death. His bow releases, the arrow flies toward me, I wonder if I will hear it before it strikes or not... The sound is that of an arrow hitting a shield. Someone is holding a shield in front of me.

Silver's lovely voice says, "Miss me?" She starts pulling me away, and more and more hands grab ahold of my robes. They pull me quickly away, and the enemy forces halt their advance. I flip the bird at them and fade away. My time to die is postponed once more.

30
THE YOUTH
CLASH OF GODS

Leaving Silver and Nathan behind does not feel right. The enemy army pushing against the shield wall, their slow and steady retreat evidently risky, and phase three still feels off to me. So many things could go wrong, and now I am sent away, unable to aid them if any of my worries come true. I run back, watching them stand against our enemies, and doubt inside makes running harder. My feet feel heavy and my strides are slow, as I constantly turn around to see if any of them tells me to stay. But they do not.

Dozens of bodies lie on the ground behind and in front of me. The battle has been crude; blood is all over the field, as well as battered swords and shields, closed eyes, and a horrid smell spreads all over the place. My steps are calculated to avoid stepping on anyone who passed away during the battle, but it is hard to accomplish with such a vast number of fallen men and women. Nausea creeps into my stomach and makes me gag constantly. This is the only reason why I accelerate my run away from my brother and my best friend. Best of luck to both.

The main road between the soldiers' houses is ready, the explosives are set in place, and most of our soldiers have retreated to their designated places closer to the collapsed wall. They are expectant, nervous, striding back and forth, looking ahead to where our shield wall is holding the enemies back. I feel like one of them, held between the urge to go and help them and the command to stay. In my case, the order to go save Mom.

Without wasting more time, I dash to the front wall and turn left, continuing my run along the wall. My endurance starts taking a toll, as I'm breathing heavily, gasping for air, trying to continue my sprint for as long as my legs and lungs allow. I am supposed to run far north before turning west in the direction of the quarry. Grass and dirt are smashed under my feet, on and on and on, my body failing to keep up its speed.

The wall is on my right as the quarry gets closer to my left. The only sounds are my breathing and my steps crashing on the ground. All enemies are away, trying to kill my brother. He is sacrificing for our family. I'm heartbroken. There is nothing I can do for him, nothing at all. This is complete bullshit, but so is life in this world.

I believe I am far away now. White Tower seems to be a kilometer away in a straight line, so I must have run about eight hundred meters north. No more houses cover me; I am wide in the open. Catching my breath, scanning everything in front of me, behind me, right and left, I crouch to start my way toward the quarry when a massive explosion goes off to my left.

My surprised eyes turn quickly, while my heart fights between joy at the plan working and worrying if Nathan was caught by the explosion. At least phase three seems to have worked. I try to connect empathically with Nate but fail. The connection seems to be lost; could this mean he is…? No, it cannot be, he is too strong to be defeated by this. Fuck, I am turning back. I cannot pursue my mission not knowing if he survived and needs my help and will die without it.

Silver's voice sounds loudly and comfortingly inside my head, "Go, Jay. I'll get him." I had forgotten we are no longer just the two of us. We are a group of leaders, we are an army, we are a community fighting together for survival and something more. I send my words to her mind, "Thank you, Sil. See you soon," before losing connection, I notice she feels concerned. What could it be?

Once more my mind tries to wander off and preoccupy itself further. My task is my task, and Silver's is Silver's. Every one of our contributions is essential to succeed, and we must not lose focus. So, I start crawling westwards, keeping my body as low to the ground as possible. The armor grazes the rocks and stale dirt underneath, making a scratching sound. It goes unheard as I am alone.

To my left, the massive smoke cloud is rising to the sky. I cannot see the enemy soldiers, as houses are blocking my view. I hope it took out most of the enemy army, and I wish for Nathan to really be safe. Silver must have protected him and taken him back. I continue my advances, looking all around to avoid being surprised by an enemy wandering off from the battle. No one is close by.

A worrisome thought comes to mind. Did Nathan send me to save Mom because he knew the fight was lost? We could have saved her after winning. Why would he do this? Damn it. I cannot go back. I wouldn't change the course of battle by myself. All I can do is go on.

A sound starts thundering to my left, and the smoke cloud is blown violently eastwards toward our army. The houses creak against the wind. The smoke starts fading away, and the battle is soon to resume. The hurricane came from White Tower, and I can see Cold standing in his scaffold and pointing toward the explosion's direction. Did he do it?

Oh, damn. This could be something terrible for our plans. Does he have powers too? Could it be possible that not only Nathan and I have them? This explosion and the excessive effort made by Nate during battle could have weakened his body. If he is weak, and Cold is rested, any confrontation could be uneven. I hope for Nathan to be resting, to be recovering his powers to kill that traitor to humanity. Time to go on. I rest my hope on Silver.

With my belly against the ground, I continue my advance. No one has seen me; the army must have been caught by the explosion, and the survivors, if any, are away from my view. Cold is nowhere to be seen. I have a free path to the quarry, where I hope to find my mother and where, in the best scenario, no soldiers are left to guard the slaves. However, this idea feels naive; Cold cannot be that gullible and shortsighted. He must have left soldiers guarding the slaves to avoid an uprising.

Thirty minutes go by as I constantly stop to scan around, to decide if I must follow straight or change my course. My heart beats hard against my armor, an echo of each beat in my ears. The helmet limits my vision ahead and constantly slides up front, covering my eyes, and making me stop. Worst of all, this crouching motion has both my legs and shoulders sore. I never expected this to be such a demanding exercise.

Sweat drops fall on my eyes, burning them and forcing me to blink wildly. Each breath seems to raise the helmet's inside temperature. All this is such a nuisance. No matter what I do or how I do it, everything seems weird, my body resents it, and my mind constantly suggests to me to stop and rest or get up and walk normally. Both ideas are stupid. If I stop, the more time I will take saving Mom and getting back to help in battle. What if the battle ends, we lose, and I get trapped behind enemy lines?

The other possibility is to stand up and walk or run to the quarry. Now that is the most idiotic idea possible. If the army manages to see me, at least two or three will come to kill me. If no one from the army sees me, any soldier guarding the slaves up ahead would prepare himself or herself and send me to an early grave. At least my self-control still works and blocks those nailing-my-own-coffin type of ideas.

White Tower is already behind me. The quarry is less than one hundred meters ahead. Large piles of gravel or some sort of powder or rock rise across the landscape. The world seems gray here, both in sight and in emotion. A place of forced labor, of slavery, of pain and misery, and tainted with the death of hundreds.

Oh, my God! I halt with all nerves in my body constricted at the sight. To my right, a pile of burnt corpses reaches a height to haunt. Those were people, not stones, and they were treated as garbage. Men, women, children. All set one on top of another. This cannot be true; this cannot be happening. Lights around me dim, as the world will never be the same to me.

I turn around and start retreating. This is not real. I must be in a nightmare...Mom. I must go on for her. I gasp for air as it escapes my grasp. My eyes squint and I frown, gulping saliva to avoid puking. I really need to go on. This is a nightmare. If I go back, Mom will die, and all these poor souls will still be gone. If I go on, I will save our Mom, and the time to avenge these martyrs will come. Nathan, this is your duty; I will do mine.

I continue my advance, shaken and weak, through the massive mounds of gravel, feeling the rugged ground on my palms, sinking deeply and making them bleed. Finally, I focus once more on what I am doing. Mom, all this is for Mom, to find her, save her, and go back to aid the army. If we succeed, not only will Mom be saved, but hundreds of people within White Tower, and thousands of people outside of it, both born and unborn. No one will ever be treated as disposable.

The blood and pain changes their meaning. This is not an irritation, this is a reminder that what we are fighting to accomplish is not easy. The road behind us has been strenuous, and the road ahead is filled with perils, but we are doing it for the right reason. So, I go on. I go past one, and two, and three piles of gravel, stacked by slaves, and I feel myself fuming. This hellhole must end, Nathan must defeat Cold's army, but that is not the end. That will be the beginning of what we must do to cleanse the world from Cold's evil and ensure nothing similar will ever return.

Behind the last mountain of painfully mined gravel, a deep mine shows the true depth of the horror Cold has created. In plain sight, hundreds of famished human beings, ribcages marked against their thin skin, legs which barely manage to keep them upright, and arms looking like toothpicks from afar. The smell of sweat and smoke and humidity blend into an awful stench. They strike the stones with pikes thicker than their biceps, and each motion they make unsteadies their stand. Those in front of me are bodies clinging to life by an almost invisible thread. More like carcasses than humans. Postponing the time when they join the pile of those who passed on.

The scene makes me puke, literally barf on my helmet. I get rid of it and force myself to search around the quarry for my mother. She is nowhere to be seen. Closing my eyes, all my energy and focus go out to her. *Where are you, Mom?* It is Jay, we have come to save you. Please shine a guiding light in your direction.

Nothing. Goose bumps across my body at the thought of being too late. We had to take our time to assemble an army, to fight for others, to do what the world needed. Was it too much time? Instead of coming straight for our mother, did we sacrifice her for this war? If so, did we make the right decision? Nathan and I could have saved her ourselves, but we could have also been caught and tortured by Cold's massive army. We could have succeeded at saving her; however, we wouldn't have sowed and grown hope in so many people. She wouldn't have appreciated our being that selfish.

Nonetheless, if she is truly dead, a part of this journey has been meaningless. Losing her the first time was harsh, but we were not certain if she survived or not. Time brought the pain, and time took it away. Now, we could have lost her, consciously aiding in her death, and it feels a thousand times worse. Why do I feel as if I am not breathing anymore? My chest inflates, and at the same time I feel choked. My veins pop out on my arms, my head aches, and my vision blurs. I kneel back down, with nothing more inside my body to puke, and yet I gag.

"Jay." A known voice sounds softly and clearly in my mind. What a lovely music to my ears; my Mom's voice brings a river of tears down my face. Not tears of pain, though. My bodily strength comes back, and I get up. I answer, "Where are you, Mom? Guide me to you and let's get back to Nathan. He is fighting a war, leading hundreds, to free humanity of this evil." Even if her words have not reached me, I feel she's proud. She is smiling from within, weakly. Part of what she projects to me comes along with her frail stamina in a battered, enslaved body.

She answers weakly, "The tunnel up ahead." In front of where I stand, down into the quarry, a tunnel goes underground. I slide down the quarry's sidewall and start running as fast as my feet can. People barely see me; a few turn around at the loud noise I am making. They are closer to death than to life. Soon we will free you, brothers and sisters, just hold on a minute longer. I dodge rocks, pikes, carts, and ladders. Behind me, alive people and dead bodies left in the ground to rot scare and anger me.

The tunnel's entrance is tall, about four meters high and three meters wide. Inside, the walls are illuminated by flickering torches. The shadows of men and women too thin to be alive dance creepily on the ground. I yell, "Mom!", and still very few turn around. They are too weak to turn, and too smart to test their luck in case I am an enslaver. "Mom!" Deeper into the tunnel, now walking to avoid missing her. Ten, twenty meters in, and no response. "Mom!" Please answer me back; use your powers or your voice as high as you can. "Mom!"

Finally, I hear a soft echo about ten meters in front and to my right, "Here, baby boy." I run to her and even though her body is a mere shadow of what she is in my memories, her beautiful face is clear to me. Her smile is weak, but real. She is sitting down, unable to stand up, her body trembling with cold. She is dying, even if her eyes are committed to life. I remove my armor to cover her with my clothes. Even I look buff compared to her, and it breaks my heart.

I take my canteen and try to quench her thirst slowly. She gurgles and spits, unable to drink water, dehydrated. Her eyes and cheeks are sunken, and some teeth are missing, but she still is the most beautiful woman alive. Once more, I try to hydrate her with small droplets of water. I moisten my hand and allow the dripping water into her mouth and face. She manages to painfully swallow, her body starts to warm up slightly, and she seems to be improving her condition.

She tries to speak and fails; her eyes must do the talking for now. She is proud, half believing it is a dream and half celebrating the possibility of all being real. More drops of water, and a kiss on her forehead to reassure her this is all too real. I sit in front of her and caress her falling hair and hold her head with my palm. She will survive, I will make sure she does. Four more drops of water.

She screams suddenly with wide, panicked eyes, "Jay!", when a violent lash cuts deep in my right shoulder. I feel the warm blood coming out of the cut and the shooting pain up and down my back. Hurriedly, I turn around and receive another terrible whiplash to my torso. Left breathless, with an indescribable pain across my body, I lower my head into a fetal position as I try to contain the pain and fail. Before another hit, I roll to my left and hear the cracking sound soaring above my head.

Over my shoulder I see him… Pete The Perpetual. He is smiling with his dark teeth, dark brown eyes gazing straight at me, with a whip in one hand and a sword in the other. His eyes are wild, and his head dancing from side to side crazily. He raises his terrible right arm, readying the whip again, but he stops. He mutters, "Wait a second. I know you, puny little bastard. You are James, the fucker who got away and destroyed our campsite. Well, welcome back. This time, it will be for real." He laughs maniacally, the red and yellow lights from the torches bouncing off his bald head.

Another violent slash destroys my left bicep, blood gushing out in spurts, with the entire arm numb and unmovable. I try to drag myself out of his view, but he jumps on top of a rock and sends another unforgiving slash in my direction. It fails by a centimeter, and he laughs louder. My mother is staring at me with panic in her eyes, trying to get up to help me, but failing with her weak famined body.

Oh, God. I am done. How stupid of me to run here, to stop doing everything I was trained to do. He must have seen me run across the quarry, into the tunnel, and he just waited for the moment to... Another violent strike on my back and my vision starts to obscure from the colossal pain. He is destroying my body and my armor is lying beside my Mom, reminding me of how idiotic I am.

He says evilly, "Don't you pass out on me, James. We are in here for the long run. Happy, happy, happy birthday to me." He smiles with the evilest grin imaginable, his eyes showing me his mind is riled up with ideas of how to torture without killing me. His steps toward me are chilling, both his whip and sword down, and I cannot move from where I sit. His skinny hand grabs me by the ankle and pulls me violently toward him. I slip and hit my head, blood starts running, and I fight weakly against his hold, unable to use my left arm.

I hit against rocks and pikes, as he pulls me over dead bodies and liquids on the ground, I dare not imagine what they are. I puke again, and my heart is racing the fastest it has ever. The end of the tunnel is near, both really and figuratively. He is pulling me outside, probably to the place where he tortures his slaves. My mom is getting farther and farther away, unable to do a thing, and suffering from my stupidity.

Thirty meters to the exit of the tunnel. He stops, turns around, and lashes another excruciating hit on my legs. They burn, ache, and suffer for about ten seconds, making me cry my eyes out before they turn numb. A cut about two centimeters wide across my thighs immobilizes them. The injury is terrible, I can see my flesh within, blood coming out from yet another gash. He is killing me slowly, cut by cut, a butcher.

He grabs my ankle once again with his skeletal hand and turns to continue our terrible path. He is whistling, content at the evil he is doing. What a disgraceful piece of shit. He does not deserve to live, and I have fucked up the chance to catch him by surprise and end his sorry ass life. Fuck me, this is on me. Once again, my stupid kid's naivete decided to go ahead and screw everything up. Two doors, Jay, two fucking doors. One leads to death and one leads to saving your mom and killing a pest from the face of the Earth. Which do you pick? Of course, you pick… death.

He continues walking slowly; every centimeter of my body is either numb or aching horribly. His body moves as if dancing, jumping content at his prey. He is… A ray of fire bolts through his body, opening a wide hole straight through his torso. Side to side… he falls down dead. At the tunnel's entrance, a horse whines, and Nathan's transformed body fumes with his red leering eyes staring at me. He exhales heavily while he dismounts and walks toward me with an extended hand to help me up. I smile stupidly; an angel from heaven with hell's fire by his side.

I should have known he would save me. He always has. He looks tired, walking heavily with a hunched back and weary face. His hand comes closer, offering me aid once more to get up and keep going. This is how it will always be; my brother will always be at my side, helping me to get up and go on with my life.

As our fingers touch, he flies back, sucked by some invisible force, and falls heavily on the ground. His body is writhing with pain as rocks dig deeply into his back. He rolls over and pushes himself up with his weakened arms. He stands staring with wrath at the tunnel's entrance, his body growing larger and larger, fire surrounding him as a force field, his shoulders dancing up and down with his ireful breathing. "Well, well. So, this is flame boy."

Chills make me contort at the sound of that hellish voice. Each word is a knife to my back. Cold is here.

Nathan lights both of his hands up, fire revolving around his open palms, growing larger by the second. He throws a fire ball at Cold, whose imposing build and stature blocks our only way out. A whirlwind wards off the fireball easily, Cold barely moved, and his laughter echoes creepily across the tunnel. One shot from Nate's left, and another from his right hand, and once more Cold's powers block the attack. They must be testing each other, a fight to the death about to erupt.

Nate's right hand signals me to retreat. He seems to be wary about his enemy's capacity, and it frightens me. Until this moment, I would have sworn my brother was the most powerful being in the face of the earth; but now, even he is doubting it. Using all my remaining fortitude, I start coiling and crawling back to our mother. She is unconscious. Screaming and trying to help me must have been too much for her. Her body is not cold, and her breathing is normal. She will survive... if Nathan manages to protect us.

Once more he goes on the offensive, but this time there is no contention. He holds both hands forward, with an open stance, and fire starts pouring nonstop toward Cold. Nathan gets a firmer stance, as he knows the testing is over, and the real deal is commencing. Fire wraps Cold, shut in by a massive fiery outbreak. However, he remains unaltered, with his glaring light blue eyes and his evil grin seen between the flames. Nate stops; he knows this approach will exhaust him and leave all of us unprotected.

Cold's voice thunders past my brother, the tunnel walls amplifying his wickedness, "Is that all? Is Phoenix such a weak opponent?" Cold stares at Pete's body, almost destroyed in half by my brother's anger. He smiles at it, even though he was one of his right-hand men, and sends it flying away with a powerful wind. The body crashes unpleasantly against a stalactite, waving wackily and falling hard on the rock ground. "Puny." Cold despicably disregards Pete and focuses once more on my brother.

This deplorable act has angered him further. Fire whips are dancing around him, his legs are completely covered by them, and his closed fists contain a massive force whose heat can be felt even from where I am lying. Nathan's right arm shoots a fire whip, galloping on the tunnel's wall, branding it with a dark mark, and shooting straight toward Cold's body. He turns to his left and starts protecting himself from the renewed attack. Both of his hands forward, fighting to keep his ground, gritting his teeth, and frowning strongly. He is not finding it easy.

Simultaneously, my brother's left arm shoots the same attack across the tunnel's other side. Diverting Cold's attention with the first attack, the second attack seems to be completely surprising. The flames advance quickly, jumping on the wall, moving forward toward Cold's back. He is completely unaware; he is about to be charcoaled for good, for being naive. This is it, my body strengthened by the sight, the luminescence of the whip on Cold's back, dashing toward him, two meters to go!

He turns his head slightly toward his right and blocks the attack completely, as if his eyes scared the fire off toward another direction. Cold closes his fists, crossing his arms over his chest, and extends them swiftly while sending a massive wind burst in all directions. Nate is lifted and sent five meters backward, hitting hard on the ground and contorting at the pain of rocks jutting into his back.

While he spits blood on the ground, words with an increased cadence challenge my brother, "You don't know the full extent of my powers. I believe you don't even know the full extent of yours. Do me a favor and kneel to me. I could kill only one, your mother or brother. You choose." A maniacal cackle is followed by a challenging hand pointing at my mother and me.

My brother stands up weakly, supporting himself on rocks. He is battered, his back is hunched, and his head is lowered, staring at the ground, thinking. I connect with him, and a second before it happens, I hear his laughter. Laughter? Why is he even laughing? I ask into his mind, "Nate, are you okay? What are we going to do?" He does not answer. He simply opens his right palm in my direction, indicating to me everything is all right. I don't understand what is happening.

His laughter finally sounds, and Cold's face becomes more serious. His confusion is palpable; he believed my brother to be done, his body succumbing to a more powerful opponent.

Copying his enemy, Nate holds both arms crossed over his chest, and shoots them quickly outward. A massive fire blast advances toward Cold. He blocks it with wind. The power clash sends flames back toward my brother, over Cold and out of the tunnel, and sideways, heating up the entire tunnel.

Nathan lunges and digs both feet deep into the gravel, shouting loud with effort, putting everything he's got into the attack, which grows larger and larger. Cold screams back, demanding more strength from his body, seeking for a way to halt Nathan's surprising comeback. The torches hanging on the tunnel walls join the attack, their flames being sucked into the raging wave. Cold is backing up slowly, step by step, trying to exit the tunnel, his body trembling at the effort, incapable of deterring my brother's assault.

Nathan starts advancing, and his hands start moving in a circular motion. The fire blast starts revolving, a tornado of fire directed from his hands to Cold's body. It strengthens the attack, concentrating all flames on the same target, losing less power from the blocking. The crash site of fire and wind starts growing larger, and the entire tunnel's temperature is rising, the walls grumbling and small debris falling from the ceiling.

Nathan's head turns slightly, we make eye contact, and our connection returns. He shares his plan, "I am going to push this fight out. Do what you can to escape with Mom. Hydrate her and escape. This is not your fight." His voice commands me in my mind. I answer, "Noted. Now go and kill that bastard." He smiles lopsidedly, winks at me, and turns back toward his enemy. Pushing harder and harder, each step clearly taking a toll on his body, using all his endurance. Nathan has used his powers far beyond any threshold he had experienced, and I am afraid for his health. Each step shows how he is burning out, but his body is not his mind. Each step seems to strengthen his mind.

Cold is retreating steadily, incapable of escaping the tornado revolving around him. Nathan is already under the tunnel's exit, and my time to act has come. With my canteen I splash a few drops of water on my mother's face, trying to wake her up, moving her softly side to side and speaking to her. "Mom wake up. It is time to go." But nothing seems to work. Her face is calm and peaceful under wrinkles caused by years of grief.

I try to get water into her mouth to hydrate her back into consciousness. Nothing seems to work. Think, Jay, think. A wheelbarrow is on the wall to my left; I could try to put her in it and push her out. No, my legs are still numb, the cuts are deep, and the pain in my exposed flesh is unbearable. I will not be able to stand, no matter how much I try. God, please guide me. What am I going to do? The clash of powers outside of the tunnel sounds colossal, high-speed winds and fire creaking strongly, the ground shaking incessantly, and gravel flying in all directions.

Nathan's attack will not last long. He is using all his strength to give us a window, and I am not taking it. Anger clouds my judgement. Focus, Jay, try to fight the urge to nervously collapse. How am I to communicate with my mom when she is unconscious? And that is when I understand it. I must communicate subconsciously. "Mom. Let's go." Her eyes open wildly, hearing my silence, and she smiles at my sight. "Let's go, baby boy."

She looks at my injured body, at the cuts and scrapes, the bruises and blood all over it. Her eyes are about to shed tears, but her dehydrated body has no water to spare. She swallows hard, even though it is air. Her mother heart is taking control, and her strength is coming back slightly. I say, "Drink some water, Mom. Nathan's saving us; we need to go." She swallows a few drops of water slowly, breathing strongly without moving her eyes off my cuts. She mumbles, "What happened before I passed out?"

Nathan's scream outside of the tunnel sounds desperate. The power wrestle outside seems to be close to an end. I hear him inside my mind, "Use your fucking powers, Jay. Now!" I focus. I connect with my Mom's mind. I can see what she sees, I can see what she feels. The gruesome sound outside of the tunnel vanishes, and I am silent. Our connection grows stronger by the second, I can feel her seeing my mind, looking at my memories of the path we have traversed to come here.

She is understanding what is going on. A war, yes, she sees the war we have led. The pain, I see the pain she has felt. Physically under slavery, punishment, being whipped, punched, pushed. Mentally, with humiliation, being spat on, ignored as a human being, disrespected. Too long she has suffered. A light, both Nathan and I have been her guiding force. She never lost hope. Dad flashes by, and she blocks the memory somehow. Weird. Where is Dad?

Both of us open our eyes and exchange curious looks. She answers, "I don't know, Jay, we got separated a long time ago, when all this started. We will look for him in time, but first let's go. Focus." Her voice sounds more familiar, more composed, and stronger. With my eyes closed, I can see her body, feel her hands as if they were mine. Our minds blend, so that the place where her thoughts end and my own begin is nonexistent. Our hearts, our breaths, our strength synchronize. The addition of two into one.

We open our eyes at the same time. I raise my left hand and her left hand mimics mine. I turn my head right and left, and she follows. The connection is complete; we are one, and our strength is one as well. Sharing the connection, we both manage to get on our feet feebly. We walk toward the tunnel's exit. We walk! The water she drinks hydrates me, the gravel under her bare feet scrapes my soles. The light outside of the tunnel dazes our four eyes, and the explosion of fire and wind warms our bodies.

We continue our stride, slowly but coordinated. Cold and Nathan look at us, but neither can do a thing about it. If either stop focusing on his enemy, the attack could be unforgiving. Cold shouts at us with his menacing voice, "You are dead!" Nate answers, taunting him, "Go, kill them if you can. You will be burnt to ashes before you manage to even blow their hair, fucking wimp!" Nathan laughs at Cold's amused gaze. He knows he cannot waiver a second of his defense, or he will be defeated.

We continue walking away from them, to the west. Heated gravel is flying all around us, and the ground rumbles under us. We walk up the quarry's sidewall slowly, placing each step strongly before taking the next, avoiding a slip. My mom and I walk in unison, each with an arm around the other's shoulders. We push together, and we fight together.

As soon as we reach the top of the quarry and White Tower can be seen to our right, I say, "Mom, I need you to go. Walk straight to the wall and turn right. I will share half of my strength with you. We will not break our connection, but I cannot leave. Nathan could need me." She stares at me with both pride and fear in her hazel eyes. She nods, understanding, and I sense within her the pain of doubt, of the possibility of losing us again. I send her these last words to her mind, as she starts walking toward the wall, "We won't."

I peek down into the quarry. The confrontation is starting to fade. Both are losing powers swiftly. Nathan's breathing is heavy, one of his hands is already down, and his attack is being held only by his right arm for now. Cold sends a perpendicular gust of wind toward Nathan, gravel striking his body fiercely and blinding him. He uses his right to protect himself from the unexpected attack, and his fire strike ends abruptly. Cold pushes strongly with both hands toward Nathan, and an impressive wind force sends him flying outside of the quarry, in the opposite direction from my lookout. His body is stiff, trying to control the frenzied spinning to fall without injuries. He hits the ground and bounces beyond my view.

Oh, no! I cannot sense Nathan. His body has never endured this long. I cannot see him either. Where are you? The seconds go by as if hours, and his body does not reappear on top of the quarry. Cold is staring in his direction, panting, moving his head from side to side, trying to find him. Nothing comes back from Nate's direction. A minute or so has passed, and nothing. No connection, no movement. What am I supposed to do? There is no way I can face Cold; it would be suicide. Mom is using my strength to escape; I cannot risk losing our connection.

Cold turns around and spots me. His eyes pierce me, and terror gets a strong grip on me. I cannot move; he is just staring at me, thinking about how to end me. One step in my direction, and his body is visibly exhausted and in pain. Another step, and I cannot do a thing. If I turn around and run, I give up on Nathan. If I stay, I give up on Mom. A third step and gravel start flying weakly toward me, hurting my eyes and face. I block it with my right arm. With every step, the wind blowing toward me strengthens; he is toying with me. He yells, "You stupid kid. Did you really believe flame boy could…?"

Nathan's back; his uncontainable anger spikes inside of me, and he is standing on the quarry's ledge. A wave of fire pours down on Cold, as he barely turns around and builds up his wind defense once more. His feet are pushed into the ground; lower and lower he goes, while Nathan's red glaring eyes, menacing from above, stare straight at his target. His face contorts, and he gives a wrathful screech, the wave growing larger and larger, uncontrollable, shooting in all directions out of his body, and concentrating around Cold's miniscule figure.

The attack loses momentum, as his body is suffering fatigue, about to collapse. In my mind I read his thoughts; he is preoccupied, he is squeezing every ounce of strength out of his body, willing to die for us if he takes Cold with him. I cannot allow him to do it. For too long I have dismissed this, but the time has come to do something I have feared for too long. I turn my sight toward Cold, and without losing my Mom's connection, I connect empathically with this monster.

Visions of horror run across my mind vividly and messily. Torture, death, war, raping, pillaging, evil all bundled up in one sick mind. The images make me cry; my heart feels weak as if bleeding out. My throat is sore as if I had been crying my entire life, and I swallow painfully at the revulsion. The moment the connection kicks in I feel Cold's body. I cannot control him as he does not allow me to, but I can feel it. He is growing weaker; he trembles inside out; his arms are heavy and screaming for a rest. Both Nathan and his body are exhausted, both bodies broken.

At the same time, both put an end to their powers and fall on their knees. They keep their gazes on each other, distrusting and filled with distaste. Cold takes his massive sword out of its scabbard, the blue stripes reflecting the sun, and Nathan concurs by taking his out of the sheath, with its red details yearning for fire. Nate slides down the quarry's wall and walks shakily toward the center of the quarry. Cold is stumbling his way toward him. They halt their steps and stand face-to-face three meters away.

This is it. My God, this is the end. Anxiety controls my body and mind. Nathan is barely standing up, he is most definitely not ready for a sword fight. He is fighting on by heart, not physically fit to move a muscle, but proud and moved by an immeasurable loyalty to all of us. Mom arrives at our camp, and she sees how the fighting has ended. I can see it as well. Our enemies are kneeling, surrounded by our few survivors. Silver is there, the leader of our army in this last stand.

She turns around and sees the frail, skeletal woman walking toward her. She dashes toward her, grabs her by the waist, and my mother collapses. She has fallen unconscious, and our connection is lost. The pain in my entire body comes back in a rush. I shriek at the burns of all the cuts and gashes. Now, I am useless to Nathan. The end is getting closer and closer. I'm a bystander of a clash of gods.

Both remove their armors since they are not capable of holding such weight much longer. The metal protection falls to the ground, sounding like aluminum foil being wrinkled. Their bodies are covered in sweat, shivers running through their legs and arms, tired physically to an extreme, but holding up with hate against each other. These two men are willing to die here. Only one will survive, that is certain.

Unexpectedly, Cold attacks first, dashing lightning quick and striking a heavy blow at Nathan. He parries it with a swift defense; the swords crash for the first time, and the metal cringes at the force. One strike above, another below, two right strikes, one left strike, the velocity of the battle is amazing. From here it is difficult to see the motions; the sound is what allows me to identify when an attack is done. Their feet are hard on the ground, moving like a choreographed dance, circling around each other, never losing sight of the enemy.

Nathan is defending himself with all the strength left in his beaten body. Sweat covers his face, his thorax rising with every difficult breath he takes. Cold is not fit for this battle either. His support leg trembles with exhaustion, his blade's strikes lose strength with every try. He quickly changes his stance, pushing his body against my brother, and tries to prod Nathan with the sword. It scrapes my brother's abdomen as he was not able to dodge in time. He squirms in pain and blocks a subsequent attack from Cold.

This time the swords don't bounce off each other; they stay together, and Cold starts pushing my brother. His piercing blue eyes are set upon my brother's red luminescent ones. There is hatred in both gazes. He takes small back steps, trying to hold his ground and failing since Cold is a larger and heavier man. Rapidly, my brother falls to the ground, rolls sideways, and sends a blow to Cold's left leg. He is saved by a shin guard, but it causes severe pain. Cold's glaring blue eyes are filled with loathing as he grits his teeth painfully.

Nathan stands up and jumps toward Cold, landing a heavy blow down on him that he manages to block by holding the sword with both hands. It ricochets and hits his forehead with the plain side of the sword. Nathan does not lose time and tackles him to the ground. He tries to penetrate his side with the sword, but Cold grabs his hand and contains it. They are fighting with all the strength remaining in their bodies, screaming, trying to end the fight and failing.

Cold finally shoves my brother off him with brutal force, and Nathan falls by his side. A massive kick from Cold lands on his right thigh. Suffering, he tries to get back up and moves, limping away from his enemy. His body weight is supported by his left leg, and he's unable to strike, so he waits for Cold's reprisal. The pain is evident in his face, and he's trying to move the least possible amount as the soreness remains. He is breathing through his clenched teeth, staring at Cold with hatred and indecision at the same time.

Cold is standing up, grinning, staring at my brother's pain with penetrating eyes, waiting for the moment to strike. I try desperately to stand up, to run to my brother's aid, to distract Cold's attention, but fail. The amount of blood I have lost and the deep cuts in my back, legs, and torso have me immobilized, useless. There is no way I am going to get to my brother in time. This could be the end. My jaw jitters as tears start rolling down my cheeks. The impotence has me destroyed. What if he dies and I was not able to do a thing about it, just stare and get the most important person of my life ripped away from me?

With each of Cold's steps toward Nate, my panic rises, delves deeper, and makes me cower. Another step. Please, Nate, do something; you can turn the tables. A third step. Please, God, do something for him, protect him, grant him another ounce of strength. Cold is speaking to my brother, boasting. A fourth step, he is at sword's length. Nathan looks at him, fearless, ready to die, but with his sword at the ready. His eyes move toward me, he sees me peeking over the quarry's edge; he smiles and nods. A farewell…

Wait. I can help him; it is not in anyone else's hands to aid my brother. How idiotic of me. For one last time, I connect with Cold's reckless and evil mind. I see the thoughts of death and murder in his mind, I see my brother's weak body in front of him, his ideas on how to make him suffer. Should I cut a leg and watch him limp and bleed to death? Should I prod and penetrate his limbs with my sword? Should I kill him with my own bare hands? A mental laugh reaches his lips and erupts. He screams for me to hear, "So how will I kill this boy?" His voice and words don't impress my brother. He remains still, supported on a leg and waiting for Cold's move.

I close my eyes, trying to focus by blocking everything around me. Cold and Nathan, nothing else. This is my world now. Through Cold's eyes, staring wickedly at my brother, I manage to get into his mind. Nathan is staring at Cold; his thoughts are at peace, he is certain this is his death, but at the same time he is proud of giving his life for humanity. He thinks of me, and pities not being in my life anymore. However, he feels joy at my mother's salvation and reinsertion in my life. He thinks about Silver, how much he loves her and how much he will miss her. He sees her clearly in his mind, I appear in the image with my mother placing a hand on my shoulder and another on Silver's. A new family, he thinks.

I speak to his mind, "Brother. Listen to me. I can see Cold's mind. Let me guide you in this last battle, so you manage to stay one step ahead of him. We are a new family, with you in it." He looks at me once more, with a sarcastic grin and devious eyes saying, "I'm ready." As his voice resonates inside my mind, he moves a step closer to Cold, challenging him, "Come on, filth." He raises his sword, holding it with both hands, and taunts him with a crack of his neck.

Cold feels amazed by my brother's resilience and his spirit. He is going to strike a hard blow toward Nathan's left side and follow it quickly with a slice toward his right disabled leg. Nathan hears his thoughts through me. A lightning quick blow to his left is parried, followed by impressive reflexes at blocking the right strike. Cold is awestruck by the defensive speed. Two blows to his right, one straight to his head, and a deep prod to trespass his abdomen. Ready, brother, here he comes.

Nate blocks twice to his right, dodges the overhead blow and evades swiftly the unsuccessful protrusion. Cold's anger starts building up, and the clouds above them start twirling as weak wind gusts start emanating from his body. He is too feeble to use his powers, but the same as Nathan, rage seems to fuel them. A fury strike, right, left, right, left, Nathan foreseeing each move, blocking, dodging, evading by the minimum. He is working patiently, unaltered, and I am nervous to death at the miniscule margin of error. He is unable to move his right leg, his movements severely limited. Each strike and prod miss him by centimeters. What to do?

Cold crashes swords with Nathan, spits on him, and tries to grab his hilt. Nathan, knowing his intentions, moves the blade slightly and cuts his left palm. Cold backs away, grabbing his heavily bleeding palm, while winding his sword on his right hand. He runs toward Nathan, intending to tackle him while blocking any possible blow from above with his upheld sword. He moves amazingly quickly for a man his size, bolting toward my brother's leg, and missing it as he moves it away a split second before.

Cold's large body crashes heavily on the gravel. He rolls to his right, evading a nonexistent attack from my brother, and he stands up again with his sword ready. Nathan, completely unable to move more than a few centimeters, did not even try to attack him when down. Nathan's possibilities to succeed are minimum, if even existent. His right thigh's quad must be shattered, and his body is on the verge of fainting to exhaustion. I can feel it through his mind; he is not expecting to win, just expecting to give Cold the worst time of his life.

Another right blow to his head, a left to his torso, another to his shoulder blade, a prod to his abdomen, a right attack to his thigh, and each one is parried or dodged with movements difficult to follow by gaze. My brother's speed is amazing, always standing on his healthy leg, using the least motion possible to overcome Cold's intentions. Cold cannot believe what is happening. Before and after each move, he feels fear and confusion. He is truly having the worst time of his life. Dying to kill my brother, but completely unable to even scratch him.

Right strike, left strike, deep prod, twirl around him, left strike, and final blow to his ankles. Cold dashes forward, sending a massive right blow that crashes against my brother's upheld sword, an impressively quick strike to the left, parried by my brother's precise block, a deep prod to Nate's abdomen that misses by a couple of centimeters and makes Cold move forward toward him. A twirl of his massive body to the right, around my brother's body, evading Nathan's counter, and sending a deathly left attack that crashes against my brother's impressive recovery from a missed attack. As Cold's sword bounces off the block, he uses the motion to speed his shoulder's rotation and send a huge and lightspeed cut at my brother's ankles. He lowers his sword to protect his legs, and a powerful hand grabs him by his neck.

Nathan raises his gaze and sees Cold's proud smirk, his deep blue eyes penetrating my brother's red stare, death covering both men's minds. There is no fear in one of them, and in the other joy, revenge, and cunning take hold. What has happened?

I can listen to Cold through my brother's mind, "So, your brother can read minds?" Cold's cruel voice sends shivers down my spine. He looks at me while holding my brother's weak body, choking him. He smiles wickedly and points at me while sending a message to my mind. "You are next."

He tosses Nathan's body violently to the ground, leaving him squirming and breathless. I lose the connection to both Nathan's and Cold's mind. My brother must have fainted. He is doomed. This is the end. I scream for help desperately; please Silver, please Bull, please Em, please Rick, please Dan, someone please save him. My pleas are answered by no one; we are all alone, the three of us, my brother and I at the mercy of the evilest man alive.

Cold raises his sword with both hands, ready to kill my brother. Why didn't I bring my quiver and arrows? Why didn't I protect myself better against Pete? Why did I leave my brother to die? My brother left helpless at his mercy, Cold uses every ounce of strength in his body to drill down his sword at Nathan's helpless body. The strength is exaggerated; he wants to cut my brother in half. I am witnessing the death of a hero. My heart broken, my hope vanishing, my fear nonexistent.

I will not live in a world without him. Come for me next,

Cold. I will not defend myself. Without my brother all is lost. Humanity has fought valiantly, but Cold is simply too powerful to be defeated. All our armies are at his mercy. This maniacal son of a bitch will retake the ground we recovered, and fuck with it. I only hope when his death comes, his final judgement will punish him for his sins.

Cold's blue sword runs perpendicularly toward my brother's unconscious body. All of Cold's muscles tense to ensure the strike is deadly. Farewell, my brother...

A fire shield appears out of nowhere, covering my brother's body, raging with blinding flames of white, red, and yellow. Cold's sword strikes the shield, and nothing comes out of the other end. His sword melts up to the hilt; he shrieks in pain at the burning metal and throws the remnants of his sword away. He backs away in fear. His eyes stay on Nathan, while his legs start backing away. His body moves up and down with every surprised and panicked breath, dumbfounded.

His awestruck stare is followed by negating head motions; he is feeling what he has caused so many innocent people to feel. Nathan's body starts transforming slowly. His body grows larger every second, the blood covering his body evaporates, and fire dances around him, waiting for his command. He is still unmoving, eyes closed and apparently unconscious. Fire starts covering his body, like an army of ants marching from his toes, up his shins, across his thighs, advancing on his abdomen, covering his neck, and finally surrounding his peaceful face.

Cold turns around and starts running in despair, afraid to death of what he is seeing. A coward undeserving to live, running to hide and survive, away from an enemy for whom he was never a match. Nathan's red, glaring, luminescent eyes open suddenly. He stands up slowly, no limp left in his right leg, staring straight at Cold's terrified run. Cold is running as quickly as his legs carry him, twenty meters away from my brother, desperately trying to reach the quarry's wall to start climbing in retreat, escaping from his well-deserved destiny.

He is running toward White Tower, desperately trying to return to his army, ignoring that they are defeated. As he strides quickly away from my brother, White Tower's never-ending fire starts flowing like a river toward the quarry, dancing over the field and the gravel mounds, shining brightly. The fire starts accelerating toward the quarry in a circular motion, loudly burning, creaking heavily toward Cold.

A wall of fire lands in front of Cold's frantic sprint, made from the fire he so loyally idolized as a beam of his prowess. He halts at the massive obstruction, his body illuminated by the raging symbol in front of him, his large shadow behind him, flickering, showing his fearful stand. He walks away from it slowly, in panic. The fire starts closing in around him as he yells fearfully.

His body is abruptly surrounded by a tornado of fire, three times taller than the quarry's edge, turning around and around, illuminating far more than the sunset on the horizon. White flames, yellow flames, red flames, and blue flames are intensely scorching the source of all evil. He does not even scream in pain as the fire consumes him. An immediate death.

I look back at my brother and connect with him. He does not enjoy killing, not even celebrating Cold's demise. He will never forgive himself, but it had to be done. The world will forgive him. He is doing this for all of us, at the expense of himself. Sadness is ten times as powerful as the joy he is feeling. Death should never be the answer, but sometimes your decisions are made by someone else. Cold decided to die fighting against humanity. My brother was simply the executioner of his will.

All the fire in the quarry vanishes brusquely. Nathan is back to his normal self, arms hanging motionlessly at each side; his back is hunched up, and his head is moving drunkenly side to side. He faints, and his unresponsive body falls to his side heavily, crashing against the ground unmoving, no strength left inside. His work is done. Humanity, rejoice.

31
THE ELDER
AN END FOR A NEW BEGINNING

I KNOW I AM CONSCIOUS, OR at least starting to come back from a dream. My eyelids are heavy and dry, sticky, unable to be opened. I swallow once and twice to no avail; my mouth and throat are dry. Pain starts creeping in from several parts of my body, my lips are cracked, my elbows are hurt, and the back of both legs sting. All my muscles are sore, and a pulsating headache hinders my thoughts.

Where am I? What happened?

Memories start coming back slowly and blurrily, complicating my understanding. Yes, I do remember my brother James. The world collapsed. Yes, nature is everywhere, and humanity has taken a step back. We speculated about how everything crumbled, how we were sent back to our roots, to survival, to getting behind our house walls and rejecting everyone who dared get close. The intrinsic selfishness of humans led the way for many years.

We survived for a long time by ourselves. The horrors we have lived, the things I have had to do for his sake, for his sanity, will forever scar me from within. He was abducted once. I had to kill so many people to get him back. Fire, fire is my ally, fire is at my command. I have used my powers to protect him, to save him, to get him back home. But it was not only me. He has grown in cunning and skill. It was partly of his making and partly of someone else's.

A woman. What a beautiful woman. Red hair, white face, soft and delicate lips, piercing and lovely green eyes. A sharp and upturned nose, a few freckles on her cheekbones, and pale pink cheeks. She is a warrior, she is...she is the one I love. Silver is her name. This woman has saved Jay, and she has saved me. Her strength, her intelligence, her skills, and her perseverance have been a blessing since she walked into our lives.

We had such an amazing time back home, the three of us. For a long time, I had not felt truly happy, enjoying life and not thinking about survival, death, horror. We did not stay there, did we? No, we moved on from that perfect moment, to save our Mom. My brother connected to her, we called it...

Damn, my memory is fading, but he could see into her mind.

For seven years we thought Mom was dead; we gave up, we retreated to our den as cowards. We chose to act, we chose to face the music, we chose to do something to change our lives. And we changed so much more than that. The floating bodies at the most peaceful place we had been since everything collapsed come back to my mind. So many lives lost, so many men and women and children who wouldn't live to see another sunrise. The mixture of pleasure and shock, the disgusting sense of never being able to lower our defenses, both mental and physical.

The village up on the hill, victims to an enemy so evil, so despicable, we decided to change the world. Our mom was a lighthouse to a vessel of courage, and we were not alone. Valor came along, the amazing people of a village with no practice or skill at battling, willing to give up everything to avenge their neighbors and protect their children's future. Behind them, more and more villages joined in. Strength with their battle-worn soldiers, Stealth with their invisible shadows, Range with their unerring marksmen. Hundreds of people willing to march behind me, behind us, a trio of unknowns.

Their leaders, their leaders joined us. We were not alone;

they guided their people, a sword in one hand and a promise in the other. We sparked hope, we showed them a dream at arm's length, and we departed to make it happen. The waterfall was our last stop, the mist blending with our first deaths. Water and blood, an eye opener of what we were doing and how challenging the next steps would be.

And they were. A battle of massive scale, swords crashing against each other, armor bent and broken, shields with arrows sticking out of them, deceased bodies of both allies and foes sharing the field, a massive wall. White Tower, the city of evil, the pinnacle of humanity's debacle. Its imposing front gate blown up, a cloud of debris, and a dead friend. Khan was his name; he gave up his life for us. I remember his funeral and how we said goodbye to those who had fallen to our cause.

The final day. A confrontation of good versus evil, of humanity against lack of humanity, the dichotomy of what we can be. Our free will allowing us to choose two divergent paths that only meet when one must overcome and destroy the other. We lost many men, many women, and with them the possibility of a future where they lived happily, contributing with their capabilities, personalities, and dreams. With each loss, the road toward the future we strode for lost a brick, making it harder to reach and weakening its construction.

The hardest loss was that of a mentor, of a leader by people's choice. Dan was a man of wisdom, capable of understanding people, humanity, past, present, and future. He was slain, even though he was not supposed to be fighting. However, he wanted to and probably knew it would be his end, and he took it into his own hands. The wisdom of a man who understands life and death. I will forever remember him. Wherever I go and whatever I do, I will act based on his teachings, on his knowledge, and on his memory.

A plan that worked changed everything. A last explosion, men and women lost physically, even though they were lost mentally long ago under a tyrant's leadership. A man whose evil had to be cleansed away from the Earth, even beyond his death. My brother went to find and save our mother. I stayed behind to guide our army and succumbed to the overuse of my powers. The beautiful woman, Silver, saved me. She led our people when I was done, battered and weak.

But my brother needed help. He was suffering, his body whipped and cut, bruised and harassed by a terrible enemy. His suffering gave me my strength back; at least my resilience came back, even though my body was at the verge of collapse. I charged at the enemy front line, killing them one by one nonstop, dodging the attacks directed at me without hindering my advance. I toppled an enemy from a horse and rode away, our army led by Silver, Rick, and Em. Bull was down, a friend, an ally, a role model, and a beast.

I did save my brother, barely. A second longer and he could have been dead. I will never allow myself to expose him again to such a close call. We had to part ways, as the future of humanity and the survival of our mother were priorities. He took into his own hands the second road, so I had to lead the way in the other. Cold must have followed me, disregarding his army and the battle, uninterested in the result at the field. He wanted to kill me, he almost did, and we fought to the death.

Cold is dead.

I open my eyes as if waking from a nightmare, my heart rushing, my body moist with sweat, and my breathing accelerated. By inertia, I try to sit up, afraid of not knowing where I am or if everything I just thought of was real or not. Nathan is my name; around me stands a bunch of blurry figures. They are surprised by my intent, and they hold me back. Hands are on my forehead, my arms, my legs, my torso, and I start to get riled up.

I feel fire within me, raging, about to explode uncontrollably. When a pair of the most gentle and soft lips kiss me lovingly, slowly, and familiarly. My voice sounds shaky and dry, worn with disuse as I whisper, "Silver." My eyelids start fluttering and the blurry figures come into sight, clearer and clearer by the second. I know these people…they are my life.

Rick and Em hug each other excitedly, celebrating I am awake. My mother cries immediately. Silver is still leaning on top of me, staring with those puppy, enamored eyes. Em comes forward and gives me a dagger, a beautiful one with the shiniest metal blade I have ever seen. Red gems are welded into the hilt, and the blade bears the inscription "Phoenix."

She kisses my forehead and says, "Strength recognizes you, Nathan, as our leader and our beacon to the future. Thank you from past, present, and future." She is as excited as she will ever show. Her firm grasp on the hilt of the knife is unsteady with emotion. I answer with difficulty, "Thank you, Em. You are a leader I will follow gladly to the end of the world if you ask me to." She bows and leaves the room.

Rick takes a step forward. His eyes get watery, but he holds his composure while saying, "My friend, you have given me the only thing life can never take away from me… hope. My family will never come back to this world, but when I meet them again, I will tell them the story about a young man and his family who dared everything to change the world." His words move me, and we share tears together as friends, as brothers. I answer with a hoarse voice, "Tell them their father built the future where no one else will suffer what they suffered. He used their memory to empower humanity and change the world. Tell them who their father is, and how without him the world wouldn't prevail."

Rick takes off a wicker bracelet he has always worn around his wrist. He grabs my hand and places the bracelet on my wrist while saying through tears, "This was a gift from my children. They would have wanted me to give it to you. Thank you for what you have become in my life, and in so many lives." Rick exits the room visibly moved and proud.

Before anyone else speaks, heavy steps sound outside of the room. A mountain of a man enters the door, lowering his head to avoid the door's frame. Bull comes in limping, in pain, touching his ribcage with an arm and holding a small leather bag in the other. He says, "I am touched by the speeches of those who came before me. There are no more words to share. Only this." He gives me the leather bag with a solemn face. I open it and a small bit of horse shit smears on my hand. His deep laugh fills the room with joy, and Silver and Mom join in.

I toss the horse shit toward him, and he moans in pain at the effort to protect his face from it. We laugh it out; the best gift anyone could have ever given me. A soldier from Range enters the room and hands Bull a bow and a quiver. He continues saying, "You have led us away from our bubble, our unreal grasp of the world, and given us the chance to help build a better future for humanity. May your aim never err, as your judgement has not."

Bull shares a few enlightening words as he gives me the bow, a beautiful art piece made from onyx stone and a metal thread. The quiver is a leather case, as dark as the night. Both designed to endure fire, if I ever need my powers again. We shake hands weakly, unlike the past handshakes, and nod at each other. I respect this man to my core.

A sudden sting to my heart reminds me of all those we lost to be here celebrating. Dan and his wisdom will endure through us and the way we decide to lead our people. Khan's courage took his life away, but it must be a guiding light when tough times come our way. We must fight with our lives to protect the world we have built and will continue building. I will make sure we will never forget those who lost their lives for our cause, for our future.

A couple of tears slide slowly down my cheeks, when Silver jumps on me and kisses me lovingly. She says happily, "I am sorry, I did not know we had to bring gifts." We share a laugh at her comment. "I love you, Nate." She is such an amazing woman, unbreakable and fearless in the battlefield, loving and charming when needed, cunning and perseverant always. She makes me a better man. My happiness is only strengthened and multiplied by her. Life is fleeting, and time cannot be wasted. Once you know, you know, no need to lose time pondering about scenarios. The best hint is when your significant other makes you think more about tomorrow than about today. I will marry her.

My mom stands silently staring at me. She is way healthier than my memories at the battlefield. Her skin is no longer pale, her brown hair is growing back, her lips and cheeks are blushing, and her beautiful long fingers are losing the wrinkles caused by her suffering. She walks toward me, kisses my forehead as only mothers do, and whispers at me.

"Thank you for taking care of your brother. Thank you for everything you have done, well beyond saving me. You have saved humanity. I am sorry for the many years you had to endure by yourself, learning to survive and protect your brother at all costs. I know the things you must have done to survive, and how they took part of your heart and soul. You are a soldier, a survivor, a leader, and a guiding force. I cannot be prouder of the man you have become. Your father will be as well." She sits at my bedside, and I cry inconsolably, finally feeling her love again.

She continues, "I was never able to communicate with the two of you. At first, both your dad and I tried constantly to enhance my power but failed. We were then separated, enslaved, and sent apart. I continued to try every single day, but I was never able to succeed. My powers are child's play next to yours, my children. We will never be separated again." The possibility of Dad being alive excites me. If we are to build a better world, he should have the possibility to live and enjoy it with us.

Mom adds, "I am also sorry for Chrissy. I know how much you must have suffered. James told me about what happened and how it changed you. We will never forget about her, as her passing was caused by the same evil we will never ever allow to flourish again. With her memory we will fuel our efforts to prolong what we have built for eternity." I nod, thanking her, feeling her sorrow and support in my heart.

Finally, she says, "You have given hope to thousands of people. In the hands of a young man, the world changed forever.

Without knowing it, you took destiny into your own hands, and now you will never be forgotten. The lives of countless men, women, and children, alive and unborn, have been touched and forever improved by your deeds. And last, the death of thousands did not go unpunished, and their memories will never fade, as their fall is the base of our new world order." Mom kisses my forehead and stands up.

She turns around and starts walking out of the room, leaving me alone, but moving my soul with each word of love and encouragement. Her pride is everything I ever wanted. She is the reason why I live and why I decided to go beyond the path laid upon me. She is a woman of dreams, of courage, of love to everyone around her. With her being here, I feel my life is resolved and finally on track to something beyond survival.

James walks into my room, and my heart feels a shock of pride and love. He is crestfallen, with countless scars on his face, on his uncovered legs and arms; the result of his saving our mother, of following my orders and becoming a hero. I say, confused, "Why do you walk in here with your head down, Jay? You ought to walk in here proudly as you have become a soldier, a leader, and a hero." He looks at me surprised, while his face blushes from my unexpected comment.

He answers, "I thought you were going to die, brother. It has been almost three months since the day when you saved me, when you killed that filth and cleansed the Earth from his evil." In his voice, a mixture of hatred, fear, and joy blend inexplicably. I am surprised by how long I have been unconscious.

I say, "Jay, you should never be ashamed of speaking your mind to me. We are in this together. Also, by now you should have understood a simple and obvious reality… I will never die." He stares at me annoyed and laughs with his low and husky laugh. He answers, "You better not die, Nate. At least not today. Follow me." He turns around, while his words sound far more serious.

Uncomfortable and exhausted, I say, "Jay, I am tired and in pain. Can we do this another time?" He shrugs and nods. While his back is turned toward me, his voice sounds loud and clear in my mind. "Wimp." Empathic connection, that is what this bastard's power is called. I chuckle at his comment and tell him audibly, "You are dead, you weak son of a b…."

Our mom peeks in the door at the precise moment and says with a confused voice. "Aren't you two coming?" Confused, I sit up and drink a glass of water on my bed table. The flow of cold liquid wets my dry lips, mouth, and throat pleasantly. I pour a second glass and use it to wet my face and hair. The water drops caress my body and drip on the floor. I stand up beside the bed and test my legs; they are sore and weak but capable of holding me.

Each step feels easier than the last, my strength coming back to every muscle. James is holding me up, walking with me, supporting my frail body. Even the fire inside sparks and rages once again. My body is coming back to its regular self, my mind getting clearer by the second. The wind blows on my moist face refreshingly, ahead my mother is walking toward a stairway.

We walk up the stairs with difficulty. I have no idea where we are. Jay has a mischievous grin in his face that turns to a face showing his effort when I support my body weight on him as my legs fail occasionally. Ahead an open door lets a glare in. The light entering from it blinds me, so I exit the door while covering my face from the bright sunlight. My mother is standing to my left and my brother to my right, staring into an open field.

While my eyes adapt to the illumination, a massive roar erupts. The sound of a thousand voices soaring together to the heavens. From a balcony I see a horde of people staring at us, cheering at us, dancing, jumping, and fist-pumping. A party simply because of us. To my left White Tower still stands, but the red dashes have been cleaned off and inscriptions have been chiseled on its walls. Jay says, "The names of the fallen, to never forget them," as he notices I am staring at White Tower, and his comment fills me with hope and joy.

Beyond White Tower, the wall is still erected, and the front gate has been rebuilt. However, it is wide open as this is not a fortress but a city for all those who want to come and build a new future. Dozens of buildings are being built simultaneously; farms are being plowed and seeded; a stable is built, and horses and cows are grazing together by it. A city of the future made by everyone for everyone. This is what we fought for, what so many gave their lives for. Tears of joy splash my face at the sight of what we have achieved.

Outside of the gate and all the way into the forest, dozens of people are coming toward the city, with their carts filled with their belongings and with products to sell. Fruits, vegetables, artwork, and more. It is the result of human effort entering our city to strive. The cheers continue and increase, people are staring vividly and motionlessly at me. Jay looks at me with an obvious look; he knows what they want me to do.

Extending my arms, I send two massive flares out to the sky, illuminating the horizon as they explode as fireworks. Peoples' eyes shine at the luminescence, and their roar reaches deafening levels. I take one more look at the crowd and those coming toward our city. Welcome to your future, humanity.

Please share your thoughts, comments, criticisms, and praise about *Tale of Two Brothers* by returning to the retail site where you purchased the book and writing a review.

ABOUT THE AUTHOR

Hello, my friendly reader! My name is Daniel Fernández, and I am from Costa Rica, a beautiful, paradisiacal country in Central America. I live with my parents and younger brother. Working together in our family company has taught me to value their effort to raise me and give me all the opportunities to become a better man. Thanks to them, I am bilingual and studied engineering, and been able to travel abroad and understand the world just a bit better.

This book is a personal project that started as a hobby to practice English while studying at the University of Costa Rica, and soon became a passion. Also, writing an entire book in my second language was a challenge I deemed almost impossible, so I did what I usually do when challenged... face it head-on. Writing for countless hours, staying up nights, and working long days to create the best story possible. It is my first book, so you may not like it, but do not give up on me. Send your feedback and sit back, as I will strive to make better books every day for you to enjoy.

I sincerely hope you enjoy this story of love, of family, and of survival, where I explore topics about human selfishness and kindness, our deepest dichotomy. We are in this world to help each other, to become better every day and serve to improve our surroundings. This book tries to make us analyze why we are alive and how we should use our lives for a grander purpose.

Daniel

Enjoy!
December 3rd, 2018

Follow me! I'm on Facebook as Author Daniel Fernandez Masis and Twitter as @FernandezAuthor